"Emanuela Barasch Rubinstein is a unique voice telling a unique story with universal relevance. In beautiful, precise prose, *Intimate Solitude* explores a society and a history unlike any other with compassion and humanity. An important book for our time."

— Robert Peett, Holland House Books

"From the opening sentence, *Intimate Solitude* pulls you into its world. A culture fraught with pleasure, pain, envy, and the consequences of betrayal, as well as love, bravery, hope, and disappointment. You experience the depth and warmth of passion shared by the protagonists—for their families and their country. The two young men move from their childhood friendship through rivalries, success, and antagonism towards eventual reconciliation. This is a book of sharp images beyond the lives of aging childhood friends. We see a new and inspiring country gaining energy from pioneers followed by refugees from the Middle East and Europe arriving in pain with different expectations and values, each one of them fighting prejudice to ensure the survival of their religious, social, and political beliefs. An intriguing insight into life in a vibrant but troubled world. It is the tale of human strength and frailty that you cannot easily forget."

— Paula Nicolson, Emeritus Professor,
University of London

"Jerusalem nurtures writers and poets. The author created a captivating drama starting in Beit HaKerem, her childhood pastoral Jerusalem neighborhood, culminating in the world of Wall Street. The book provides an intimate glimpse into the lives of many Israelis during a period of intifadas, wars in Lebanon, and political and social upheaval since 1977 as well as food for thought about the future of Israeli society."

— Prof. Ariel Rubinstein, New York University
and Tel Aviv University

T0278066

Intimate
Solitude

A N o v e l

Intimate Solitude

A Novel

Emanuela Barasch Rubinstein

ACADEMIC STUDIES PRESS

BOSTON

2024

Library of Congress Cataloging-in-Publication Data

Names: Barasch-Rubinstein, Emanuela, 1959- author.

Title: Intimate Solitude / Emanuela Barasch Rubinstein.

Description: Boston: Academic Studies Press, 2024.

Identifiers: LCCN 2024006114 (print) | LCCN 2024006115 (ebook) | ISBN 9798887195049 (hardback) | ISBN 9798887195056 (paperback) | ISBN 9798887195063 (adobe pdf) | ISBN 9798887195070 (epub)

Subjects: LCGFT: Novels.

Classification: LCC PR9510.9.B37 I58 2024 (print) | LCC PR9510.9.B37 (ebook) | DDC 823/.914--dc23/eng/20240401

LC record available at https://lccn.loc.gov/2024006114
LC ebook record available at https://lccn.loc.gov/2024006115

ISBN 9798887195049 (hardback)
ISBN 9798887195056 (paperback)
ISBN 9798887195063 (adobe pdf)
ISBN 9798887195070 (epub)

Book design by Kryon Publishing Services.
Cover design by Ivan Grave.

Published by Academic Studies Press
1577 Beacon Street
Brookline, MA 02446, USA
press@academicstudiespress.com
www.academicstudiespress.com

Contents

A Historical Note   1

1. 2003   5

2. 1968   7

3. 1970   9

4. August 1974   13

5. 1975   17

6. Fourth of July, 1976   21

7. May 1977   25

8. 1982   31

9. February 11, 1983   35

10. 1984   41

11. May 1, 1988   45

12. April 2, 1990   51

13. Summer 1991   55

14. 1992   59

15. 1993   63

16. December 1995   67

17. May 1996   73

18. September 1996   81

19. 1997   85

20. April 1998   89

21. September 1998   97

22. January 1999   103

23. September 1999   111

24. October 2000   117

25. September 2001   121

26. 2002   129

27. January 30, 2003   135

28. February 2003   141

29. February 20, 2003   149

30. Early March 2003   159

31. Late March 2003   163

32. April 1, 2003   167

33. April 13, 2003   173

34. January 2004   177

35. August 2005   183

36. July 2006   189

37. February 2007   193

38. March 2007   201

39. December 2007   205

40. May 1, 2008   213

41. January 2009   219

42. February 5, 2009   227

43. December 2010   235

44. August 2011   241

45. April 2012   251

46. May 2013   257

47. August 2014   261

48. August 2, 2015   267

49. May 1, 2016   273

A Historical Note

The unique history of Israel and its political implications often take center stage in world news. The Arab-Israeli conflict provides ample opportunities for media coverage. However, significant social tensions and animosities within Israeli society are rarely portrayed. Though acknowledged by most Israelis as the source of political developments, Sephardi-Ashkenazi relations are almost never addressed in the foreign press.

Israel is a country of immigrants. Since the awakening of Zionism, Jews from around the globe have left their homes and traveled to this remote land in the Middle East. The immigrants who came to Israel were part of two distinct groups: Ashkenazi and Sephardi Jews. The Ashkenazim are Jews of European descent, coming mainly from East and Central Europe and America. European traditions shaped their views and habits. Ashkenazi Jews who came to Palestine in the late nineteenth and early twentieth centuries wished to establish a modern, secular Jewish state. Some were socialists; they created the kibbutz movement that has had a significant impact on Israeli history.

In the mid-twentieth century, a massive wave of Jewish immigration came to Israel; some of the immigrants were from Europe, but most were Sephardim from North Africa, Jews of Mediterranean descent. In their Arab homelands they faced growing antisemitism, adopted Zionist ideas, and immigrated to the newly founded Jewish state. They had an entirely different lifestyle from their Ashkenazi counterparts: they were religious people with extended families and traditional customs. Most were not as educated as the Ashkenazi Jews. Since the State of Israel was in its infancy, they were placed in temporary refugee camps, where some stayed for years. As they moved to the cities, most lived in poor, crowded areas for several decades.

Israelis can easily discern between Ashkenazi and Sephardi Jews by their appearance and surnames. Ashkenazi Jews have European surnames (Stern, in this novel); Sephardi Jews carry Mediterranean surnames (Haddad, in this novel). In the first years of the encounter between the two groups, they differed in various ways (food, dress, religious habits, musical taste, and more).

One cannot overestimate the impact of the tension between these two factions on Israeli society, both past and present. Sephardi Jews believe they could have done much better had they not been discriminated against by the Ashkenazi elite; that Ashkenazim, who were primarily secular, ridiculed and belittled the traditional values of the Sephardim. The majority of Sephardi Israelis support right-wing parties, mainly the Likud, feeling they have no place in the Labor Party. They were never inclined toward socialism and sometimes regarded it as a sort of scam or deception. The rise of the Likud Party to power in 1977 illustrated the Sephardic Israelis' determination to find a political outlet for their values—values that were, and still are, foreign to liberals.

Ashkenazi Israelis, on the other hand, felt that the Sephardic immigrants were undereducated and needed to enter the modern Western world. Believing that the latter had come from underdeveloped countries, they urged Sephardi Jews to acquire advanced professional education and not settle for biblical studies in yeshivas. Ashkenazi Israelis were convinced that their economic advantage was a result of a higher level of education, which provides better professional opportunities.

The conflict between the two groups is very much alive today, though I believe it is not as bitter as it once was. It remains true that the majority of voters for liberal parties are Ashkenazi Israelis and that right-wing voters are Sephardic Israelis, but, today, counterexamples can easily be found on both sides. Also, marriage between the two groups has increased, thus blurring the line between them and creating a generation of Israelis who do not feel solely Ashkenazi or Sephardi. Despite having Sephardi or Ashkenazi surnames, their worldviews and values cannot be characterized as either Western or non-Western.

However, the cultural struggle between traditional religious views and liberal values is ongoing in contemporary Israel. The Tel Aviv area (sometimes described facetiously as "the state of Tel Aviv") represents a liberal secular culture; Jerusalem and some remote parts of the country are characterized by a more traditional religious lifestyle.

There is, however, a minority of Ashkenazi Israelis who have adopted a religious existence. They are either ultra-Orthodox Jews or more modern religious people who are supporters of the right-wing political agenda. Known as "settlers" (since some settled in the West Bank), they have a growing influence on Israeli politics. Until the 1967 war, they were a negligible minority, perceiving themselves as inferior to Israelis serving in the army. But the Six-Day War generated a profound change. This group is now entirely devoted to settling the West Bank and promoting religious values.

The protagonists of this novel reflect the various segments of Israeli society. From an elemental framework of Ashkenazi-Sephardi relations, they slowly drift into a super-capitalist way of life, which blurs social conflicts yet undermines the emotional support that the group provides to the individual.

Hopefully, this short note will assist readers in understanding the events and conflicts depicted in the novel.

2003

The slow, effortless descent of the elevator from the fortieth floor to the lobby came to an abrupt halt, with a slight vibration and an almost silent whistle. In the plunging cube stood a man of about forty, tall and slender, his forehead pressed against the elevator's wall. He muttered to himself, "It can't be true. It simply can't be true." His hands were clenched in his pockets, cold sweat ran down his back, and a sheer drop might have trickled down his cheek onto the brown carpet. But, as he felt the movement before the doors opened, he straightened up, tucked his shirt into his pants, ran his hands through his hair, and adopted a practical expression. His face was thin and delicate, his skin smooth, and his eyes nearly black. Though he was used to being the center of attention, the thought of people looking at him now was terrifying.

As the doors opened, he stepped into the lobby. Men's suits, women's dresses, a scent of perfume all merged into a crowd of strangers hastening into the elevator. *I need to get out of here quickly*, he thought, *before anyone sees me like this.* But as he took another step, avoiding the people entering the elevator, he saw a familiar face. A petite woman about his age with chunky glasses looked at him. Her smile resembled a twitch, the lips turning downward rather than up. Ofir couldn't remember who she was. He turned around to take another look, but with a soft clunk the steel doors closed, and the elevator ascended.

He found the heavy air in the underground parking lot nauseating, the dim orange light sickening, and the filthy concrete walls repellant. The parking lot was empty. He walked alone, hearing the tapping of his shoes echo and watching his long shadow clutching his keys. Suddenly, he heard a cat yowling. He turned around, and through his tears, he saw a kitten sitting in a corner, meowing in desperation from the bowels of the earth. *To hell with the money! But the insult, the betrayal, the long years of friendship . . . And why? Why?* From the heavy air came a strange sensation of disintegration, potent yet elusive. What has been will no longer be, the past evaporates, gone and forgotten, replaced by a sour, pragmatic spirit that makes him feel all alone in the world even as he prepares to step into his car, drive home, and have dinner with his family.

1968

A close friendship between children is akin to a blood covenant; they are totally devoted to each other. But the friendship between Ofir and Ben was enigmatic. Two separate parts, a square and a triangle, connected and made a harmonious whole. These boys, with such different characters, spent countless hours together. Ofir was nervous and restless, Ben was quiet and composed. Ofir was a quick thinker, shifting from one topic to another; following his train of thought was practically impossible. Ben's thinking was well-organized and structured; he progressed from one step to another until he reached a reasoned conclusion. In first grade, in Beit Hakerem Elementary School in Jerusalem, the teacher entered the classroom, trailed by a slim, hesitant boy. His blue eyes moved anxiously from side to side, scanning the class with apprehension. His lifted shoulders and pocketed hands created an impression of confusion. His left foot moved slightly as if his shoe was too small and he was trying to remove it. In her husky voice, the teacher introduced him: "This is Ben, a new addition to our class. He's moved to Beit Hakerem[1] from another neighborhood." She prompted the children to welcome him and directed him to sit beside Ofir.

All eyes turned toward Ofir's desk. This time, though, they weren't observing him in their usual manner. And Ofir, accustomed to all his classmates wanting to be his friend, realized they were now entirely focused on the new boy. No jealousy arose, but he felt a new humility, unfamiliar and pleasant; he already liked his new classmate. As the bell rang, Ofir turned to Ben and said, "See the line in the middle of the desk? This side is yours, and this is mine. But you can use my side, and I can use yours. You can also use my markers. Are you coming to play soccer?" Ben responded with a shy smile, happy at the invitation, but refusing it; he didn't like sports. Ofir, now eager to befriend him, insisted: "Come on, try it, it's fun; I'll teach you how to play, I'll help you." But later, in the dusty schoolyard, full of children shouting, he saw the new boy running oddly; his legs were almost straight, as if he were leaping

---

1 An upscale secular neighborhood in Jerusalem.

over hurdles. His body was covered with sweat, his face flushed and then pale, and, after a couple of minutes, he left and vomited next to the fence.

The friendship between the two became well known in school. The two boys were inseparable, sharing everything, laughing out loud on the way home, stopping to buy falafel, eating in silence on the bench next to the shop. Ben never complained that Ofir copied his homework. When two bullies picked on him on his way home, ridiculing him for being short and weak and for his strange run—"as if he has crutches"—Ofir came to his rescue. He followed Ben from a distance, and as the boys closed in, pointing at him and snickering, Ofir showed up, tall and muscular, yelling at them that if they picked on his friend one more time, he would make sure it would be their last. Ben looked at him with gratitude. The broad smile that spread across his face as the two boys fled in panic gradually turned into a look of relief.

In those days, Jerusalem was a hectic city. After the Six-Day War, people from all corners of the globe came to visit the city—devotees waiting impatiently for the coming of the Messiah, adventurous young men wishing to explore the Old City, and eccentrics gathering in budget hostels. Arabs came to the western side of the city looking for work. New buildings sprung up in the Jewish neighborhoods. The municipality repaired roads and sidewalks, and ditches began to appear in different districts. The shock created by the war was sublimated into agitated and restless activity, as if an event that was supposed to occur in the far future had unfolded prematurely. It seemed that the military victory was so inconceivable that roads and buildings had to be constructed to prove that it did, indeed, take place.

Ofir and Ben strolled along Herzl Avenue, the central road crossing Beit Hakerem, finding their way between the ditches. The avenue had been expanded to include a new lane, bus stops were relocated, and traffic lights were replaced. Traffic was diverted to the side, and an old house at the junction was taken down to create space for a new building. Ofir stopped before a ditch, his body tense, and then leaped up high, legs together. As he landed on the other side, he cried to Ben, "I only wanted to be sure I could do it," but Ben could hardly hear him. He hurried to the pedestrian crossing, walking rapidly to cross the street and meet his friend on the other side of the ditch.

1970

The sign above the little convenience store that opened in the small shopping center of the Beit Hakerem neighborhood read: Merceria—School Equipment. But, besides paper products, pens, pencils, erasers, markers, and staplers, it sold key rings, game cards, small housewares, sewing materials, shoelaces, baby toys, and cigarettes. At the entrance to the shop was a stall with colorful candies, black and red licorice, honey-coated peanuts, and snacks. Around noon, when school was over, children gathered around the stall, putting the candy in small plastic bags and waiting for their turn to pay. The seller, a cheerful, full-bodied blonde woman, collected coins and handed change back with swift movements. Her husband, a thin, short man, stood at the other side of the shop, watching so no one would steal.

Ben's parents had left Kiryat Yovel, a neighborhood inhabited mostly by new immigrants and impoverished people, almost all of them were Sephardi. His father, David Haddad, had immigrated from Libya, and his mother, Sophia, from Romania. Their three children were born in huge, tall, and graceless buildings, dirty and neglected. First came Ben, followed by Isaac and Ada. Sophia was very strict about cleanliness, scrubbing the floors and washing the children's clothes so often that sometimes they fell apart. She felt that the dingy stairway, rusty railing, and rats scurrying through the yard late at night were the outcome of life in Israel—a harsh, dangerous, and poor desert land. She tried to replicate the home in where she had grown up; tapestries adorned the walls, plastic flowers sprouted from a decorated vase, books were neatly stacked on shelves, and an embroidered tablecloth covered the kitchen table. She taught Ben to read at the age of five and looked after the children until they went to school. When Ben entered first grade, she realized she couldn't raise her children in isolation from their environment.

Unlike his wife, David always knew that living apart from one's neighbors is impossible. Every evening, coming home from work, he was appalled by the immense buildings—austere and threatening concrete blocks. Shouts and stifled crying always emerged from somewhere; teenagers smoked on the stairs. *We have to get out of here*, he said to himself every evening. *We need to move to another place as soon as possible. It would not end well here.*

When his neighbors began to talk openly about their hatred of Ashkenazi Israelis, he decided to leave.[1] Not that he didn't understand them. More than once, he'd been treated in an insulting and condescending manner. He was asked if he wanted to "sign with his finger" in the post office, and his physician had told him that in Israel "we use real medication, not your grandmother's potions." But still, he thought that uniting in hatred toward others was damaging and wrong. At the age of ten, he immigrated to Israel alone after his parents were murdered in Libya. He'd been a fragile boy with blazing eyes, anxious about the new country. The lack of a family instilled in him a deep conviction that he needed to take care of himself, and that no one would help him. "People look only after themselves," he often whispered to himself. Passionate speeches about an egalitarian society, leaders calling on young people to sacrifice themselves for their country—David thought this was nothing but boundless hypocrisy. In his eyes, they were nothing but cunning, devious ways to help someone else and not him. And he felt the same about the Sephardi leaders who were always calling for a united stand against discrimination. His wife watched them anxiously and murmured something in Romanian, and he only said, "Every person should look after himself."

Eventually, he gathered up his courage and decided to move to Beit Hakerem, where professors, lawyers, and doctors lived. He rented a small store in the shopping center and placed a sign above it, written in Hebrew and Italian—Merceria—exactly like the one over his parents' store in Libya. After a couple of months, the business was thriving, and the family moved to a larger flat.

In the afternoon, the store was bustling. Children stopped to buy candy after school; people came to purchase stationery. David added tiny pots, miniature cacti, and succulents in small cans to the inventory, which sold immediately. Sophia and David got to know many customers, greeting them by name. By midyear, they'd brought in foreign newspapers, as some regular customers requested them: the *New York Times*, the *Guardian, Der Spiegel*, and others. The wife of a renown surgeon requested a journal with stories about international celebrities, and David went out of his way to obtain it.

The hustle that filled the store was lively and pleasant, but there was dead silence one Thursday afternoon when a man wearing an army uniform

---

1   In the '70s, a split opened up between Ashkenazi and Sephardi Israelis. Sephardi Israelis felt that the Ashkenazi elite discriminated against them.

came in. Smiling amiably, the paratrooper colonel stood in line for candy behind some children. As he asked for a pack of cigarettes, only chewing and whispers from the back of the store could be heard. "He commanded the force that liberated the Old City and the Wailing Wall," a customer murmured. Sophia's hands shook as she gave him his change, and David, against his better judgment, wiped a tear from his eye and adopted a serious expression. Everyone watched the colonel as he went out. In the street, he opened the pack, lit a cigarette and disappeared into a military vehicle that sped away with a vroom. Even as the car vanished at the end of the road, the customers remained still and silent. Only after a few moments had passed did a young boy ask if he could please have some licorice.

August 1974

A small fir tree and a vine climbing up the fence could be seen from the window. Purple and white flowers covered the bare bricks, concealing the stairs that led from Hakhaluts Street to a small alley. A key turning, a door sliding open, brisk steps to the kitchen, a fridge door opening and closing—Ofir's father listened silently to his son gulp water. He knew Ofir assumed that no one was home; at this early afternoon hour, he would usually have been right. The toaster beeped, plates rattled onto the table, cutlery clinked, and the aroma of warmed-up food filtered all the way to the study.

Joseph stood at his study door, neither going to greet his son nor sitting down. He was irritated by a disturbing and unpleasant hesitation: Should he remain silently in his room, wait to see what Ofir was doing, or let his son know he was at home? An obscure hatch opened; Joseph could watch his son without him being aware of it, and he found it hard to do the proper thing and close it immediately. Would Ofir turn on the television? Call Ben? He heard his son tossing his backpack onto the floor in the corridor and going into his bedroom; then came strange creaks followed by a thump. He figured Ofir had flopped onto his bed, as he always did. He never sat on it before lying down; rather, he collapsed onto it with his whole body all at once, with the bed emitting a sigh.

Go and say hello, he reproached himself. *He'll be offended if he finds out you're at home.* But after a couple of steps towards Ofir's room, he halted. His heart was pounding rapidly, as if weighed down by a massive burden. *He will ask why I'm at home*, he thought, *and I'll have to explain, elaborate, justify. I'll need to say there is a solution and eventually everything will be fine, but he'll look at me with those dark vibrant eyes and pose countless questions. "So, you're not fired? What exactly is an 'examination?' What's wrong?"*

As he returned to his study on tiptoes, he contemplated what he would say later. He knew how clever his son was. He usually found this pleasant, even admirable, but Ofir's sharpness also contained a hidden threat. If he casually mentioned "financial mismanagement" at the university, Ofir would wonder out loud if "someone had misappropriated funds." If he said the problem was erroneous documentation, his son would say that apparently it was intended to conceal a fraud; any technical mistake could disguise malicious intentions. When he had been appointed chief financial officer of The Hebrew University in Jerusalem, Ofir had smiled at him and said, "Watch it, Dad, you are in charge of a lot of money; someone may set you up." He'd chuckled, winked, and replied, "Don't worry, Son. I make it my business to know where every shekel is!"

But now the idea of having to explain to Ofir that he would prefer to stay at home and avoid the embarrassment, waiting until the missing money was discovered, brought him to tears. He stood motionless for a brief moment, peering around. The beautiful apartment exuded an air of dignity and elegance—furniture crafted of fine cedar wood with beautiful moldings, pricey Persian rugs he had bought in London, an antique bookcase full of books. It was clear to any visitor that the inhabitants were cultured. Adorning the walls were paintings by well-known painters before they gained recognition, and a large window overlooked the garden. Even the light that filled the room wasn't overly bright but moderate and pleasant. Every Saturday afternoon, he had esteemed guests in his living room: famous professors, high-ranking Jewish Agency officials, the heads of cultural institutions, and occasionally even politicians. He was especially proud of a unique friendship with a feted general, a companion from his time on a kibbutz.

But now the charm of the house had become annoying, even revolting. Joseph felt that its dignified character was artificial and marred. The dining room table was too big—how had he missed this? It made the elegant couch next to it appear too small. The golden picture frames—such negligence!—struck him as cheap. The small carpet didn't complement the big rug at all. For a moment, it seemed that this whole disarray of the missing funds had been created because his living room wasn't elegant enough.

"Dad, I didn't know you were at home. Is everything okay?"

In an instant, Joseph was jolted from his reverie, from contemplating the apartment as if he were a stranger, and he turned to his son. *Strange how muscular he is*, he thought as he observed the shirtless boy. A couple of days ago, Ofir had celebrated his twelfth birthday. Now his father gazed at him in astonishment, as if he had just discovered that his son was not a child anymore. Another thought surfaced and faded: *He is not a good student*. Ofir leaned against his desk, body tense and uneasy; he expected an answer.

"Ofir, when did you come home? I didn't hear you."

"About an hour ago. What are you doing at home? Are you sick?"

"Sick? No."

"Dad, what's going on?"

"Ah, nothing. A problem at work."

"Problem?"

"I need to review some financial reports to locate a missing amount. It was probably entered in the wrong place in the accounts; but right now, I need a short break."

The look on Ofir's face seemed like a blend of astonishment and suspicion. Joseph couldn't tell if his son grasped the true meaning of his words or if he believed his lame explanation. Ofir scrutinized him for another brief moment, and then, to Joseph's surprise, he said, "Well, I'm heading over to Ben's," and left the room. Joseph sagged slightly with relief as he heard the door close and feet jumping down the stairs and walking away.

Fourteen days and six hours after everyone had heard about the missing money, Joseph was summoned to the university president's office and forgiven. "Mr. Stern, we'll patch things up now, but you need to make sure the problem is solved." The president wore a heavy sweater and coughed into a handkerchief. Part of the money had been located in various accounts, and a smaller amount was still missing, but it was not entirely clear that it had actually gone anywhere at all. It was possible that a more forensic investigation would locate it. The president patted him on the back and said in a friendly tone, "Oh, well, this war really did disrupt our lives in so many ways, but we shouldn't allow it to dominate us."

And indeed, though nearly a year had passed since the Yom Kippur War, the horror it created was evident everywhere. The need to find the source of the failure, remove the threat, brought forward scrutiny of every nook and cranny, inspection of each intricacy, a search for the hidden error that had rekindled old anxieties of diaspora and extermination. It seemed that the feeling of security and indestructability that followed the rapid victory in the Six-Day War had disappeared without a trace. A veteran sat on a street bench outside Joseph's house every night, staring at the trees, afraid of their shadows. For months the soldier had struggled to close his eyes. Eventually, he had disappeared. He'd left for South Africa, vowing never to return. Other soldiers took to the streets and vented their fury at the nation's leaders. The unexpected terror created profound skepticism, a notion that one had to search in every corner to unearth the source of evil.

This frantic state of mind also infected the university administration. Without being asked, they initiated a thorough examination of all past financial reports. It was discovered that money intended to purchase books had mysteriously found its way into the construction budget. When Joseph was approached and questioned about the confusion, he blushed, as if he had been found guilty of stealing the money. Nothing frightened him more than harm to his reputation. Joseph Stern, with his dignified appearance of high status but with down-to-earth manners, and jacket worn even in the blazing heat of summer, was willing to defend his good name fiercely. When he came to his senses, he decided to confront the allegations. He appointed a team of three auditors to investigate the matter. Initially, he came to the office every day, concealing sleepless nights and pretending that a simple explanation would be found in no time. But as the examination went on, he only went to work in the afternoon, and sometimes even stayed at home, ruminating about who could have stolen the money.

But now he had been pardoned.

The president had patted Joseph on the back again, sneezed and blown his nose loudly, and said, "Well, it can happen. When running large institutions, things tend to get complicated." In an instant the fears of the last weeks evaporated: a newspaper article about corruption at The Hebrew University, Joseph being summoned in for questioning and dismissed, his children looking at him bewildered and anxious, his wife asking why he hadn't been more vigilant with the money, and the house engulfed in silence on Saturday afternoon.

He smiled at the president. "I see you caught cold. This winter is especially harsh," he said, dispelling the remnants of the threat and replacing them with a friendly conversation. No one knew how to steer a conversation better than he did; people talking about daily matters found themselves in a discussion about substantial policy, aggressive debate turned into shared laughter about foolish junior officials. Now he examined the president, tracking every muscle in his face—his eyeglasses placed on his fuzzy nose, mouth slightly open—seeking confirmation that the chance that his reputation would be harmed and his life destroyed had finally passed. The president smiled, and the brief conversation about the weather deepened the calm spreading inside Joseph, removing the anxiety of an abrupt upheaval of his life.

1975

They were both in love with Adi. Two pairs eyes were fixed on her: Ofir from close up, Ben from afar. Ofir tried to talk to her while Ben took a couple of steps back. She always seemed engrossed in a dream, waking occasionally, looking around, smiling, and then withdrawing into an isolated inner space. Shaking her shiny black hair and opening wide her almond eyes, Adi walked around in school as everyone watched her.

The two boys followed her around at school—admiring, inspecting, speculating. Finally, Ofir managed to start a conversation with her. They were in eighth grade; she was a year younger. A nearly arbitrary combination of words had been created in the schoolyard, something about how crowded it was, nowhere to sit down. Ben only smiled, leaning against the bench so as not to faint. The conversation, about nothing in particular, went on. All sorts of words came up—the math teacher, the principal, her girlfriend, gym—forming sentences that became a short dialogue, which led to another exchange on the following day.

After a couple of days, they began to hang out together. Ben got slightly used to her presence, translating his anxiety into questions about teachers, her class, homework. Ofir was the leader: tomorrow we'll go to the movies, then eat at the café; or, after school, you'll come to my house. Adi and Ben complied as if it had been decided that he was in charge of this small group. They often sat on the old benches in Gan Ha'esrim, a small park in Beit Hakerem, looking at the flowers around the monument. Behind the fence, Orthodox young men had settled in an old crumbling house with cracked walls and a roof missing a couple of shingles. As praying voices reverberated from the house, the three of them giggled; for some inexplicable reason, these ultra-Orthodox men were determined to breathe life into gloomy scenes from history books.

On weekends, they rambled through the Old City. Amidst the crowds of people, they strolled in the market's narrow alleyways that were filled with the aroma of spices and steaming Arab coffee. The Arab merchants watched them suspiciously, but persistently offered their merchandise, blocking the way and presenting carved wooden animals, ashtrays, and small pieces of glassware. Ofir went first, Adi followed him, and Ben was last. In the center of the market, the alleys were so narrow that passing through them was nearly impossible.

In one passage, they walked by a butcher's shop. Huge, skinned beasts were hanging from the ceiling, dangling almost to the floor, immense slabs of meat seen through the wide-open door. An iron hook was stuck in the bare red, glistening meat; drops rolled down it, but it remained still and motion-less, indifferent to the buzzing flies. Adi turned her head away. "I can't look at this." Ben peeked and then looked the other way; only Ofir examined the enormous skinned bodies with curiosity.

They stopped at a café in a narrow alley, sitting on small straw stools, trying to sip the boiling Arab coffee. The smoke of hookahs filled the place, and loud Arab music streamed from a small radio. The three gazed into the alley that was nearly dark but for a few light beams penetrating the many awnings and casting orange patches on the peeling walls.

The time they spent together was enjoyable, but also irritating. Sometimes Ofir was sorry Ben was there with them; if he hadn't been, he could have tried to kiss Adi. A strange turmoil overtook him when he thought about it, making him shiver. He imagined her breasts, and then he suddenly recalled he'd forgotten to lock the door before leaving the house. He stood a breath away from Adi, trying to catch her perfume in the air, and then he real-ized it was time to go home. Finally, he told himself it was better to have Ben around. They could wander together for hours, and his odd comments went unnoticed. Embarrassment made him say things like, "Girls are a different kind of human being" or "people are simply cultured animals." Ben, on the other hand, wished to become a sort of secret adviser, knowing everything and repeating nothing. But Adi didn't need a confidant. As she saw how hard he was trying to please her, she smiled kindly, and tossed her black hair.

Adi sauntered, lost in daydreams, with one boy on each side. At first, she thought she might grow close to Ofir; his untamed nature was alluring, his restlessness exciting. But walking around in the streets of Jerusalem with both of them was very pleasant. Adi, dressed in tight clothes and wearing makeup, went to the cinema with the boys, the Tea House, the Old City. After a couple of weeks, she began smiling at other boys.

As school year was over and summer vacation had begun, they sat in small chairs in the courtyard of the Tea House in Ein Karem. On the table, there were all kinds of tea blends. They listened to pleasant music and gazed at the hills. When evening falls, the Judean mountains glisten with a bluish light and the purest air fills the sky. At the table next to them, a lively discussion was unfolding: the impact of the war, government corruption, and above all, the bare animosity between Sephardi and Ashkenazi Israelis that surfaced in a flash, erupting after simmering in hidden places. But surrounded by silent hilltops, swathed in bluish-purple haze, it all seemed distant and unreal. Night fell and darkness enshrouded the hillsides, and from afar jackals' howls could be heard, as affecting as a newborn's cry.

Fourth of July, 1976

Late at night, after the sun had set and darkness spread in the sky, Ofir and Ben lay on their backs, gazing upwards. Summer breezes caressed their young bodies; they smelled the scent of freshly cut grass. The sky was filled with fireworks: red, white, and blue droplets of light splattered everywhere, explosions echoed and sparkling streams enveloped them. Astonished, they watched tiny balls shoot up into the air and then break up into brooks of glare. They had never seen so many fireworks.

Adi had abandoned them.

On the way back from the swimming pool, Ofir said casually, "Today we meet at my place, at seven o'clock." Adi looked at him as if she had woken up from an afternoon nap, smiled, and said, "Sorry, I can't. I'm seeing someone." Silence descended. Ofir and Ben looked at her with surprise that immediately turned into restrained anger. Ofir, moving from side to side, opened his backpack, pulled out a bottle of water, drank some, put the bottle back, and then pulled it out again. Ben kicked a tiny stone on the curb, and said nothing. "I'm going out with someone. You don't know him. Never mind. See you tomorrow."

She shook her dark hair, smiled gently, said goodbye, and went home. They were left mute, perplexed, and unable to look at each other. Ofir opened his backpack again, as if he were looking for something, and then zipped it up in haste. Ben watched him and finally said, "I can't believe we knew nothing. Who's she dating?" They kept walking, deep in thought. An escalating anger tormented Ofir, transforming into something akin to pain. *I'm such a fool*, he thought. *How did I let the opportunity slip away? I should have made Ben leave and tried to kiss her.* He stepped off the curb, up again, and back into the side of the road. The thought of her kissing someone else was unbearable.

Ben ambled slowly, his eyes fixed on the sidewalk, as if he had lost something. A candy wrapper, a cigarette butt, a dark stain on the asphalt— it seemed as if he'd failed in an important mission and would now have to face the consequences. Adi had been entrusted to his care and he'd left her behind.

So they walked together as a profound silence fell between them. Pain and envy rendered them mute.

After a few minutes, Ofir said unexpectedly, "You know, today the bicentennial celebrations of the United States are taking place at the university stadium. I've heard it will end with amazing fireworks."

"But we don't have tickets. It's only for invited guests."

"We'll sneak in. What's the problem? We'll jump over the fence."

"How? I can't."

"No problem, the compound is encircled by barbed wire. We can jump over it."

"You can. I can't."

"C'mon, I'll help you. If we try and can't make it, we'll go home."

"I'm not sure."

"C'mon, let's try. There's nothing to lose."

He's right, there's nothing to lose, Ben said to himself. The thought of Adi meeting someone kept shifting, taking on one form and then morphing into something new, striking Ben time and again. All he could imagine was a hand touching her hair, her body. *Her smile has been more radiant lately*, he thought. But, suddenly, the hand that kept touching her body seemed fitting and just. *Serves him right! Ofir always thinks he's better than me, constantly implying that he would have kissed her if I hadn't been around.*

Ben's pain blended with his envy of Ofir—and for a couple of minutes, anguish turned into a strange pleasure; though he knew it was warped and disgusting, the pleasure gradually spread, drifting into narrow inner channels.

In the evening, Ofir left home, leaping down the stairs, and went to Ben's house. Tall pine trees cast shadows on the quiet streets of Beit Hakerem. Hakhaluts Street wound between new buildings constructed with smooth Jerusalem stone, and old, decaying villas of the first habitants of the neighborhood, their backyards full of thorns and broken bottles. He had slept about three hours in the afternoon, and now he was too alert, both sullen and sharp, in pain and nervous. He walked briskly. If he had been sure no one could see him, he would have walked on the stone walls as he had done years ago, leaping from one to the next.

When he had got back from school, he had almost called Adi. He would have yelled at her that there was no need for her to come along; she could go with her boyfriend if she wanted to. But anguish and fury were exhausting. He sank onto his bed—which groaned loudly and then was quiet—and fell into a deep, dreamless sleep. When he'd awakened, he'd set out for Ben's, unconsciously making his hands into fists. *It's all because of Ben*, he thought. *If we weren't hanging out together with Adi, I would have kissed her. I've seen her look at me. But Ben is always there, making conversation, asking questions.* His body tensed as he continued to think about it; the image of Adi with another boy was so frightening that he could barely take it. He squeezed his fists even tighter and nearly closed his eyes as he walked, as if he was about to see them together.

But at Ben's front door shame took over him. Through the door, he could hear voices coming from the radio, praising the heroic rescue operation in Entebbe.[1] He stood alert and motionless, head bowed as he moved the doormat back and forth. *This pain is distorting,* he said to himself. *It makes me angry at my best friend, who is not to blame.* I waited too long, that's all. It was so comfortable to hang around together. He leaned against the door, and a thin, nearly unnoticed, thought drifted by: *I didn't want it badly enough.* This love brought pleasure simply because it existed, like a story that could be written without being read.

Around seven o'clock, Ofir and Ben went to The Hebrew University stadium in Givat Ram. Many people were milling about, soldiers in their dress uniforms; there were official cars, United States flags everywhere, loud music was booming, and people were rushing to the magnificent ceremony. The two friends were surprised by the commotion. The festive spirit overtook them, eradicating their sadness. Ofir walked fast, almost bounding. Ben could hardly keep up, running in his strange way, his knees almost unbending. "We won't be able to make it," he said. Ofir answered, "Sure we will. There must be a hole in the fence." They went to the other side of the compound; it was surrounded by barbed wire. Ofir examined the fence, his dark eyes following the twisting wire, finding a place where it was low.

"Let's get in here."

"Impossible. We'll get caught."

"No one's looking. I'll step on the wire here and you can get through."

"Ofir, it's impossible. It's barbed wire."

"So what? No problem. Let's give it a try."

Ofir put his foot on the barbed wire so Ben could get over it. One step after another, Ben was very cautious, trying to keep his balance and not fall. His face was full of excitement, his blue eyes shining; as daring and manly as Ofir, he was stealing into the stadium without getting caught. His racing

---

1   On July 3–4 1976, an Israeli commando squad released 103 hostages kept in Entebbe. A French airplane was hijacked en route to Israel.

heart and intoxicating pleasure left him dizzy and careless—and the wire cut his thigh. He turned pale as blood ran down his leg. Almost immediately, he regretted the adventure, but Ofir reassured him: "Don't worry, it's nothing. It's a small cut. One second and we'll be in."

When they were through, they ran toward the center of the stadium, quickly mixing with the crowd so no one would notice they had sneaked in. Joyful and high-spirited, they laughed loudly. "We made it," they cried, and dropped onto the grass. The speeches were over and cheerful music was playing; the sun had set and the full moon was ascending, huge and yellow, surrounded by a halo.

Their backs were damp from the moist grass and their heads were resting on the green when the first volley of fireworks was fired. Red, white, and blue flamed in the sky, and between them gold and silver. Slivers of light washed across the sky, stormy and turbulent, scattering and never seeming to fade.

An entire hour went by and the fireworks continued to illuminate the sky. The boys watched them, tracing the mesmerizing, sparkling streaks, laughing, cheering. Their sadness disappeared and was replaced with a certain comfort. Here, together, they managed to surmount a hurdle, overcome another obstacle on the crooked path from boyhood to adolescence. Adi's presence faded away; their juvenile spirits bested their suffering and inserted a flicker of happiness into four eyes watching the endless steams of flame. When silence finally fell and only a pale moon was left in the sky, they too were silent, closing their eyes and inhaling the scent of a freshly cut grass.

May 1977

Envy has two heads: one sullen, the other smiling; one with sharp, serrated teeth, the other extending an embracing arm—a dual-natured creature, slashing and enchanting, ripping and captivating. And neither head can exist without the other. Hatred is wrapped around enchantment's neck, as the horrible pain assumes the form of a friendly countenance. If envy had only one head, it would be possible to tame it, turn it into a nice pet. The overwhelming urge to emulate someone else might prove beneficial. And self-doubt, which sometimes transforms into jagged self-hatred, could be tamed, moderated, even slightly changed. But the mixture of the two is a bitter solution, distorting and inflicting harm.

Ben's day started on a very positive note. As the schoolyear approached its conclusion, tenth-grade students were deeply engrossed in their study. In the advance math class, the teacher moved among the students, assisting some, suggesting a different solution to others. He never lingered next to Ben; there was no need. No one worked harder than him, and his grades were exceptional.

A tap was heard on the classroom's door, and the secretary entered, asking Ben to come to the principal's office. She was on the phone as he entered her office, but she smiled at him warmly. The room was pleasant and well lit. Facing a computer screen, the principal sat at the head of a long table with eight chairs. She invited him to sit down and kept talking, saying several times, "But it's a ridiculous decision. I simply can't accept it." A slightly squeaky woman's voice came from the phone, objecting to the principal's words. Ben looked around: a book cabinet, curtains with a delicate green pattern, photos of students hanging on the walls next to thank you letters, and nearly parched potted plants. Finally, the call ended; the principal frowned and murmured, "Ah, they can't be trusted," and turned to Ben.

"We decided to give you a special prize for outstanding academic achievement. No one deserves it more than you. We are very proud of you; your achievements are exceptional." She smiled at him kindly and explained how worthy he was of the prize. Ben could hardly follow. The thought of telling his parents was so pleasing, especially after the bitter argument they'd had the day before.

Ofir's delight in learning about his friend's future prize was both flattering and annoying. The lack of envy added a bitter drop to the back-slapping and shouts of "My genius friend!" *Perhaps he is pretending not to be jealous,* a thought passed over Ben and was pushed aside, piling on wariness and animosity that better be kept out of sight. But Ofir's hug was so supportive that Ben willingly surrendered to its warmth.

Ben hoped this joy would help him overcome what he knew would happen at the end of the school day: Ofir had a girlfriend. They were always touching and kissing each other at the school entrance, leaving Ben standing next to them with strange twitch on his face, his mouth smiling yet his eyes filled with tears. Dana kissed Ofir in a showy manner, and Ofir, exasperatingly, was very fond of her, leaving Ben by himself during afternoons. When they met, Ben had to compete for what had always come naturally: Ofir's friendship, the affinity between them, spending the afternoons together. Their conversation now had a discordant tone, every sentence was tested. *Maybe chatting with Dana is nicer? Perhaps Ofir would rather be with her than idly talking to me?*

Ben stood by while Ofir and Dana kissed in front of him. He watched them, undecided whether he should avert his gaze, and finally left without saying goodbye. He walked home slowly, angry at himself and Ofir, stifling a strange nausea. His skinny body suddenly seemed ridiculously childish, repulsively weightless. As he struggled to shake off the self-loathing, he could hear his father's voice echo from yesterday—"I knew this would happen"—and then his own protests as he swallowed his tears, arguing that his father had got it all wrong.

At first, the conversation with his parents had developed smoothly, giving no indication of the acrimony that would later erupt. While his mother was serving dinner and encouraging his little sister to eat, she asked Ben why she hadn't seen Ofir lately. Ben stifled his embarrassment and said, "He's got a girlfriend." His parents' eyes opened wide in surprise. His father cleared his throat, and his mother smiled and asked: "Really? Who is she?" "She's a year younger than us," he answered. "He met her at a party."

"I knew this would happen," his father said, his voice rough and determined. Ben turned to look at him. He had a resolute expression, as if he were unearthing some primal truth that was self-evident but that everyone chose to ignore. His sharp jaw jutting out, eyes half closed, and hollow cheeks sucked in, Ben's father's countenance revealed an intention to say something he knew would provoke resentment.

"Dad, what do you mean? What 'happened?'"

"He can't be trusted. He's not a true friend."

"What?! What are you talking about?"

"You know very well what I'm talking about. All those professors' sons; they can't be trusted. They only look after themselves."

"His father is not a professor. He's the university's chief financial officer."

"Same thing. This Beit Hakerem bunch, always protecting each other."

"Dad, what's with you? He did nothing wrong. It's not a crime to have a girlfriend."

"She's Ashkenazi, isn't she?"

The sigh his mother let out, accompanied by a couple of words in Romanian, filled the room. She tossed a bowl on the table that made a sharp, unpleasant sound, as if about to break and spill the food on the table. "What do you want from him?" she said in a loud voice. "What's the problem? We also live here."

"You can pretend as much as you want, but deep in your heart, you know I am right. Ofir is your friend only when he needs you. That's the way it is here."

"I can't believe you're saying this! We've been best friends since we moved here from Kiryat Yovel."

"But he doesn't need you anymore when he has a girlfriend. Now we'll see if he's a true friend."

Ben looked at him, his heart pounding and a film of tears covering his eyes. A years-long friendship was being trampled, endless moments together depicted as a minor adventure, secrets shared washed away in an obscure flood of grudge and insults. His father was not only disparaging the intimacy between Ben and his friend, but was implying that there'd been nothing more than exploitation and cold-blooded selfishness. In a minute, tears would have slid down his cheeks. He looked at his mother, but she carried on washing the dishes with her back to them. His father went on. Ofir was now part of "them," one of those cold and manipulative individuals, indifferent to others, perpetually striving to take advantage of any human interaction for their own gain.

He is so obvious. The thought appeared, spiraled, almost disappeared, and then resurfaced. *His envy is so apparent, his lack of sophistication embarrassing, he can't conceal his frustration. He's been living in Beit Hakerem for years, and still feels inferior, despite his success that's envied by many.* Ben's gaze swept the kitchen: an oversized, luxurious refrigerator, an oven that was a rarity even in affluent homes, an elegant dining table, above it a large tapestry framed in an ostentatious gold frame; a tablecloth decorated with a colorful pattern, a vase with artificial flowers standing on the kitchen shelf.

He looked back at his father. *He is trying hard not to say "Ashkenazi,"* Ben thought, wondering for a moment whether the desire not to upset his mother outweighed his feeling of being excluded from the "Beit Hakerem bunch." But his father's unabashed and undisguised sense of inferiority made Ben angry. He suddenly seemed so thin and fragile, his silver hair making his skin look browner, two dark arches under his eyes, rogue eyebrows. Even his clothes were somewhat wrinkled. Ben was shaken to see his father like that, embarrassed by his weakness. Out of his pain a thought surfaced. *Maybe he is right. Perhaps all these years Ofir did take advantage of me, and now I am of no use?*

Ben was deeply agitated. He nearly hated Ofir for having a girlfriend, for kissing her and making him uncomfortable, for spending time with her rather than with him—for making him see that he was more successful. Since he knew the anger was showing on his face, Ben looked down, trying to conceal it.

But his father saw his son's changing expression. He felt that he'd struck a chord and said in a loud voice: "I remember that even when you were kids, he would call when he had nothing better to do. He wouldn't take the trouble to see you if he was busy. That's the way it is here; people only look after themselves. They're only your friends when it suits them. You should be the same; do what's right for you. And, by the way, even though you're an excellent student, I bet they favor the professors' children at school." Ben knew his father wanted to say "Ashkenazi," but that he was afraid that his wife would rebuke him. He kept talking about "them," as if everyone knew who "they" were. Finally, Ben's mother turned around from the sink, wiping her hands on a kitchen towel, her fair hair disheveled and her dress stained from cooking, and said loudly, "What do you want from him? And who the hell are 'they?' Do you really want us to live here like they do in Africa? You were the one who wanted to move to Beit Hakerem, saying that if we stayed in Kiryat Yovel, the children would grow up to be criminals. So why are you complaining now?"

Ben escaped to his room. He sprawled on his bed gazing at the ceiling, his heart pounding. He closed his eyes and saw Ofir kissing Dana; his tall muscular body tense, his straight hair falling forward while holding her. Once again, envy raised its two heads: the more attractive Ofir was, the more skinny and flabby his own body seemed; and the thought of Dana succumbing to Ofir became a serrated knife slicing through him, an element of self-loathing, yielding despair and hatred.

Never mind, he'd said to himself.

He's my best friend.

Nothing else matters.

He's my best friend.

1982

It's strange how crossing the border makes the landscape appear so different. Though Southern Lebanon resembles the Galilee—a region extending through parts of the Middle East, its land covered in bare rocks and thorns, jagged mountains and cedar trees, hidden caves, and some greenery clinging to the round hills even in midsummer—it seems unfamiliar, still. Ofir's rifle strap is wet from the sweat on his hands, his uniform moist; he looks around wondering how the familiar light of a hot summer evening is so intimidating now. Orange rays of the setting sun, dust hanging in the air and blurring the bright light, a slightly smoky odor coming from an unknown source; if he hadn't known he had entered enemy territory, he would have thought he had gone hiking with friends. But his cautious steps, as if he weren't carrying the bulky RPG on his back, his gaze wandering vigilantly from side to side, the cough he stifles all indicate that he is a soldier at war.[1]

The villages on the way look deserted. Only rarely does a surprised face appear in a window and immediately disappears. Dogs bark at the soldiers walking on the broken roadside, cocking their ears and listening to the footsteps. Grazing goats briefly raise their heads and return to nibbling on the yellowish grass; crows soar over, emitting horrific caws. The soldiers are getting closer; enemies await them somewhere along the way, concealed on the slopes, hoping that the evening calm will lull the Israelis. But Ofir and his comrades are alert and tense, wavering between fear of the hostile surroundings and inexplicable excitement at the approaching battle.

Ofir's red military boots are coated with dust; every now and then he lowers his gaze and looks at them traversing the broken asphalt. *One step after another, don't look down, a good soldier is ever vigilant.* In the distance, a small village can be seen, with a handful of partially built houses revealing bare, graceless concrete. On the left-hand side, olive trees stand; the soldiers are

---

1 In 1982, Israel launched a military operation in south Lebanon in retaliation for PLO attacks on Israeli soldiers and civilians. Israel invaded south Lebanon, wishing to establish a new political order. It began as a limited operation, but ended up as a full-scale war. This strategy divided the Israeli public.

cautious, wary that someone will open fire. Every moment contains a struggle between watchfulness, palpable in the temples, and an inherent need to downplay the danger, detach oneself, insist that the enemy is not here, isn't hiding in the dump on the right, and isn't lying in the ditch at the side of the road. A moment of tranquility almost makes Ofir smile.

Suddenly, the commander drops to the ground, and the rest swiftly follow. Ofir looks around but sees nothing out of the ordinary. The mountains appear serene. A light breeze stirs the treetops, orange-purple feathery clouds cover the sky, a verdant valley stretches off into the distance; the captivating view makes it difficult to grasp the looming threat. But being the experienced soldier that he is, the commander noticed a glint of light reflecting from someone's watch in the distance—a brief glint on the next hill—and he immediately comprehended where the enemy was, instantly bringing the force to a halt.

As Ofir and the other soldiers storm up the hill, throwing hand grenades and shooting toward the rise, they see the trap they evaded: many PLO men flee, overwhelmed by their exposure, not knowing where to run. *War is fickle. One moment, you think you have the upper hand, then suddenly you find you were deceived.* Ofir pushes the thought away and takes part in the fight.

Later, when he recounts this to Ben, he'll say that the commander is truly remarkable. They all would have been killed if he hadn't spotted the light reflecting from the watch. The soldiers follow him through thick and thin. But now, though exhausted from the battle, the relief that spreads within him resembles pleasure: the first battle is over, he is alive, his friends are safe; they prevailed, killed some of the enemy, and took some prisoners. At last, he can lie on the ground, set his rifle aside, and close his eyes for a moment.

A couple of days pass by. The soldiers get accustomed to the peril, struggling to keep scrutinizing every bend. Climbing on the Shouf mountains is slow and exhausting. In summer, tall thorns blanket the slopes, dust envelops the dark green leaves of the cedar and cypress trees, bare rocks shine in the sunlight, and greenery flourishes only in the valleys. For hours and days, Ofir and his comrades trek forward, advancing toward the place where they know Syrian soldiers are positioned.[2] Approaching a battle creates shortness of breath; for a moment he is nauseated, but he knows that the dread he felt before his first battle has dissipated, that the fear he has now is different, more

---

2   Some Syrian forces joined the PLO in the battles against the IDF.

familiar. Rapid breathing, a subtle need to vomit, hands slightly quivering. He is well acquainted with the signs; they always appear in a specific order. *I wasn't careful enough in the first battle*, he reproaches himself.

"Enemy ahead, enemy ahead. I repeat, enemy ahead. We're walking into an ambush. Get the hell out of here! Now!" The yelling reveals the panic. "Retreat now!" a young officer shouts, and soldiers immediately turn back, wondering which way to run. A Syrian tank appears before them, the steel gleaming in the sunset, a giant iron beast hurtling toward Ofir and his comrades. The whistling of bullets is heard everywhere, cries of soldiers escaping, garbled voices from some radio, and suddenly Ofir sees a huge shadow looming directly above him.

Later, when he recounts this to Ben, he'll say that he failed to understand that the tank was so close; it was impossible to see it through the RPG's telescope. Syrian tank drivers sit inside their tanks and therefore can't see who they're confronting. But right now he crouches without moving, as if his legs are planted in the ground. Around him people are screaming in croaky voices, the tank's chains creak eerily, and a smell of burnt dust fills the air; soldiers fall, get up, keep running, and equipment is scattered everywhere; someone drops a bandage that rolls right next to Ofir—who isn't moving. A strange plan is unfolding in his mind, developing despite the cries of horror all around. "Fall back, everyone. That's an order!" he keeps hearing; and a junior commander shouts at him, "Stern, get the hell out of here. What are you doing? Don't you get the order? Move!" But Ofir is in some kind of bubble, a hush prevailing despite the deafening roar all around.

Ofir rises, his legs quiver so much he is afraid he'll fall; they're almost unable to carry his body. In a minute he'll crumble, lie on the ground, and the tank will roll over him. He takes the RPG off his back and loads a rocket. He peers through the telescope but sees nothing besides an opaque brown color. "Stern, don't you dare! It's a violation of orders. I'll put you on trial and you'll never escape this," the junior commander screams in a high voice, nearly crying, desperate to save himself but not wanting to leave a soldier behind. The humming of the vehicle becomes louder; Ofir points the weapon at the advancing tank and fires.

"Damn it, I've missed. I can't believe it," Ofir cries to the junior commander. But as he turns to the superior officer, he realizes he's been left alone. *Too late to escape*—and nausea overcomes him. The stink of burnt rubber fills his nostrils and mixes with dust the moving tank disturbs; the terrifying noise of the iron chains interweaves with the shriek of flying bullets. The tank's turret swivels, trying to locate the origin of the rocket. Ofir, now completely exhausted, manages to load a second rocket, gets up—his shaking knees prevent him from standing erect—aims, and fires.

Later, when he recounts this to Ben, he'll say he didn't understand at the time how close he was to the tank. But now he is standing motionless, his ears deaf from the thunder rolling between the mountains, watching the tank go up in flames—a blaze roaring a whisper, enveloped in black smoke. The incinerated metal is glowing in a hue he has never seen before. Inhaling the smell of fire, sensing the heat on his face, watching the sparks fill the air, he's eager to feel some joy. But a strange emptiness takes over. *I wish I could sleep now.*

After three weeks in the Lebanon War, Ofir is headed home. Twenty days of battles, twenty nights of short, fitful sleep. Deadly fear, heroism, hunger, exhaustion, dirt, enemies' dead bodies, people holding white flags, thirst, a foreign land, and fatigue he had never experienced. He is hitch-hiking in north Israel, stretching out his hand, and waiting for a passing car to stop. Anyone can tell he is a soldier returning from war: his uniform is torn, his eyes are bleary, and a rifle hangs on his back. Cars drive by, but don't stop. One slows down; in a moment it will halt. Instead, it speeds up and disappears. He's been standing here for half an hour, waiting in vain. Luckily, the exhaustion mitigates the anger. Soft clouds cover the sky, moderating the blazing summer sun and producing a pleasant light. Empty bottles roll down the sidewalk, and an old newspaper, its headline announcing a military operation to protect the Galilee, is flapping in the breeze. No one stops. A soldier returning from war, weary and drained, and no one is making the slightest effort to help him get home. He stands there thinking that when he eventually gets home, he'll have dinner, take a short nap, and then go to Ben's. There is nothing he wants more now. Together, they will watch television, staring at the screen, lost in thought. No need to speak; only with a childhood friend like him is it possible to spend hours and hours together without saying a word.

February 11, 1983

Rain trickled down Ben Yehuda Street in downtown Jerusalem, flowing slowly, accumulating in small, murky puddles. People hurried, looking for shelter, entering a building or a shop. Empty cans rolled along the pavement, a newspaper dissolved in the wet, a broken bottle sat at a doorway to an old building. Gloom permeated the street, which was normally vibrant and full of life even in the chilly Jerusalem winter. A young woman was cleaning the window of a lingerie shop despite the rain, moving the sponge from side to side as though that would stop the rain. At the entrance to the bank stood a man watching the rain fall, moving his head from side to side as if only now he realized it was winter. An old woman walked a shaggy brown dog, letting him lead her anywhere he wanted. The dog sniffed at some bits of food on the pavement, sticking his nose into a soggy package, and the old woman just stood there, vacant, immersed in thought.

At Ben Yehuda and King George Streets, Joseph Stern appeared, wearing a new raincoat. Although he'd typically be in his office at the Mount Scopus campus in the morning, he had decided to skip work and go to Atara Café. He sauntered, head down, staring at the pavement and clutching his unopened umbrella, letting the rain fall on his head. Every couple of steps he coughed, not because he needed to but out of a certain embarrassment, uncomfortable for preferring to spend time in a café rather than at work. Though no one was looking at him, he pretended to have caught a cold, clearing his throat and blowing his nose, making it evident to some imaginary spectator that a slight sore throat had forced him to miss work and drop into the café. *What can I do?* he thought. *I simply can't go on as if nothing has happened, I simply can't.*

As he opened the café door, he was relieved. A warm and agreeable scent filled the space—coffee and cooking. He inhaled it with pleasure, enjoying the homey ambiance. He crossed the narrow corridor by the coffee machine and walked into the spacious room, the back slightly higher; he would have to climb three steps to sit there. The far corner of the room, on the right-hand side, was the most popular area; it was always filled with intellectuals passionately discussing current affairs. It was buzzing in the evenings and on Friday mornings. There were political debates between leftists and Labor Party members; jokes and anecdotes were told, gossip was exchanged, and people made observations about "our life in this place." They recounted stories about current leaders and made valuable connections. The loud voices blended into an agreeable commotion.

But now it was silent.

Only a couple of tables were occupied. One waitress—an older woman who usually bantered with the customers—took orders without a word. Onion soup—the café's specialty—vegetable pie, sweet pastry, steaming cappuccino—they normally sounded so seductive; but today they were just dull and empty words, a collection of syllables, and nothing more.

Joseph sat at the table farthest from the entrance, in the corner of the upper level, leaning his head against the wall and closing his eyes. He couldn't help repeating in his head what he'd heard yesterday, one slur after the other, curse after curse—"Son of a bitch," "Motherfucker," "Burn in hell," "Go back to Auschwitz," "It's a shame the Germans didn't finish you all," "Who needs you here?," "We'll throw you out." He tried to understand how he had found himself in this horrible event that had ended in an explosion, screaming, and the horrifying wailing of an ambulance. A tiny tear found its way down his wrinkled cheek, and from there to his mouth, which was now quivering. *I can't believe it. I simply can't believe it. Why on earth did I go to that demonstration?*[1]

A sudden impulse had made him go. Despite his embarrassment, a sense that his dignified appearance would be somewhat redundant, he'd decided to go to the meeting place and march with the demonstrators without telling anyone. He left the house in haste, wearing the elegant raincoat he had bought in London and underneath it only a worn-out shirt reserved for home use. The distress he'd felt in the weeks after Ofir returned from Lebanon had gradually turned into overwhelming outrage, which at certain hours resembled a bout of nerves; he paced for hours in the long corridor between the kitchen and the living room, contemplating the lies, the futile war in Lebanon, the pictures of the Sabra and Shatila massacre, and the recollection of that late Friday night knock on the door, which had nearly made him faint.

The knock came from the front door. Joseph's stomach had shrunk, his hands limp and shaking, drops of sweat accumulating on his forehead.

---

1   After the massacre in Sabra and Shatila in Lebanon, the Left organized a rally in Jerusalem. It ended in the government compound, where a Jewish supporter of the Right threw a hand grenade at the demonstrators, killing Emil Grunzweig and wounding others.

He moved slowly, trying to walk normally despite his stiff knees. Ofir had been dispatched to Lebanon, a distant battlefield in a pointless war and, despairing, he didn't know how to save his son from his harsh fate, which seemed to him so inevitable. He dreaded the messenger carrying dire tidings about his son; he stood at the door, reluctant to open it. He peered through the peephole. Darkness. Nothing. His hands trembled so badly that he struggled to turn the key. He leaned against the door frame so as not to collapse when he got the tragic news—and opened the door.

It was the woman from next door, looking at Joseph with surprise, wondering why her amiable neighbor was so pale. She was very sorry, but she couldn't find her key. Could she possibly ask for the spare key she'd left with them? As he brought her the key, Joseph shouted to Sarit, his wife, "Everything is okay!," feeling that a ray of light emerging from an unknown source had touched him, spared him this time, saved him from an abyss; but there was no knowing if he would be offered such grace next time. And though he reproached himself like a teacher scolding his student, still he mumbled to himself that one had to be extra careful these days.

Later, when he told Ofir about the incident, Ofir had smiled and said nothing. After weeks in Lebanon, his eyes contained a new sadness. Joseph added that he had just heard that the military operation was about to expand. "Ariel Sharon announced that our troops would reach deep into Lebanon in a couple of days." This sentence made Ofir burst into laughter: "Dad, you're not serious, are you? We were already in downtown Beirut by then."

On Saturday evening, February 10, Joseph found himself walking the streets of Jerusalem with thousands of people, their faces marked by determination and gloom. They marched down Bezalel Street, turned into Sacher Park, and made their way to the government compound. All the way, people around them were swearing and threatening; an unrestrained mob that, if left alone, would have beaten the demonstrators brutally. Indecent gestures, insults—some uttered in unknown languages—spitting, bottle throwing; screams, intimidations, shoves, beatings, mocking laughter. Mute and motionless, the police watched the crowd and the excited mob. A short man with a wide, vulgar face and wild beard snatched Joseph's eyeglasses, smashed them to the ground and stepped on them, screaming in a cracked voice, "Go back to Auschwitz, you filthy Ashkenazi. We don't need you here."

The waitress served Joseph steaming onion soup silently. He stirred the brown liquid with a piece of hard cheese; he cut it into tiny pieces and waited for them to melt. *I once sat at this table with Shai Agnon,*[2] he suddenly recalled. Years ago, Joseph had joined the renowned author and a couple of professors from The Hebrew University, everyone listening to the writer with admiration. They would usually openly disparage the administrators of the university, but Joseph was always welcome. His natural tact, his capacity to adapt to any situation, the gossip only he knew, someone always pulled a chair out and asked him to join the party. But on that day, they all gathered around Agnon, listening eagerly to his acerbic observations on the changing nature of The Hebrew University. Sitting close, enjoying himself, Joseph had felt that a hidden, slightly mysterious, aspect of life in Jerusalem was gradually being revealed, something he would cherish for years. But now the memory made him smile bitterly. He rested his head against the wall and closed his eyes.

In the square outside the prime minister's office, voices, intermingling with hostile cries directed at the demonstrators coming from the megaphone, demanded the government take responsibility for its actions. Protest chants were mixed with yelling, profanities, vulgar hand gestures. In the tumult, Joseph was surprised to be struck by a stone on his back. *That's strange*, he thought, assuming that only fellow demonstrators were behind him. But, as he was wondering who had thrown the stone, there was a loud explosion, a hand grenade hurled at the rally, and then the wailing of an ambulance blending with the cries.

When Sarit, a thin woman with a sharp face, her countenance betraying constant hesitation, opened the door, she saw her husband like she had never seen him before: he was pale, his glasses broken, dust covering his hair, his lovely raincoat stained and dirty, his elegant watch smashed, and drops of wax on his shoes. Although she was a reserved woman, she stretched out her arms and hugged him close without saying a word. They stood in the doorway, Joseph shaking, Sarits caressing his head, and only after a couple of minutes did they go inside.

A deep voice on the TV announced: "Emil Grunzweig, born in Romania, the son of an Auschwitz survivor, a math teacher who wrote a thesis on the philosophy of science, a divorced father, a combat soldier . . ." The words came quickly, one after the other—the bright, beautiful face of the murdered young man filled the screen. Joseph stared at the images, attempting to understand what had been said, but all he could

---

2   Shai Agnon was a distinguish Israeli writer and a Nobel Prize laureate.

hear were syllables that didn't amount to words. Only a trace of a thought crossed his mind, an unpleasant flash that faded before casting its light, something about regret that his children were growing up in Israel and that perhaps they should move to the US before it was too late. He was left feeling nauseated and empty. *It's a shame, what a shame*—these were the only words in his mind; he couldn't explain to himself what exactly it was that was so regretful.

"Excuse me, are you okay?" The waitress touched his arm gently, bending toward him, looking at him with concern. Seeing such a dignified man leaning his head against the wall with his eyes closed made her anxious. "Yes, yes, I'm fine," he replied out of habit, straightening up and asking for the bill. A full-figured, middle-aged woman with heavy make-up, a slight mustache visible above her lip, thick eyebrows, and greasy hair pulled back, she looked at him and said, "Yeah, I also want to lean my head against the counter and cry. What a shame, isn't it? God, what a shame."

1984

The Computer Science Department of The Hebrew University was located on the old Givat Ram campus, surrounded by lawns and trees. At noon, students often sat on the grass, absorbing the pleasant winter sun and the light breeze rattling the faded green leaves of the mulberry trees.

Dark clouds appeared in the distance, but the sky still had a fresh blue hue. Ben sat with other students. Together they laughed, joked about some professors, and discussed math problems. A cheerful spirit, snacks shared, bright green grass, and trees casting a dappled shadow over them—everything was peaceful and tranquil, creating a sense of calm. Five young men sat together; four relaxed on the grass, one upright and tensed. And though Ben took part in the conversation, he was clearly upset. His blue eyes couldn't stay still; they flickered quickly from side to side, examining his friends. He seemed strained, as though he was in a hurry to get somewhere. The blond curls on his forehead emphasized his serious expression, and his thin body was alert, as if he were about to leap up any minute.

At first, his friendship with Michelle had been easygoing and pleasant. A tuition business was looking for students to instruct middle school children. Ben taught math and Michelle English, and soon they were engaged in conversation. A petite young woman with straight hair, a slightly childish face, small eyes encircled with black pencil, glasses perched on her nose, a few freckles, pinkish skin—you would have thought there was an air of innocence about her were it not for her strange, round mouth that twitched as she spoke, oddly curving down rather than up when she laughed. The sly lips moved constantly, arching and straightening, stretching and shrinking, hostile and gloating. Normally, Ben would have been intimidated by a woman wearing a very short skirt and low-cut shirt, but Michelle was very talkative, she laughed and told funny stories, and so a good-humored friendship formed between them.

In the evening, the children were gone, yet the odor of sandwiches and peeled oranges remained in the room. Ben and Michelle joked about the students; he told her about a boy who didn't know even the simplest arithmetic. She repeated a sentence in broken English, the errors creating a new, funny meaning. They went to the café next to the school; it offered tasty tomato soup, despite its scruffy appearance. They had dinner together a couple of times, laughing and having a good time. But the conviviality evaporated at once as one evening as Michelle suddenly asked him, "How come you're working? Why didn't you get a scholarship?" Though the question was casual in tone, the touch of mockery in her eyes made him slightly suspicious. He began a long explanation: undergraduate students rarely get financial support, and even with his excellent grades it was practically impossible. He had asked the department's secretary, and she'd said he could submit a form, but the odds were slim.

Michelle listened attentively, with an unpleasant sparkle in her eyes. The left side of her mouth was pulled down, betraying her disbelief in his explanations. When he concluded, she said with a smile: "Maybe you didn't get a scholarship because you don't have an Ashkenazi surname?" It was as if Ben's weakness had been exposed and there was no way to conceal it. He was utterly taken by surprise and kept quiet. Aside from his father, no one had ever explicitly suggested that he may have been deprived of anything because of his background. An outstanding student, he was always praised and rewarded. He found his father's claims of discrimination lame, betraying nothing but an envy he tried to conceal. But now, watching Michelle look at him with a touch of contempt, he felt himself flush. Out of embarrassment and confusion he blurted, "What do you know about it? You're a hundred percent Ashkenazi, aren't you?"

"Yes, but I know how things work."

"How do you know?"

"Trust me, I know. I observe life from the same side."

"Which side?"

"Of those who don't have doors opened for them or a red carpet stretched before them."

"What are you talking about?"

"If your surname were Rabinowitz and not Haddad, you would have gotten a scholarship. But don't be naïve; it's not only about Ashkenazi and Sephardi. Some people have everything without even trying, and some have to keep struggling. That's the way it is. And we are both on the same side."

"I don't understand what 'sides' you are talking about."

"That's life. The world is divided into those who have and those who don't have; those who everyone wants to be their friend and those who need to suck up; those who get even and those who shut up when offended.

Don't tell me you disagree. I've seen you with your hunky friend, the one who studies economics."

"Ofir? I didn't know you knew him."

"I don't, but I've seen you hang out together. Anyone can tell he's someone who doesn't need to make an effort."

An obscure distress, unsettling but lacking definite form, took hold of Ben. His feeling of lightness and innocence began to loop and thicken into a dark, murky steam. For a moment, this description of winners and losers made perfect sense, as did being a part of a group that needed to sweat to make its way. It was even slightly comforting. An army of deprived and rejected people began to form in his mind: he was walking in a crowd of people with visible faults; he was one of many; no one was falling for their charm or asking to be their friends. They all wished to climb, but no one was handing them a rope or a ladder. He bowed his head, sipping the soup that was left in the bowl, fearing to look straight at Michelle. They said nothing. Finally, as he turned his gaze to her, he saw her strange mouth curling up in ridicule. She stretched out a feminine hand, touched him, and said softly, "My place?"

As she took off her clothes, Michelle's face betrayed determination, as if having sex was a rebellion against a predetermined fate. Her naked body clung to his body; every movement she made was touched by intention, a desire to reveal something far from naturally succumbing to pleasure. Ben looked at her, bewitched by her small figure, ignoring her treating him as if he were an inexperienced child. His observation, made despite his sensual delight, that there was something evil about her only intensified his satisfaction.

But later, lying on the narrow bed covered with a slightly shabby duvet, he observed the room with some disgust. Though it had appeared clean at first glance, he now saw spider webs on the ceiling, rust on the window hinges, a couple of broken tiles in the wall facing the bed. Even Michelle's body, resting in his arms, seemed slightly unclean, though he kept telling himself that it was impossible. As he freed himself from her embrace, got up and dressed. He heard her quietly saying, "Next time you see your friend, ask him to do something for you that he really dislikes. You'll see what happens."

As the students rose from the grass, Ben strolled to the cafeteria to meet Ofir. After their trays were full, and they'd paid and sat at the table, Ben said quietly, "Listen, I need help. I must copy a friend's notebook and return it within two hours. The photocopy machines in the library are broken. I won't make it if I do it by myself. Can you stay with me for two hours and do half the copying?"

"In handwriting? Do you mean read and then write it?"

"Yes. I have no choice. The machines aren't working."

"Gosh, that's a bummer. Two hours of reading and writing?"

"Yes."

Ofir looked at him and broke into laughter.

"Oh, what the hell. But you know, I have a terrible handwriting. Are you sure you would be able to read what I write?"

May 1, 1988

It all began with an argument between Ofir's parents. He had joined them for dinner a couple of days after he had completed his master's degree in economics. The odor of spring filled the kitchen; the Brunfelsia blooming outside the kitchen window had an intoxicating scent that mixed with the cooking aromas. Children's voices came from the street, a light breeze moved the gray curtain above the kitchen window, and tinkling music came from the radio.

When dinner was ready, beeps sounded from the radio: the news. In a deep, masculine voice, the announcer stated that May Day, International Workers' Day, was celebrated all over the world. In Tel Aviv, workers paraded in the streets and then participated in an assembly organized by union leaders. Ofir's mother burst into quiet laughter. "May Day? I can't believe it's still commemorated. What exactly is there to celebrate?" The daughter of a wealthy family, she found the idea of solidarity between workers strange, even somewhat ludicrous.

But Ofir's father, who had joined a kibbutz after immigrating to Israel and left it with a heavy heart after seven years, protested. "What do you mean? It is a day to celebrate the unity of workers all over the world. People who need to look after themselves because no one else does." Despite his polished appearance and elegant home, the passionate socialist speeches he'd heard in the kibbutz were fixed in his memory; creating a vague yearning for the group of young people he had been part of. More than once he'd reflected that their naïve belief that if they tried hard enough the future would be better, generated simple, straightforward happiness—an emotion rarely mentioned nowadays. As the chief financial officer of The Hebrew University, he took extra care to prevent any exploitation of the institution's workers, double checking that their pension money was secure, an employee who lost their job would get full compensation, a pregnant woman would receive all her entitled benefits. But his wife found the idea rather silly. In a tone that tried to conceal her previous mirth, she said: "I don't understand. What do the workers in the Soviet Union have in common with those in Western Europe?"

"They both have rights that must be protected."

"But these are completely different societies. What do the workers in China and the US have in common?"

"In both places, people are trying to exploit them."

"But their conditions are so different. You can't look at the laborers regardless of where they come from. Should Israeli workers fight for the rights of those in China? Surely, you'll agree it makes no sense."

Joseph looked at her and his blue eyes revealed a surge of anger. A wrinkle contracted on the forehead; his gray hair was slightly disheveled; the shirt made of fine fabric suddenly seemed a bit crumpled. He said in a strange, low voice, a sort of whispered shout, "What have they got in common?! What have they got in common?! How can you say that? What do workers here and in other places have in common? Why don't you tell me—what have I got in common with the people living in Israel? And what have I got in common with the university's employees? And now that I'm thinking about it, what have I got in common with any human being other than myself? How are the two of *us* connected?"

There was utter silence. Ofir's mother, now adopting a somber expression, served dinner, and the three of them sipped their soup without a word. The news was over and music came from the radio, cheerful tunes in stark contrast to the gloom that filled the kitchen. Joseph's words were left unanswered, echoing in the room. Sarit seemed deep in thought, and her husband did not conceal his distress. Ofir waited quietly for the conversation to resume.

When they finished with the soup, his mother removed the plates and brought freshly made schnitzels, potatoes, and a green salad to the table. This dispelled some of the gloom, and soon the conversation resumed. After a few minutes, as Ofir felt that his father's questions had dissipated and disappeared, he decided it was the right moment. He had some water, cleared his throat, and said, "Ah, I want to tell you something. Ben and I decided to start a business together. He began his doctoral studies in computer science last year, but he's unhappy. I've just completed my master's. Ben has an idea how to use robotics in medicine; he thinks we can make a lot of money. I'd handle the financial side."

Ofir's parents stared at him, thunderstruck.

Though he'd feared their response, their speechlessness made him smile. The first-born son, he was aware of their high hopes. His younger sister found school difficult. His younger brother was inclined toward the arts—at a young age, he had stated he wanted to be a painter. His parents smiled, but when he's left the room, they murmured that they would need to provide for him and better start saving money right away.

But not Ofir. A gifted young man, daring and hardworking, charismatic and smart. It seemed as though he had been shaped into a spacious and shiny template—pleasant and silky like an overcoat that fits perfectly: emphasizing his nice build without being too tight, keeping him warm but not causing sweating. Made of fine fabric but not overly fancy, it covers him so softly that he would never want to take it off. He was always in search of a mirror that would reflect his own loveliness. But recently, it had grown somewhat uncomfortable, constraining his movements. To his utter surprise, despite its elegance, he felt compelled to take it off—to go without the cover that people admired so much. "Ben is very gifted, you know that. He thinks robotics isn't used enough. He wants to develop something for orthopedic surgeries. If he succeeds, the demand will be huge."

Joseph put his knife and fork on his plate, looking at his son as if he had just found out he was sitting next to him. He drank some water, put the glass down carefully, waited a moment, and then said in a restrained tone: "But what happens if you fail? Then what? You are two gifted young men, and you can easily find good jobs. Ben can be part of the aerospace industry. I'm sure they are eager to hire people like him. And you, such an accomplished economist, you can do anything. The Ministry of Finance, government companies, the private sector, you'll be choosing among excellent options. But if you waste a couple of years, it won't be the same. People will always wonder why you didn't find a job right after school."

"Dad, there's a good chance it will work. It's an original idea; it can completely change orthopedic surgery. There are some things the human hand is incapable of doing, even the best surgeon's. It's an entirely new field with almost unlimited possibilities. And I know how to run the financial side. You know, if it does work, we'll be wealthy people . . ."

Sarit, who was listening to the conversation silently as her gaze moved back and forth from her husband to her son, her usual hesitant expression transforming into unconcealed childish amazement, suddenly broke in, without waiting for Ofir to finish the sentence: "But a job is so much more than that, Ofir. It's financial security, a way to secure your life. If you're tenured, you'll have a monthly salary for the rest of your life. You could buy a flat, settle down, save money."

"That's true, Mom, but I hope to make enough money to have financial security anyway."

"But a job's a bedrock. You work with the same people for years; some become your friends. You are part of something."

"You can't stand the teachers you work with," Ofir said.

"Most of them," his mother replied, "but I also have friends. And it doesn't matter, I am part of the school. If I ever need help urgently, I'd ask the principal. And I should add, even though I don't like some of the teachers, I can't imagine my life without the school. I get up in the morning to go to work."

Ofir's father added in a humorous tone, "Clearly, you could live pretty comfortably from a salary, if you know how to manage financially," winking in an effort to make the conversation lighter. But a hard, fixed fact had come into being, rooting itself and growing: Ofir was about to stray off the road. Turn onto an unfamiliar path. He looked at his parents attentively, trying to respond to their arguments, and to appear practical and calm, but his eyes were already aglow in an unfamiliar light. And though he thought his parents' arguments made sense—he, too, was troubled by financial security—his plan had already turned into an independent and uncontrolled creature, seductive and frightening. He could see the offices they would take in Tel Aviv, the clients who would compete to get their robot first, hospital managers from all over the world on their doorstep, the huge profit, money that would become a source of pride and evoke admiration, meetings with senior businessmen, with the minister of finance—these images transformed his parents' gloomy expression into a flaw that would be fixed over time. And his mother's words about work being "life's bedrock" assumed a new, unexpected meaning.

Sarit got up and removed the plates from the table, her face betraying hesitation. Joseph sat quietly, immersed in thought. The sun had set, the street was quiet now. Again, the radio beeped. The eight o'clock news. John Demjanjuk was appealing his conviction, arguing that he was not Ivan the Terrible. "The Supreme Court will consider his appeal with five judges on the bench," said the radio.

Joseph breathed a deep sigh, almost groaned, and stood up. Every time the Holocaust was mentioned, his face lost its gentle expression and became gray and contorted. The dignified countenance of a successful man vanished, replaced by apparent fury. His eyes, normally so warm, were enraged as he said in a shrill voice, "Appeal? Why? May he rot in hell, the bastard. Even if he was only a guard in a concentration camp, he deserves to die. The scum!" A bleak atmosphere, full of nightmares and horror, filled the kitchen at the words "Ivan the Terrible." Ofir and his parents listened to the radio without speaking, as if in a moment it might turn out that a concentration camp still existed somewhere and Ivan the Terrible was about to return to it. Only as the news finished did they move again. Ofir said goodbye and left as his exhausted parents collapsed onto the comfortable sofa in the living room.

April 2, 1990

The small office on the ninth floor of Clal Center in downtown Jerusalem emitted a peculiar smell of glue. In each room, the carpet was gray, the walls plain; a cheap cabinet tucked in the corner bore a bulky fax machine and paper was scattered everywhere. A private detective had an office next to them. Loud voices and yelling often came through the thin walls. The detective, a young man around Ofir's and Ben's age, was inclined to talk about his problems with his girlfriend, like a doctor explaining that he had caught the disease he was treating. Ben sat for hours facing the computer screen; Ofir wrote letters and called various companies, closing the door between to avoid disturbing Ben.

This morning, Ben was the only one in the office. The snow that had begun falling at dawn, piling up on the city's rooftops, had left the Clal Center nearly empty. The excitement the white covering created, so different from the regular ashy coating on the streets, hadn't stopped Ben from going to work. He'd walked for half an hour to the office, thinking how pleasant the quiet the snow created was. A strange calm filled the center of the city, which was almost empty. As he knew he would be by himself all day, he bought fresh rolls at a small bakery on the way, and hot chocolate from a booth next to the tower. Ofir had been called to Defense Forces reserve duty in Gaza for a week. Every time he called, Ben felt relieved. During the day he managed to do away with the fear of what might happen in the narrow alleys of Gaza City, but at night he thought he could sense Ofir in pain. Ofir called, made some jokes, and immediately inquired about progress, asking questions and awaiting detailed answers. The goal they had set for themselves, the production of the first model of the robotic arm within a year and a half, was utterly absorbing.

Two months before, Ofir had managed to persuade an American businessman leading a group of entrepreneurs to invest in their project. A somewhat mysterious man, Dan Pearson from New York listened to Ofir patiently, asked a couple of questions, and said in a practical manner that he needed "to think it over." Ofir called him twice, but was always met with hesitation. As he began to lose hope and was looking for another investor, the phone rang at home late one night. Dan had arrived in Israel without prior notice. "I'm here in Jerusalem and would like to visit your offices early tomorrow morning." Panic made Ofir say, "Sure, we'd be glad." But when he hung up, he collapsed into the big blue armchair in his room and buried his head in his hands. *It's all lost,* he thought. *When he sees the neglected office, he won't even consider investing in the project.* He immediately called Ben. "Ofir? Are you okay? What's happened?" Ofir told him, and they both sank into despair. Finally, Ben suggested they go to office early in the morning and tidy up. At least the piles of papers on the floor would be out of sight, and they could try to clean their desks.

Dan Pearson got out of a taxi in front of the Clal Center. He was a tall man with wild, curly hair and reddish pockmarked skin. He shook Ofir's and Ben's hands, his eyes inquisitive. They suggested a tour of the area, but Pearson asked to go immediately to the office. As they went in, Ben muttered something about "a temporary place until we get going" and Ofir said, "We couldn't find anywhere else in Jerusalem." Pearson sat down heavily and began to study the technical aspects of the future robotic arm. His questions revealed a profound knowledge of robotics; Ben couldn't answer some of them. After about an hour, the American stood up, smiled, and said, "I like it. I'll send you a draft of an investment proposal. My lawyer will contact you. He'll work out all the details. But I want you to send me a detailed monthly report tracking your progress. And as it will take years to get FDA approval, I suggest that for the time being, you develop a robotic arm for surgical procedure simulations. When you get the approval, it could be used for actual orthopedic surgeries."

A couple of months went by and the robotic arm gradually came into being. Programming became very complex. A young orthopedic doctor was hired to demonstrate how it would operate during knee surgeries. Ofir and Ben worked hard to make the robot easy for surgeons to use. Dan Pearson agreed to hire a computer engineer, Abraham Weinstein, a young, religious man who asked to be a partner. Ben and Ofir looked at each other. Ofir winked and Ben said, "We're sorry, but if we do well, you'll have the option to buy shares." Abraham smiled and said, "With God's will, you'll change your minds later on," and immediately got back to work. On this snowing morning he stayed at home with his three little children, leaving Ben by himself in the office.

Ben went to the window and looked out at the rooftops of Jerusalem covered with snow. From the ninth floor, he could see the outdoor food market and the neighborhood behind it, with its small stone buildings. The whiteness concealed the city's dirt, the black and mildewed walls, the broken gutters; it introduced an airiness, illuminated Jerusalem. An unfamiliar light emanated throughout the city. Children threw snowballs at each other, the lone cypress tree near the office building was dotted with white, the streets lost their usual bleakness and adopted a graceful appearance. Even the people, who normally rushed along with a sullen look, smiled today. Maybe this made Ben think of his night with Michelle without the irritation that always surfaced in the morning—though he never could decide who he was angry with.

Her wiliness, her joy in ridiculing weaknesses, her need to provoke— another man might ignore them, plunge into her naked body without paying any attention to the sneer on her lips. But not Ben. He saw her with depressing clarity. Sometimes he thought she had a grain of pure meanness in her, but she became his partner, nonetheless. Not a spouse—despite the nights they spent together, she taking off her clothes and lying on the bed in an alluring manner, as though she was expecting gratitude for allowing him to use her body to satisfy his lust—but a sort of secret friend, a spin doctor one didn't want anyone to know about. Ofir had seen them together only twice. When he'd asked who she was, Ben had replied, "Just a friend. We work together," turning his head to conceal his blushing cheeks. Sometimes he stared at Ofir in shame, thinking of what Michelle always said: He's using you; he expects you always to be there for him but he isn't helping you; he's having a good time with women but never invites you along; don't let him step on you; don't give up; we need to look after ourselves because others won't; everything comes easy for him but not for us. A feeling of sour betrayal filled Ben, yet it dissipated every time Ofir had a new girlfriend: a beautiful Swedish student, a dancer from Tel Aviv, a poet with large eyes. Then the double-headed jealousy rose again, more agonizing than ever. As he lay in bed at night, imagining Ofir with one of his girlfriends, he felt he might disappear, disintegrate into minuscule particles, swallowed up by the vision of Ofir's masculine body with women who would never give him a second glance. Then Michelle's words turned into a bitter medicine removing his despair from his thin body. Us and them: we fight for everything, while they have the world spread out before them; our life is a constant battle, while they always win. And though these arguments seemed so true in the darkness, they did not overshadow the stressful and ominous shame that always followed them in the morning.

Ben stretched his arms, determined to get rid of his agitating thoughts and get back to work. There was no use in staying in the office on a snowy day if he wasn't getting anywhere. He got back to his computer screen. Before they manufactured a robotic arm prototype, the program needed to be perfect, without a single error. He always felt happier when he was immersed in the project; his anger was replaced by images of success. A powerful creature materialized in his mind, developing into triumph. *Ofir and I are not only old friends*, he thought, *but also a great team; we complement each other. My caution balances his daring; my thoroughness enhances his creative ideas.*

After clearly articulating this to himself, a sense of relief washed over him. He made a cup of tea and walked slowly to his desk, leaving a trail of drops on the dark carpet. He removed a few of papers from his desk, making room for the steaming drink. Before I start working, I'll wash the cups in the small kitchen next to the elevator, he thought. He went to the door, opened it, and was taken aback.

Because of the cold weather, the Clal Center's management allowed homeless people to enter the tower. The space in front of the elevator was filled with dirty men dressed in rags, lying on the thick carpet, some covered with filthy blankets. They didn't utter a word, each one absorbed in his world, indifferent to others. Even when they saw Ben leaving the office, they did not respond. Only one man lifted his head and looked at him. He wasn't old, about forty, with messy hair, a wild beard, and small dark eyes. He stared at Ben without lowering his gaze. His face was wrinkled and exhausted, his supine body limp. His huge hands were covered in bruises and bloody scratches, and his fingernails were black. A dog with muddy fur slept next to him. The man looked at Ben with anticipation, as if he was about to reply to his question.

Ben leaped back into the office and slammed the door behind him, frightened, breathing heavily.

Summer 1991

Some people are excited by speed. A rushing car, a train hurtling on the tracks, an airplane about to take off—an inner thread is stretched and strained, creating an alert anticipation in a hunter's soul. Ofir was standing by the window in the new offices, looking out on Ayalon highway winding between the towers of Tel Aviv. Though the window was closed, and he could hear nothing, frenetic alertness filled him as he saw the vehicles accelerating below. The fast traffic charging forward, a constant flood of cars speeding to their destination, a raging stream generated fervor. He felt that he, too, would like to leap forward and break an invisible block, dash in haste to an unknown place.

Handex's offices spread out in five spacious rooms. Ofir, Ben, and their twelve employees filled every corner with papers, computers, robotic arm parts, and huge screens. The secretary sat in the entrance hall, fastidiously answering phone calls. Ben warned her to be careful about what she was saying; one can never be certain who is on the other side of the line. Three engineers, two doctors, and six programmers—all occupied from morning to dusk with enhancing the robotic system. The first stage had gone exceptionally well; the robotic arm did much better than expected. The rumor of the medical robot spread like wildfire. Hospitals from the US and Europe took great interest in the new instrument; conference organizers begged Ofir and Ben to present the new tool, medical journals asked for photos. Two hospitals in the Boston area were the first to use it. The surgeons kept praising the robotic arm, capable of doing "what our best experts cannot do."

When Ofir's parents visited Handex, they looked around with admiration. A modern commercial building with an elegant entrance, the offices were roomy and well lit, the furniture made of fine wood. Ofir's mother kept murmuring that "every room here is like a hall." His father walked around, asking everyone what they were doing, receiving polite explanations. Ofir had invited them, wishing to ease their concerns. Whenever he came for a visit they would ask him in a skeptical tone, "Well, so how is it going?," trying to collect details on the company's profits. And his mother would add in a slightly whiny voice, "You do put some money to one side, don't you?" Though he never specified numbers or said how much the company was making, their eyes betrayed relief when they saw the commodious offices. He thought their apprehension had lifted slightly.

Moving to Tel Aviv was very positive. Jerusalem had become an austere and isolated city, lacking the European atmosphere which the founders of The Hebrew University had granted it in the first half of the twentieth century. Young Orthodox Jews could be seen everywhere; old buildings were torn down making room for new synagogues. Even in Beit Hakerem, an entirely secular neighborhood, a yeshiva replaced a teachers' college. A different spirit was gradually taking root, fanatic and uncompromising, in line with the ancient and tortuous history of Jerusalem. Many secular young people were moving elsewhere, mainly to Tel Aviv.

Ofir had rented a renovated flat in the center of Tel Aviv, in an alley shaded by two tall sycamore trees. To embrace the invigorating change in his life, he got rid of the old furniture and filled the house with super-modern stuff, which he'd purchased from an expensive home design store. When Ben came for a visit, he looked around, bewildered—his own flat was so ordinary, like his parents' house. Ofir's neighbors were artists: she was a painter, he was a musician. In the evenings, he enjoyed the loud jazz coming from their flat; it demonstrated the blessed change in his life. He found Tel Aviv pleasing—a beach town with people spending time by the sea, in cafés and restaurants. A city with a relaxed, moderate attitude. On Fridays, at noon, he walked along the streets, passing by people walking their dogs or older ladies, made up and well-coiffured, on their way to meet friends. And into this very pleasant life came Laurie.

Late one Friday night he passed by The Penguin, a bar with vibrant music and enjoyable company. The place was packed. Ofir examined the young women sitting at the table next to him with an experienced eye. Glasses of beer were lined on the table one after the other, the talk was somewhat tiresome.

Suddenly he saw her.

Shining black hair, very fair skin in mid-summer, round brown eyes, a small nose, and a full mouth. She wore a black sleeveless dress, tight around the neck, revealing her bright and beautiful shoulders. She was pretty in an unusual way. Even her hair, bangs and a ponytail hanging down her back, were different; a woman attractive in an old-fashioned way, looking like a painting of a princess. Five young women sat at the table next to her having a lively conversation, sometimes laughing, sometimes serious; but he couldn't figure out what they were saying.

An invisible muscle was slightly strained, ignorant of its future outburst. Desire mixed with curiosity, masculine arrogance with a touch of innocence. As she got up and went out, he decided to approach her when she returned. An experienced man who seduced women easily, he waited for the right moment. As he saw her walking back to the table, he approached her, adopting an amused expression—though not too amused—and said what had never failed him:

"Hi, I hope I'm not interrupting anything. I noticed you and I . . . I'm not playing games. It's not my style. I would really like to get to know you."

"Sorry, I don't speak Hebrew."

Overwhelmed, this totally unexpected response left him speechless. He often thought that he had heard every possible answer or joke, but he stood there mute. And though he spoke English very well and could easily repeat the sentence in English, he stared at her, returning a forced smile to the small white teeth peeking through as she smiled, and remained silent.

He went to The Penguin often for a couple of weeks, hoping she would show up. Another Friday, he went earlier than usual, but in vain. Hours of anticipation, looking at every woman entering the bar, glasses of beer downed in haste, almost thoughtlessly, turned into gloominess. He kept telling himself he only wanted to complete the seduction, erase the embarrassing memory. But all these detailed and well-founded arguments disappeared in an instant when someone touched his arm—the fair skin and gleaming small teeth almost made him mute again.

Laurie came from London. A young woman with a certain age-old acumen, fashionable clothes that looked classy, a childish mischief concealed by British manners. When she let her hair down and then gathered it again with a black velvet bow hairpin, her porcelain skin looked remarkably clean and fresh. Her straight dress emphasized her curved figure. Tall and erect, she sometimes adopted a detached, skeptical expression. A Jewish woman who had come to Israel driven by disillusioned idealism.

On the street in Hampstead where she'd grown up, silence had always prevailed. Only rarely were a passing car or church bells heard. A house made of brown bricks, almost at the top of the hill, surrounded by a garden with a moldy wall. At the garden's center stood a magnolia tree, blooming every spring. The family watched the first buds turning into white flowers, wine glasses with snowy nectar, withering before summer.

Within an educated, affluent family, Laurie's life seemed to stretch into a very comfortable future. She was admitted to Oxford, got a good degree, and then went to law school. But she found the legal system somewhat tedious, and a years-long affair with a friend from school ended in misery. Thus, the option of immigrating to Israel, which had always existed, arose. Her parents had never considered leaving Britain, but every visit to Israel produced either overstated enthusiasm or distressed disappointment. She knew they would take her resolution with both apprehension and some pride, but since she had made the decision, she was determined to avoid unnecessary sentimentality and to cope with the new country with humor. She wouldn't be daunted by government bureaucrats whose rudeness was common knowledge or be deterred by the aggressiveness of some Israelis. Everything was known beforehand; she was moving to Tel Aviv with eyes wide open, with no illusions or false hopes.

Laurie's naked body on the bed seemed to Ofir like a figure from an old picture. Her black hair on the pillow resembled bold brush strokes, her pink nipples looked like a touch of pigment dispersed in water, and her pubic hair was like delicate lines made with a charcoal pencil, a quick but accurate sketch. He looked at her, slightly trembling. All his ideas about the female body—categories and subcategories, side and front views, the desired proportions between the breasts and the torso, the significance of the legs, face versus body, curved or elongated body type, short or long hair—they all vanished, taking with them the comfortable distance he had developed, the confidence of a man who had known many women. He now stood there like a boy seeing a naked woman for the first time, anxious and astonished.

A moment before he lay down beside her a thought crossed his mind, something about a path from which there was no turning back. A small wooden bridge, maybe even made of ropes, materialized in his imagination; a pass from desert to green meadow or perhaps from rocks to plowed field. For a split second the bridge assumed a clear, well-defined form, and then faded away and disappeared.

1992

The setting sun cast golden light into the café on Hayarkon Street in Tel Aviv, reflecting in the glass plates and cups on the table. Late in the afternoon, the breeze made the smell of the sea much stronger. Warm salty spray brought a primordial odor, creating tranquility; ancient water crashing onto the beach and fading away, crawling onto the hot sand, changing its mind and sliding back.

Next to Ben sat a pretty woman with long blond hair, big blue eyes, and an oval face, wearing a white dress with generous cleavage revealing full breasts. Ben looked around curiously, searching for people watching her. He smiled with satisfaction when he saw a couple of men looking at her keenly. He stuck his fork into a slice of rich cheesecake, taking a bite of the three layers, cheese, chocolate, and cake dough, eating voraciously, exhibiting his pleasure to an imaginary spectator. The pretty woman smiled at him, as if he were a cute little boy gorging on desert, while sipping from her small cup, leaving behind traces of lipstick.

Earlier that day, they had visited a high-end jewelry store located on Dizengoff Street. The assistants had been very accommodating; only last week they'd bought a bracelet at the same shop. The place was spacious and bright. A beige-colored carpet, off-white walls, beech wood display cases full of jewelry, lit by numerous tiny lamps; and on the wall were screens with videos showing beautiful women wearing earrings, chains, necklaces, rings. In the center of the store was a round glass display case filled with diamond jewelry.

The pretty woman turned to the diamonds. Smiling at Ben, leaning on his arm, she rested her head on his shoulder as though she needed support and led him directly to the diamonds. An assistant offered to help; the woman smiled again, pointed at Ben and said, "He wants to buy me earrings." Immediately, trays lined with burgundy velvet were taken out: earrings round, square, long and short, studded with diamonds. The pretty woman examined the earrings, touching some with her long fingers that were tipped with well-groomed red nails. While Ben waited, as if he happened to be there by mere coincidence, she asked to see a couple of pairs, and finally picked out one with three miniature diamonds. These were removed from the tray and disappeared into a red box, wrapped with cellophane.

"Forty-five hundred shekels, sir," the assistant said to Ben, as if there were no point in bothering the pretty woman with money; clearly, he would pay whatever they cost. Ben handed over his credit card, and in a minute or two the couple walked toward the exit, the pretty woman smiling at him cheerfully. As they left, another couple entered. The man glanced at Ben's partner with desire. His gaze, so clear and exposed, made Ben glad, as if he had managed to overcome an opponent, to progress toward a triumph he would never quite achieve.

Earlier that day, before they had gone to the jewelry shop, the pretty woman had come to Handex's offices to get Ben. Rather than wait in the car, she had come into the offices, per his request. Michelle had suggested this. When she saw the pretty woman, she whispered to herself that her physical relationship with Ben was over and that she'd better focus on her role as a secret consultant. "Make sure Ofir sees her as much as possible," she said quietly, explaining repeatedly that one shouldn't give "them" the feeling that they were the only ones doing well. The pretty woman often came into the office to pick up Ben, smiling at Ofir. He greeted her nicely, suggesting they all go out together, complimenting her on her blouse or jewelry; but after she and Ben left, he sank into his chair, leaning back, closing his eyes, adopting a worried, even pained, expression.

The pretty woman and Ben stopped for a while at his place. Without him suggesting it, she took off her clothes in front of him and waited for him in bed. He gazed at her with both pleasure and a touch of resentment. "Carine, you're so beautiful," he always said, wondering if his words were aimed at flattering her or himself. She smiled at him amiably, as if he were a naughty boy, and pulled him toward her. Every time they had sex, he slightly overcame his two-headed envy: Carine's beauty removed his detestable slimness, which remained unchanged despite grueling workouts at the gym, and made Ofir an equal rival. And Michelle's words about "they" and "we" made perfect sense, in a vague and undefined way.

Early in the morning ten months ago, he had stopped by the bank. Handex's account belonged to both him and Ofir; only the two of them could access it. The bank teller, an older woman always wearing dark clothes, greeted him and asked how she could help. "I need to transfer money. Could you please transfer nine thousand eight hundred and eighty shekels into my personal account? Put it under "clearing and management services."

For ten months, he'd been transferring money to his personal account, without telling Ofir.

Money that had become compensation for insults, transforming shameful memories into events that could be avenged. Words blending into each other made stealing appropriate and just. The growing need to explain their friendship—why Ofir hung around with a guy like him—became a constant pain. The women who never wanted him, the lack of masculinity he always felt, and his father's words about the cold-hearted Ashkenazi who wasn't a true friend created a void that could easily be filled with money.

The first time he'd spoken to the teller he'd been trembling. *Petty thief, that's what you are,* he said to himself. Rather than asking Ofir to raise their salaries, he transferred money behind his back. Ofir never refused his requests. They ran the company in perfect harmony, in good spirits, with no arguments or quarrels.

After leaving the bank in the morning, he was highly agitated; he was angry about a traffic jam, the doorman who didn't greet him politely, the secretary who confused incoming and outgoing mail, the programmer who suggested a mechanical aspect of the arm needed improvement. Unlike his usual self, he called the cleaning lady to show her the space behind the file cabinet that wasn't clean enough. As the daily meeting began, he was impatient, but later he fell into thought and heard nothing.

At noon, he didn't join everyone for lunch at the Bulgarian restaurant around the corner. He drove quickly to the bank, wanting to cancel the money transfer and alleviate his growing anxiety, which had evolved into an unexpectedly burdensome anguish. The teller wasn't there; her young colleague offered to help. "I'm sorry, Judith was sick and had to leave. Is there anything I can assist you with? I also handle transfers." He hesitated for a moment and then decided it would be better not to involve anyone else. It was bad enough that the other teller knew about it, though she seemed utterly indifferent. He thanked the woman and said he would return tomorrow, when Judith was there.

But he did not go back the following day.

He returned at the start of the following month, making the same transfer again.

Over ten months he'd transferred nine thousand nine hundred and eighty shekels into his personal account. In the second month, the older teller suggested setting up a direct debit and he agreed immediately. He would be spared the embarrassing monthly encounters with her, although she looked exhausted and uninterested in his requests. He exited the bank and stood on the sidewalk, unsure where to go.

The morning breeze blew through his blond curls, now with a few silver threads, and dried the small sweat drops that rolled down his back despite the chilly morning. As the money was moved, he felt a minor physical agitation. His heartbeat, his hands slightly quivering, sweat. His body exhibited the fear he wished to ignore. Against his will, he envisaged Ofir's response when he discovered the theft; his dark eyes would look at him in a bewilderment that would thicken into exasperation. He would yell or perhaps keep quiet—it would be better if he shouted!—and then storm out of the room, slamming the door behind him. Ofir would want to dissolve the company, sue him, demand that he returned the money.

Tears filled his eyes as he stood in the street, staring at the passing cars. *Ofir, my best friend, my buddy since early childhood, will yell at me, disgrace me, destroy me.* His future suffering became so tangible that in felt like bursting into tears. *Michelle is right,* he thought. *We shouldn't give up. We have to stand up for ourselves. They always put us down, always win.*

Shaken, Ben began to walk down the street toward his parked car. A man walking quickly almost ran into him. A woman with a tight dress walked beside him, trying to catch his eye, but he saw nothing. While thinking about the potential threat, he suddenly saw Carine's body as she'd lain upon his bed yesterday. She seemed alive and real before him: heavy but rounded breasts, a slim abdomen, a full bottom that narrowed gracefully to long legs, delicate hands that looked so elegant with the many rings he had bought her, and protruding lips always colored with red lipstick.

As he started the car, a smile began to spread on his face. *What's the big deal?!* He talked to himself, as if he were sitting in the back seat of the car. *Why am I making such a fuss about it? The company is doing great and will probably make more money in the future, Ofir and I run it perfectly together, we're good friends and we complement each other. When the robotic arm becomes commercial, we'll have so much money no one will notice that some of it is missing.*

The sun had almost set, dusting golden powder along the horizon. Ben and Carine were looking at the sea that had assumed a metallic blue hue. She smiled at him sweetly and clung to him, her left breast pressed against his body; she shook her mane of blond hair and said gently: "Next week, will we buy my engagement ring?"

1993

A last-minute hitch. An unexpected obstacle. A plan that went awry. Just before the commencement of the commercial production of the robotic arm, a defect was detected. Perhaps a specific condition hadn't been properly defined. It turned out that in a single situation—an extremely rare one—the robotic arm malfunctioned. The problem was detected almost by chance; a junior doctor in a Boston hospital had practiced using the machine. He'd tried to use the robotic arm in every possible way and found that the arm moved in the wrong direction when at a specific angle never used in surgery.

The machine was disabled at once. The hospital director called Handex, alarmed, describing the problem and suggesting that he would reconsider purchasing it. His wheezy voice came over the phone, with almost no breath between sentences, spraying furious words into the room. "I'm sure you understand that we can no longer use the robot this way; there is no point if it doesn't work properly. It's a shame, really—our doctor got used to training with the robot. It's very difficult to go back to train manually. Nearly impossible." Finally, he stopped his brief rant, having spoken one sentence after another; Ben began to inquire what exactly had gone wrong, asking for accurate data and a detailed description of what had happened when the machine malfunctioned. He asked the director to take photos of the robotic arm at this unusual angle: "We will work day and night," Ben promised, "until we find the problem, and then we will send a team to Boston to fix it. Please give us a couple of days to get to the bottom of this."

Ben and Ofir called a staff meeting. "There is no question of assigning blame," said Ofir in an authoritarian manner, leaning against the desk with his arms crossed. "We're all doing our best. Our only mission now is to locate the problem and solve it in the best possible way, so that the hospital will keep using the arm." But despite these words, a new, unfamiliar tension materialized in the company's offices, a hostility people were eager to conceal. The pleasant atmosphere, the sense of joint effort in which everyone participated, slightly dissipated, leaving a sour spirit and discontent.

The programmers, now twelve people, were more anxious than anyone. The head of the department was Nava, a forty-year-old woman with a PhD in computer science. Clever, determined, capable of solving any issue, she now sat at her desk from morning to dusk, diligently trying to find the error. Her eyebrows drew closer, creating two wrinkles between them, she bit her lips all day long, and her eyes moved for hours from left to right, following the numbers.

The entire programming department was under strain. Abraham, the first computer engineer Ofir and Ben had hired, went into the programmers' office every hour, staring at everyone. Once in a while he couldn't stop himself from asking, "So, did you find anything?" His hands went through his hair, taking off his kippah and putting it back on his head, straightening his shirt, which always seemed too small, and tucking it into his pants. The fifth time he entered the office, Nava lifted her eyes from the screen, gazing directly at him and said in a restrained tone, "Will you please leave us alone? Can't you see we're working?"

"I see, but I don't see any results."

"Excuse me? What is that supposed to mean?"

"That you're looking, but can't find anything. Maybe you're looking in the wrong direction?"

"Will you stop giving us advice? We don't need this now."

"I think you do."

Nava's eyes widened. She had never liked Abraham—a religious man, a settler, flaunting his devotion to his family as if it were a rare jewel he had inherited. "You like to give advice, don't you? Even when no one's asking for it. Maybe you caused the problem?"

"Typical left-winger . . . blaming everyone else."

"And the settlers, as usual, think they're the only ones who know what's right."

"In this case, it's clear you're not right. Otherwise, this whole mess wouldn't have been created."

"You know what your problem is? You can't function if you're not hating someone. Arabs, supporters of the Left, as long as someone is the bad guy and you can tell yourself you're the good ones and others are evil."

"You know what your problem is? You can't admit you're wrong. As simple as that. You can't say 'I thought something but found I was mistaken.' If you could, you would have done so long ago. The problem is that due to your stubbornness, your prime minister is about to give parts of our sacred Land of Israel to our enemies, and unfortunately, much blood will have to be spilled to recapture it."

"Sacred?! To whom?! Rabin will make peace, that's what's bothering you. He wants to solve the conflict with the Palestinians, and you simply can't handle life without conflict. What will you do without enemies? You'll be lost."

"I'm not worried. Trust me, it's not going to happen. With God's help, the Land of Israel will be Jewish forever. We are stubborn, you know. And we live together and struggle together, unlike you guys—living alone, without a big family, with different friends all the time . . ."

The argument between them, now loud, drew everyone to their room. People stood silently, listening to the insults they hurled at each other. Finally, Ben and Ofir arrived. They managed to hear the last sentences, but as they entered the room, the yelling ceased and only echoes of insults were left. Nava and Abraham lowered their eyes, both embarrassed by the political argument which had erupted almost against their will. Ofir asked in a slightly threatening tone, "What's going on here?" No one answered, and everyone went back to their work, leaving Nava looking angrily at her computer screen.

As they walked together to Ofir's office, a silence settled between the friends. A printer's buzz came from one office, a telephone rang, the humming of the robotic arm moving from side to side, and nothing more. They entered the room. Ben sat on the armchair next to the window and dropped his head back on the headrest; Ofir collapsed into his fancy swivel chair and closed his eyes. An overbearing silence filled the room, nearly tangible, spreading to the walls, clinging to the window, filtering out through the closed door.

The two childhood friends, running a promising company, didn't say a word. Each one was eager to explain, argue, yet they remained mute, afraid not only of the unexpected hitch but also of some obscure fissure that had been suddenly unearthed. Not arguments, different stands or viewpoints, but disintegration, a splitting into divisions and subdivisions, depletion, dilution, a process that results in every individual being alone. An onset of an unknown road; it was still possible to believe that it can be forsaken, exchanged for a different path. Ben stuck his nails into the wood of the chair; Ofir gripped the desk. They were both frightened of the shadow they felt was approaching them, having no idea how to fend it off.

After a long while, Ofir opened his eyes and saw Ben staring into the distance. The need to cling to mundane problems made him say, "I understand Nava. Abraham is annoying. And I also agree with every word she's saying. But if we allow political arguments here, we're doomed." He looked at Ben, who was absorbed in thought, his eyes blank.

"There is something condescending about her," replied Ben in a slightly hoarse voice, as if he were struggling with tears and hadn't heard Ofir. "She speaks as if she knows everything better than you. But I also don't like Abraham's self-righteousness, constantly implying that being religious is some kind of advantage. He never speaks about himself; he always says 'we are like this . . . we are like that . . .' Sometimes I feel like asking him why he never says 'I am . . .'"

Ofir looked at Ben, bewildered. "We simply can't allow political arguments here. We won't be able to run the company if we do."

But Ben was self-absorbed, hearing nothing. "My dad says the Land of Israel should not be given to the Gentiles; my mom says we shouldn't take their land, and do anything to prevent soldiers from dying. My dad wants me to accompany him to synagogue on Friday; my mom asks me if I have enough time to read books." His eyes were wide open, but looking at nothing. For a moment Ofir thought tears made them shine.

To further validate his words, Ofir stepped forward and stood by Ben, saying, "Listen, everyone here has their opinion. Since my last reserve military service in Gaza, I've prayed that Rabin will reach some kind of agreement and we'll give them back the occupied territories. I don't want to set foot in those alleys again, chasing children throwing stones, wary of terrorists. I want them to be there and us here, and that's it. I'm not sure Rabin will succeed, there is so much resentment against his actions. And by the way, it will be good for business if he does. But that's irrelevant now. To solve our technical problem and for the sake of our company, we need to generate a sense of togetherness."

Ben looked at him, saying nothing. Ofir was waiting, turning from side to side, walking to the door, changing his mind, and standing by the window, observing the highway. But he turned around in complete surprise, almost stumbling, as he heard Ben say with a stifled voice, "But how? How are we going to do this? We don't work together. Each one is working for himself, for his own success. The company is nothing but a vehicle, not an end in itself. If our employees—including Abraham—are offered another job at a more successful company than Handex, they will quit right on the spot. Every person seeks to maximize their utility. So how exactly will we generate a feeling of a joint effort?"

December 1995

Traveling to Israel always made Natalie, Laurie's mother, excited and somewhat anxious. Once a year, she went with her husband to visit his brother Harry, who lived in Ness Ziona.[1] His house, single-storied and old, was surrounded by a large garden, where they had dinner. Harry took pride in the farmhouse's construction by the first Jewish pioneers in the area during the late nineteenth century. And though it was shabby and nearly falling apart, he was determined to neither change it nor sell it to builders, who offered a fortune. In spring, the nearby orange grove gave off an intoxicating aroma of blossoms, so unfamiliar and invigorating that it stirred within Natalie a yearning for excitement she had never known.

But this time, breaking their routine, they had visited in the winter to meet the family of their future son-in-law. During the flight, Natalie was restless. Her husband fell asleep immediately with his legs stretched out. Turning from side to side, she tried to sleep, but in vain. She then thought she might watch a film, and after a couple of minutes decided to read, but the thought of their approaching encounter with Ofir and his parents took over. She had met him three times on her previous visits. He was first introduced as a friend, then as a boyfriend, and finally Laurie indicated they would move in together. But when Laurie told her parents they were about to get married, Natalie was taken by surprise. It seemed that Laurie's marrying an Israeli man had caused unexpected turmoil.

Laurie described Ofir's parents in detail, but the more Natalie attempted to picture them the blurrier they became. His father was a senior administrator at The Hebrew University, his mother a teacher. Their house in Jerusalem, Ofir's brother and sister—though Laurie portrayed everything with vitality and humor, Natalie felt something crucial was lacking. Years ago, she had visited Beit Hakerem, but couldn't remember anything. Though she kept thinking about what the conversation would be like, in her mind the

---

1   A town in the center of Israel. It was founded as a farm by the first Zionist pioneers in 1883.

entire encounter, which was meant to be filled with happiness and joy, was enveloped in a vague desolation.

After dinner had been served and the trays collected, the flight attendants closed the window shades, leaving the airplane in darkness. Natalie loved dusk, but she found this irritating. As she couldn't fall asleep, her thoughts traveled to her parents. Her mother, who had moved from Germany to Britain when the Nazis took power, didn't want any Jewish friends. But when Natalie was about five years old, images of the Red Army entering Auschwitz appeared in the newspaper. Her mother looked at them, crying out loud, wailing and holding her head, indifferent to her young daughter watching her in horror. "God forbid, God forbid," she kept yelling as the faces of the survivors emerged, skulls with human eyes, looking out at the world as if they were blind. Though she came from an assimilated family and Zionism was strange to her, and had never even considered immigrating to Palestine, the broken people she saw in the paper created unfamiliar fear. While the UN voted for the partition of Palestine and founding of a Jewish state, she remained seated by the radio set, counting the votes. Upon announcement of the decision, she emitted a strange sigh, sank into the armchair with her head back, lit a cigarette, and exhaled the smoke in an pronounced manner.

In the first years following the war, Natalie's mother had begun to light Shabbat candles on Friday nights. First, she placed them on the dinner table and watched them with glazed eyes. She then carried them carefully to the pretty oak chest in the living room and returned to the dining table. After a few minutes, she walked embarrassed to the living room to check that the candles hadn't gone out. Very carefully, as if she were carrying fragile ancient treasures, she moved them back to the kitchen, monitoring them every couple of minutes with both admiration and discomfort. She tried to keep kosher, leaving one shelf in the refrigerator for dairy products and one for meat, as though it were necessary to prepare for a terrible disaster and store food. Occasionally, she visited the Conservative synagogue close to their house, but always came back home weary and disheartened. After a year, she stopped going, but she gathered every available piece of information about the Holocaust and the State of Israel, reading three newspapers, so as not to miss a single detail. The concentration camps, the process of extermination, the survivors gathered in camps, the Balfour Declaration, the War of Independence—she knew all about the process that she felt was both tragic and heroic.

Natalie was born in London. Her parents had done well; they lived in a beautiful neighborhood and she attended good schools. She sometimes felt the red and brown bricks had become part of her body. The family joined a Reform community and were surrounded by Jewish friends, dining together on weekends, inviting each other for Passover and Rosh Hashanah. It never crossed her mind to marry a non-Jewish man. Eric had grown up in a different part of London, but ever since they had met, they'd felt like childhood friends. There was no need to plan their home in Hampstead; a polished pattern, reserved and somewhat elegant, was ingrained in both of them, keeping their lives within boundaries they both knew perfectly well.

The singing in the Belsize Square synagogue on Friday night and Saturday mornings was crystal clear. The pleasant voices of seven women—one of whom was Natalie—and six men blended perfectly, echoing harmonious prayers and chants. Initially, they all sang in unison, then diverged into twos and threes, and finally came together again, ending the song in complete harmony. The synagogue would be nearly full; many went to listen to the choir, known for its enchanting sound. Some people closed their eyes, surrendering to the music; others followed the conductor attentively—his sharp movements stood in contrast to the soft music.

Natalie had often thought that it was only through singing that a sense of the divine was formed. The sight of the ark, the rabbi praying, the synagogue packed on Yom Kippur—they all left her unaffected. But when the choir sang, she felt a different light, dim but glowing, filling the space, spreading slowly from the singers to the audience and shrouding them with mysterious splendor; their faces indicated that a radiance had saturated them, and that they'd given themselves to it with profound awe. Chant after chant, the choir and the audience melded into a single entity, unified by the clear voices reaching out to God, praising Him and asking for His grace.

But the last time Natalie had gone to the synagogue on the Sabbath, the light had faded. A new spirit, gloomy and bitter, had taken over the place. Since the assassination of Yitzhak Rabin, the transparent bubble enveloping the community had burst, leaving its members speaking quietly, almost whispering, as though they wished no one could hear them. "Jews murdering their own prime minister—it's unbelievable," a friend from the choir said to Natalie somberly. "I can't sleep at night. It's all I think about. What a disgrace. What will people think of us now?" Time and again the word "unbelievable" was spoken, followed by "God forbid" or "who could believe this could happen?" The eyes of the community members betrayed a horror which normally remained unseen.

On the morning after the murder, people gathered in the room next to the sanctuary, standing and watching the news in silence. Facing the TV some held their heads, one woman cried quietly at the side, and two men wore prayer shawls. A girl clung to her mother in fear. The rabbi was slumped in a chair. For years they had been grappling with accusations that Israel's military force was excessive, that it was reluctant to end the occupation, finding every argument both just and absurd. Israel's brilliant victory in the Six Day War has already been forgotten—how Holocaust survivors became heroes. But now, in an instant, their sense of being unique was shattered. Like any other people, they turned against their leader and killed him.

Against her will, Natalie thought of her friendly neighbor. "What are you celebrating? Do you keep kosher?" the woman would ask. More than once she'd enquired about Israel, and Natalie always gave a balanced view: it's important that Israel exists, but it should withdraw from the occupied territories. Jews need a national home, but not at the expense of others. But now, thinking about the questions her neighbor might ask, a deep anger surfaced, grew, and solidified, becoming a mass that could not be ignored. She imagined herself raising her voice to the bewildered neighbor: *Israel? I'm British, just like you. Why do you keep asking me about Israel? Do I enquire where your parents came from?* Israel is a distant country, somewhere in the deserts of the Middle East, a Jewish state that was established for good reasons, that veered off course after the Six-Day War, and occupied another people. And now a Jewish man has assassinated Rabin, our hero. What is it that you want to know about Israel? I'll tell you what kind of country it is: over there, no one asks me how I celebrate, and what do I do. They simply let me be Jewish, without asking too many questions. I don't have to justify myself, to explain myself to my neighbors. I speak the little Hebrew I know there, but no one understands me . . .

"Natalie, Natalie, wake up. You've been talking in your sleep. We'll be landing shortly. Did you have a bad dream? You kept turning from side to side." Eric shook her gently, attempting to get rid of the nightmare. The window shades were now open, and a different light entered the plane. It was sharp and yellow, with neither mist nor clouds. Unmasked sun shone in the sky. Natalie looked at Eric, astonished, pulling herself out of her dream, and then she realized she would see Laurie in a couple of minutes. Complete joy swept over her; she looked through the window with a smile.

The Mediterranean Sea stretched all the way to the horizon, a vibrant blue, fresh, and invigorating; and Tel Aviv's shoreline could be seen in the distance. She combed her hair, tucked in her blouse, took a look at her watch and said to her husband, "Ah, I must have slept for a quite some time. We'll be touching down in a couple of minutes, won't we?"

May 1996

A bride and a groom under a canopy on a balcony overlooking the sea. Laurie, the bride, is wearing a simple, graceful dress. A soft shining fabric envelops her tall body. Her light, glowing skin is more radiant than ever. Her beautiful shoulders, previously bare, are covered by a veil; her lips are red and full, and her round eyes are wide open, slightly anxious, almost wary; they wander from one guest to another. Small white flowers are woven into the ebony hair falling over her shoulders. For a moment, she looks like a little girl dressed up like a bride, wanting to take off the costume and escape. But as she turns to Ofir, her future husband, a smile creeps into her eyes, a mischievous sparkle. She examines him from head to toe. He's dressed in an elegant suit. She smiles to herself with contentment. A bride painted in black and white, with gentle brush strokes; clean, simple lines that curve like an old Japanese painting. But her red lips lend an air of earthly sensuality to the delicate image.

On her right side is Natalie, her mother. A woman in in her fifties, she is tall and slightly awkward. Though her skin is smooth and unwrinkled, it seems as though she grew old years ago, when she was still young. Her brown hair perfectly done, she is nicely made up, and wears a long purple dress and lovely gold earrings—if the heavy movements of her body could be ignored, she'd be attractive. She smiles, but her eyes reveal panic. People had asked her if she was afraid to travel to Israel, where suicide bombers blow up buses; she'd replied that she would be extra careful. But strangely, now, under the canopy, she feels the danger acutely and turns toward the sea. The sun is setting, the horizon is deep orange, a purple stripe above it, and the sky is blue gray. The intense colors make her shiver. The view is spectacular and foreign. The scent of the sea is primordial. Alarmed, she turns to Eric, her husband, and sees a film of tears in his eyes.

To conceal them, Eric touches his face casually. But after a couple of moments, he sees it is useless and lets the tears roll down his soft, round cheeks. He is a full-figured man of medium height, with a protruding belly. He wears glasses with gold frames, which he pushes up occasionally. His hair is slightly long and graying, and his eyes small and intelligent. The bride's father, the excitement leaves him in tears. Against his will, he is thinking of his parents, who couldn't fly from London to Tel Aviv due to old age and poor health. "I wish they were here," he murmurs to himself. "I wish they could see this beautiful couple getting married. Laurie, sweetie, what a lovely bride she is. I wish my grandfather could have seen her." Though the rabbi has already begun the ceremony, Eric is thinking of his late grandfather, who was a rabbi in Golders Green. As a child, Eric used to attend marriage ceremonies presided over by his grandfather, and he now recalls one in particular: a very young couple, maybe eighteen years old, the groom's face was nearly as flushed as his red hair, and the bride's face completely concealed as she was led to the canopy. His grandfather's deep voice echoed as he recited the blessings, but the grandson watched the bride with trepidation, wondering if the groom knew what she looked like . . .

Eric now wards off the memory and is present again in the wedding. At last, he stops crying and manages to smile faintly. Though he can see Laurie's happiness clearly, his heart aches. He fears he won't see her again after the wedding. In a moment she will be married to this handsome young man standing beside her and she will completely disappear from his life, forget he exists, cut all cords linking her to her family, and settle in this country, which he loves dearly but is still a foreign land to him. She will even begin to behave like the locals, who are loud and too resolute. These thoughts, which he knows are odd, make a broad grin appear on his face, as if he has just discovered he's attending a joyful event. He looks at his wife, signing how happy Laurie is; he examines the groom, no doubt a good-looking man, and then turns his eyes to the groom's father—*that man's too vain. His excessive amiability and well-prepared jokes; he's always offering to help. Underneath it all there is great pride*, but Eric isn't sure about what.

Harry, Eric's brother from Ness Ziona, stands in front of the canopy and crosses his muscular arms to show his reservations about the ceremony. *What have I got to do with all these stylish folks, and the psalms and prayers the rabbi is uttering?* A farmer, a man whose daily routine is shaped by forces of nature, he finds the rabbi's remarks redundant and annoying. He's never married Nurit, his partner of thirty years, who is standing next to him dressed in an embroidered blouse that Russian farmers' wives used to wear. Her hair is gathered simply on top of her head, she is tanned and wrinkled, but in her eyes there's the freshness of people who live in nature. She looks at the groom and bride, smiles, and then puts her arm through her partner's.

Joseph looks at Ofir with satisfaction and then examines the guests. When he sees an unfamiliar face, he tries to figure out who that person is. Here is the president of the university, the provost. His friend the general is wearing his uniform and everyone is impressed by him. Famous professors, officers of the Jewish Agency—he counts the important guests with satisfaction. The young literature professor's jacket is too sloppy, he thinks, putting it down in an imaginary notebook, making a note to joke about it sometime in the future. Men, women, children, elegantly dressed and smiling—Joseph looks at them and sees deep pillars holding a robust, durable structure, an accepted order fostering security and peace of mind. Family members stand close to the canopy; behind them are people of social standing, and then the young friends of the bride and groom (apart from Abraham, their religious employee, who is right in front of the canopy with his wife and five children). *It has always been like this, and always will be. It is my good fortune,* he thinks, *that I made such good connections, a spider's web that envelops me and my family and secures our future. Though Ofir doesn't need them to succeed, they may prove helpful for my younger son and daughter and perhaps also for "the British branch of the family."* Joseph likes to call them that. Though his son is getting married, the thought of him being able to use his connections to assist Laurie and her family fills him with a complete and childlike joy.

Sarit, standing next to her husband, steals a quick look at Laurie's mother's dress, wondering which is prettier. *Mine.* Her dress is dark blue, straight, with almost no decoration; Natalie's is purple, fashionable but not as classy. As the rabbi tells jokes and reads the blessings, Sarit wonders if she should have worn a more glamorous dress or whether the one she has on is best—it emphasizes her slender body. Pondering this question, she suddenly sees the rabbi facing her. Dark eyes and a smile that reveals crooked teeth, she observes him with aversion. *This entire event is preposterous,* she thinks. *It's strange that people ascribe so much importance to ceremonies. Laurie and Ofir have been living together for over a year now, so why is all this necessary?* Everyone is thrilled and in tears, yet she thinks it is a sign of weakness, ideological confusion, even giving in—yes, succumbing to primitive fears that ought to be conquered. *They could throw a party,* she reflects. *Why a religious ceremony?* Arriving here from Russia at the turn of the twentieth century, my mother's parents wouldn't have even considered having such a religious wedding. Socialist pioneers, they despised religion; it was their revolutionary spirit that transformed Zionism from a mere idea to reality. And my father's parents, secular assimilated Jews from Germany, they wouldn't have had a religious ceremony, either. Ah, the increasing susceptibility taking over this place, giving fear unrestricted control, never restraining it, permitting all sorts of rabbis to enforce primitive ideas. The furrow between her eyebrows disappears, and her thin lips are tighter. Her face reveals determination. But as she sees the gleam in her son's eyes she shudders, and for a moment she thinks she is about to faint.

Ofir towers over everyone else; his head nearly touches the canopy. His hair is slick with sweat, probably due to the excitement, and his dark eyes are radiant. He smiles at Laurie, she blushes, and then he listens to the rabbi's words. They are strange, ancient and obscure. Ofir finds the rabbi pale and clumsy, but he is exhilarated, feeling nearly reborn. Not only is he about to marry his beloved Laurie—who, for a fleeting moment, he believes is eyeing him seductively—but the firm is on the road to success.

How did I come up with this idea? he wonders with delight. *It was a flash of inspiration!* For months, the computer people scrutinized every line, rewrote the entire program, wholly committed to resolving the issue, yet feeling it was hopeless. They endlessly blamed one another, convinced that all their effort and hard work would amount to nothing. And suddenly, it occurred to me that problem wasn't in the program: it was in the hardware. They went silent when I raised the possibility. Ben leaped up and ran to his office, shouting to Abraham, who followed him out of breath: "I will do this by myself, thank you." Ben had locked himself in the room for hours, examining every part of the robot with his well-known perfectionism. At midnight, he'd opened the door, pale and exhausted, but his eyes bright: "I found the problem."

Ofir wants to wink at Ben now, express the intimacy between them. He looks for him in the crowd. He sees him standing at the back of the balcony, almost next to the wall, with his parents. *Strange that he isn't standing closer to the canopy.* For a moment, the thought overshadows Ofir's joy, casting a shadow which then sinks and disappears. *Abraham, of all people, is standing right in front of me, as if the fact this is a religious ceremony makes him a close relative,* Ofir thinks with resentment. He carefully suppresses the thought, cautious not to dim the inner light within him.

Abraham is standing next to the canopy; by his side is his pregnant wife and children. His smile is more of an expression of triumph than of joy. Once in a while he touches his kippah and mumbles the prayers along with the rabbi, showcasing his familiarity with the text. Every now and then, he adds "amen" with confidence, relishing the surprised faces of those around him.

Eventually they all go looking for the rabbi, he thinks with pleasure. Those secular guys from Tel Aviv reject any imposition of religion, yet at the moment of truth they wish the rabbi to marry them. Observing the canopy, a pleasant warmth spreads within him; his cheeks flush and his eyes shine. He believes that in this moment, Ofir has found an inner truth, a hidden light he will always cherish, even if he won't admit it. And he's the only person from Handex that Ofir could share this light with. The image of the rabbi will be an enduring memory for him, an unforgettable part of the wedding.

But as Abraham notes a hint of laughter in Ofir's and his father's eyes—they are looking at each other and maybe even winking—he stops smiling and is on the verge of tears. As a child, he was ridiculed by secular children in the neighborhood. Now these past insults surface; he can almost hear them shouting "Dos,[1] dos, Weinstein the dos" as he walked home. His parents had decided to live in a secular part of Petah Tikva, confident that his religious upbringing would make it easy for him to meet the secular environment. But the boys living in his neighborhood were stronger and more agile than he was. In the summer, he watched them enviously in their shorts and tank tops, their bodies tan and their hair wild. Now, for a brief moment, Ofir morphs into a boy who ridiculed him when he was a child. The boy would leave school and jump easily over a fence; meanwhile, Abraham would struggle with the fence and walk home slowly and heavily. In a minute, Ofir will leap from the canopy and sprint off to play ball, leaving Abraham, as always, in the dust.

As he shuts his tear-filled eyes, Abraham hears the rabbi reciting the seven blessings; his heart trembles. "Blessed art Thou, O Lord our God, King of the Universe . . ." echoes up to the balcony, ancient words that Abraham thinks cannot be repudiated. All those childhood insults disintegrate and turn into silent shadows that follow him, mirrored wherever he goes yet never becoming light. As a matter of fact, he murmurs to himself, I should be grateful for these insults; I should disregard the childish tears and recognize that they pushed me toward the right path, lifting me beyond human weaknesses, which we all share. I learned religious devotion and a steadfast belief in the redemption of the holy Land of Israel.

An odd thought emerges, assuming a clear shape and vibrant colors: *when Hebron is entirely Jewish, I will invite Ofir and his family for a tour of the*

---

1   A derogatory term for an Orthodox Jew.

city and to my home in the settlement. Their mocking smiles and concealed dislike toward us will fade, giving way to sheer amazement.

At the side of the balcony, almost behind all the other guests, stands the Haddad family; it's hard to tell whether this is a result of emotional distance or a profound affinity that requires no confirmation. David, Ben's father, looks around nervously, like a man in company he doesn't like. His thick white hair looks almost like a crown. Though he is thinner than ever and slightly bent, leaning on a walking stick, there is a touch of grandeur about him. Dressed in an elegant but old-fashioned suit, his vibrant eyes examine the guests one after the other. *Almost everyone here is Ashkenazi,* he notices. The rabbi sings an Ashkenazi tune, which he finds charmless and dull. He is absolutely certain that the Sephardi synagogue's cantor in Beit Hakerem would have made this wedding, which he thinks is too quiet and restrained, livelier and more cheerful.

When Ben told him he intended to start a computer business, he hugged him and kissed his forehead. His son was so gifted, such an excellent student; he had no doubt it would go well. When he discovered that it would be with Ofir, disappointed, he took a step back. *Once again, this vain and unreliable Ashkenazi, pretending to be his son's best friend.* For years he had told Ben not to fall for empty slogans about sacrificing yourself for other people. Every man looks after himself and his own family, and no one else! This partnership with a childhood friend is nothing but a deception. And now, disguising his bitterness, he is a guest at Ofir's wedding, two months before his own son's marriage. If it had been possible, he would have avoided attending this wedding altogether. He has no desire to be anywhere near a family that he finds condescending and devoid of compassion.

Sophia, his wife, is standing next to him, wearing a slightly gaudy dress with a flower pattern, her lips bright pink. Her body is heavy, her arms full, her feet swollen, but her eyes are full of light. The wedding makes her happy and tears roll down her cheeks. *The young couple is so beautiful,* she thinks. *Ofir is so tall, and Laurie so delicate!* She turns to her son and his future wife, who looks stunning in a black dress and glittering earrings. The proud mother then turns back to the canopy and the vibrant sea behind it, which gradually turns dark and secretive, and feels that a worthy cause has been found; a source of solace, a seed of goodness that always prevails—even if implicitly—is now entirely visible to everyone.

Ben looks at Ofir and Laurie and flushes. His parents assume it is the excitement; his best friend is getting married. Ben's fiancé thinks it is too hot on the balcony; they should have had the ceremony indoors. The Handex employees smile at him, certain that he is picturing his upcoming wedding, only a few months away. And he says to himself: *The shame, God, the shame— I can hardly bear it. A sort of enormous leech, slimy and repulsive, stuck to my body, feeding on my guilt.* The fear that Ofir will find out, the self-hatred that grows stronger and stronger at night, the contempt for the money he doesn't need but keeps stealing; the unbearable moments of joy when he feels more powerful than Ofir, the pain he can impose on him, the eyes that will finally stop smiling at him; the muscular body that will crumple, his own body that won't seem so skinny anymore, the triumph; his sobbing when he confesses, the ridiculous excuses he will use, describing his future wife's uncontrollable desire to buy clothes and jewelry, stuttered words about her not wanting him if he doesn't have money; nausea, the strange pleasure he takes in purchasing things for Carine, which demonstrates that his life depends on money that could disappear one day, a life filled with anxiety; fear of a comfortable but degenerating daily routine, a profound dread of the justice that will eventually win out, the prayers he whispers on sleepless nights, asking God to forgive him, searching for the appropriate words to address the Almighty but never finding them; his self-justification while looking at the sky, especially on cloudless nights—

"If I forget thee, O Jerusalem, let my right hand forget her cunning. Let my tongue cleave to the roof of my mouth, if I remember thee not; if I set not Jerusalem above my chiefest joy." A sound of breaking glass and loud voices congratulating the bride and the groom.

September 1996

In the evening, chilly air filled the garden around Harry's house in Ness Ziona. A light breeze played through the trees. A lemon tree, its tiny yellow fruit hiding in the drying leaves; an orange tree, its fruit so heavy they bent its thin branches; a tall tangerine tree, its green-yellow leaves full of shimmering light; and at the far end of the garden, a gloomy olive tree, with grayish leaves and a gnarled trunk. Next to the fence were green bushes, tall and wild. But the fragrant wildflowers transplanted from nearby meadows were the heart of the garden. Some were still blooming at the end of the summer; others bowed their heads as they felt the winds of fall.

During the daytime, the flowers were captivating. Yellow, red, purple—stains of intense color surrounded by green foliage. But as darkness came on, the garden lost its appealing nature and adopted a mysterious air. The flowers looked dull and somewhat lackluster. Yet the philodendron at the side of the garden, previously only a background to the blooms, suddenly seemed vital, reaching out its outstretched palms to the trees, trying to sense their presence. A small myrtle turned its myriad ears, listening to the hum of the breeze, which grew stronger as darkness fell. A round blue ranger looked like a huge hedgehog trapped at the corner of the garden, hunching its back, stretching its long spires, its petals like crowns placed on invisible heads. The fruit trees weren't so inviting anymore; the fruits turned invisible, the leaves dark, a wild thicket that might cover anything.

Natalie and Eric sat on the porch, facing the garden. Above them loomed a darkening sky with small clouds; a full moon, yellow and round, slowly rose from the horizon. They looked around, trying to figure out what made them feel like strangers. The new scent? Air full of dust and minuscule drops of water? The grayness that contained a hidden ray, lighting the sky, though it was impossible to tell where it came from? After a couple of minutes, Natalie relaxed in her chair and said quietly, "This is so different from our garden at home, isn't it?" The one in Hampstead appeared in her mind as she closed her eyes; its tranquility expanded across seas and continents. The smell of leaves on the ground, the cool, humid air, the flower beds with their variety of plants. She suddenly recalled the daffodils she had planted before traveling to Israel, the magnolia tree, its leaves orange in the fall, the climbing vine that clung to the house. For a moment, she felt she could smell the fresh scent of her garden in London. When she opened her eyes, the scene seemed wild and slightly frightening.

In the morning, they took a trip north to Galilee. Every time they traveled with Harry and Nurit, Natalie gazed at the view with admiration and a touch of panic. Mountains, valleys, desert, and sea, her brother-in-law kept saying "our land," and Natalie looked around, trying to locate the origin of this affinity to the land. He called it his own. Natalie liked Harry's direct and honest way of talking, his generosity, and his silence when he had nothing to say. He once drove her from the airport to his house saying nothing all the way. With anyone else, she would have been brought to tears—but not with him. His silence was natural and good. But as he said "our land," she felt an inexplicable abyss opening up between them.

When she toured the green landscape of Britain, she never felt it was hers. A couple of weeks ago, they had driven to Bamburgh Beach. The old castle faced the pure blue sea. Haze concealed the horizon, wide meadows curved down to the glittering sand, bushes swaying in the wind. Natalie had stood there, overwhelmed, breathless. A massive dome enveloped the world, the sea stretched to the horizon, and a variety of plants danced in the wind together—forward, backward, forward again. She closed her eyes to breathe the fresh scent of the sea, enjoying nature, giving in to the consolation of its omnipotence. One woman, standing in one place, taking in a very small part of a huge, immeasurable, space.

This morning, as they drove to Galilee, she first enjoyed the beauty of the landscape. The small car driving northward along the coast began to climb the mountains around Haifa, turning eastward toward the Jezreel Valley, and then to the Galilee mountains. The old Renault struggled uphill, faltering but gradually climbing the rocky mountains, with scattered plants turning yellow at the end of the summer. One hilltop and another, hidden caves, bright rocks—Natalie was so absorbed by the wild landscape she could hardly follow the conversation. Bare land, burning sun, hilly slopes, birds circling in the sky, a herd of cattle trying in vain to find shade under a single tree—a region she felt was primordial and elemental.

They reached the summit—and as the car descended the hills, suddenly, unexpectedly, Natalie was astonished to see a blue lake nestled in the mountains. The Sea of Galilee stretched out before her, tranquil and enlightened, refreshing water in between bearded hills. As her brother-in-law saw her expression, amazed and admiring, he smiled and said, "Yes, this is incredible. We have a beautiful country, don't we?" interrupting her strange daze, as though it were a vision she was seeing and not a lake surrounded by hills. At once the envelope of misty air was ruptured, a winding road ending in baptism, mountains cradling water, and again Natalie asked herself in what way was this place "ours."

While sitting in a restaurant in Migdal, plates of hummus, tahini, and salads on the table, she looked at her husband and his brother talking. Nurit remarked quietly, "These two brothers are both very similar and different." They both had round faces, small, intelligent eyes, fleshy noses and soft, straight gray hair. But their appearance revealed their different ways of life. Eric was slightly bent, his body slack as he leaned against the backrest, observing his brother with humor. Harry sat straight, his muscular hands veiny, his face wrinkled from hours in the sun, and his gaze direct, perhaps even forthright. The two women gazed at the brothers, smiling at each other.

"You are from somewhere around here, aren't you?" asked Natalie.

"I'm from a kibbutz not far from here. I was born there and left only when I was twenty-five. My parents were part of the group that established the kibbutz. The beautiful valley we saw on our way here used to be one big swamp. They drained the water and planted eucalyptus trees to dry the land. They worked in unbearable heat and suffered from malaria. Fortunately, they both survived. They were so scared when I was born, fearing that children wouldn't make it through the harsh conditions. I have been living in Ness Ziona for more than thirty years now, but this place is my home. My parents turned the place from a wasteland into a blooming valley."

A thin, invisible needle of envy pierced Natalie; she thought she could feel it burning. Passion, devotion, hard work, difficult conditions that created profound intimacy, a shared destiny, an unreserved commitment to the idea of a Jewish state, a brave life lacking hesitation—looking at her brother-in-law's partner, her eyes betrayed a hidden yearning. For a moment, the present was forgotten—the murder of Rabin and the occupation. She wanted nothing more than to be a part of the group of pioneers who dried out the swamps. But as she turned her eyes to her husband, she thought she could smell the fresh scent of her garden in London. Young seedlings that may have sprouted while she was away, the magnolia tree whose leaves would fall before the winter, the daffodils she planted before the trip—though she kept listening to the stories of making the wasteland blossom and nodding politely, again the mountainous landscape turned into an estranged land. Desert next to a sea, a lake surrounded by hills, the blazing sun and verdant valleys, wild, primeval natural forces, unconquerable seas and continents stretching to the horizon and beyond. The longing for the small garden on the hill in Hampstead brought tears to her eyes, despite her silent, repeated self-reproach.

1997

Michelle closed her apartment door, went down the stairs, exited the building, and began to walk swiftly. As she knew her husband was watching her from the window, she turned right, pretending to be on the way to her office. But down the road, she was planning to turn in the opposite direction, to Ibn Gabirol Street. There, she would take a taxi to the restaurant where she would meet Ben. Now a successful lawyer, she wore a very tight suit and high heels, modern, orange-framed glasses resting on her childish nose, and her strange mouth, covered in bright red lipstick, was constantly twitching as though it were an independent creature.

When the taxi stopped at the restaurant, she sneaked in hastily. She found Ben seated at a side table, reading the newspaper. Only when she stood right next to him did he lift his eyes, smile, and call the waitress. As Michelle ordered coffee, she noticed him openly checking out the young waitress. He asked her in a humorous tone if she made enough money and if the owner of the place took care of his employees. When she brought the food he joked again with the young woman, while Michelle looked at him in bewilderment.

"So, everything is okay at Handex? I assume the troubles are over?" she asked in a provocative tone.

"Yep, everything is fine. We've resolved the issues and now we're in the process of manufacturing a couple of new robots. We hope to sell them quickly."

"I'm sure they'll be snapped up. You said the director of the Boston hospital was thrilled when he heard the glitch had been fixed."

"Yes. The simulation of surgeries with our robotic arm is very user-friendly."

"You don't look so happy."

"I am happy."

"It sure doesn't look like it."

"Yes, everything's good. We're making money. We hired another engineer and a programmer."

"So?"

"So what?"

"So why aren't you happy?"

"To be honest, I don't know. When I think about it, I see everything is progressing smoothly.

"Do you have a problem with money? Your wife doesn't."

Ben smiled faintly. His bright eyes followed children jumping and laughing in the street and a silver car driving quickly, finally returning to Michelle almost in desperation.

"The truth is that now when everything's fine, I feel like something is lacking."

"I can't believe you're saying that. You kept telling me that people were quarreling and blaming each other."

"That's true. They did quarrel and blame each other."

"Do you miss that? Are you out of your mind?"

"It's strange, but, despite the quarrels, which were unpleasant, I felt we were all trying to solve the problem together."

"I don't get it. You said the very opposite: before the glitch occurred, everyone wanted the project to succeed, and the problem made them turn against each other."

"Frankly, I thought that by the time we fixed this complication, we'd get back our old atmosphere. But it never happened. Something changed. I'm not sure what, but it's not the same. The feeling that we all want the company to do well is gone."

"I don't believe there's a single person there who isn't in it for the money."

"Everyone wants money, but there was always something else, and it's gone."

"You kept ridiculing Ofir for trying to generate a fake notion of partnership. You said he acted like a spoiled child, trying to live in an ideal world."

"That's true. But maybe he had a point. Something has disintegrated, and it doesn't fit together anymore. I'm not sure what it is. People work together, but each one is alone. It's not all bad. In fact, we are more productive this way, but it's not pleasant, that's all."

"It's better that way. My boss keeps telling us that a law firm requires cooperation, that lawyers should consult each other, and so on. I think it's his way of exploiting us. It makes it harder to ask for a raise."

A minuscule and almost imperceptible spark of laughter flickered in Ben's eyes and immediately faded as if it had never existed. His thin hands grabbed the mug and turned it. Sitting bent over the table had wrinkled his white shirt. His soft curls, with plenty of gray, fell across his high forehead, now marked by a new horizonal line. He wore a strange expression, a mixture of pain and pleasure, as though he found his own suffering amusing. He ordered another cup of coffee and again joked with the waitress.

Michelle noticed he was in a strange mood. Though he kept smiling, his enmity surfaced against his will. She watched him intently, her mouth twitching, smiling as her mouth turned down. This may be an opportunity to generate animosity, she thought. I can weaken a years-long partnership, and manipulate Ben into distancing himself from his successful friend. The right side of her mouth turned down; she lifted her eyebrows and adopted a severe, dignified countenance.

"Oh, come on, it's about time you grew up," she said. "You can't hold onto these childish affinities for friends and colleagues. It doesn't work that way. Trust me, I know. I understand life without metaphors or tropes. Life smiles at some people, and then there are all the rest of us. It's that simple. And if you're not fortunate enough to be born a winner, you must do whatever it takes to make it. And there's no solidarity or friendship, only personal interest."

"Oddly, you sound like my dad. He keeps telling me that everyone looks after himself, his family, and no one else."

"Family? Maybe children and parents. If I had to choose between my husband and my professional success, I have no doubt what I would choose. I was the one who wanted to get married—and I don't want to divorce him. But there is simply no choice. If you want to make it, it has to be at the expense of others."

A group of elderly women entered the restaurant and sat down beside them, the sound of dragging chairs, loud voices, the smell of perfumes blending together. Ben and Michelle watched them sit down, smiling kindly at the waitress and debating what they should order. One asked if the omelet was made with herbs, another wanted spelt bread, and the third asked for chamomile tea with milk. Michelle followed the women with interest, but moments later, as she turned her gaze to Ben, she saw him looking at her intently, immersed in thought.

"Want to come to my place? Let's have some fun."

"What?! Where is Carine?"

"Went to Paris for a week. Shopping with a friend."

"Are you inviting me to your home?"

"Yes. Why not? It won't be the first time you've come to my place."

"Your apartment?"

"Yes. Do you mind?"

Not a single word was said on their way to Ben's place. The elegant car drove on Ayalon highway, crossed the narrow streets of central Tel Aviv and finally stopped smoothly in a parking place in front of a beautiful building. The entrance was made with marble, the elevator very spacious, on the top floor they stood in front of a door with gold-lettered plate that read "Haddad." As they entered, her breath escaped her. Though Ben had told her Carine kept renovating the apartment, she had never imagined he was living in such a swanky place. For a moment, she thought perhaps he was no longer part of the vast and indistinct group of gray people who have to struggle for everything. She walked from one room to another, looking around bewildered: a vast living room flooded with light, almost all white except for a couple of colorful cushions and a huge painting adoring an entire wall; the kitchen was a mixture of shiny marble and bare concrete. The remaining rooms exuded perfect harmony. And here was the bedroom, the colossal bed with a light gray cover, an oversized mirror gracing the wall, bell-shaped lamps on both sides of the bed . . .

Michelle was pushed from the back and fell hard on the bed. Ben leaned over her, tearing at her clothes, breathing heavily. And though she felt a certain thrill of triumph, she was horrified as he asked her if he could tie her to the bed. "What do you say? It's not for real, you know. You can always say 'no.' I feel like running wild."

Her heartbeats were razor-sharp; she could hardly feel his body. Her sarcasm, mean comments, her desire to manipulate everyone, her insatiable need to dominate, they all disappeared at once as paralyzing fear filled her, the horror of an animal caught in a hunting net, kicking at the threads that only tightened further around her body. She stopped herself from asking Ben not to hurt her, closing her eyes as his sweat dripped on her body. If she had opened her eyes, she would have seen first his intoxicating, sharp pleasure, a strange expression, flared nostrils and eyes half closed, and a triumphant smile; finally envy had been eliminated, Ofir evaporated like he had never existed, and only Ben's body was left in the bedroom, strong and uninhibited. But then his mouth twitched slightly, his body became slack, his eyes closed, and the wrinkle across his forehead deepened. His hand ran through his sweaty curls. He opened his eyes for a second, looking at her with surprise, and then he closed them again and bent his head forward, remaining motionless—maybe sinking in an inner abyss, maybe praying.

April 1998

The tall tower rose high above the buildings of Tel Aviv, a glittering lighthouse in a sea of urban lights. Even before the Azrieli skyscraper was open to the public, Handex had rented offices on the fortieth floor. The equipment had been shipped and unpacked in the new spacious place. An unsettling spirit filled the old offices before the move: loud voices, the screech of desks being dragged across the floor, the sound of breaking glasses that had been carelessly placed near the corridor, the constant laughter of the Russian-speaking movers, the muffled sound a pile of paper made when falling off a cabinet onto a dusty floor, the rattle of the windows the programmers slammed in haste, the thud the telephone made when it fell from the corner of the desk the secretary had been pushed into.

Spring sunlight, a draft that made computer printouts billow, a wastebasket upended—when the company vacated its offices, a certain framework was dismantled and the self-imposed discipline dissipated. On the floor were fragments of the initial model of the robotic arm, folded envelopes, and napkins, along with previously concealed coffee stains on the carpet.

The new offices had better lighting, vast windows, and the smell of fresh paint. The wall-to-wall carpet was bright and clean. The Handex offices had a nice glass entrance, but the office sign hadn't been placed on the door yet. In the first couple of days, construction workers filled the corridor. Some elevators were out of order, and daily power outages made the employees get up and turn toward the windows to look out at the city spread beneath them: winding roads and tall trees that rattled in the spring breeze and cast shadows over buildings. The sky was clear and lucid, very light blue with hints of hidden pink, not yet illuminated by the blazing summer sun.

Abraham got a very spacious office next to Ben's. The company's senior employee, he walked around the corridor checking every room, asking if everything was okay, perhaps someone needed assistance? Even before the company moved, he had started using a fatherly tone and addressing others as though they had asked for his advice, giving guidance on teenage sons, warnings about rent hikes, and suggestions of reliable places to purchase a

used car. He always wore wide trousers and a plaid shirt with a slightly yellowish collar and straightened his kippah as he talked, smiling at everyone.

But immediately after the move, he went excitedly into Ben's office and
said that a mezuzah must be affixed to the main entrance and to every office
door. Engrossed in the software, Ben lifted his gaze from the computer screen
for a moment. "Yeah, sure. The tower's maintenance company will do that,"
he said, and immediately went back to work. But Abraham stood at the door,
leaning against the doorframe and stretching a little, not leaving. When Ben
realized Abraham was still watching him, he relaxed, leaned back in his office
chair, turned to Abraham, and waited in silence.

"I don't want to bother you," Abraham said. "I can see that moving the
offices is quite a hassle, but I think we need to hold a ceremony for affixing
the mezuzahs and invite everyone. I understand the offices will have mezuzahs anyway, but there is something symbolic about it. God is guarding us
from all evil with a mezuzah on the door."

A faint smile spread on Ben's face, momentarily replacing his serious
expression and blurring the long wrinkle across his forehead. He ran his hand
through his hair and blinked.

"Come on, Abraham, you can't be serious. Not that I object to God
guarding us, but still, think about all the trouble people with mezuzahs have
had." For a moment, he seemed taken by a mischievous spirit, as if he was
finding humor in the idea of unfortunate people affixing mezuzahs to their
doors. They had experienced illnesses, orphanhood, bankruptcies—all with
a mezuzah. He swung his legs with an odd sense of delight under the desk,
like a toddler seated in a highchair.

Abraham was taken by surprise by Ben's response. A couple of times he
had discussed the Sephardi synagogue in Jerusalem with Ben's father, and he
naturally assumed that Ben would gladly accept his suggestion. Though still
leaning against the door frame, he straightened up, for a moment holding
his breath, wondering if Ben was about to say that he was only joking. "Of
course, there is no insurance; every believer knows that. It only means we
place our trust in God. Well, you know, like your father says."

As Abraham uttered the word "father," a hidden string in Ben's body
stretched, making him strangely alert. He stopped swinging his legs under
the desk like a child, put down the pen he was holding, and directed his gaze
at Abraham. His eyes resembled those of a blind man attempting to see in the
darkness; though he is bound to fail, he still strains, eager to absorb objects

around him. Ben's smile disappeared completely as a hidden pain bled into his lively face.

"My father also thinks people should care for themselves and not others," Ben said. "He says we must never follow politicians who try to persuade us with all sorts of rubbish like 'the public good' and all that. Every person should do whatever is best for them. It's better that way."

"He's right! Trust me, he is right!" Abraham added quickly, feeling that he would find common ground with Ben here. "Those supporters of the Left keep talking about the benefit of society, how they support the workers, but the truth is that each one of them cares only for himself. Look where they live, where their children work, and you'll understand who it is that they really look after. All this nonsense about the rights of the workers—the only rights they ever care about are their own. Look at Ehud Barak—he's a millionaire!" Abraham kept talking, going on about it, explaining how the Labor Party convinced people to join social struggles and wars, and every time he said the word 'socialist,' an expression of disgust spread across his face. Ben set there, saying nothing. When Abraham was finally silent for a moment, his excited speech leaving him breathless, he raised the kippah and put it back on his head carelessly. Ben said quietly, "But you are just the same, aren't you? Only you replace 'society' with 'God.' I mean, if you look at history, more people have been sacrificed for God than for any other the goal."

"No, no, that's completely different," Abraham replied vehemently, delving into a long and complicated discussion on the essential difference between supporting an argument and the belief in God—who is eternal; has stood the test of time; is fully articulated in the Bible, the Book of Books; and exists in light and darkness. People have willingly sacrificed themselves so not to desecrate His name and Judaism had survived only due to an encompassing, uncompromising belief in the Almighty; otherwise the Jewish people would have vanished long ago. Only the lofty principles of Judaism kept it together. A belief in God implies high moral standards and an affinity among the believers. "We," he finally concluded, "live together as a community, unlike secular people, where each person lives by himself, distant from other people."

As he enunciated the last sentence, Abraham realized how blunt and tasteless it was. Ben watched him with such hostility that his lips tightened further and the right side of his mouth contracted in contempt. Ben said nothing. Silence fell. Abraham stood embarrassed at the door straightening his kippah, coughing slightly, looking down.

"Oh, well, never mind," Ben finally muttered. "Do you want to have a ceremony for affixing the mezuzah? That's okay, I don't mind. Invite everyone and we'll propose a toast." He then turned to the computer and began working. Abraham stood at the door for a few moments, consumed by a turmoil he didn't quite understand. He turned around and walked back to his office with heavy steps, dragging his feet on the shiny new floor.

Laurie's pregnancy filled Ofir with joy. As he took the elevator to the fortieth floor, he looked at his reflection and realized he was smiling. His mirror image in the elevator doors was distorted and his body seemed twisting from side to side, but his face looked bright and clear. A natural smile, born in his eyes, spread gradually to his thin cheeks, and then to his mouth. For a moment a mischievous child emerged despite the straight sharp nose, high cheekbones, and pointed chin. It had been years since this particular jolly spirit had filled him, this plain, innate happiness. Alone in the elevator, looking at his reflection, he made a funny face at the mirror and burst out laughing.

When the elevator reached the fortieth floor, he went to Ben's office. As he opened the door, he immediately noticed Ben's sullen look. His shoulders lifted slightly, he tucked his hand into his pocket, and his left foot moved like the shoe was too tight—his childhood friend's body revealed his distress in a familiar manner.

"What's wrong?" Ofir asked immediately. "Listen," Ben replied, "Abraham wants to have a ceremony for affixing the mezuzahs to the main entrance and to every office doorpost. I don't mind that we have mezuzahs; on the contrary, I called Azrieli company to ensure they would be affixed. But he wants a big ceremony with everyone taking part, and of course he will run it. You know, I'm not sure why, but I find it annoying."

"Ah, here he goes again . . . whenever something even remotely associated with religion comes up, he behaves as though he were an expert and the only one to be consulted. If he wants mezuzahs, he should approach us and say he thinks it's important."

"That's what he did."

"No! He wants us to have a big religious ceremony with everyone taking part, and he would conduct it. In short, he wants to impose religion on others."

"He's not imposing anything on me. I also want the mezuzahs. I did ask the maintenance company if they'd take care of that. But there is something annoying about the way he talks about it, with a condescending tone. It's like he's holding some absolute truth and I only have opinions. It's ridiculous.

My dad talks like that. My mom reads books, and he keeps telling her that the only truth is in the Scriptures."

"Your mom is really well read."

"And she keeps apologizing: 'It's good to see different perspectives, to know other people have similar problems, it's interesting to learn about other places.' Endless explanations. He always looks at her and smiles affectionately as if she were a cute child, sometimes caressing her, saying it's all in the Bible, no need to look elsewhere."

"I think Abraham's problem is that he can't accept the possibility that he may be wrong. You know, even when I am absolutely sure about something, I still know I may be wrong. But for him, it's different. What he believes in is absolute, and others may be right or wrong."

"Yeah, same with my dad. You know how he talks. Whatever is good is from the Bible and everything else is secular and corrupt. It's strange, he came to Israel by himself at a very young age, but he kept his family's values. They are so deeply embedded within him, there's no point in discussing them. My mom simply lets him say whatever he wants and doesn't respond. From his point of view, there is simply no way he is mistaken; at most, he failed to explain himself clearly."

"Frankly, what I can't stand about Abraham is the connection he makes between religion and politics. I mean, as far as I'm concerned, he can believe whatever he wants, but when it gets to this madness of the Greater Israel[1] I am in despair. If he wants a religious lifestyle, and he's sure God is on his side, that's fine with me. But when it means I have to do even more reserved duty in the army and risk my life to guard those horrible settlements, I have zero patience. It is exactly this attitude—of people who think their beliefs can't be doubted—that led to the murder of Rabin."

"It's not easy to live with a person with no self-doubt. On the other hand, it creates a sense of stability. Everything is simple; there are clear rules. My dad always knows who is a good person and who isn't, without any doubt. In a way, you can argue he is a better person than I am."

"Better person? I can't believe you're saying that! What are you talking about? First, there is the fundamental question of the interpretation of good

---

1   "Greater Israel" refers to the territory of biblical Israel, including Judea, Samaria, and the Gaza Strip. The right-wing settler movement aims to restore this territory.

and evil, every person sees it differently. And also, there is a question of following your own moral standards."

"True. But clearer rules make the right choice easier. Secular people,
especially skeptical ones, tend to do things they consider immoral."

"What?! Do you seriously think you're not as moral as your dad?

"Yes."

"Why?"

"I cheat when it's worth it."

"How do you mean?"

"Remember Dan Pearson, our first investor?"

"Yes."

"I cheated him."

"What? How? You never told me this."

"He was really an expert in robotics, he could foresee potential problems. He had asked me if we have addressed different software errors, and I
said we had, even though that wasn't the case. I prayed he wouldn't inquire
about the solution. I shamelessly told a lie. If he had found out the truth he
would have left, and we wouldn't be here today."

"Why didn't you tell me this?"

The blue eyes that gazed at Ofir from across the desk seemed oddly
luminous—wide open cracks that revealed upheavals but also tranquility,
torments abstracted into a determined resolution that can't be overturned.
The curls around his head seemed made of wires, and his always-tight lips
became even tighter, but a shadow of a smile emerged. Ben's thin nose looked
sharp and unpleasant, his skinny body both lax and tense, and his left leg kept
moving nervously from side to side, evidence of an ongoing turmoil.

As Ofir turned around and left the room, he thought he heard a choked
chuckle, though later, when he thought about it, he was positive there had
been silence in the room. The sound of the closing door, his steps on the
smooth floor, his office's door sliding too easily, pushed forward though he
meant to open it carefully, the squeak of his office chair as he sank into it, the
garbage can he kicked—

He found his own elaborated explanations rather hollow. Ben wanted
us to succeed at any price, he didn't want to put me at risk, he was positive I
would agree, he knew I know nothing about it so what's the point of asking
me—the sentences emerged and disintegrated, dividing into words without
context, and into single syllables, then silence fell. Ofir felt slightly nauseous.
Something had been fractured, slightly split, a hole as small as an eye of a

needle had been created in the past extending from childhood to the present, which until now seemed so perfect, a fine, immaculate weaving.

He sat in his office for an hour, thinking about it over and over again, seeing Ben's face, wondering if he were smiling. Soon I'll go home, he thought. Laurie is expecting me for dinner. But a forlorn spirit overwhelmed him. Annoyed and distressed, he told himself that it was nothing but a slight disappointment that would soon dissipate. He sat motionless in his chair, listening to the voices from the corridor gradually fading away, wondering if when he left the office he might find that everyone had disappeared and he was all alone in the tall skyscraper.

September 1998

Laurie found the narrow stairs leading up from the street to the building, concealed by tall trees, to be somewhat precarious. Nine months pregnant, she walked home slowly, taking small steps, bending her body slightly backward so as not to lose her balance as she wiped the sweat off her chest and pulled at the thin maternity dress that clung to her body. She had been living in Israel for seven years now, but still couldn't get used to the steamy Mediterranean summer.

In the first year, she had felt the summer was a sort of adventure; somehow, she had found herself in a distant, exotic country, wishing to take off her clothes and sigh with relief. Over here, everyone walks around wearing rubber flip flops, sweat removing any trace of makeup and ruining any hairdo. When Ofir saw her returning from the sea for the first time, he burst out laughing and kissed her. The young Brit had lost her elegant appearance. Her hair was messy, her fair skin turned pink, her light dress wrinkled and stained, and she sauntered with her flip-flops full of sand. "You know, the sand should be left on the shore" he'd said, amused, explaining that there were water faucets on the shore for washing it off. She smiled shyly, trying to conceal her exhaustion.

But as the years went by, summer became more oppressive. Though she was determined not to spend all day in air-conditioned places, she often avoided going outdoors. The Tel Aviv Museum was dark and cool, but she was struck by the sweltering Mediterranean heat and scorching air every time she left the building.

Today she left the museum later than usual. Illusive afternoon rays, pleasant looking yet parching; fresh trees casting shade through their dark green dust-covered leaves; oranges cut in half and placed in a bowl at a kiosk selling fresh juice, the heat making them look glossy, lovely, and disgusting; lively streets with graceless buildings. A woman strolled in front of her with two dogs waggling their tails joyfully and sniffing every corner, urinating on the sidewalk and walking away quickly; a boy walking briskly beside her brushed her accidentally, looked at her, but didn't offer an apology—only a couple of streets left, she'd be home in about ten minutes.

As she walked past a nursery school, a sudden memory of the kindergarten she attended in Hampstead crossed her mind. London seemed so far from the street she was on, but the childhood memory transported her to the serene neighborhood on the hillside. The kindergarten was not far from her home. The yard was a bit small, but the room had plenty of toys. The full-figured teacher had a Black assistant, a reticent and pleasant woman with a translucent scarf tied around her head. She was very gentle, whereas the teacher was somewhat loud. A thought about kindergartens in Tel Aviv surfaced; for a moment, Laurie thought she heard screaming and crying, but as she kept walking, they vanished.

Passing by a supermarket, she decided to purchase some dairy products. Hunger struck her, a pregnant woman's need for apple-flavored yogurt, to bite down on hard cheese, to dip a roll in fresh cottage cheese. She entered the store and tossed goat cheese into the red basket, cottage cheese, mozzarella, natural yogurt, fruit-flavored yogurt, fine gouda, cream cheese. The basket was so full Laurie struggle to fit the cheddar in. Finally, she turned to pay.

The cashier, a young woman with heavy makeup, was chewing gum audibly and reclining in her chair, her leg near the products. After scanning the containers and casually tossing them aside, she engaged in loud conversation with a young man standing in the corner. As she tried to scan the mozzarella cheese, the cash register began to beep. She looked at the scanner displeased and said to Laurie, "This one can't be scanned. Get another one," and went on joking with the young man as Laurie walked slowly back to the dairy products shelves.

A long thread of insults, made of bountiful knots, was gradually tightening. James mocking her, a friend from elementary school who made fun of her in front of everyone, a boy who snickered as he looked at her small breasts, long and short strands clinging onto one another and turning into a long cord of offensive, abusive words. And though it was impossible to set the strands apart, and hard to remember how each one had been created and what tears had given it its special texture, every insult pulled the thick thread, joining the strands together. Laurie, faltering as she went to get another mozzarella cheese, was trying to remove the insult with self-reproach: *She is just a silly girl, rude and lazy, that's all.*

But as she returned with another cheese, the cashier still couldn't scan it and ordered her to get another one, the thread clutched Laurie's throat and she felt the tears in her eyes. "Excuse me, could you possibly bring another one?" she said in Hebrew with a heavy English accent, but the girl replied, "Lady, we're not in America. You fetch it." Laurie could feel the tears running down her cheeks.

As she left the cashier and walked out of the store, she heard an elderly man also waiting in line shouting at the cashier: "Shame on you! Asking this pregnant woman to get the cheese! I'll complain to the manager." Her legs carried her heavy body quickly; she was anxious to leave the store and go home. She couldn't stand this place anymore. The heat was unbearable, sweat was rolling down her back. The rudeness of the young woman, a run-down park she passed by on her way, a street that looked as if it hadn't been cleaned in years, loud Mediterranean music coming from somewhere, and then her foot hit a stone on the pavement and she almost stumbled and fell down. At the very last moment, she grabbed a bus stop pole.

Laurie sank down on the bench at the bus stop and closed her eyes.

After a couple of moments, the long thread had loosened, the knots unraveled, and every strand was moving by itself. She opened her eyes. The rude cashier became silly and unimportant again, with her stupid gaze and coarse facial features. *In London, she would have been kicked out at once.* The thought of the disrespectful girl being fired disgracefully in London almost made her laugh. Here, she gets a job in some grocery store, speaks impolitely to the customers, and the manager asks her to come to his office. There he says quietly but firmly that she is dismissed; it is unimaginable that a person who behaves so rudely would work there. She tries to argue, but after a couple of sentences she understands that it's hopeless, and then she walks away, swearing loudly—not to be heard but so she could say to herself that she was not dumped in disgrace and kept her dignity. Laurie smiled with satisfaction: In the world I come from, a cashier would never have brought me to tears.

She now noticed a tall tree casting a shadow on the bus stop, a light breeze rustling the thin leaves, dark green lady's fans whispering. A white cat with shiny fur jumped on the bench and lay across it, rubbing its head against the peeling wooden beams. The street was quiet; soft music came from somewhere. The evening's blue hue spread across the sky, spilling a tiny cool drop into the burning atmosphere.

It wasn't such a bad day, she thought. *Against all odds, I've managed to convince the photography curator.*

Joseph's social connections had gotten her a job at the Tel Aviv Museum as an assistant to the contemporary art curator. Friends introduced him to museum donors who had been amazed by his young daughter-in-law—an

Oxford graduate!—and who had approached the museum director to suggest he should hire her. She had spoken English with the curator, and whenever she needed to speak in Hebrew, she wrote the sentences down first, anxious not to make mistakes. Once in a while, people smiled as she spoke; she would blush and lower her gaze, apologizing for her Hebrew. But now, two years later, she could easily make conversation and could even laugh if someone pointed out a mistake.

A couple of weeks ago, she attended an exhibition of Arab-Israeli artists in Umm al-Fahm.[1] One of her British friends wanted to see the exhibition and asked Laurie to join her. "Don't worry, we'll drive slowly so the car won't bump," her friend said, suggesting they go on Saturday. The gallery, which had opened two years before, invited artists to present their works on the Arab-Israeli conflict.

I wish I hadn't come, she thought as they went in, breathing heavily from climbing the stairs to the gallery, one step after the other, often halting to hold her protruding belly. A sculpture of a soldier hitting a boy, an abstract picture, a mixture of strong colors with a black stain at its heart, a display imitating spilled blood—it was all so expected and banal, utterly tedious. *I could have guessed this is what it would be like,* she said to herself. She wandered around, moving from one room to another, putting on a severe countenance and peeking at her watch once in a while. But for a moment, she found herself a small room without her friends, facing a side wall dedicated to young artists.

Four of Hamid's works were exhibited on a side wall, small black-and-white pictures: the cheerless face of a young boy, an elongated shadow of a soldier next to a small fence surrounded with grass, a full-figured and wrinkled Arab woman looking into the distance, and a deserted house on a hillside. Later, on the way home, she thought there was something familiar about the photographs, as if she had seen them before. But when she had first looked at them, she had been overwhelmed. They were very simple, with no excessive details; people living in a space with nothing but sky and stony ground, looking around not with desperation but with perplexity, with only a hint of the lack of safe haven. Laurie was looking at the photos when her friends found her. "Come on, let's go to eat," one said, taking hold of Laurie's hand and pulling her out of the gallery.

---

1   A city in Israel populated by Arab citizens of Israel.

When she told the curator about Hamid's photos and suggested a small exhibition at the Tel Aviv Museum, the curator's eyebrows lifted, and she said in a sarcastic tone, "Oh, well, you know you would have to ask the photography curator—horrible person. I can't imagine how she became a curator. She has absolutely no relevant education. No one can stand her. But if you want to try, go ahead. I don't mind. But remember that I warned you!"

When Laurie knocked softly on the photography curator's open door, a hoarse voice came from the office. "I'm busy," and then silence. As she stood there, hesitating whether she should return to her office or persist, the curator appeared: a woman about fifty years old, with heavy, purple-framed eyeglasses and strange makeup. She looked ashen, her eyes surrounded by a thick black line, almost mask-like. She wore a black dress with an asymmetrical cut and heavy black combat boots. Laurie recalled how the curator had been ridiculed for her need to assume an avant-garde appearance, for saying things like "art is not a respectable concert hall." She looked down on them, convinced that her passion for art was genuine while they were merely comfortable. In a condescending tone, she said to Laurie, "What did they send you to me for?"

Laurie stood face to face with the curator. A blush spread across her cheeks as she involuntary straightened her hair, a quiver in an unidentified part of her body, her mouth dry. She briefly pondered whether she should turn and leave or attempt to explain why she had come. The curator stared at her, saying nothing, and then, fueled by embarrassment and anger, came the sentences in English, one after the other, a chain of enthusiastic words depicting Hamid's photos. His unique viewpoint, unusual angles, minimalistic perspective, monumental spirit apparent even in bare soil—Laurie spoke quickly, almost without taking a breath between sentences.

The curator removed her purple-framed glasses and listened attentively. As Laurie stopped to breathe, she said: "Send me his works. If I like them, I'll arrange a small exhibition here."

Oh, well, it's time to go on, Laurie thought. I've rested for a while and now I'll go home. As she turned to the stairs, she took off her sandals and climbed up barefoot. Ofir was expecting her at the door, smiling and hugging her. "Laurie, I thought you'd be at home. I made dinner." On the table she saw a bowl of salad, fresh rolls, all sorts of cheeses, fresh orange juice, and her favorite apple pie from the nearby bakery.

January 1999

Sophia, Ben's mother, walked slowly out of the hospital, carrying a heavy plastic bag and a small pink purse. *Poor thing*, she thought. *Why did it have to happen to her?* At noon the entrance hall was crowded with visitors, patients going out of the hospital to get some fresh air, and doctors and nurses on their way to have lunch. Sophia walked amidst the crowd, making her way to the bench located right outside the entrance door. A full-bodied woman, her swollen legs in flat shoes that seemed too small for her, wearing a colorful dress topped by a blue rain coat. Her blond hair was carefully combed, her cheeks slightly wrinkled, but her eyes remained always full of light.

This was the third miscarriage. Something must be really wrong with her, she thought. She looked so healthy, with rosy cheeks and glowing skin, but three pregnancies ending in the first term was no coincidence. Sophia had just left the gynecology ward, with Ben sitting next to Carine. She lay in bed awake, eyes closed, saying nothing. David had left the room a couple of minutes earlier, looking for the hospital's synagogue for *mincha* prayer. Sophia had decided to go out for a while to ease her distress. She sat on a bench at the entrance plaza and pulled out an apple from her plastic bag.

A pleasant winter sun came out from behind the soft clouds. Pure light filled the sky, mixing with a fresh scent of last night's rain. A young tree at the hospital entrance shed transparent water globules, falling silently on the ground. *Strange, so strange*, Sophia kept a lively conversation with herself. *I wonder if it's genetic. It must be. A young woman who seems so healthy, something must be wrong with her family.* Well, we hardly got to know her mother, since she lives somewhere in Galilee, and Ben says her father disappeared when she was a baby. Sophia kept contemplating this in hopes of dispelling her sadness and erase the memory of her son's eyes, full of pain and suppressed anger.

She pulled a knife from the plastic bag and began peeling the apple, removing the thin green skin slowly and putting the pieces into the bag. *Something must be wrong with Carine.* Her mother seemed so healthy. Not as pretty as she was, but strong and robust. Sophia kept delving into Carine's family history, trying to understand what Ben had said, which had previously seemed vague and meaningless—someone from Russia whose asthma awakened in the fall and the spring, a hint that the father had a mental illness—all her attempts to render Carine's life from birth to the present were futile. A beautiful woman, pleasant and smiling, Sophia had never witnessed a single quarrel between her and Ben; Carine's presence was all about the now, not the past or the future. Had it not been for these miscarriages, Sophia would never have attempted to reconstruct her life.

David, returning from the synagogue, was pacing slowly in the hospital's corridors, his gaze lowered, pausing once in a while to blow his nose. When Ben first told them Carine was pregnant, David burst into laughter, bewildering his wife and son. A childish joy had filled him—in a minute, he would jump in the air or burst out singing—he wanted nothing more than another generation of Haddads. The very idea that his son would have a child made him so happy despite his profound reservations about Carine. If he had to find a wife for his son, he would have chosen another woman. Not that he wanted a Sephardi woman—he had married an Ashkenazi woman. Sometimes, watching his three curly blond children made him chuckle. But he had wished Ben had married a religious woman.

Sophia is a truly devoted mother and a loyal wife, he kept reproaching himself, emphasizing each word to intensify his own message. Years of living together, and she always offered a hand. But he was saddened by the stacks of books next to her bedside, her deliberate avoidance of any religious practices, and her consistent efforts to seek rational explanations, never attributing anything to a divine force. On one occasion, all the clocks they had sold stop ticking simultaneously—because the batteries weren't compatible with the clocks. The sign above the entrance suddenly plummeted and crashed into pieces—because the rain had loosened the screws holding it in place. On the day Ben and Ofir had initiated Handex, the refrigerator ceased cooling and the entire store flooded—the result of a short circuit. When Ben told them he was getting married, a forgotten deposit in an obscure bank account came to light—the bank issued a special notification after ten years. Sophia left no room for the influence of Providence. She was a practical woman, always seeking a logical explanation. This made David's religious belief appear redundant, almost ridiculous, a sort of strange, nearly childish insistence that a supernatural force shapes our lives.

But David was utterly convinced that Sophia failed to see the heart of it all. All those seemingly solid explanations were nothing but a veil, the connections a mere facade, not because they were false but because they exemplified a hidden power, a transcendent entity manifested in endless shapes and forms. The Almighty establishes order and then disrupts it, fashions both laws of nature and miracles, instils belief within a man's heart and then puts him to test. There was no need to look for the footprints of the King of Kings; only a blind man failed to see that whatever happens to us, is evidence of the power of God.

For Ben and Carine's wedding, David had insisted that Rabbi Bakshi-Doron[1] perform the ceremony. With the help of some friends from the synagogue and a generous donation to Binyan Av,[2] he had convinced the Sephardi Chief Rabbi to come to Tel Aviv and officiate at the wedding. There is no better time to support our rabbis, he thought, now that they are scrutinized and interrogated by the police. He found the accusations of Arie Deri[3] stealing money as hollow as any other claim that prioritized the welfare of the public over personal gain. Every person takes care of himself, he thought, reading the newspaper headline with disgust, eager to toss the paper into the garbage can so no one would see it.

The lavish wedding hall, the elegant guests, Sophia who looked as if she was about to faint at any moment, the rabbi's voice echoing in the hall— David experienced a new, unfamiliar elation. He was filled not only with joy but also something resembling fear, an awe, as if the *Shekhinah* was present as the ceremony took place. He wondered if it was only the normal excitement of a father as his first-born son wed or a divine sign. Ben's curls looked like a crown, the veil covering Carine's face resembled the curtain of the ark, Sophia's eyes were shining like glittering diamonds, and he thought he had heard obscure syllables as the rabbi was praying. Even Ofir, standing with his wife close to the canopy, seemed enigmatic. *Maybe it was all a sign*, he thought, a signal from God that this marriage would prevail, perhaps Carine would be a worthy wife. He had disliked her from the very first time they met. Her glamorous beauty embarrassed him, her dresses with deep cleavage made him look at her with lust, her expensive jewelry drove him to despair; clearly, she was only after his son's money. Though she always smiled pleasantly, she never offered Sophia any help, and had no interest in women's things: raising children, cooking, cleaning. But under the canopy, he thought

---

1   The Sephardic chief rabbi of Israel between 1993 and 2003.
2   A major Sephardi Orthodox yeshiva in Israel.
3   Arie Deri is a prominent Sephardi public figure and has been a minister in several Israeli governments. In 1999, he was convicted of bribery and fraud.

he saw tears in her big blue eyes, and Carine's mother seemed thrilled. The soft light, the blessings the rabbi was mumbling, Ben who suddenly seized Carine's hand—*Maybe it was all a sign from God,* he thought, evidence of an obscure and ancient wisdom creating unusual matches.

But now, pacing in the hospital's corridors after praying *Mincha,* a sense of despair enveloped him. *I knew this would happen,* he reflected. It was crystal clear. She wasn't the right match for him, not dedicated to raising children. And she was too pretty, yes, *too.* There's no need for that, it would have been better if he found a nice warm woman who would support him the way Sophia supports me. He could envisage those embryos that refused to adhere into Carine's body, ejected before three months, children that would never be born because of an error, a discrepancy, a distortion, something that didn't unfold the way it should have. And all those discussions on medical history and hormonal therapies were such nonsense, it was so obvious that a simple and clear truth had been revealed for the third time. A profound mismatch materialized in Carine's body, and who knew? Maybe they will separate, perhaps Ben will find the right woman for him. Though David kept reproaching himself that it was inappropriate to speculate about this as Carine was hospitalized, he couldn't help but admit that thinking about it made him somewhat hopeful.

Punishment. Divine punishment. A reckoning for my wrongdoings. Carine's miscarriages are retribution for my misdeeds. Ben sat by Carine's bed, his head back against the headrest, his arms limp next to his body, and his legs spread forward. His left leg was jittering as though it wasn't part of his body. He looked at the ceiling, focusing on an old, damp stain, and then turned his gaze to her, lying in bed motionless. Her eyes were closed but her countenance indicated she was not asleep. A delicate contour, long blond hair spread on the pillow, in a hospital gown, her body suddenly looked small and nearly childish. Strange, without the jewelry, makeup and trendy clothes, she seemed fragile; for a single moment she looked like an abandoned child, left alone in the hospital.

A couple of days ago he had brought her there, bleeding. Returning home late in the evening, he'd opened the door and heard her moan. At the center of the bed was a puddle of blood, neither dripping nor absorbed in the bed, and her pale face revealed blue veins at the temples he had never seen before. The doctor who came with the ambulance immediately asked if she was pregnant and ordered her to the hospital.

The first miscarriage hadn't seemed like an omen but a one-time mishap. The second one generated a profound dread, prompting appointments with the family doctor, two gynecologists, a genetics expert, a nutrition consultant, a fitness trainer, and a midwife promoting natural birth. Carine underwent various tests—hormone assessment, a chromosome check, immune system evaluations, an examination of the uterine structure—but no problem was found; everything seemed fine. Every positive result ended in a jewelry store: huge diamond earrings, a necklace made of rare pearls, a couple of golden rings with precious stones, and an eighteenth-century bracelet that perfectly fit Carine's delicate wrist. Ben no longer waited for her to pick a piece of jewelry but made suggestions: this ring looks fabulous, the necklace is unique and very expensive, maybe those earrings?

A couple of days later, upon arriving at Azrieli Towers parking lot, he realized Laurie had just happened to park next to him.[4] "I drove Ofir to the office, and I'm going to the mall," she said shyly, lifting a beautiful baby from the car seat and placing her gently in a stroller. A big head with soft black hair, huge dark eyes looking at him bewildered, fair, nearly transparent skin—the baby looked like a porcelain doll, her chubby body dressed in a pink outfit from which two bare feet protruded, swaying from side to side as Laurie tried to put them in socks.

For a second, he couldn't breathe. Though he smiled at Abigail—the baby in the stroller—he felt he suffocated, wondering if it was the heavy air in the parking lot. The adorable baby almost made him faint, with her miniature pinkish feet and impeccable small toes; he leaned against a car so Laurie wouldn't notice. But she was preoccupied with dressing the baby, and as she managed to put on the socks, she smiled at him and left.

He locked the car and walked toward the elevator. The dim, orange-toned light sickened him; he thought he saw garbage piling up next to the filthy concrete walls, but as he focused his gaze, all he could see was the shadow of a cat leaping and disappearing into an invisible crack. Only his own shadow could be seen, long and distorted. *To hell with it,* he said to himself. *Why is he always ahead of me? Why does he get to have more?* For a moment, he forgot he was in a parking lot; an obscure road stretched before him, mountainous and rocky. *I wish I'd never known him. I wish he wasn't such a good friend,* he thought, feeling how envy's two heads were awakened at once, crawling from their

---

4   There is a large shopping mall on the ground floor of Azrieli Tower.

hideout and opening mouths full of filthy, rotten teeth. The beautiful baby blended with the memory of Carine's miscarriage and made him remember bleeding embryos that were discharged before becoming human, doomed to be destroyed and never turn into a chubby baby with a sweet smell—

"Hey, watch it! Where are you going? I almost ran you over!" he heard a man shouting, and then realized car horns were blowing all around him. He waved his hand apologetically, turned around, and walked back to his luxury Volvo, which a couple of seconds later sped back and turned to exit the lot.

Ben arrived at the bank branch five minutes before closing. He managed to sneak in before the doors were locked. He looked for the older teller responsible for Handex's account. After a couple of minutes of wandering around, he realized she wasn't there. "She left. Retired," a young teller said. "I took her place. May I help you?"

"Every month, around ten thousand shekels are directly transferred from Handex's account to my personal account. I want to make it twenty thousand."

"Are you the sole owner of the account? Ah, no, I see there is a . . . Ofir Stern. Is he your partner?"

"Yes. But there's no problem. We both want to make the change."

"He will have to sign."

"I can assure you it is a mutual decision."

"Did he sign the forms last time? I can't see his signature."

"He did. You should have the signed forms."

"Oh, well, given that I wasn't the one to make the direct deposit, I'll assume he did sign. I'll make it twenty thousand, but I'll give you the forms, and he needs to sign them. You can then fax them to me."

"No problem. You'll have the signed forms as soon as possible."

A couple of minutes later, the luxury car sped back again and turned towards Azrieli Tower, gliding softly on the road. Rain splashed on the windshield and slid slowly downward. Ben held the steering wheel with one hand and wiped the sweat off his forehead with the other. I can easily forge the signature, he thought, and send in the signed forms. But maybe I won't do that. I won't send the form. It's better this way. The bank teller may just call Handex, asking why she never got the forms. The secretary will tell her she has no idea what this is about and will suggest she speaks to me. The teller will respond that she prefers to talk to Mr. Ofir Stern, as his signature is necessary. Ofir will say he has no idea what she's talking about, the firm has a bookkeeper or she can speak to our accountants. She will insist, your partner was here and said you would sign the forms. Ofir will be taken by surprise: Why on earth was my partner dealing with this? Are you sure you're not confusing him with someone else? No, she'll respond. He was here at the branch and modified the monthly direct to his account, increasing it from ten thousand shekels to twenty thousand.

An old man trying to cross the road waved his walking stick, and Ben stopped abruptly. *In a few years, I will look like him,* he thought, *bent and leaning on a stick.* Carine will be old, and her rare beauty will be replaced by a countenance of sour impatience. We will be rich and childless. My parents will be gone, my brother and sister will have big families, and only I will live in a secluded villa with Carine, who will wear designer clothes and expensive jewelry. We will take part in fundraiser events for sick children, invite ministers and businessmen to our home, establish a charity for the poor of Tel Aviv. We will be lonely. Childless. Desolate. Solitary. People will find solace in our life: Money can't buy happiness. These rich folks have no children. Friends won't invite us to bar mitzvahs or weddings, to spare us the pain.

But not Ofir. He will always be my loyal friend. He will invite us to every holiday dinner and family events. Make us part of his family. Abigail will call me Uncle Ben. He will smile at me joyfully whenever he sees me, pat my back, his eyes shining as always, bright and blank. His gaze is sharp and dumb. He is a brilliant stupid man. He can crack mysteries but he doesn't understand the suffering he inflicts on me; endlessly devoted and can't see how his dedication torments me. Sometimes I want to fall into his arms, to give into this pleasant intimacy, but then, in an instant, at the very same time, I want to hit him.

Enough!

I am tired of this friendship.

I've had enough of this adolescent naiveté. School days are long gone, and the freedom of solitude is intoxicating, invigorating, igniting the imagination. I don't need this childhood friend, reviving irksome memories, iron chains that prevent me from moving fast without inhibition.

I won't send the teller the signed forms. I hope she'll call Ofir, and he will discover I'm stealing his money.

While driving to the office, he kept elaborating to himself how he would manage to break free, tear the invisible screen around him and move forward, finally leave the depressing group of people who are second, deputy, devoted assistant, supportive friend, escort—and join the leaders, those who are being followed by others. He may even start a new company that only he would lead.

But, as he went up the elevator, the imaginary thread that led him to all those exciting pinnacles he couldn't fully understand was suddenly cut, and embarrassment took over. The thought of meeting Ofir in a minute made him blush. He looked at his reflection in the elevator doors and once again thought how slender he was, and then thought that he hadn't seen Michelle for a couple of weeks. He checked his cell phone, though he knew no one had called him, and placed it back in his shirt pocket. As the elevator reached the fortieth floor, he wasn't sure what to do. As he saw no one was around, he remained in the elevator until the door shut. He heard a subtle ding, and the elevator slid back slowly to the entrance floor.

September 1999

Insomnia is strange, thought Ofir. Sleep is like an invisible, odorless cloud that suddenly disappears, drifting to another place, perhaps to another home, another person facing a mute television at two o'clock in the morning and can't fall asleep.

It had been a couple of weeks since he found it hard to fall asleep. He, of all people, Laurie laughed, who always dropped on the bed and fell asleep at once, even without a couple of minutes of relaxation, was now walking around the house at night, wide awake. When it happened for the first time, he was slightly amused, thinking that since he became a father, he seemed to have adopted the habits of an anxious parent, getting up at night to check that the infant was breathing normally. Time and again, he went to Abigail's bed, watching her childish body lax in sleep. She looked almost angelic, like pictures of saints he had seen. But over the following nights, he realized it to be an enduring insomnia. He went to the nursery, then to the kitchen, back to the study, and then to the living room. Every now and then, he would lie in bed, but he found Laurie's deep breathing and her curved body wrapped in a colorful blanket irksome. Her tranquility seemed to emphasize his restlessness. Immersed in deep sleep, she was oblivious to him pacing around the house, wondering why he was awake.

After two weeks of insomnia, where he would fall asleep around three in the morning and rise at seven o'clock to head to work, he began to question this strange alertness. Late at night, he would have some fruit, read every page of the newspaper, try to read a book but always halt after a couple of paragraphs, and then decide to get some work done. But he'd become very tired after a couple of minutes and watch some television series that always ended with an implausible family complication. He'd switch to a sports channel broadcasting soccer matches from the eighties. Nothing worked; his life had been disrupted. His body neglected the need to be awake during the day and asleep at night.

He speculated that it might be a result of his last army service duty, which at his age would probably be his last—years of service in Gaza made the place both familiar and alarming. A couple of days before he'd had to start his service, a certain tension began to materialize, an invisible shadow following him throughout the day, making every decision or action complicated; kissing on Abigail's moist cheek, immersing into Laurie's body in a way that saddened her, his hectic work. Every problem had to be solved at once; time was scarce. The new model of the robot had to be ready, some repairs to the arm must be accomplished swiftly, and developing the new robot for abdominal surgeries must progress. Eventually, it was Ben who'd say softly, "Relax, Ofir, everything will be fine. Nothing will change here until you return."

The first day of the reserve duty was always the hardest: the military camp in the Negev where soldiers organized, heavy equipment and uniforms, the transformation from Tel Aviv to the bare desert landscape, the rigid military atmosphere, military boots, loose pants, green shirt, the rifle on his shoulder, people running around checking the equipment, getting into vehicles and driving to the Gaza Strip. Every move required self-control, restraint, overcoming an urge to eliminate the threat or escape.

After a couple of days, laxness prevailed, a false sigh of relief. Children played soccer nearby; women talked and watched the soldiers with hostility; a barrage of stones came from a hidden rooftop; elderly men crossed the road and lowered their gaze; younger men hid. Conducting house-to-houses searches at night drove Ofir to despair—knocking on the door, waking a family. Women covered themselves with blankets and men looked at them with loathing. Sometimes, adolescents tried to escape and, as the soldiers stopped them, women's screaming filled the house. Ofir couldn't wait until they would leave the houses and walk in the narrow alleys.

Every time he served in the reserves, he wondered how he kept going whenever he was called, despite detesting Gaza. The last time he served there, a few weeks before being discharge from the reserves, they had been searching for a Hamas man. They knocked on the door and woke the mother, who opened the door, pale and tired. They passed from one room to another, checking who was there, examining every corner—the bedroom, two nurseries with three children in each sleeping on mattresses on the floor, an empty room for visitors, another empty room, the kitchen, a huge living room, and finally the last room at the end of the corridor. A squeak was heard and an old woman opened the door, alarmingly wrinkled, short and bent, wearing a black nightgown—she fearlessly leaped on Ofir, hitting him with her fists and screaming in a harsh voice; the only word he could understand, *yahud*,[1] was repeated over and over again.

---

1   A Jew in Arabic.

"Push her away!" was cried out. "Watch it, you don't know who's hiding here, don't let her touch you!" But Ofir stood motionless, letting the old woman beat him without pushing her away, clinging to the rifle without moving, watching her frenzy silently. For a split second, everyone disappeared: the family, the Hamas man who may have been hiding in the house, and the other soldiers. Only the old woman cursing him was left, a ghost who beat him again and again. Finally, another soldier came, yelled at her to leave, and pushed her abruptly aside.

In his sleepless nights, Ofir recalled the old woman. He tried to think of the dark narrow paths, eyes full of hatred, a stone that hit him in the eye and left a small scratch on his cornea, his uniform always soaked with sweat . . . but in vain. Only the bent old woman appeared, and every time he thought of her, more details surfaced: her hands were twisted and the nails black, her thin, pointed nose complemented her sharp features and toothless jaw, her bare arms looked like an ancient scroll, and her voice—he felt it was echoing in the living room—strident, sharp, like a knife scratching a plate. Ofir would close his eyes and toss his head on the headrest, thinking how fortunate he was not to return to Gaza. We should leave that place, pull out, he mumbled repeatedly, end the occupation and return to the 1967 borders. In order to silence the old woman's voice, he turned to work.

Handex's income and expenses from recent years appeared on the computer screen, divided by month. In February and March, their income saw a significant boost as they sold two robotic arms to French hospitals, and in December another one would be sent to a hospital in Canada. The colorful diagrams across the screen illustrated the company's success: sales were rising, a few orders awaited final approval, the company was expanding, salaries were increasing, and two fresh recruits have been brought in: a senior doctor and a programmer, together working from daybreak to nightfall to develop the robot intended for actual surgical procedures. He contemplated the possibility of expanding the offices in Azrieli Tower. Sometimes three people shared a single office, and that affected the quality of their work.

On the other hand, certain problems that impeded overall progress needed to be solved. There was always a divide between the computer people and the engineers. Discussing certain issues, it seemed that around the meeting table people were speaking two different languages. The programmers saw a process: one command leads to another, and then to another. Engineers saw materials: contraction and expansion in heat, flexibility, endurance. Ben was the only one who could act as an interpreter between the two languages.

His thorough, systematic thinking formed a pattern that merged process and material aspects, finding convergence between the two. But the disputes between the movement people and material people remained unresolved in his absence. Then there were the medical guys, assertive and decisive, declaring without a doubt what the robot should do and how to operate it. Clearly, they had been trained to think in a logical, structured manner, always making progress through elimination; they moved from one step immediately to another without taking offense or clinging to their mistakes. They were not as stubborn as the programmers and the engineers but more arrogant, believing only they truly understood the implications of using a robotic arm.

Ofir stared at the colorful screen for long minutes, but suddenly he realized that a strange feeling was growing and expanding within him; *an anxiety about something vague and undefined that was about to unfold.* An undesirable development, a trouble, collapse, maybe even a catastrophe—he couldn't tell what it was that he feared, but he knew the future was holding an unavoidable detrimental event. To remove his apprehension, he kept examining the financial data—the company was doing very well, no doubt. But still, an obscure path into the future had been unveiled, a hidden window with a clear view; only in rare moments of heightened consciousness could he glance through it hastily before it closed. Ofir saw something foreboding, though he couldn't figure out what it was.

He got up, walked around the house, and then collapsed on the sofa in the living room. A flash of cold light he had seen with his eyes shut was terrifying. An obscure glint signaled something and immediately disappeared. For a moment, he thought he was plummeting to the floor. Immediately he began to speculate: the robotic arm would suddenly move in an unexpected, inaccurate way; the company would go bankrupt; he would catch an incurable disease; Laurie would leave him; a rare genetic disease would be found in Abigail's little body; he would be drafted for war time and die in battle. More and more catastrophes materialized, and although he rejected each one, reassuring himself that the likelihood that they would actually occur was so small as to be negligible, he was left with a profound impression that calamity was nearing, yet he couldn't figure out where it was coming from, or in what form.

Ofir got up from the sofa, went into the kitchen, drank a glass of water, and took Abigail's milk bottle out of the fridge. In a couple of minutes, soft whimpers would come from her bed. He would lift her gently, and together they would sit in the armchair. He would put the bottle in her mouth and she would drink it eagerly without opening her eyes. He returned to the living room and sat heavily on the sofa, staring at the window. Night after night, he gazed at the changing light, the starry darkness fading gradually, and only when a touch of orange hue blended into it, a nearly invisible ray heralding sunrise, would he fall asleep.

Damn darkness, he thought. *The darker it gets, the clearer the view becomes. Like an owl at midnight turning its head around and seeing the forest sharper and better than in daylight: thick, menacing, graceless.*

October 2000

Natalie was standing on Ibn Gabirol Street looking from side to side with apprehension. Dressed in a black pleated skirt and a freshly ironed blouse, she searched for the bus stop where she can catch a bus to Laurie's home. Commotion filled the street, graceless buildings surrounded with rustling trees, dust blending with the scent of cars, the bustle of a busy avenue. As she saw the bus stop, she began walking briskly, though a closer look would have revealed that each of her steps was smaller than usual.

Tomorrow, Abigail will be two years old. Natalie had just left a toy store up the road, having decided to add a present to the ones she had brought from London. Her bag was heavy: a doll with brown hair and rosy cheeks, a doctor's kit, and a plastic palace with miniature kings and queens. When Laurie saw the presents, she burst into laughter and said they would keep Abigail busy for a year.

Her decision to travel to Israel for her granddaughter's birthday had generated some concern. The Intifada, terrorists exploding in buses, in malls, in the streets—the situation was volatile, people were afraid to go out to restaurants and cafés. Everyone asked her if she was sure she wanted to go. She repeatedly explained that Laurie and her family didn't travel by bus, that she would be vigilant and take taxis.

A guard stood at the entrance to Abigail's nursery school. It was possible to be careful, to decrease the chances of getting hurt, and there was no danger at home. From a distance, things often appear worse, but in the end, people continued their daily routine, only more cautiously. She repeated the same simple yet detailed explanations so many times that they became a solid wall encircling her. She answered every question clearly and without any doubt, as though she were taking a history exam and needed to write a well-reasoned essay.

Standing in the queue at Heathrow airport, a hole had suddenly formed in the wall. Natalie shuddered, felt dizzy and a bit nauseous, like a soldier on the way to the battlefield. Eric held her arm and spoke softly: "You can still change your mind. You could go in a couple of months when things calm down." But the queue went surprisingly quickly, the ground attendant called one passenger after the next, and suddenly she found herself handing over her luggage and bidding her husband farewell.

On the flight, she practiced her responses to questions about recent events in Israel, repeating them over and over again, word for word, one sentence after the other. But arguments that had previously seemed solid now appeared somewhat absurd. Terrorists can explode their bombs anywhere; it is practically impossible to defend oneself; there is no escape. Tel Aviv stretched out in her mind with narrow, shaded streets, the promenade along the seashore, polluted streets; an imaginary walk in the city turned into a defense plan against an unknown enemy. On side streets, it was possible to hide behind a fence or in the gardens. In an open space, it would be wise to run away, escape, maybe even run into the sea. In a mall, if she heard a shooting or an explosion, she would hurry into a dress shop, find refuge in the fitting rooms. Though she couldn't tell the exact nature of the lurking danger, she kept searching for possible escape routes in public restrooms, stairways, parking lots, fitting rooms, restaurant kitchens. All these inelegant spaces now seemed like perfect shelters from a hidden threat, one that despite her efforts to imagine in detail always ended in explosions.

"Let your thoughts go to what will happen there," her friend Susie had told her a day before she left for Israel. Susie's parents had survived World War II and immigrated to the UK, where she was born. "I've heard my parents' stories about the Holocaust. They tried to tell me it would never happen again. We are safe in the UK. But I always wondered about one thing," she said, turning her head and falling silent. After an embarrassing silence, she answered an unasked question, "What would I have done in their place? Would I have tried to escape? Hide? Revolt? For instance, when assembling the Jews before deportation, would I have tried to hide or go along with the others? On the way to a concentration camp, would I have attempted an escape or preferred to stay with my parents and two brothers? Run away or see them beaten and humiliated, perhaps even murdered?"

Natalie looked at her, astonished. Her heart was pounding, and she wished she could overcome her anxiety, which gradually turned into an obscure substance that spread within her. It never occurred to her that her friend was contemplating such questions. Susie smiled again and said, "I know it sounds terrible, but there is also something positive about these thoughts. The Holocaust is an immense darkness overshadowing us. It becomes more tangible in that way; a phenomenon made of distinct details. Strangely, it creates a sense of security: I feel I am more prepared for future calamities. But of course, new catastrophes might be entirely different," she said, and burst into laughter.

Recalling this conversation, Natalie felt somewhat relieved. All through the flight, she visualized the streets of Tel Aviv—buildings, restaurants and cafés, nurseries and schools, bus stops and train stations—in each one a hiding place, a back door, a private passage, a small gate into a garden, spaces where she could find refuge if needed.

As Abigail saw her at the airport, she stretched out her chubby arms towards her. Dressed in a red and white outfit with a glowing face and a red ribbon in her hair, she hugged her grandmother, who held her tears back. Ofir immediately took her luggage, Laurie held her close and didn't let go—making all those imaginary explosions vanish. Simple happiness, innocent childish exhilaration dispels fear; light abolishes darkness, pushing it into crevices and gutters from which it will later emerge.

Natalie kept walking southward on Ibn Gabirol Street. She was in a hectic mood, wishing to go into shops and look at different products. An urge took hold to take side streets and then return to the main road, seek a new and previously unknown path to Laurie's house. First, she went into a bookstore and examined some history books, then bought a cookbook. In a housewares store, she found a grater like her mother use to have. A money changer in a tiny shop converted pounds to shekels at a favorable rate, but a nursery on the other side to the street was a complete disappointment with a small selection of plants at high prices, and in an apparel shop she bought Laurie a nice blouse. As she exited the boutique, Laurie called, and Natalie told her about the day. Laurie suggested an excellent confectionery, then added: "Mom, be careful. When you're done shopping, take a taxi home. Remember, don't take the bus!" Natalie nodded in agreement and hustled into a pet shop.

One step after another, a shop and another shop, Natalie's legs carry her almost against her will; she can't understand why she is so energetic. Her arms reach out to grab things. Her head swivels constantly from side to side, her eyes scanning the street with unfamiliar curiosity, moving quickly from people to objects, carefully checking the shop windows. Her legs move with surprising agility as she hops onto sidewalks and crossroads. For a moment, as she stops in front of a restaurant, she thinks she can smell food that she had never smelled before.

Again, she wonders what is happening, why she is flushed, why she feels as though she can detect the smallest details on the street. The paint under a shop window is peeling slightly; a street cat is sitting in a hidden corner near a fence; two tiny stones lay on the sidewalk; an oil stain mars a strip of the crossroad; a heart is carved on an electric pole. *I look as if I've lost something and I'm trying to find it, as if I'm looking for something, as if—Danger. I'm looking for danger. To see it. To confront it.*

In a split second, she realizes that her wandering in the street is nothing but a bizarre desire to face the peril, one that she doesn't quite understand. A suicide bomber, an explosive device—she has no idea of the shape of the threat she feels lurking on every corner. The childish will that overtakes her generates panic. She reproaches herself, warns herself that this adventure will end in disaster, and anyway, it's ridiculous that a woman her age should behave this way. It's sheer madness. It would have been better if she didn't walk in the street at all. She should have stayed at Laurie's house, but she keeps walking briskly, panting and erect—then she sees the bus stop.

The bus screeches to a halt right in front of her, and the doors open with a thump. She hands the driver a one-hundred-shekel bill. He grumbles and gives her change, bills and coins. She takes few steps and decides to sit next to the back door. The door closes, and the bus moves on. She gazes at Ibn Gabirol Street passing, buildings covered with gray haze, green trees along a busy street, restaurants, cafés. The bus stops again. Natalie looks anxiously at the door, and examines everyone getting on the bus: an elderly lady with shopping bags, there is nothing suspicious about her; a dark young man wearing a tight shirt who sits next to the driver and they begin to talk. Again, the bus is moving, here is another stop. This time, two young girls with backpacks get on, students returning from school, and after them is an old man. One stop before Laurie's house, many people get on the bus: school boys, three elderly men, two elegant ladies, and a young man, wearing a bulky coat, walking heavily.

Natalie can hardly breathe. Should she call the driver? Everyone looks watchful, examining the man with the coat carefully, but he walks slowly and stands at the center of the bus, facing the door, indifferent to Natalie's pounding heart. Her hands are shaking, sweat rolls down her back, her jaw is so tight that her teeth are grinding, but she is resolved and doesn't take her eyes off him. Are there any strange lumps in the coat? Someone rings the bell. The bus stops. Natalie's legs can hardly carry her, but she rises and hops off the bus. The door closes behind her and the bus drives away. She strides briskly and then stops, trying to catch her breath.

After a few minutes Laurie calls. "Laurie, did something happen? An explosion on a bus?" she asks, almost shouting, and Laurie answers, "No, thank God, nothing happened today. Why? Mom, are you okay?"

September 2001

A bright light, intense and cold, filled the afternoon sky. No soft clouds could be seen on the horizon. No breeze, not even a light and undetectable one, moved the leaves of the ficus trees down the road. No reviving sound of water emanated from the small fountain at the side of the street standing dry and cracked in the sun. No child's laughter, not even one resembling a whimper, emerged from the nearest nursery.

Over and done with.

What has been will no longer be, the past disintegrates and dissipates, and in a moment, it will be gone and forgotten. Events, each abundant with details, will vanish as if they had never happened, swallowed by the darkness of oblivion, and only at old age will they raise a smile; ah, yes, I'd forgotten, this took place before I was forty years old. What unfolded yesterday no longer exists today; what happened today will be rubbed out tomorrow. The passing moment is all that is left, and it transpires unnoticed. People once cherished beautiful moments, collected memories that would comfort them in the future: a first kiss, a farewell from a lover, an affinity between friends. As time goes by, these moments would surely bring about a pleasant longing. But embracing the passing moment voids the memories, leaving them bare and faded, almost redundant and oppressive.

And now it was all over.

The marriage was terminated. Ben and Carine had left the Tel Aviv Rabbinate after the papers had been signed and the divorce came into effect. They embraced each other, kissed on the cheek, and said goodbye. Carine crossed the street and disappeared into the black Mercedes awaiting her. Ben began walking without knowing where his feet were carrying him. One step after the other, the shaded street led to wide avenues. He kept strolling as if once he stopped, he would no longer be a married man, and the divorce would be finalized.

After four miscarriages, they stopped trying to have a child. The gynecologist instructed them to take a break, allow Carine's body to recover and gather strength. He didn't suggest any treatment, as no problem had been found. "All the tests indicated that everything was fine. I've seen similar cases," the doctor said in a contemplative tone. "We don't always understand the human body; there are unknown factors not necessarily related to medicine. You can try again, look for a surrogate mother, and perhaps even consider adoption. If you do decide to try again, wait at least six months." Ben looked at him with resentment. Bringing up adoption seemed ludicrous. *I would rather be childless than pretend a strange boy was mine,* he thought. Carine gazed at the doctor indifferently, examining her red nail polish as he elaborated on the options provided by modern medicine.

As they left the clinic, Ben suggested he would buy her "a small gift." She smiled as always and accepted his offer at once. As they left the jewelry store, he proposed having dinner at a fine restaurant but, to his utter surprise, she refused—she was tired, all those appointments with the doctor were exhausting, she wasn't hungry, would he mind if she went to the spa? She needed some relaxation, maybe a massage, an appointment with the beautician and the hairdresser. Ben consented, relieved that he wouldn't have to conceal his despair.

In the coming weeks, Carine was often away from home. Shopping, the beauty salon, the gym, meeting friends, frequent travel abroad—every time a new excuse came up. In the evening, the apartment was dark, and the curtains were drawn. Every time a terror attack took place, he called her, and she always answered quietly and politely: I'm not in the street and not in a restaurant. The spa is located on the top floor of a tower in central Tel Aviv, the gym is in another building, I'm safe here, don't worry. Aloofness was expanding and growing, gradually becoming irreversible. At first, he thought she was depressed and wished to forget the miscarriages. The focus on gynecology was so oppressive, completely removing the vitality of the reproductive process and turning it into a study of organs. But he had to admit that Carine didn't look sad at all.

At night, when she was home, he tried to caress her body, but she murmured something about being tired and fell asleep, and he was left awake, looking at a sky that sometimes seemed alien and distant and occasionally illuminated and soft. Once in a while, he muttered apologies toward the sky or observed it, mute and feeble, thinking about his life with Carine, Jerusalem, and childhood memories that always mingled with the image of Ofir. He reflected on his parents, how his mother made him read books and his father told him biblical stories, bringing every character to life, giving each protagonist specific appearance, habits, and emotions.

One night he recalled how his father told him about Abraham, describing him as a man with a long white beard, big eyes, rough hands, wearing something like a long robe. And his wife, Sarah, was a bit plump, his father chuckled, but beautiful and very lovely. Dad, what was she wearing? A red dress. Red? Why red? I don't know, because Abraham loved her very much. Strange, if he loved her so much why did he care that they didn't have children? Children are very important, Ben. People live for their offspring. There is no life without children. Mom and I would do anything for you, you know that, don't you? So, Dad, why didn't he leave her and marry Hagar? If children are so important, he should have found a woman who could have children. God forbid, son! God forbid! It's a sin to leave a barren woman. God would never forgive that.

Ben wiped the sweat off his forehead as he recalled his father's expression at the thought of Abraham leaving Sarah for her infertility: a sort of disgust, as if he had seen a revolting sight accompanied by a stench. But why not? he thought, listening to Carine's peaceful breathing next to him. This was not a marriage of love but of comfort, a practical agreement, economic affluence linked with a beautiful woman; he had never told her he loved her and she had never expected it. She was indifferent to any expression of affinity aside from the gifts. Why not leave her? Life with her is a contract, nothing more.

Ben kept thinking about his relationship with Carine, reconstructing every step, how they'd met, moved in together, got married, connecting various events, wondering how one had led to the other, following a twisted thread that kept spinning, leading to an obscure source, deeply implanted and sprouting everywhere. Eroding envy, vanity, an urge to conquer, to be wealthy were all part of this marriage. But not love. And even though he kept thinking about it, persuading himself that there was no reason for them to stay together, he couldn't remove the image of his father's countenance at the thought of leaving a barren woman.

After a couple of months, Carine stayed away more often at night. A women's meeting, traveling with a girlfriend, visiting her mother—the excuses she uttered quietly, without embarrassment. Ben said nothing. At first, jealousy surfaced, anger at her cheating on him. He lay in bed, his body tense and his left leg quivering for hours, imagining Carine with other men, coarse masculine hands groping her body. But he told himself, in the voice of a steadfast old teacher reprimanding his student, that he *did* consider leaving her, and had she given birth, it would have never crossed his mind. *Carine's affairs are a fitting punishment,* he thought, and so the jealousy died out and he was left awake in bed, gazing at the sky as always, muttering some explanation and apology.

After an hour of wandering along the beach, he decided to return to his office. *Enough! This marriage is over,* he told himself. *Even if I walk for hours, it won't be reversed.* Tears filled his eyes, and he wiped them with his sleeve like a toddler. *Over and done with. This chapter in my life is terminated. Carine and I are no longer married.* The pure blue sea stretched onto the horizon, and from the place where sky and water merged, soft, pleasant clouds materialized. A small sailboat drifted slowly, and migrating birds gathered into a giant arrow flying south, away from the snowy winter. *Only work can help me now,* he thought. *It diminishes distress, creates a worthy cause, implants hope, making my life enviable.* At last, the FDA had approved the robotic arm for knee surgery. This fantastic achievement and the success it heralded made a small smile mix into the tears, and he began to walk back to his car.

On the computer screen in his office, a 3D drawing appeared. Handex had invested years into developing this program. Ben decided to examine whether it was possible to improve a specific component. Plunging himself into programming was always pleasant: following a logical thread removed worries, stray thoughts, daydreams. He was engrossed in work as if he had not gotten divorced today when he heard a knock on the door.

Abraham. He entered the office without being invited. Embarrassment made him raise his kippah, brush his hand through his hair, and put it back on his head. Ben watched him silently.

"There's a problem with the operation of the robotic arm in the hospital in Ontario. They're confusing different commands and as a result the simulation of the surgery failed," Abraham said.

"We have representatives there. Can't they solve the problem?"

"Apparently not."

"We'll send someone to assist them. Does anyone from the Training Department want to go?"

"Maybe Sarit or Saul. I'm not sure. I don't understand what the problem is. We've already sent Sarit once, but they can't seem to get it right."

"Why don't we send Nava? Even though she's part of the development team, she has an in-depth understanding of the program."

Abraham's face twitched, revealing profound discontent.

"Nava doesn't explain very well. I mean, she provides a great explanation but, eventually, people don't get it and repeat their mistakes."

"Really? Why? She knows her stuff."

"Of course I'm not saying this isn't true, but something about her explanations makes people miss the point. She's arrogant. She gives the impression that it's quite complex."

An almost invisible smile spread on Ben's lips, the wrinkle across his forehead seemed somewhat smoother. He twiddled the pen he was holding from side to side and said, "You've got a point. There is something arrogant about her."

"God forbid, I'm not saying she's not a great programmer. And it's not because she is a liberal. But she is lofty and condescending. If you want people to understand what you're saying, you need to be vivid, not cold."

"What do you mean?"

"Well, you know, people are not rational machines. One can understand on different levels, even when it comes to a computer program. It has to be illustrated, difference scenarios should be displayed, you have to make the person you're speaking to want to get it right."

"But she does all that. I've seen her instructing doctors at a French hospital, and I was very impressed. She begins with the details and gradually develops the logical structure until she reaches the very basic rules of operating the robot."

"That's not the point. Of course she understands the program perfectly. But it's a question of her attitude toward people. Human beings need a different kind of explanation, not only a logical description of the facts. Think, for example, about commentary in the Talmud: 'What is the source of the question? What would it solve? Is there any novelty in it?' Almost always you'd find a comparison to similar questions. This provides an entirely different perspective. It could have been expressed in very few sentences, but the reader's comprehension would have been very different."

"Abraham, the Talmud deals with different problems with complex solutions. The robot is a machine, and in order to operate it, its logic should be clear. That's all."

"It doesn't matter. I'm talking about humans processing information. Nava thinks that it's enough to describe every component, show how it is connected to the other components, and that's it."

"She's right. That is all that's needed."

"No. You have to make people understand. Human beings are complex creatures, it's not enough to provide certain facts and they'll go on from there. It's a lot more complicated. Can you say you can grasp anything through the intellect? There are things beyond us: there is Providence, there are urges we are unaware of. Rational thinking can't solve everything."

The tears that filled Ben's eyes almost fell down his cheeks, full of deep, vertical wrinkles. To conceal them from Abraham, he closed his eyes, pretending to be immersed in thought. In a minute, he would have needed to lift his hand and wipe his eyes with his sleeve, but he grabbed the chair trying to mask his pain. How on earth was it possible to understand why he married Carine and why he divorced her? How had envy of Ofir led him to this relationship, which now seemed so futile and even somewhat bizarre? For a moment, he felt like an incomprehensible fate had tossed him into a hidden vortex that he was unable to escape.

Abraham thought that Ben's silence and closed eyes indicated that he was contemplating his arguments. Finally, the moment had come to convince Ben to choose the right path, to prove that the liberal's superficial view that man should rely on rational analysis is nothing but an infatuation, an empty faith, a broken reed. Once he accepts this, with God's help, he will find a path to a true religious belief, comfort in a different lifestyle away from Tel Aviv.

"Look at your father, for example. A wise, God-fearing man who began with nothing and was able to support his wife and children, providing for a wonderful family. Still, he was a religious man, keeping the Commandments. Does this mean he isn't an expert in practical issues? That he can't follow pure logic? Of course not. It only means that he knows there are things beyond reason."

Abraham raised the kippah, placed it back on his head, and smiled at Ben, but to his utter surprise he saw Ben closing his eyes again. For a single moment, he thought something twitched in Ben's face; his mouth stretched and his chin quivered as if a tiny animal was running inside him, unable to escape. Then the face became smooth, the wrinkle along the forehead disappeared, the thin lips loosened, the cheeks relaxed. Ben opened his eyes. The blue eyes peering at Abraham seemed too bright, a mixture of sparks of fire and drops of ice. Though it was clear that Abraham's words had created turmoil, Ben looked at him and spoke quietly in a serene tone.

"First of all, not only my father provided for my family—both my parents did. They both came to Israel empty-handed and together raised the family. My mother worked as hard as my father, and her common sense was very much the reason for their economic success. And also, what supports you and me is the success of Handex. The robot is a result of a systematic logical thought. The idea wasn't enough; without the rational structure we developed, the robot wouldn't have come to life, and there is absolutely nothing here beyond reason. The logic behind the robotic arm is all that is needed to explain how it operates, and nothing more."

Abraham was embarrassed by Ben's firm answer. The intimate atmosphere he had tried to create disappeared instantly, along with his evocation of Ben's father's religious belief and their shared conviction that relying on nothing but rational thought was an illusion. As Abraham was about to reply, muttering something about "occurrences that human beings don't always comprehend," Ben looked at him, detached, and in his eyes was a glimmer of contempt.

"Of course, of course, I'm not saying it's not true," Abraham began to say, trying to explain that he didn't mean that reason isn't necessary—after all, he is a computer engineer, and he only meant that we are all vehicles in the hands of the Almighty. But Ben stood up facing Abraham, as if a duel were about to take place. He stuck his clenched fists into his pockets and spoke quietly, almost whispering. "Ask Nava if she wants to go. If she does, we'll send her at once."

2002

A sunny morning filled the long balcony overlooking the street. Leaves falling from a nearby tree spread on the bright, comfortable deck chairs. A half-full cup of coffee sat on a small table, and on the floor were Abigail's dolls. Laurie stood by the rail and observed the street, a light robe enveloping her body. She inhaled fresh air saturated with the smell of leaves and gazed at the blue, cloudless sky. A police siren broke the silence—due to the fear of suicide bombers, the police quickly approached any suspicious object, any strange-looking man—but the sound died out quickly and quiet spread again in the street.

Ofir was left naked in bed. *Not like that,* Laurie thought. *Not like that.* An echo of a voice she had heard years ago surfaced, the odor of a room that became disgustingly familiar, another man's deep voice which she used to obey. Even the former gratitude suddenly materialized, mute yet unforgotten.

In the last couple of months, a somewhat sullen, gloomy spirit had come over Ofir, so different from his usual energetic nature: quickly changing subjects, laughing one minute and turning serious the next. A song on the radio could prompt him to seize her and start dancing; a passing remark could send him diving into a book—he was constantly changing, perpetually altering himself. But lately, he was a bit down. Somewhat indifferent and lacking his usual vitality.

At night, Laurie heard him walking around the house; the fridge door opening and closing repeatedly, the clinking of glasses, sometimes a rustling of food wrappers. A drawer in the kitchen cabinet creaked every time it opened. Although Ofir tried to pull it out quietly, it whistled faintly. Once in a while, the bathroom door opened and closed. Ofir's collapsing on the sofa in the living room made the sound of a muffled thump. The glass he placed on the table was barely audible. The chair by his desk grated as he rolled forward and backward. The computer made a constant humming noise, quiet but unpleasant. The balcony door slid back and forth; sometimes Ofir's foot hit the track. Only rarely would she hear his steps approaching the bedroom, and after a while she would feel his hand touching her back as he whispered.

"Laurie, are you asleep?"

At first, his hand gently caressed her body, and then it began to pull at her gently. His gloom created a slight urge of domination: grabbing replaced a light touch, clenching replaced caressing, and for brief moments, demand replaced his usual charm, and Laurie yielded without hesitation. She gazed at him, astonished, anxious but giving in to pleasure. But the memory of those days in Oxford began to spiral and swell, spread in the bedroom, threatening to make Ofir's body unfamiliar, even repellent.

Anthony, a student at Oxford, had straight blond hair, a booming voice, and a somewhat childlike appearance. A handsome man from a wealthy, non-Jewish family, their relationship could never ripen into marriage. After she had broken up with a boyfriend, he appeared: amusing, somewhat immature, highly educated, and infatuated with her. When she told him she was Jewish, he smiled sweetly and asked if her father was a doctor or a lawyer.

There had been a bit of dampness in his room, and the plaster emitted a moldy odor. The high ceiling was slightly filthy, the furniture dark and heavy. The bedding had a flowery pattern, and books were scattered everywhere. After they'd had sex for the first time, he looked at her, sweating, and said, "Laurie, you really are a liberated woman. I'm crazy about you." And so, it was established that she was a modern, permissive woman, enjoying bodily pleasures without hesitation. Laurie lay in bed beside him and smiled, as proud of the compliment as if she had won a prestigious award. As she got up, she knew his eyes were following her, but she left without looking back, closed the door, and chuckled.

A body merging with another body. Each time they met, she felt a need to match up to the compliment, to show that her yielding to pleasure was deep and uninhibited, a young woman who thinks that sensual freedom made for equality. Her body bent and stretched, curled and straightened, spread out and contracted, emitted moans and became silent—and Anthony's deep voice followed it, first with admiration and later suggestive: "Maybe like this? Or perhaps like that?"

What had been born of a quest for freedom gradually turned into a sort of obedience. Adhering to permissiveness produced conformity, and the constant need to prove the lack of inhibitions created submission. Anthony suggested, and she didn't refuse; Anthony said, and she agreed; Anthony demanded, and she consented; Anthony resolved, and she became a shadow, a woman who satisfied his wishes. The room in the dormitory turned into a prison in which they were both incarcerated, tied by chains of their own making, enslaved by a narrow and sour spirit that sanctified bodily pleasures and left them both extremely weak and dreadfully similar to each other.

When Laurie left the room for the last time, she felt she was about to collapse. She could hardly walk along the corridor leading to the exit. The clicking of her boots seemed sharp and frightening, her coat too heavy, and her leather gloves shiny and gross. The young woman reflected in the window looked pale; her eyes had a blank, desperate expression. Only as she left the building and the cold wind hit her face did she take a deep breath and sigh with relief.

A couple of days later, they met as usual in the pub, having a beer before returning to his dorm room. But this time she looked straight at him, and despite feeling she was blushing said quietly, "I don't want to come to your room anymore. I like you, but not like this." Anthony looked at her with anger. He put down his glass, got up, put on his jacket and swiftly left. But later that night she got an email: "Laurie, I'm really sorry. You're right. I'm glad one of us is smart. I never meant to hurt you. Yours, Anthony."

Ofir's light sadness made Laurie compassionate. On the couch in the evening, facing the television, she embraced him, asking him why he seemed so sad and smiling at his vigorous denial—he was tired, overworked; though the project was exciting there were obstacles, and now that they'd gotten the approval of the FDA, he felt he was facing another huge challenge. Maybe they were too ambitious and should have settled for less; meanwhile, only a few hospitals had acquired the robotic arm for knee surgery. The excuses he provided did not even slightly disguise the lost look he was trying to hide. But late at night, the tenderness of the evening was replaced by an impatient mood. It seemed that if only Laurie would yield to his grasp, which was a little too fierce, the gloom would dissipate and his vital spirit would return.

This morning, Ofir didn't wake up at seven o'clock, stretching his long arm over the blanket to turn off the alarm clock. As Laurie was about to leave for work, he hugged her in the kitchen and whispered, "Laurie, why don't you stay at home with me for a little while? Call the museum and say you'll be late today. You'll find an excuse. Let's have some fun." The sudden wailing of police cars coming from the street left her breathless, rising and falling, echoing among the buildings, deafening and abrasive, barging in through doors and penetrating closed windows. Though she'd been living in Tel Aviv for a couple of years now, she was left horrified every time a terror attack took place, attempting to conceal her tears. But this time, Ofir embraced her and said casually, "They'll be leaving soon. Come here," and she let the wails fade away without following them as she usually did. As she turned around, he chuckled and said, "If there is a terrorist here, I hope he leaves soon. We have better things to do now."

A hand moving over her body, touching her as if she were a stranger. Fingers followed an imaginary line stretching from her head to her toes. A man and a woman intertwined with each other, female and male; sometimes it was impossible to discern where one body ended and the other began. And though a certain apprehension prevailed in the room as if it were a third creature—Laurie looking aside for a moment, trying to capture it—pleasure made her ignore it and pretend that it had evaporated. A thread woven in her body, gentle and invisible, golden and transparent, was slowly stretching, twirling and tightening, folding and straightening. She felt Ofir's sleek body emit a dim light, his muscles fully strained, his heavy breathing audible, a sliver of fire reflected in his eyes.

For a single moment, madness prevailed. An inner image was fading, its outlines vanishing, replaced by breasts and pelvis. Ofir's breathing was so rapid it seemed he was about to choke, and then, in a simple natural move, he grabbed Laurie's hair—

"Not like that, Ofir. Not like that," a voice came out of her, words articulated, though she felt she had never said them. The memory of Anthony's body surfaced, leaving once again a sour sadness. Ofir looked at her as if he had just woken up and found her lying there beside him, surprised and slightly discomfited. She got up, put on her robe and went to the balcony. Quiet blue sky, a street left still, almost lifeless, Laurie's gaze wandered from the building facing her to the ficus tree with its twisted trunk, and then to the narrow street below. Anxiety and a slight queasiness spread within her. An inner tapestry with a delicate pattern was slightly unraveled; only one thread was pulled out, a warp thread loosening a weft thread, leaving it undone, demonstrating that the entire weave could unwind if only certain yarns were pulled. She turned around to observe Ofir. His eyes were closed. Looking at him from the balcony, she could tell he was wrapped in thought, pretending to be asleep.

Laurie stood there for a long time, staring at the street, reconstructing the last minutes. *Hampstead. I wish I were in Hampstead now.* A yearning was born, making her throat tight. She closed her eyes and recalled the green garden and the magnolia tree at its heart, the gray air, the lovely entrance to the house, the pleasant hall, the spacious living room, her room, the wardrobe still full of her clothes, the upper-left drawer with her childhood memories, the old photos, the teddy bear she got as a child and went to bed with for years, the red ribbon around its neck, the white fur, the more tattered it was, the more she loved it—

A fair forehead on twisted, feminine arms, hair black as coal sliding to the side, a tear running down the cheek, a robe wrapped tightly around a quivering body all concealed a thought she was determined to repress: *Maybe I shouldn't have come here. Perhaps it was a mistake.*

January 30, 2003

At four forty-three, on Thursday afternoon, twenty-two minutes after the weekly staff meeting ended, fourteen minutes after Ben had gone back to his office, and seven minutes after Ofir returned to his office, sank into his chair, and inspected once again the company's credit line, Ofir's phone buzzed loudly, like a bee in pain. His secretary whispered into the handset that the young bookkeeper was asking to meet with him privately.

"Yes, I suggested she approach the accountant but she insists on talking to you. No, I have no idea why, but she won't accept anyone else. Yes, I know you are extremely busy, but she won't take no for an answer. Just for a couple of minutes? Sure, I'll send her in."

A young woman entered the room and greeted Ofir with a heavy Russian accent. She had fair skin, short dark hair, and heavily made up green eyes. She wore tight black jeans and a black leather jacket. Though her countenance betrayed a certain determination, she hesitated whether she should sit down, looking at the chair facing Ofir but remaining standing until he invited her to sit. He wondered if she was about to ask for a raise only two months after starting her job. The former bookkeeper, a long-time employee of Handex, had moved to the United States, and Ofir had decided to hire this young woman who only recently obtained her bookkeeping certification.

"Listen, I looked into the records of previous years, as you've requested. I know you said I should only take a brief glace for a general understanding, but I examine every figure, more than you suggested. I am not sure why; I wanted to be sure I was on top of things. I don't know how to say this but . . . I think some money is missing from the company's account."

"What do you mean by missing?"

"From 1992 on, there is a yearly discrepancy of around a hundred and twenty thousand shekels, and from 1999 on around two hundred and forty thousand shekels are missing. It adds up to almost two million shekels, which is, of course, only the nominal amount. I double checked my calculations a few times."

"Are you sure?"

"Yes."

"Maybe you made a mistake?"

"That was my initial assumption. I was convinced it was an error. So, I recalculated everything from start to the finish three times and came up with the same total."

"How is that possible? So where is the money? Maybe under the wrong entry? It happens rather often."

"True. At first, I thought more was missing, but I found part of it under an incorrect entry. Still, a lot is simply missing."

"So, what is the explanation?"

"I'm not sure, but maybe . . ."

"What?"

"It's possible that . . ."

"That what?"

"In one place, I found a note that the former bookkeeper had written in handwriting: 'transferred to Ben Haddad's private account.'"

"What?!"

"Yes. She'd written this in pencil in the margin, in very small handwriting. And next to it was the number of his bank account."

"Are you saying the money was transferred to my partner's private account? That's impossible."

"I've double-checked it. It's true."

"It is impossible! I'm sure it's a mistake."

"I'm afraid not."

"Are you absolutely sure?"

"Yes. Definitely. Apparently, the former bookkeeper knew about it and said nothing. She worked here for years. Anyway, that is the explanation. The money was transferred to Ben Haddad's private account."

Her pale face became nearly transparent, her green eyes looked sunken, like a skull's orbital cavity, and her thin fingers passed through her slightly oily hair. "I'm sorry, excuse me. But I thought I had to tell you" she said, getting up quickly without looking at Ofir, leaving the room, silently closing the door behind her.

It seemed that a cold and biting current of air pressed Ofir into his chair. He was looking up at the ceiling, still and inert, utterly lifeless, yet his body twitched and jerked, and then was still. His straight hair fell back, his hands jittered, and his left knee moved from side to side, but his right knee looked as if it had been fixed to the chair and couldn't be moved. A tiny spider was crawling on the lamp, moving its legs in perfect coordination. Ofir followed the moving legs. After it crossed the lamp, it leapt into the air, but Ofir's gaze remained fixed on the lamp, his eyes open without blinking, his mouth gaping.

Half an hour later, he managed to get up. Though his heart was pounding rapidly and he felt the room was becoming blurry, he closed his briefcase, turned off the light, and left the office. Voices came from the corridor, he thought he could hear Ben speaking, but he hurried to the elevator, wondering if he would faint by the time he reached the fortieth floor. *Damn it, damn it,* he said to himself. *Ben has been stealing from me for ten years. I can't believe it. Ben has been stealing from me for ten years. I need to go home to Laurie.*

The fancy SUV began to crawl up the winding tunnel of the parking lot, merging into a line of cars, finally reaching the gate. As the car exited into the busy street, a light hit Ofir. Though it was twilight, Ofir saw a strong glare, blinding and oppressive, making it hard to drive. For a moment, he thought he was wrong about the time. Had he left the office too early? Was it noon now? Maybe he never went to work today? No, that couldn't be true, he was sure he had had lunch with Ben and two other engineers, and after lunch, the weekly staff meeting had taken place, so apparently it was Thursday, otherwise the meeting wouldn't have been in the afternoon. It must be almost evening now, but for some strange reason, intense light was apparent everywhere, white and reflecting, a radiation creating a cold glow, white and noxious.

Dizziness overtook him, a kind of strange density, as if every passing moment encompassed hours, days, even years. Evening contained morning, the speeding car stood in endless spaces, yet it dashed ahead, the buildings on the sides of the street disintegrated into walls, windows, balconies hung loosely in the air. The strange light circulating in the sky was transparent yet overbearing. The car accelerated, but he thought it was standing in place, and his attempts to determine when he would get home were futile. For a single moment, a thought passed, a crust of logic prevailed—he should tell Laurie he would be late so she wouldn't worry—but it sank in a bottomless pit, dark and illuminated.

A wind penetrated the car through the open window, carrying a strong smell of sea; rain splashed on the windshield; silhouettes passed on the side of the road. Memory upon memory, laughter blending with pain; there is Ofir the child, maybe three years old or even younger, going to the nursery, a woman bending over to him saying, "What a cute boy! What's your name?" He's looking at her, in her eyes he sees how charming he is; as she smiles cheerily at him, he can see her big teeth. He thinks she caressed him, maybe only exchanging a few words with his mother, saying how charming he is.

For a moment, he was overwhelmed with glee, as if that woman is with him in the car, and in a moment, she will pull a lollypop out of her purse and hand it to him to show how cute he is. Even now, as an adult, he remains incredibly attractive; women always desire to be near him, even when they notice his wedding ring. Maybe this woman is interested in spending some time with him?

The old memory stretched and widened, expanded and became more tangible; his mother was smiling heartily at the woman, glad to see that her son produced such admiration. The street was nearly empty. He went with his mother to the nursery, where the teacher warmly greeted them and invited him in.

Along the passing view, beneath the overbearing light Ofir couldn't quite figure out, his early childhood in Beit Hakerem unfolded: narrow streets with trees casting shadows, Hakhaluts Street winding between aging villas, and the nursery he once attended. Despair made him eager to mingle there now, to become once again the toddler the teacher favored above all others. He grinned as he thought of the teacher, as though she were now right beside him, loving him more than anyone. He succumbed with pleasure to the old appreciation that he was such a charming boy.

The rain had become so heavy Ofir could hardly see; hailstones pelted the road, making a gentle sound. The cars slowed down and drove carefully, and he clung to the memory, reviving every small detail. He giggled like a toddler, burping out loud and laughing; in a moment he would jump in place, amused, turning the steering wheel from side to side and making the sound of an engine like a child driving a toy car. But a dark, obscure shadow with ragged ends slowly materialized and blended into the strange light without dimming the horrifying gleam. Something bad happened after nursery school, but he can't quite remember what it was. An accident? A disaster? Maybe someone died?

A deep sharp cut, like a jagged whip that struck him strongly only once, slashed the living flesh and exposed the inner organs to absorbing air. His lifelong friend, a part of him, his partner in a life project, had cheated, deceived, betrayed him, lied, stolen, pretended to be a soulmate, a brother, but acted like a foe. An overpowering weeping overtook Ofir. He yelled and screamed, exploding with crying, sobbing uncontrollably. If the rain hadn't been so heavy, his wailing would have been heard outside the car, but rolling thunder drowned it in the storm's pounding drums. His weeping grew louder, mixing with cries of "Mommy, Mommy," as if he were a young child again leaning against her apron. Through his tears the road seemed like a path on a lake, sometimes covered in water, sometimes ascending over it. But out of cries of pain suddenly emerged a bewildering thought, a sort of a smart trick: maybe it's an error? A mistake in calculation? The bookkeeper was young and inexperienced; could the desire to please him, to show what a devoted worker she was, create a miscalculation? Perhaps she even misled him deliberately, deceived him to come across as trustworthy?

Though he wasn't sobbing anymore and he'd fallen silent—a stillness he was eager to break—again the jigged shadow materialized, weaving into the oppressive light, an entity that was all heaviness and despair. *Of course, it was not a mistake*, he yelled at himself in the speeding car. *Of course not!* He was eager to hear a human voice, even if it was his own. Out of the mutilating pain, with tears running down his cheeks and dripping on his shirt, he began to plan revenge: I'll steal his money; I'll tell his parents that he is a thief; I'll make a pass at women he dates. Ofir could feel his body shaking and twisting at these plans, he was suffocating, he could hardly breathe—

The sea.

I need to go to the sea.

I have to smell the sea; salty, misty, wild, primordial.

There is a right turn here, then I'll take a left turn and continue straight ahead. I know the sea is on the west side.

The SUV almost turned over as he suddenly veered off. At the intersection, Ofir took a left turn and began to speed on the narrow road leading to the beach. The peculiar light seemed to him even stronger, almost blinding, and for a moment he thought it might be emanating from inside him. A couple of minutes, later he reached the beach. He stopped, turned off the engine, took off his socks and shoes and got out of the car. After a couple of steps on the seashells he felt acute dizziness. His legs were shaking, he breathed heavily, he moved his hands in the air, but as he tried to walk toward the water he tumbled and fell, his face sinking in the wet sand.

A concerned citizen from Kfar Vitkin[1] called the police, saying he saw a suspicious person on the beach. He drove an SUV, turned it off, began to walk toward the water and disappeared. Despite the storm, and fearing terror attacks, a police car had been sent to check out who was there at the waterline. As the police officers lit the beach with flashlights, they saw a man lying

---

1   A village on the seashore, north of Tel Aviv.

on his back and gazing at the sky despite the pouring rain. They approached him carefully, fearing he was a suicide bomber, but he didn't look suspicious. When they stood right next to him, they asked for his name and what he was doing there. At first, he stared at them with a glazed expression and said nothing, and then he asked to be left alone, he was dealing with some problem and they were preventing him from solving it.

"Just a nut," the police officer reported on the radio, and asked if he needed to call someone to have him hospitalized.

February 2003

Even though two full weeks had gone by since the police officers had brought Ofir home, Laurie was still moving around on tiptoes, closing the windows carefully and the doors silently, asking Abigail to turn off the television. She felt that if she could only remove the daily hassles and let silence fall, Ofir would recover.

Abigail, however, was utterly oblivious to her mother's efforts to adjust their home to Ofir's condition. In the morning, after the police officers brought him home, she'd crawled into their bed as she did every morning, and kissed him on his cheek. "Daddy isn't well. He has to rest," Laurie cautioned her, trying to conceal last night's horror: Ofir couldn't be found and didn't answer his phone. Ben had no idea where he was. He failed to find him. She was holding herself back from calling his parents. At midnight she called the police and said her husband had disappeared. The police officer suggested she waits for a while before declaring him missing. She was terrified thinking he was hurt, lying injured and no one offered help, collapsed in a puddle of blood, maybe even dead, murdered, gone, attacked when he was by himself, stabbed, choked, a body tossed into a ditch, she would be left alone with Abigail—for hours she paced back and forth at home, put Abigail to bed, called Ben time and again, and her British friends; they all said that they were sure everything would be fine but had no idea why Ofir wasn't answering his phone. Finally, when she opened the door and saw only the older police officer, she nearly fainted and shrieked in English, "What happened? What happened?" Then she saw Ofir pale and completely wet, leaning against a younger police officer, who led him directly to the bedroom as if he knew where it was. The older police officer said, "What happened to him? We found him on the beach in Kfar Vitkin. I believe he is not in a good mental state. He asked us to take him home. Call a doctor." He left the car keys on the table adding, "We brought the car and parked it in the street," closing the door behind him.

Ofir's eyes were wide open, looking at Laurie with anticipation as if he had asked her a question and was expecting an answer. And though she caressed him and waited for him to say something, he gazed at her in silence, as if she were the one who needed to clarify why she had chosen to spend a winter evening at home instead of on an unfamiliar beach in the midst of the storm. "What happened, Ofir, what happened?" Tears covered her face, but he watched her distantly, examining her and waiting for her to say something. "Did something happen to you?" she kept asking as he opened his dark eyes expectantly, looking for her to answer her own painful questions so he would find out what had gone so wrong. Only as she got up from the bed to call the doctor, turned around and walked toward the door, did she hear a voice behind her, impartial and detached. "Ben has been stealing from me for ten years," he said, closed his eyes, and fell into a deep sleep.

The psychiatrist who came the next day at noon looked at Laurie intensely and asked what had happened. A man of about fifty years old, bold, wearing round eyeglasses placed on a small nose. He asked for a glass of water, sat on the living room sofa, stretched his legs out, and pulled out a small notebook. Though he spoke to Laurie in a soft, sympathetic manner, he started asking about Ofir, writing in his notebook without raising his eyes. Was he inclined to changing moods? Did he experience pain? Trouble sleeping? Is he a healthy man? Taking any medication? How does he function as a father? Laurie found all these questions odd and unnecessary, completely unrelated to her husband lying motionless in bed in the other room, hearing nothing. Only his wide-open eyes following her with anticipation indicated he was present and aware. His long, muscular body was feeble, his feet bare and his hair full of sand. Two seashells fell out of his pockets, but he appeared completely unaware of that.

Laurie tried to answer the doctor's questions but, after a couple of words, a whimper arose in her throat and her voice turned into a loud moan. The doctor raised his eyes from his notebook, looked at her sympathetically, nearly smiling, and said, "I'm really sorry, I know how hard this must be for you. I know these questions seem unnecessary but they are crucial for reaching a precise diagnosis of your husband's mental condition." When he finished writing everything down, he closed the notebook, tucked it into his backpack, and asked to speak with Ofir in private. He went into the bedroom and closed the door behind him. Faint voices came from the room, but she couldn't make out a single word.

After about ten minutes, he came out of the bedroom and walked back to the living room. He sank into an armchair, had some water, stretched his legs, crossed his arms and said quietly, "Ofir has undergone a severe mental trauma. I understand he discovered that his partner, his childhood friend, has been stealing from him for ten years. Clearly, this is a substantial crisis, not only due to the implications on the future, but because it makes him perceive the past in a new light. It is a very complicated life event; I would compare it to the loss of a loved one or a traumatic breakup from a partner, as someone close to us for years and is part of our self-perception turns out to be not who we thought he was. And it's not only about missing them, but suddenly the part of us relating to them collapses. And because this partner is a childhood friend, it makes him see his entire life differently." As he spoke, he looked directly into Laurie's eyes, taking in her tears yet adopting an impartial tone. The quiet words, he knew, would eventually help family members deal better with the crisis.

"I don't see a need to hospitalize him at this point," he added cautiously, aware that mentioning hospitalization might create panic. "I don't think he's a threat to himself or others. He's gone through a very traumatic event and he is processing it slowly. Normally the first phase of shock lasts up to two weeks, and then begins the complex process of dealing with it. I left him pills he is required to take once a day, and he reassured me he won't forget. I suggest considering psychological treatment, sessions with a therapist, but of course, his consent and cooperation are essential. In the meantime, he should rest. Make sure there is food and drink within his reach, but there is no need to push him to eat. Of course, if there is any change, contact me immediately, even during nighttime."

Bewilderment crept into Laurie's eyes, which were full of tears. With eyes wide open, she asked, "Did he answer you? Did he agree to take the medication?" and the doctor replied quietly, "He's not detached from reality. He knows what's going on. However, communication with other people is extremely difficult for him, especially with you, being so close to him. He feels that if he talks to you, he would have to explain, and currently, he is incapable of doing so. Often people in this state prefer to talk to strangers, especially doctors. I believe he will take the medication, but call me if he doesn't."

Laurie felt that the door closing behind the doctor was heavy and noisy, as if a huge iron gate had been slammed and could never be opened again. The steps he took toward the elevator sounded like muffled knocking, the elevator's bell a disagreeable buzz. Laurie crept silently into the bedroom and saw Ofir deep in sleep, softening his straight facial features. She closed the door cautiously and went slowly into the living room, looking around as if the apartment were unfamiliar. The pretty Persian carpet spread across the floor suddenly seemed vulgar and too colorful, the brown leather sofa, expensive and comfortable, reminded her of some beast, and the mahogany coffee table she had sent from London was now unbelievably distressing: a bunch of sticks tied together, graceless and commonplace. The bright kitchen seemed too metallic, a vase with flowers ridiculous, unbecoming for the room. She went to the balcony and collapsed onto a deck chair despite the cold and the pouring rain that splashed on the white rail.

An inner space had stretched and twisted, contracted and straightened, assumed a long shape, and then spread into a sort of circle that curled into itself and became a small and condensed point: The first time she'd met Ofir, a tall man with a gentle face and Israeli manners, Ofir crying when Abigail was born; Ofir on a trip to the Alps, carrying her on his back when she couldn't walk anymore; Ofir at a French film, mimicking the protagonist in the dark cinema, making her burst into loud laughter, alarmed by reproachful looks; Ofir's naked body on the bed, slim and muscular; Ofir running the company with Ben with such wisdom and talent—

The tears that ran down her cheeks made Laurie get up and return to the bedroom; a mechanical movement, as if someone were moving her. She opened the door cautiously and softly walked in on tiptoes. The air in the room was thick and heavy, mixed with Ofir's breath and remnants of the scent of the sea. Despite the dim light, she could see he was sound asleep. His body was limp in an awkward way, as if the organs were connected in an obscure manner. Sand that had fallen off him surrounded the bed.

As she stood by the bed, Laurie kneeled and bent her head down, her black hair covering Ofir's face, her tears dropping on his cheeks. Grace, compassion, fear, and love blended as she kissed his lips, an innocent, unreserved kiss, but he only moved his body slightly in sleep and turned limp again.

The phone ringing in Hampstead two days later broke the pleasant morning calm. Eric was engrossed in his newspaper at the dining table, while Natalie, in a robe with hair disheveled, made breakfast, glancing once in a while at the blue sky of the pleasant winter day. She looked at the garden with contentment. Green shrubs were planted as to create an impression of a wild meadow, a mixture of green-toned leaves, and colorful daffodils spread among them. Fresh dew on the leaves, first blossoms from the bulbs she had planted, a climbing ivy that sent out another tendril during the night that was now clinging to the fence—she felt a simple joy as though she hadn't looked at her garden only yesterday morning. She prepared two cups of tea and let the tea brew for a couple of minutes, made scrambled eggs and added basil and chive, placed freshly cut whole wheat bread in a straw basket. As she was turning the eggs with a wooden spoon, the phone rang. Positive that it was her friend, she answered the phone saying, "Hello Suzie," but to her utter surprise she heard Laurie choking, "Mom? Are you at home? Can we talk?"

A sobbing voice, congested and breathless, was swallowed in weeping and then resurfaced again. Natalie heard Laurie crying and initially couldn't comprehend what she was saying. "What happened? A terror attack?" She screamed in horror, "Is everyone okay?" A question followed by another one, her hands were quivering as she held the phone, trying to find out the nature of the disaster that had taken place, to figure out the speechless weeping coming from the phone. She felt dizzy, leaned against the door, and didn't protest as Eric grabbed the phone. Trying to sound composed he asked, "Laurie, what happened?" His contracted face gradually relaxed, losing its anxious expression and adopting a calmer countenance. His eyebrows loosened, his mouth softened and was now even slightly open; habit made him push up his glasses, and finally he said, "Sweetie, relax. It will take some time but he will recover. Would you like Mom to come? Why don't you come here?"

Eric and Natalie sat in silence. Natalie tightened her sloppy, light-blue robe. Eric brushed his hair back. The smell of burned scrambled eggs filled the kitchen. The tea turned black, the slices of bread were left in the basket as both of them sat silently, self-absorbed, with eyes closed. One thought went round both their minds, the sort of consideration that gradually becomes an idea, existing simultaneously in two minds of two different people, a mother and father, exactly in the same way. *It's a shame Laurie moved to Israel and never had a family here in Britain. I wish she hadn't left the UK and settled in Tel Aviv; at the very least she could have lived with Ofir in London.* And though they both knew that the crisis in Ofir's life could have taken place anywhere, they often heard of partners falling out with each other, at that very moment, they felt their daughter was suffering only because she'd decided to live in Israel. The unfamiliar landscape, an army occupying another people, Tel Aviv scorching in the summer heat, Abigail going to a noisy, crowded nursery—everything could have been better.

But here their thoughts split into two brooks, each turning in a different direction. Natalie moaned out loud. Ever since her last visit to Israel, an insistent spirit had taken her over. Upon her return to London, she had approached her pestering neighbor and began to describe Tel Aviv in great detail: the beach, the restaurants, the constant fear of terror. No need to apologize, she kept muttering to herself. *I am against the occupation but*

I support the Jewish state. And there is also no need to apologize for being a British Jew. But now she felt betrayed. The life of her daughter who'd settled in Israel had come to a crisis and she had no idea how it would be resolved. Eric, unlike her, blew his nose, pushed his glasses up, and thought of the fundamental difference between his life as a Jewish man in London and the lives of Jews in Israel. He was truly fond of Ofir. When he had described the way he ran his company, Eric was full of admiration, yet in every single moment he knew Ofir was unlike him, different, lacking a certain hesitation he believed was somehow necessary. And now, as he learned of Ofir's mental breakdown, a dread which he couldn't quite figure out overtook him. He kept telling himself that he was only worried about his daughter and granddaughter, but a faint inner voice reproached him and determined unequivocally that he was lying.

Three days later, the phone rang in the evening in Beit Hakerem. Joseph Stern wanted to hurry to pick up the phone, but lately he'd been limping and had to use a walking stick. Since his retirement, a variety of ailments had appeared. A chronic pain in his right foot, an infection in his hip, a stiff neck—the doctor insisted that they developed gradually throughout the years, but Joseph had never felt them before his retirement. His wife, who had retired years ago, volunteered in an animal rescue organization. He was left alone at home, listening to the radio in the morning and meeting some friends in the afternoon. As he heard Laurie's voice coming from the phone, more muted than usual, saying, "I want to tell you what happened to Ofir. I'm afraid it's not good news," he immediately called Sarit. Together they listened breathlessly to the voice coming from the receiver, saying: "It's impossible," "This can't be true," "Ah, who would have imagined that."

When she was done, they asked when they could come; they would like to see Ofir at once. Laurie replied that the doctor suggested only one of them should come for half an hour, it was impossible to tell how he would react, and anyway he was asleep most of the day. She suggested tomorrow they could both come to Tel Aviv. Joseph would wait in the café next to their house and Sarit could visit their son. Joseph asked hesitantly how Abigail was taking it. She was told her daddy was sick, but she slept by his side in the mornings, talking to him though he didn't reply, pulling on his shirt as she always did. Once he embraced her.

The shock left them sitting silently next to each other. Sarit covered her face with her hands and Joseph dropped his head backward to stop the tears from running down his cheeks. The heartbreak immediately created thoughts about Handex, the emblem of Ofir's unfortunate choice, insisting on setting up his own company rather than taking a job at a bank or a government office, which at this very moment made both of them aghast and embittered. All sorts of sentences were emitted, poignant and painful, and it was impossible to tell who actually said them: this foolish resolve to turn away a solid position, all this wouldn't have happened if he were an employee and not self-employed. Who knows what will happen now? The firm will collapse, the tremendous efforts will all have been wasted. People with tenure have financial security; they aren't reliant on their friends, and therefore experience no such disappointments. They may have less money, but a better life.

Finally, Sarit got up and went to the kitchen and set the kettle to boil out of habit. The tea bag sank into the full glass, sugar dissolving slowly in the hot water; the teaspoon stirred quickly, creating a misty vortex. *I was wrong, so wrong,* she thought, *it's all my fault, I didn't bring him up the way I should have; like everyone else I was captivated by his charm, feeling he was so strong—I didn't teach him to be careful, vigilant, look after himself.* She felt the entire disaster was a result of faulty shaping of her son's character, preferring ambition over the elemental instinct for self-preservation. And, even though she knew well that friends betraying each other has always taken place, in her mind this theft was the result of an unsuitable relation, an abominable mixture of friendship and economic interests. Why, Ben is not a criminal, she kept thinking, he also fell into this trap. She thought of him as a mischievous child who had taken a toy from Ofir. And the more she examined this turmoil the more convinced she was that turning away from the proper way of living, one that separates between the workplace and friendship, was the source of this misfortune. Her son and his best friend were reborn in her mind: one was an economist at the Ministry of Finance and the other a computer science professor. For long moments they led interesting conversations, watched television, traveled together until she got tired and decided to go to bed.

Joseph was left sitting on the sofa, his head reclining and his eyes closed. *What's the point of all my connections,* he thought in pain, *if I am unable to protect my son?* The network he had created diligently over many years was now unraveling gradually. At first, a few fibers fell off the threads, then the ties were loosened and, finally, huge holes were made, and the entire network was almost useless. A line of people materialized in his mind: prominent professors, high government officials, socialites, generous American donors, army men, heads of cultural institutions—all so fond of Joseph, asking for his assistance, and he was always willing to help. An unwritten list of people who might prove useful, and now they all turned into faceless silhouettes, and his past efforts to assist them seemed futile and unappreciated.

For a moment, he was overwhelmed by an acute nostalgia for the kibbutz, which had begun to surface in the last year. The memory of the green lawns and communal dining room brought tears to his eyes. Friends who sat together in the evening, deep in conversation, once in a while singing late into the night. He told himself it had been a mistake to move to Jerusalem; he should have grown old in the kibbutz. Life was better there, he thought, brooding, and then he grunted and waved off his useless contemplations.

February 20, 2003

A spring stretched to its very limit, slightly corroded but still flexible, its spirals large and heavy and turning into a long, iron wire, nearly breaking—then one end is released. The twang of the instant contraction is quiet yet shrill, strangely resembling a whine. The end hitting Ben's heart is like a rusty nail stuck into living flesh, splattering blood and skin everywhere.

Though Ben had been anticipating this moment for years, Laurie's simple and direct words—"You're a thief"—were overwhelming. Not "Some money is missing from the company's bank account" or "We found that you've transferred the money into your private account." Not even "How could you do this to your best friend?" Nothing but a couple of words in English, neither threatening nor admonishing, but simply stating a plain objective fact: he was a thief. And the conversation was over. He was left staring at his phone in astonishment, and only eventually did he place it on the coffee table in the living room. He then lay down on the sofa and remained motionless, apart from the uncontrollable trembling of his left leg.

Since Ofir had disappeared three weeks ago, Ben suspected his partner had discovered something. That night, Laurie's voice on the phone had sounded more and more like sobbing; she begged Ben to find Ofir, and asked him to call the police. She was afraid her Hebrew would be unclear and that the police officers wouldn't understand her. She later called and said, "Ofir is here. The police brought him. I don't know what happened." She hung up and never called again. It made no sense that Ofir would disappear if he had found some money had been stolen. He would probably suspect other people, not Ben. And if he thought it was Ben, he would ask for an explanation. Why would he vanish without a word?

But after a couple of days, with neither Ofir nor Laurie returning his calls, a new suspicion emerged—not certainty that Ofir knew the truth, but a confidence that a meaningful event had occurred. From a phone conversation with Ofir's mom a couple of days later, Ben learned that she didn't know where her son and Laurie were. On Sunday morning, the secretary called Ofir to ask why he hadn't come to work. Laurie answered the call, saying he was sick. "I have no idea when he'll feel better, and I don't know if you should reschedule his appointments."

One day after another, Ofir didn't go into Handex or call. Ben told himself that he needed to visit him to find out what had happened, but fear confined him to his office, home, fancy restaurants. On Tuesday, February 11, Ben finally mustered the courage to drive to Ofir's house. Parking the car, he felt that his pounding heart could be heard loudly. He then walked cautiously to the building's entrance and rang the bell. Silence. He rang it again. A buzz was heard, nothing else. The front door didn't open and no voice came from the intercom. He could see lights on in Ofir's apartment, and his car was in the parking lot, but no one invited him in. Before he left, he looked up again to the top floor. A shadow crossed the balcony and vanished.

The whispers at Handex gradually became louder and louder, turning almost into yelling. Ofir wasn't coming into work, and no one knew why. At first, rumors circulated about illness. Was Ofir unwell? His wife? Probably cancer, but they're still not sure; an accurate prognosis hasn't been made yet. Then there was talk about him being heavily in debt. Someone heard that people from the gray market had visited his residence, demanding such an exorbitant sum even Ofir couldn't pay it; neighbors said they'd smashed up expensive pieces of furniture. "Maybe he's gone underground," one programmer murmured. Then a theory about a quarrel between Ben and Ofir emerged, but it was immediately ruled out. Even if it was true, why should Ofir disappear? After investing so many years in the company, a disagreement wouldn't prevent him from working.

The speculations grew and evolved, each taking a specific form with concrete details lending them more credibility. A cold and suspicious spirit overwhelmed Handex. Doors remained closed, many avoided going to lunch, Ofir's name wasn't mentioned at the weekly staff meeting. Ten days after he disappeared, Abraham opened Ben's office door without knocking, closed it behind him, and remained standing, crossing his arms and watching Ben as if he expected an immediate answer.

"What's going on with Ofir?" he asked, narrowing his eyes and following every muscle in Ben's face. Silence. Ben's gaze was fixed on an invisible spot on the wall; he remained silent. He had a sour expression as if he had eaten spoiled food and the bad taste hadn't yet gone away.

"Why isn't Ofir coming to the office?

"I think he's sick."

"You think or you know?"

Ben raised his eyes and looked at Abraham with reproach. He was pale, his eyes grew bright, a hidden muscle twitched. The sharp look left no room for doubt; he wasn't going to accept Abraham's aggressive tone. Abraham felt Ben's reservation and addressed him more gently: "Will Ofir come back to work?"

"I hope so."

"We finally got the FDA approval. It'll be a shame if everything falls apart."

"I agree."

"He doesn't want to sell the arm anymore?"

"I don't know."

"He wants to close the firm?"

"I don't know."

"Do you think Handex will survive?

"I don't know that, either."

"When will we know? I don't want to be pushy, but I'm sure you understand . . ."

"I hope the situation will become clearer soon."

"You know I provide for six children?"

"Yes."

"I'm not the only one who is worried. People are asking questions."

"I understand."

Abraham's aggravation was evident. His back curved, his round belly protruded. He ran his hand through his hair and played with his kippah. His thick hair was now gray. Without his smile, which was usually so joyful, he seemed older. His face betrayed the acrimony he normally concealed. "Do you remember that when I took this job I asked to become a partner? I saw you winking at each other. But now it would have been very useful, wouldn't it? We could control the firm, maybe even kick Ofir out." Ben looked at him and said nothing. He was frozen; he twirled the pen in his hand, observing the ink sliding from side to side.

Dark clouds converged outside the window, containing seeds of a severe winter storm. In a moment, petrifying thunder would sound, pouring rain would beat on the buildings, water would flood the streets, the wind would shake the trees until some would crack with a moan; the Ayalon River would overflow and fill the wide road. But now, annoyingly, the clouds merely intimidated, neither fulfilling their potential threat nor drifting away.

"I'm sorry, Ben. I didn't mean to talk to you like that. But I'm so worried about the future. It's killing me. It's not easy, you know, when you provide for a wife and six kids."

"How old are the children?"

"The eldest is eighteen. He's in the army. Joined the paratroopers."

"Paratrooper? Like Ofir . . ."

Pride flickered in Abraham's eyes; for a moment they appeared moist. The thought of his eldest son resembling Ofir pleased him. But as he saw Ben's bitter smile and recalled that a complication in Ofir's life might be taking his job, his satisfaction was replaced by frustration permeating throughout the years. It had always been there—even before he had met Ofir. "I don't know what his problem is, but he is being irresponsible. He needs to understand that people depend on Handex. He can't simply walk away. He used to be reliable. But now he's living a different life."

"Different life? What do you mean?"

"Well, you know, living extravagantly in the center of Tel Aviv; it's not like the modest spirit of Jerusalem in which he grew up."

"I also live in a luxury apartment in the center of Tel Aviv. Can I be trusted?"

"He's different. You know it's true. Forgive me for saying this, but he has no respect for tradition. And his wife works at the museum—I hear she's curated exhibitions of Arab artists. Not enough Jewish artists these days?! They must be Arabs?!" Abraham looked like a disgruntled toddler whose toy had been given to another child. He ran his hands through his hair, awaiting Ben's response. But Ben was thinking about something else. *He's not listening to me*, thought Abraham. "I don't know what you mean," Ben finally said absent-mindedly. "He has money. That's all. I have money. You have money. I never heard you complain about it, even though you live in a settlement in Samaria."

Silence fell. Abraham thought of his wife, who had recently begun to shop in the upmarket Ramat Aviv mall in Tel Aviv. Without telling her friends, she went shopping for stylish clothes on Fridays. For years she had main-tained a simple lifestyle, concealing their economic success. But a couple of months ago, she had started wearing silk tops and chic skirts and jackets; now her wardrobe was very fashionable. The thought of telling her he was unem-ployed and looking for a new job was depressing. *What if I can't find a new position? What if I have to start all over again at the salary of a young engineer? Perhaps I'll have to take a teaching job in the settlement.*

He almost answered Ben. He would have said something like: "Money is not everything in life." He would say that he was working to maintain a traditional family life. Unless he adhered to the values of Judaism and supported the dream of a Greater Israel, the money he made was useless.

His community was an essential part of his life. He was on the verge of describing the profound divide between himself and the rest of Handex, explaining that he was operating in pursuit of ideals and not mere comfort. But Ben raised his eyes and looked at him. And though his gaze still held traces of fire, a cold light, blue and metallic, filled them, threatening to freeze Abraham, who swallowed his words, turned around, and left the room without saying goodbye.

It had been two weeks since Ofir disappeared. Ben tried to take his place, answer questions he hadn't been asked before, solve problems he didn't fully understand. Credit terms, partial financing, customs on robotic parts, assembling micro parts—fragments of sentences Ofir had been saying for years now turned into helpful advice. He now realized how difficult Ofir's job was. Ofir gave the impression that only common sense and sound judgment shaped his decisions, but Ben now realized that his partner was talented and was essential to the company's success. When bankers and suppliers asked him where his partner was, Ben told them that Ofir was dealing with a family problem that would soon be resolved. He tried to allay any doubts about Handex's stability. But every passing day, the office became emptier: two programmers took a week off, one engineer decided to have elective foot surgery, and the newly hired product designer called in sick. On Thursday afternoon, three weeks into Ofir's absence, Ben left early; his own footsteps echoed in the hallway.

A strange coincidence, Ben thought as he gazed at the mute television. Two unrelated facts, completely independent, yet he felt they were somehow connected. For some unknown reason, on Thursday, three weeks ago, he had invited Michelle to visit Handex for the first time.

Her small, brown eyes peered out from behind designer eyeglasses. Winking to convey contempt, twitching her mouth to reveal subtle mockery, always moving her body seductively, she spilled venomous words from her jiggling lips. He often wondered how their relationship had endured for so many years. He used to think she was a sort of sexual outlet, a woman seemingly always ready for sex, though with an affected air. Then he'd decided he needed her insights, as she often pointed out hidden motives that he had not seen. On starless nights in bed, he thought of her as Lilith, recalling a conversation with his father when he was a child.

"Beware of Lilith, Son."

"Who is Lilith?"

"She is an evil woman, a demon, inflicting pain on people, seducing men and killing babies."

"Daddy, what does 'seduce' mean?"

"She makes men do things they don't want to do."

"How does she do that?"

"She's smart, Son, she knows they have desires they're ashamed of. She tells them it's fine, they can do whatever they want."

"So why don't they kick her out if she is so bad?"

"They try, but they don't always succeed. She's very devious; she understands better than any other woman what men conceal."

And Michelle's words—"us" and "them," "losers" and "winners," "weak" and "strong," "strugglers" and "winners," "Sephardi" and "Ashkenazi," "ordinary people" and "attractive people"—were applicable to any situation, suited any person. Though Ben kept telling himself that her worldview was too simplified, breaking the world into two parts, casting shadow on one side and illuminating the other, he sometimes thought that Ofir did have an unfair advantage. Laurie had no idea what hardship was; his parents, albeit financially comfortable, were never invited to certain parties; Carine, so he had heard, spent time with a wealthy man. And he, despite his professional success, was lying in bed, looking at his thin body with hostility.

Despair had made him invite Michelle to Handex. To escape her light and darkness, he decided to expose her, make her a familiar friend; let daylight dry out her venom. But when she walked into his office that Thursday, her lips twitching and contempt in her eyes, she said, "I've seen your arrogant partner has left. What's wrong with him? He looks like a ghost." Ben felt thrown, once again, into a black and filthy corner, making him more wretched than ever.

Lying on the sofa, Ben turned to the muted television. Ariel Sharon was on the screen, frowning and sniffling, severe, but with laughter in his eyes. Photos of a bus after a suicide attack, incinerated seats and the top of the bus torn apart. Young Arab men throwing stones at soldiers, Arab women wearing long robes, running around screaming, and in the corridors of a hospital people lying in beds with tubes attached to their bodies. *It will all go down the drain if Ofir doesn't return,* he thought. The employees knew something was wrong. Some avoided going to the office—even Abraham was losing patience. *If I wait too long, the firm will collapse.* There was no other option. He had to find out what had happened to Ofir. Handex was in jeopardy.

Ben rang Ofir's phone, but there was no answer. Suddenly, he thought Ofir could be dead, and immediately dismissed it with a short chuckle. *Why dead? Illness, family crisis, a possible theft. But dead? How can I even imagine this?* His hands were shaking as he hung up. He called Laurie.

"Hello?" Laurie's voice sounded slightly choked.

"Laurie, it's Ben. I'm really worried. What's happened to Ofir? Where is he?" Though the silence on the other end only lasted a second or two, his heart pounded and a peculiar spot materialized before him. He thought a draft filled the room, though the windows were closed.

Then Laurie said in English, "You're a thief," and hung up.

Muteness. Silence. Lack of words.

Ben couldn't comprehend what had just happened. He opened his mouth, trying to say something to himself but to his utter surprise he couldn't think of a single word. He looked at his phone, then at the window, the television, and back to the phone, feeling that his capacity for speech was completely lost. Utterly erased. Despair made him try to form a sentence—just two words long, just one. But he was shocked. Speechless. Finally, he emitted a long "ah" and afterwards a sort of "harrumph," and then fell silent again.

Sitting on the sofa, his back hunched, his head bent down, his left leg trembling, he attempted in vain to find a word that would describe his condition. Now sweaty soccer players were on the television; there was a cheering crowd. A child watching the field with wonder. Ben looked at him, suddenly thought of his mother, and then his muteness dissipated. An inner dam was breached. Syllables become words, which became groaned sentences in his mind: *I deserve it. I've been stealing from him for years and now I will be punished. He is my best friend. How could I have done this? I can't stand him. He's always ahead of me. He always has more than me. Next to him I look wretched. No woman will ever prefer me over him. It's a crime. A sin. A forbidden action. Eventually justice will be served.*

Finally, he got up and went to the kitchen for some water. After the divorce from Carine, he'd rented a spacious apartment with luxury furniture in a tower in the center of Tel Aviv. He sat on chair at the bar, looking out of the window onto the roofs of Tel Aviv.

Ben closed his eyes.

Now that it was clear beyond doubt that justice would be done and he was about to be punished, a petrifying fear overwhelmed him. He was in danger. *Tomorrow, early in the morning, before going to work, I'll close the bank account. I'll transfer the money abroad or distribute it across different accounts.*

No, not a good idea—that's a mistake. I've got to find a criminal lawyer at once. I'll get advice from a friend who went to law school.

Suddenly it occurred to Ben that perhaps Ofir had known about the money for a long time. *I assumed it was the first day he didn't come to Handex, but maybe it was earlier. Weeks, months or even years—Ofir could have been watching me, aware of the theft.* Maybe he's started shutting Handex down . . . Perhaps he's filed a criminal complaint already. Maybe the police have been trailing me?

Reflecting on recent conversations with his partner, Ben now thought that every word contained a double meaning or revealed concealed activity. He attempted to piece together every dialogue, but they blurred and intertwined; it was impossible to tell where one ended and the other began. *Why's it happened now of all times?* he thought. *I'm out of luck. Why now? I have such bad luck.*

Talia had approached Ben on the street a couple of months earlier, asking if she needed a parking permit. Though she'd smiled at him, her manner was very practical. If he hadn't known the answer, she would have been disappointed. Brown eyes, small nose, wavy hair; there was something pleasant, yet limited, about her. If you buy big packages, you pay less; investment in people always pays off if you're patient; if you save a bit every time, eventually it will add up to a substantial savings; politeness makes life easier; honest people don't have a political career—she made these kinds of remarks softly and with a faint smile. Ben was relieved. Intense jealousy, crushing disappointment, an unending urge to succeed, his father's distressing advice, and the pain in his mother's eyes were supplanted by principles by which to have a balanced, enjoyable existence—a manageable life, without upheaval and bewilderment.

Almost ten years younger than Ben, Talia planned her life in a way that was odd to him. Initially, she'd studied graphics. She painted rather well, and this choice of profession suited her natural inclination for precision. Later, she decided to become a teacher: "There is no point in being self-employed if you don't make a lot of money," she said simply, as if any person in her position would have made a similar choice. She'd become a first-grade teacher. She loved children; she didn't like the lonely work of a graphic designer.

Her moderate outlook was unshaken when she saw Ben's luxurious apartment. She asked if the rent was very high and whether parking was included; it was so hard to park in Tel Aviv. Her pleasant but ordinary face, her wavy hair cut according to the latest fashion, her average height and standard body type, her nice but ordinary clothes—sometimes Ben felt she was a prototype woman, representative of her entire gender. Always making effortless conversation, asking questions and waiting patiently for the answers, she took an interest in small details he rarely noticed. She told him about her job, explained how she enjoyed instilling values in young children. When he asked her what she meant, she replied: "Children must be good, never lie, and love our country."

Ben invited her to fine restaurants; she read the menus, inquiring why one dish was more expensive than another, and whether it was necessary to reserve a table in advance? Are the fish imported? *What's wrong with this practical state of mind?*, he thought, while explaining something to her. *This pragmatic mindset is rather pleasant; every question has an answer, every dilemma can be addressed. Her questions create a sense of stability, a life without fluctuations.* Though she evoked no particular passion or exceptional enthusiasm in him, he found her charming. And she treated him with such respect—he had to admit to himself that he thoroughly enjoyed it, almost against his will.

Talia listened attentively to everything he said, every word, even the pauses between words, the short cough when he discussed his mother, the faint smile when he spoke of Ofir. When he told her about Handex, she asked why they hadn't moved to Tel Aviv earlier. Were the offices in Azrieli Tower really suitable for the firm? Could the secretary handle all the administrative tasks? Why wasn't he giving more work to the programmers? He embarked on intricate answers, yet he felt his words lost their meaning. Each word disintegrated into particles, which then reassembled themselves in unexpected forms; sentences containing all the words but not in the right sequence. And Talia's attention was always marked by a profound admiration.

Talia's body was almost homey. He sighed with relief as he lay naked in bed beside her, as if in an instant he had become a family man and wasn't looking for a partner anymore. No need to work out endlessly at the gym, he could stop scrutinizing his reflection in the mirror. It was all so clear and simple, without passion or turmoil. Envy's two heads began to turn away from each other, looking aside, keeping out of each other's way. He no longer felt like a skinny teenager. Since he'd met Talia, he hadn't imagined Ofir's muscular body even once.

Implicitly, without clear words, they began to plan their future life together: What would be the best neighborhood for raising kids?

A seven-seater car suits a big family. Teachers can devote more time to their own children. When they would visit Ben's parents, she could bake a tasty pie according to a family recipe . . . A future gradually rolled out before them, and they hadn't even said "marriage," "family," "home," or "children."

But now, of all times, Ofir had discovered his theft. Now that a paved road was visible ahead, smooth and shiny, it turned out that Ben was staring into a chasm, an abyss that would engulf him without any trace. Just like Ofir, he would disappear, and no one would know what had happened to him.

Early March 2003

Ofir sat on the balcony. At ten o'clock in the morning, a pleasant calm filled the street. The morning bustle was gone: children were at school, the traffic was quiet, an elderly man was strolling, a woman was walking her dog, a gardener was weeding. Early spring sun poured down its multicolored yet transparent beams, illuminating the glittering leaves of the ficus. A cool morning, still somewhat wintry, with a hint of mild warmth. A tinge of red spread in the sky, fused into the slowly moving clouds, sparking hope even in the gloomiest soul.

Recently Abigail had begun to hug Ofir every morning, as if she wouldn't see him when she returned home. Her dark eyes studied him, her long brown hair, smelling of fragrant soap, lay across his shoulder, her soft body clung to him, and her childish arms were wrapped around his neck, refusing to let go. Finally, she kissed him and got up. Laurie placed food beside the bed, in the living room, and on the balcony. She left a hot coffee pot and a newspaper on the kitchen table.

At first, Ofir looked at Laurie with hostility. For a moment, when he got up from bed and walked slowly to the deck chair on the balcony, he thought she was about to move towards him and embrace him. But a counterforce fixed her in place and she watched him motionless. The thought of her asking him how he was made him shudder. He might burst out crying, yell, or maybe even go back to the bedroom and lock the door behind him. But when Laurie saw him sitting on the balcony, she walked to the kitchen without a word.

He then realized she wasn't asking anything. In the morning, steaming coffee and sweet-smelling cookies appeared next to the bed, a light lunch placed on the table on the balcony, sliced fruit in the fridge, and flowers around the house; an invisible hand was trying to elicit some pleasure, create a moment of distraction. Blossoming pots on the balcony, colorful new cushions on the wide chair, the dry leaves swept away—as Ofir closed his eyes, smelling the greenery around him and listening to the chirping of the birds, he momentarily felt that maybe there was some sense in the droplet of hope he now felt had been born.

A board covering a deep abyss, strong and flexible, made of stone, wood, and chunks of ancient lava, has cracked, disintegrated, making the crevasse beneath visible. Bare teeth and drops of blood, hunger and a torn body, oblivion and lust, a hell that once exposed threatens to coat everything. The parts of the board are moving slowly, touching each other; there is a chilling tremor, and a movement backward. One piece rubs against another, jagged edge against jagged edge, stone dust and lava shrapnel. Every time the fragments touch, a horrifying cry of pain sounds out, the torments of a broken pattern that has left a gaping space, a crater of calamities. And though the parts will eventually coalesce—shedding the fissure remaining—and will once more appear polished, the abyss will always remain slightly bare. Finally, a new, comforting calm will take over, though the boards will never fully cover the abyss, with its steam and ancient dust and rubble.

What happened ten years ago? What happened? Time and again, Ofir grappled with the question, as though if he managed to understand the reason for the theft, the rest would make sense. *Handex had been doing well. The technical problem had been solved. So what happened?* But searching the past was exhausting and useless. Various memories intermingled, segments of life with no chronological order. A week with Ben in Eilat. Their plans for the new office. In Beit Hakerem, Ben had fallen and broken his leg—Ofir had carried him home. Ben's wedding, luxurious but still somewhat somber; Ben's father—always watching suspiciously. Ofir had once asked why he was so distrustful, and Ben had replied, laughing, "Because you are Ashkenazi!" Ben's systematic way of thinking, which made the transformation from simulations to real surgery possible—various events that could not be arranged chronologically. Ofir closed his eyes, feeling the light breeze fluttering on his face.

An obscure, dim memory suddenly surfaced of an event that had occurred long ago, although Ofir couldn't determine exactly when. Boys gathered around the stadium doors; basketball players from the United States had come for a friendly match. As Ofir was so gifted at sports, he had a ticket, along with a note from the sports teacher saying he could take Ben. The guard at the entrance, though, had said that only Ofir could enter. "If he can't go in, I won't," he'd declared fervently, pointing to the piece of paper. The guard wouldn't budge. "Don't worry about it, I don't really care," Ben whispered, as if talking to himself. But Ofir left with Ben. Great satisfaction filled him on the way home, almost exaltation, a sort of strange joy. He laughed out loud, mocking the guard and waving his hands while talking. It seemed that a part of him had been fulfilled, fortified, was found to be just and right; anyone could see what a good, loyal friend he was. But when he stopped laughing for a moment, he saw that Ben's eyes were filled with tears. For a moment, Ben looked at him with undisguised hostility; then he lowered his gaze.

Ofir opened his eyes. The few clouds had vanished and soft light filled the sky. Sparrows were standing on the balcony rail, making sudden, unexpected movements, chirping, raising their tails, turning their heads, and looking at him with one eye.

Ben has become a part of me, he whispered to himself, holding back his tears. *A sort of extra organ, another liver or spleen. You can't see it, but cutting it out is extremely painful.*

After a couple of minutes, Ofir relaxed. A touch of laughter was born, an amusing memory. *I wish I had gone to that game*, he thought, smiling and wiping his tears. *I wonder what I missed.* A well-known NBA player had been there. He imagined the stadium, the roaring crowd shouting "El El Israel"; the sound of drums and singing. Despite cheering the Israeli team, everyone shouted with joy when the brilliant American scored—after all, they'd all come to see him fly through the air and slam dunk. In the tumult of the stadium he could almost hear, Ofir's sigh sounded like a groan of heartbreak.

He got up, went to the kitchen, and had the lunch Laurie had left him: chicken and cheese with salad on whole wheat buns. When he was done, he ate the freshly made cookies. Finally, he drank some orange juice. *Laurie, my sweetheart*, he thought, as tears filled his eyes again. Despite the blinding pain, he could see the huge effort she was making to support him. For the last couple of nights he'd had nightmares, hearing Ben's mocking him or weeping. Laurie hugged him, her warm body enveloping him, her breath fluttering against his neck. He told himself that this was true love, unconditional devotion. Standing by him, she expected nothing in return. A tear slid down his stubble-covered cheek, dropped onto Laurie's doll-like face, and activated a hidden mechanism that made her warm body cling to him even harder.

Sometimes Ofir possessed visual images of Handex: the entrance doors, closed and locked; Ben sitting all alone at his desk. But sometimes the office was full of life and no one noticed he was gone. But these images always faded quickly and he sank into gloom again, putting off contemplating the firm's future. The very thought that he had to decide what to do, whether to meet Ben or act against him, was unbearable. Once, he found the courage to call the secretary. When she answered the phone, he hung up. The questions that might have arisen were petrifying. He tossed the phone onto the table, hurried to the bedroom, and buried himself under the heavy duvet.

Late March 2003

"Why don't you fly to Tel Aviv? You could help Laurie. You don't have to stay with them; we'll rent a small apartment nearby. You could take Abigail to the nursery and home. Maybe she could have a small room where you stay. We are, after all, on another continent. It's hard to tell how Ofir is doing." Eric kept explaining to Natalie why she should visit her daughter in Israel, persistently emphasizing that he couldn't go. Your partner in the law firm can fill in; besides, you handle all cases together, and legal processes take years. A month or two won't make any difference."

As the sentences multiplied, uttered breathlessly one after the other, every syllable merging into the next, Natalie was increasingly aware of his strange alertness. Eric kept pushing his glasses up, sliding his hand through his hair, and clearing his throat. Despite the various reasons he brought up, she felt he had a hidden purpose. Of course, he was concerned about Laurie, but there was a certain embarrassment there—his nose twitched. It's weird, she thought, he hasn't even mentioned the suicide attacks. Only two weeks ago a terrorist exploded a bomb on a bus in Haifa, and many were killed. She looked at him skeptically and said, "Sure. I'll go. I've already asked Laurie to look for a place for me. I can't stay with them now."

Eric's nose grew still and he relaxed. He leaned back in his chair, waiting for breakfast. It was drizzling outside; a cold, gray spring morning. Soon he would put on his coat and wool scarf and leave for work. "He'll be fine. It'll take some time. Laurie said he was doing better. He was sitting on the balcony now. He's even left home a couple of times," Natalie added.

"I know. But I want to help her."

"And there are no money problems, either. They've done well over the years, and can live without working for a while. Laurie has a good job at the museum. And of course, we can support them."

"It's not a question of money. Abigail is having a hard time. The teacher said she is sad. She sits by herself and won't play with her friends. It's hard to take."

"I know. It's not easy. But I think everything will be okay."

As he walked with a reserved expression to the Tube station, looking at the raindrops on the pavement, Eric's insincerity struck him. His words, intended to persuade Natalie but mainly himself, gave the impression of profound concern for his daughter. But they were crude lies, utter deception; though it appeared reasonable and well founded, the argument had nothing to do with the truth. He was suppressing his real anxiety. "The truth is crystal clear," he whispered to himself in desperation. "If Ofir had collapsed mentally in the UK, here in London, I wouldn't be so worried. If Laurie had married a British man who had a breakdown, I would support her, believing all would be well. I would offer assistance with confidence that he would recuperate. This is not the first time this has happened—friends deceiving each other, friendships ending in a quarrel, each one going his own way. *But the collapse of Ofir, an Israeli living in Tel Aviv, scares me to death.* The rain grew stronger, and Eric closed the upper button of his coat. He recalled that Laurie had told him it was hot in Tel Aviv at the moment. A warm desert wind was sweeping over the city. The balcony was covered with yellow dust. *The air here is clearer,* he thought. *In Tel Aviv, one sometimes feels stifled, as though there's not enough air to breathe.* He envisaged his daughter's home on the upper floor, spacious and cozy, overlooking a street with tall trees casting shade. And again, he felt an obscure anxiety, as if he had been told that a calamity was about to take place. *Laurie's right: it is dangerous there now, but she's vigilant. She never takes the bus and avoids public places, especially now that Ofir can't tell her where it's safe.*

A cold draft brushed against him as he went down the station stairs. He took the Northern Line to his office. The morning train was crowded, but there was an empty seat. He sat down heavily, wishing that the train's squeaking would swallow his fear. Sometimes, the swaying movement and squeaks allowed him to drift. But today, the disturbing thoughts wouldn't go away. Shamefully, he had to admit that his daughter being in some danger wasn't the source of his concern. He forced himself to picture the wreckage of bombed buses, which, after a terror attack, appeared on the news. Blurred bodies and people shouting as they carried stretchers. He even muttered to himself, "It's terrible, it's terrible," to prove to himself how dangerous it was in Israel at the moment. Yet, he realized that what truly frightened him was Ofir's mental collapse.

The train came to a halt with a screech. A couple of young boys sat next to Eric, laughing quietly. Again, he closed his eyes, attentive to the strange fear that gradually expanded within him. Suddenly, he recalled a photo he had seen in the paper a couple of weeks ago. On International Holocaust

Memorial Day, the first pictures taken in liberated Auschwitz were on the front page—live skeletons with wide-open eyes. Eric had looked at the photos for a long time, put down the paper, then picked it up and looked at them again. A body that was nothing but a skeleton, a skull-like head, he had felt compelled to look at the survivors. It was repulsive and nauseating, but he hadn't been able to look away. *Maybe you were afraid, scared it could happen to you. You could be imprisoned in a concentration camp and end up looking like the prisoners in Auschwitz. Horror made you stare at the images.*

The train halted at a station. An elegant woman wearing a sweet fragrance took a seat next to him. An elderly man was dozing off intermittently, his eyes opening briefly every now and then. As the train began to move, Eric suddenly had an insight that matured into a full understanding: he was not afraid when examining the photos. On the contrary, he was observing them at some distance. In an instant, he comprehended that he, too, possessed an aspect of Ofir's spirit. *Departures from old Jewish patterns and the adoption of new, more vital, ideals, take place outside Israel, too,* he thought. Yes, yes! He was almost laughing. I hope no one can hear my thoughts! The founding fathers of Zionism never imagined the extent to which their ideology would spread. They changed segments of the Jewish people who fully rejected their ideas. They believed only Israel would result from the revolution they sparked. But they transformed all of Jewry. A faint smile spread across his face as he told himself there was no need to be concerned about Ofir. *The process is irreversible; we've changed forever.*

Again, the train stopped at a station. A woman carrying heavy bags got off and two businessmen jumped into the car before the door closed and the train moved on with a loud rattle. Eric remembered his grandfather, the Golders Green rabbi. He could see him, an elderly man with a long, white beard, his sad eyes looking around with a mixture of pride and fear. He often talked about how Judaism was the most advanced religion, the most spiritual one—"God Almighty never frightens a Jew; He illuminates his life." But he always said it was important to be cautious and vigilant, walk with friends rather than alone, stay within the neighborhood, avoid specific streets. "Don't provoke the Gentiles—you never know how they might react." This blend of pride and fear also shaped his parents. His mother burst into tears when she learned that Laurie was planning to move to Tel Aviv.

But not me, Eric said to himself. *And not Natalie.* For years, we've followed the events taking place in Israel, every visit feeling both foreign and close. Yet we failed to see that a trace of the spirit prevailing there has also shaped us. If an ideology akin to Nazism were to grow here, we would confront with no hesitation. The words "like sheep to the slaughterhouse" surfaced for a second in his mind, vaguely assuming the shape of trains and human skeletons, and then faded away.

Just before the train came to a stop at his station, he caught sight of a headline. A man sitting across from him was reading a newspaper. Eric saw the words: "Israeli Settlement near Hebron Evacuated by Israel." There was a picture of settlers shouting and throwing stones. Normally, he groaned when he saw those kinds of photos. But this time, while exiting the train and rushing to the escalator, rage overtook him. "It's unacceptable, unacceptable," he muttered as the cold wind struck him and almost blew his scarf from around his neck. This new historical insight, which only now he fully grasped, produced a profound anger.

Jews occupying other people. A sharp and painful inner cry developed: *it's unconceivable. We, who are so sensitive to suffering, are now indifferent to the rights of the Palestinians.* All the way to the office he explained to himself how wrong and distorted the occupation was. As he opened the office door, his eyes were moist, but he smiled at the secretary and said, "How are you today?"

April 1, 2003

At ten o'clock in the morning, Joseph Stern arrived at Gan Ha'esrim, the small park in Beit Hakerem. He slowly climbed up the steps in the park and sat down on a bench under a carob tree, its dense branches shading on him. He stretched his arms across the backrest, and looked up into the canopy. The dome of foliage was hardly penetrated by the sun. He looked down and saw plenty of fallen carobs on the ground. He almost bent down to picked one up to eat, but he changed his mind, leaned back, and sighed loudly.

He could almost hear Ofir yelling. A choked voice saying that no one could tell him what to do, that he and only he would run his life—like a child struggling to hide his tears and conceal the insult that spread across his face, which had changed in the last months. Ofir was very thin; he looked taller but less muscular. His hair was dull and now partially gray; his cheekbones protruded as though they carried his entire face, and his dark eyes, which used to have a captivating, mischievous spark, looked around apathetically.

Joseph had visited his son a couple of times in the last few months, always sitting next to him while playing with Abigail. Her father's sadness was reflected in her eyes. He brought presents: dolls, handicrafts, books. She smiled gladly and tore off the wrapping, but after a couple of minutes she laid down tired beside him, placing her head on his lap. But, yesterday, Ofir seemed better. It was a pleasant spring day, so Ofir suggested they sit on the balcony. He even served coffee and cookies. A soft, red sun illuminated the sky, the air carried the scent of the first blossoms, and around the ficus tree small insects were buzzing.

Apparently, it was the spring that misled Joseph; full of light and perfume, but often hiding deep hopelessness. It made him think that it would be appropriate to hint very casually that it was time to return to normal life. As they were sitting there, he said quietly, "Well, Ofir, what will happen now?" Abigail's body became tense. She lifted her head, carefully watching her father.

Surprise spread across Ofir's face. A hidden muscle tensed at once, erasing the first signs of tranquility: a random smile, questions about politics. "Sharon says he supports the American Road Map, but who believes him?

Everyone knows it's a pretense; the last thing he wants to do is make peace;" some interest in remote family members and friends from the army he hasn't seen since he was discharged. But following his father's suggestion to return to normal life, Ofir's eyes opened, his lips pursed, and his hands gripped the chair handles. Silence fell. Abigail's breath marked the passing seconds. Joseph looked at his son, attentive; Ofir turned his gaze to the street and said nothing.

After a couple of minutes, Ofir suddenly said, "I don't know," and nothing more. Though short, his reply suggested that a conversation might develop. Only three words, but they didn't fully rule out a dialogue. Very softly and gently Joseph said, "I know this must be very difficult for you—I do understand that. I find it hard to put myself in your place. Still, you should try and think what must be done." The name "Ben" was never uttered; Joseph was careful not to mention "a childhood friend," "theft," or even "betrayal." Speaking cautiously, he avoided referring to any specific event.

Ofir said nothing. Abigail picked up her dolls from the floor and went to her room. From inside came the voices of the dolls talking to each other. Joseph said, "It'd be a shame if all the effort and talent you have invested is lost. Is it possible to divide the firm?" Again, Ofir said nothing. There was desert dust in the moist winter air. The setting sun was purple, reviving old childhood dreams and evoking hope and despair. Ofir said in a strained tone, "No, I don't think it's possible. It was a joint effort. Handex is the combination of the two of us; we complement each other."

"Do you plan to file a complaint? Maybe sue him?"

Ofir closed his eyes. A shiver passed through him, beginning at his shoulders, then moving to his chest, abdomen, and legs. Joseph almost leaped from his chair to hug his son, caress his hair, and promise that everything would be all right—all the things he'd said when Ofir was just a boy. But he held himself back, afraid he might provoke tears.

"No, I won't file a complaint. And I won't sue him. At least not now. I can't handle a trial. We'll probably close the company. I think it will cease to exist anyway. Someone told me people hardly ever show up to work." Joseph's astonishment was so apparent it nearly made Ofir smile. Joseph had believed his son was completely detached from Handex, but he realized he was mistaken. His jaw dropped as Ofir added, "I'm in touch with a lawyer regarding the company's closure. It's not simple, we need to determine how much each of us will get. Of course, what has been stolen from me would be subtracted from his part."

Joseph was astonished: "You are in touch with a lawyer?"

"Yes."

"Do you want to dissolve the company?"

"I think so. I believe it's the right thing to do. But I'm not absolutely sure."

"What will you do afterwards?"

"We have enough money."

"I know, but you have such a great talent. It'd be a shame to waste it."

"I might open a new firm."

"You could get a fantastic job, the highest possible management position, with an excellent salary."

The look on Ofir's face was bitter and sarcastic. He chuckled and then coughed, relaxed into his chair, crossed his arms, and said, "Dad, I want to be self-employed. I want to run my own business."

"But being employed implies security, stability. You depend less on others."

"Ah . . . this constant need for stability . . . No offense, but I already have enough money. I'm not worried. And I have a new idea for a business."

"Ofir, it's not only a question of financial security. Being an employee decreases dependency on others. It's a mechanism that regulates relations between people, granting them the right basis to develop properly. If you don't depend on someone, you can have a deep relationship with them. It is always true, and even more so regarding personal relations. Even when it comes to Laurie—and clearly, here we are talking about a profound love— everything would be different if you weren't married and needed her to survive and succeed. For the sake of argument, let's assume you were both a couple and business partners. Very soon emotions would fade away and you'd see each other as a means to achieve an end. Social institutions developed for a reason, you know. They protect people, making proper human relationships possible."

"Dad, I am going through a crisis, but when it's over I have ideas about the financial world. I have a novel idea, something that's never been tried. No one can provide me a place where I could develop my idea. Only entrepreneurs can do such things. Nothing compares to the sense of achievement when you realize a new concept. It feels like plenty of people, who you don't know and never will get to know, believe in you. It's intoxicating. There's nothing like that when you're an employee. And it doesn't stand in contrast to deep personal relations. Do you think there is no love in the business world? No feelings?

Joseph looked at his son, and said—openly, innocently, ridiculously direct words—"You can see how your friendship with Ben has ended. You've were close friends for many years and eventually he stole your money. This is simply a consequence of you being business partners; that's all."

He immediately regretted his words.

What a mistake! What on earth made me say this? he thought, wondering what had made him utter these insulting words. To alleviate his remorse, he reminded himself that the hardest thing for a parent is to see his child repeat past mistakes. All attempts to warn him are futile; he walks as if he were blind-folded, indifferent to the pit in front of him, just like the first time. Ofir's eyes filled their sockets; then they closed. His features seemed to contract to such an extent that his eyelashes disappeared. His mouth twisted, and he bit his lower lip.

"I'm sorry, Son," Joseph quickly said. But it was too late.

Ofir sat up straight and said, almost shouting, "Ben didn't steal from me because he needed the money. He could have asked that we take a bigger salary; he knew I'd agree. No, it wasn't a practical theft, but a theoretical one. He wanted to prove something to himself. He wanted to demonstrate to himself that he was acting only for his own good, and no one else's. Not even for the good of a close friend."

"Why did he have to act only for his own good?"

"Because that's the easiest solution for him. He's torn between two worlds, and this made it possible for him to be at peace with both of them. His mother is a practical, secular woman, his father is very religious. Ben isn't reli-gious, but he absorbed his father's spirit. Every moment, he is torn between accepting a religious viewpoint and rejecting it. There is one place, though, where he agrees with his father: acting in your own interest. His father always told him that a man must look after himself and his family. Socialism, a just society—Ben sees it as downright hypocrisy, a lie, almost a deceit. When he stole from me, he somehow—even if unconsciously—appeased his father without confronting his mother."

"Maybe he was simply jealous of you and wanted to get even? People wondered how the two of you were such good friends."

"Ah, yes, jealousy . . . It's always been there—never spelled out, but clearly felt. People tend to ascribe huge importance to jealousy, see it as a profound, meaningful motive. I think it's an excuse. A cover. A comfortable evasion. It's easier to say I don't have what someone else has than admit uncertainty. There is something so resolved and unequivocal about envy.

You'll find it's common especially where there is indecision, vacillation, an inability to choose a path."

"Ofir, look . . ."

Ofir stood and looked down at his sitting father. Suddenly tense, his hands moved from side to side as if he were wondering where to put them, and his eyes were half closed. In a metallic voice, like a train station announcer, he said: "I will do whatever I think is right, and you can think whatever you wish. You, Mom, Laurie, the lawyer; each of you has an explanation, a recommendation. But I will do whatever is right for me—only me!—and you will all have to live with it."

Joseph dropped his head onto his chest and closed his eyes. Ofir's words echoed in his mind. An inner voice contended that a change was taking place. A transformation. What has been is dead, replaced by a new spirit—efficient, practical, impartial. Each man for himself, immersed in his world, finding justification for his lack of compassion, his will to advance, achieve, win. The wolf and the lamb don't even notice each other anymore; each one proceeds on a narrow, slippery path which never splits. Devotion? Sacrifice? Magnanimity? Ah, they raise a faint smile, even quiet laughter. Yes, yes, people used to believe in them before they saw the true light of a gaze directed solely on one's own self, indifferent to any affectionate voices.

The sadness that overwhelmed Joseph made him look around. Colorful flower beds surrounded the monument in memory of the sons of Beit Hakerem who had died in the War of Independence. Tall trees created a sense of tranquility, a pleasant morning breeze lightly rustled the branches of the carob tree, which made a delightful, comforting whisper. He got up and, leaning on his walking stick, began to go home slowly, murmuring and sighing.

April 13, 2003

On Sunday morning, exactly ten minutes past ten o'clock, Handex's main doors opened, and along with a biting wind, Ofir walked in. He wore blue jeans and a light-gray sweater; he was freshly shaved and his hair was clean. If it hadn't been for his eyes, which were too bright, he would have looked like a man returning to work after a long weekend.

The secretary, reading the paper at her desk, raised her head indifferently to see who was coming in. When she saw Ofir, she dropped the paper and stood up in alarm, unsure what to do. "Good morning," he said quietly, and kept walking down the hallway towards Ben's office.

The place was half empty. Some programmers had found other jobs, a couple of engineers had taken time off and were in no hurry to return, and others had reported in sick. Even Abraham wasn't there. He was teaching in the mornings and only went to Handex in the afternoons to help Ben send spare parts to hospitals, instruct doctors, and manage the finances.

Ofir walked quickly towards Ben's office, opened the door without knocking, and entered.

Ben's eyes looked as if they were about to rupture. He was stunned. His left foot was quivering so hard that his chair was rocking. His initial surprise was due to how thin Ofir had become. His cheekbones protruding and his cheeks hollow. Ofir had always been muscular. But now he was gaunt. His sweater was too big, his pants would have fallen without the heavy belt around his waist. And his eyes: the spark of laughter and mischief was gone. Ofir stared back without embarrassment or hesitation.

Though Ben had often imagined this meeting, and had decided that he would let Ofir speak first, he couldn't have spoken even if he'd wanted to. He couldn't say a single word. He couldn't even cough or sneeze. His mind was empty and his heart pounded painfully and too quickly.

Ofir placed an envelope on the desk, turned around, and left without a word.

Ben's hands opened the envelope, moving automatically. In it was a letter from an esteemed lawyer specializing in finance: "The sum you've stolen must be deposited, with interest, in Mr. Stern's account within a week, otherwise he will turn to legal channels. Mr. Stern is not obliged in any way to avoid legal action in the future. From now on, Handex's accounts will be subject to my inspection. Any transaction will be examined carefully. Mr. Stern is willing to try to run the company together with you for a trial period of three months. If it fails, the firm will be closed and each partner will receive his share."

Horror cascaded into Ben's heart, a torrent dividing into many brooks and filtering into every opening and cleft. Different possibilities came to life in Ben's mind. Maybe the police were following him; maybe Ofir planned to blackmail him. In one scenario, short and blurred, he saw himself in prison, wearing an orange jumpsuit. The more frantic he became, thinking how to prepare for the future, the more he realized that what he found most terrifying were Ofir's eyes, revealing that a web of friendship was destroyed and that Ofir saw him now as a complete stranger.

Ofir walked to his own office; he opened the windows to freshen the room and began to organize the documents on his desk. He turned on his computer and examined the last few months' accounts. The firm's poor state was no surprise; he had been keeping tabs from home. Very soon, the company would collapse. In the last couple of weeks he was hesitating about whether to let it fall or try to save it.

At night, he sat in front of the computer, wondering what to do next. *Why not keep the firm?*, he thought, looking into the darkness. The robotic arm was doing exceptionally well. It was being used not only for training surgeons, but also for real knee operations all over the word. Ben would likely further develop it, making it suitable for other procedures as well. The potential profit was huge, so why give it all up? Reconstructing the last couple of years made him understand that an imbalance had formed, an asymmetry: Ben was part of him, his personality, his life. If asked to describe himself, Ofir would say he was Ben's friend. But Ben had pushed him away years ago; he only saw Ofir as someone he's known for years. Throughout the years, the scale had become completely distorted. One side was so heavy it always tipped the balance. The other side was light; its sole power was that, if removed, the heavy side would fall and crash.

But if I manage to extract Ben from within me, why can't we run Handex together? It has many advantages: we know each other well, we complement each other, and now Ben is anxious since he is unsure what I might do. In fact, it's better this way. Her turned to the computer, opened the email app and wrote a new message:

Dear All,

Having needed a break, I'm back in full force. Starting tomorrow, we are going to provide full service to all the hospitals that are using the arm, develop it for use in abdominal surgery, and redouble our efforts to acquire new customers. The weekly staff meeting will take place on Mondays at ten o'clock. I will run the first part of the meeting. Ben will run the second part. Good luck to us all!

Ofir

January 2004

On January 25, at the age of sixty-six, and about a month after the second marriage of his eldest son, David Haddad passed away. Though he smiled during the wedding, an almost childish snicker, when it was over, again he'd become contemplative and glum. He often sat facing the television with eyes closed, and once in a while he'd let out a deep sigh. The wedding dress had concealed that Talia was pregnant. The rabbi of the Sephardic community of Beit Hakerem performed the ceremony. The music was both Mediterranean and Western.

In his last years, despair overtook David. Though he woke up early in the morning to open the store, Sophia managed it most of the day with two young assistants and an elderly man. Around ten or eleven o'clock, David went to a café with Sephardi friends. At noon, he sauntered home, had an afternoon nap, and in the evening, he went to the synagogue for evening prayer. Later, he sank into the television armchair, constantly talking at the screen: "These Arabs, they're nothing but trouble. He remembers how they persecuted the Jews in Libya. If you turn around, they'll stab you in the back. May they rot in hell. One should always watch them vigilantly. Why isn't Shas[1] part of the government? As if they were the only ones stealing; the only difference is that Ashkenazi thieves never get caught. Who cares about these settlements that Ariel Sharon keeps talking about? The settlers are all Ashkenazi, and they don't accept Sephardic Jews. For all I care, they can be evacuated. I'm glad the Labor Party is losing the election. Who needs those leftists? They are like Gentiles. They have no respect for Jewish tradition. They got reparations from the German government and bought houses in Beit Hakerem." His complaints had intensified. He'd talk about politicians, local leaders, rabbis who failed their congregations, Sophia's negligence of religion, his irreligious children, Ben's divorce, the municipality of Jerusalem raising the property tax on the store.

---

1   A Sephardi Orthodox political party founded in 1982. As a result of the corruption of its leaders it was not part of the government formed in 2003.

As David muttered his protests, an old man's yearning was born. He remembered, hazily, his childhood and the echoes of war that had brought calamity and orphanhood. For years, he had never thought about his journey, alone, with the Jewish Agency from Libya to Israel. He'd been a scared and restless boy, worrying where he would sleep and who would provide for him. But in his later years, Tripoli had often materialized in his mind. Narrow alleys in the Jewish neighborhood, one-story stone buildings, the magnificent synagogue, the family shop with candies that made his friends stare at him enviously, his home with its colorful carpet at the entrance. From an inner space cordoned off for nearly sixty years, childhood recollections had emerged, along with his mother's voice and the sound of prayers at the synagogue. He closed his eyes, trying to gather every detail from these faint memories. *What did my and my brother's room look like? The kitchen had lovely cups, but I can't remember what they looked like. Maybe decorated blue ceramics? Or turquoise?*

Every day, David's longing grew stronger; but the details of the past were elusive. He couldn't tell if the colors and shapes he saw were true memories or a result of his desire to revive the past. A child's bed blended with a table, utensils were obscure, the smell of cooking was familiar yet just out of reach, the street noise couldn't be separated from the prayers. David sat in his armchair, eyes closed, attempting to conjure the past.

But yearning can be fickle. The silhouette of a forgotten family member can bring tears to your eyes; a particular color can provoke happiness. But memories can also carry pain that time has dampened. David couldn't remember the moment he discovered his parents had been murdered, but the loss of his mother suddenly became agonizing. He observed young mothers walking with their children, stood next to women pushing strollers, or holding a crying toddler's hand. He tried to recall how his mother had held him. For years he had forgotten he was an orphan; but now the experience came to life. Sometimes he felt that his mother had died only recently. Every aspect of his life made her absence more painful. She wasn't present when he was in elementary school, she didn't attend his wedding, she never met his children, and she would never see his soon-to-be grandson. Melancholy took root and became utter despair.

The night he died, David went to bed soon after Sofia. In the morning, she realized he wasn't lying next to her. She found him seated in his armchair, his legs drawn towards his chest, his hands crossed, his head leaning against the headrest—he passed away like an embryo in the womb, crying in pain.

Handex's employees weren't in the least surprised that Ofir didn't attend the funeral. He hadn't gone to Ben's and Talia's wedding. The rift between the partners was obvious; everyone knew they were not on speaking terms. Each one was responsible for a well-defined segment of the company; the workers had no choice but to accept this. When some guidance on management or marketing was needed, Ben said quietly, "You should ask Ofir." When a question regarding the development or activation of the robotic arm was raised, Ofir murmured, "Please direct this question to Ben."

At first, people took an interest in the rift, following it attentively, tracking their reaction to each other. While Ofir's face seemed utterly blank, Ben's revealed a certain gloom. Abraham asked Ben if they could talk about Ofir, but Ben gave him such a rebuff that he almost tripped and fell. Nava asked Ofir if the firm could operate with such tension, and Ofir simply replied, "I think so."

Some workers returned to Handex after realizing the company was functioning again. Ofir hired another accountant to examine all expenses. Ben hired a programmer and a software engineer. After a couple of months, the rift between them attracted no special attention. They didn't exchange a word; if they happened to pass one another in the corridor, they ignored each other, as if it had always been this way.

This relationship affected the atmosphere. A change had occurred, though it was impossible to say exactly what. Jokes that were once shared in the hallway could now be heard only behind closed doors. Conversations regarding family members were whispered. Suggestions about where to buy things, enjoyed by everyone, were rarely uttered, as though such talk was somehow inappropriate. At lunchtimes, many people ate in the office. Small groups still went to restaurants, but they no longer returned late due to an engaging conversation. There was a hush, a discretion.

A practical spirit prevailed at Handex now, a rather energetic one: this part of the programming must be ready by the end of this week; the metal component must be tested by the end of the month; this part of the arm must be ready within three months; we must adhere to the timetable. Even the secretary stopped chatting with her friends on the phone. She often walked around the office asking if she could help.

Nava stayed in her office and focused on developing the program for the new robotic arm. She found the atmosphere unbearable. Sometimes she felt suffocated and opened the window to hear the hum of Ayalon highway. Despite holding a senior position, she was thinking about leaving Handex.

A single mother, always saving for the future, she'd said that Handex wasn't just a workplace, but a vehicle for self-expression—a company where one could ask questions and pursue ideas that would be laughed at elsewhere. The balance between Ben's thoroughness and Ofir's brilliance freed the imagination. But the split between them, each one running part of the weekly staff meeting, disturbed the balance. It was enervating and dull, and she felt irritable and sad. Abraham had tried to raise everyone's spirits and generate a sense of unity. But even he had stopped patting the programmers' backs and asking people how they were doing.

During David Haddad's funeral, Abraham stood beside the family, participating in the prayers, saying "Amen" loudly. David's friends from the Sephardi synagogue were there, old men in dark, faded suits, wearing kippahs. Abraham stood among them, rather than with the people of Handex, his face expressing a sort of satisfaction. He acted as though it was good to depart life, even too young, accompanied by the prayers of friends. If David was destined to die before having grandchildren, at least he would be led to eternal rest with his friends citing the book of Psalms. Watching the rabbi, listening to the murmur of prayer—engrossed in the ritual, Abraham's face betrayed his religious devotion. What a shame, he thought, that neither Ben nor his brother and sister followed their father's religious way. If he had inspired them more than their mother, they would have found the right path. Ben supported Sophia, who could hardly stand, his glance shifting from one person to another.

The unfamiliar feeling of being fatherless made Ben dizzy. The people in front of him seemed blurred, the whispered prayers incomprehensible; his mother leaning against him with tears running down her cheeks looked strange, and the facial features of the rabbi tearing his shirt were too big. The memorial room was packed. It was a cold winter's day in Jerusalem, and everyone was wrapped in heavy coats. But Ben sensed an obscure light filtering in, maybe through the door, maybe from somewhere else. A soft ray had touched him, filled with burgundy capillaries, pure light that also contained darkness. The ray caressed his face, but no one else could see it. Sweat ran down his forehead, his eyes were full of tears. The beam enveloped him. Primordial, it stamped him: a man without a father. A person who would say: "My father is gone." A pendulum of an obscure clock began to swing from side to side at a steady tempo, making an inaudible ticking. A new count, which he still couldn't fathom, thickened the pain, making it unbearable.

Realizing that something was forever lost and would never be replaced made him look desperately for Ofir. But he wasn't there. Sensing the constant, heavy swing of the pendulum, Ben knew that it was over and done with. What has been will no longer be.

August 2005

Dark eyes surrounded by thick, curved eyelashes were observing Laurie. Hamid sat in an old office chair, his body slightly loose, a young man whose face revealed curiosity and sadness. He inspected Laurie's office at the Tel Aviv Museum; the shelves were filled with art journals, exhibition catalogues, and books; photos of statues covered the walls. Amidst the multitude of artwork visible everywhere, it was practically impossible to distinguish any single piece.

Laurie leaned forward—it was clear she was pregnant. With understanding, she said softly, "Don't worry. We'll make sure that the exhibition will be impressive. We'll invite journalists to review it. I don't understand why you're hesitant?" She had invested a lot of effort into organizing the solo exhibition—it was an outstanding achievement for a young, unknown artist. She had first approached the curator of contemporary art, who had no objection. She discussed it with the photography curator and showed her Hamid's work; finally she spoke with the deputy director. Though the museum's schedule was full until next year, Laurie persuaded her that now was the right time for this exhibition. An entire room would be devoted to Hamid, the exhibition would be called *The Conflict: Different Angles*, presenting the photographer's unique perspective, lacking clichés or propaganda.

Hamid shifted uneasily in his seat, looking aside without saying anything. Finally, he muttered, "I don't know. I don't want to stand at the heart of the conflict. People always suspect Israeli Arabs and think we are all terrorists. It might cause opposition, and I don't have the energy to face it, to keep trying to explain myself."

"I don't think there is any problem in presenting your perspective in Tel Aviv. I'm sure many will come to the exhibition."

"Maybe. I'm also not sure my people will like it. They expect a more unequivocal statement against the occupation."

"I think your work is unequivocal enough."

"Yes, but people want me to show blood and tears. My perspective is different, and people get angry. And also, my family doesn't like it too much."

"Really? Why? Your work is wonderful."

"They don't see it that way. They want me to run our furniture factory. It's the most important thing for them, and if they think the exhibition will jeopardize it, they will definitely object."

"Listen, Hamid, it's your decision, of course. But I think it is a unique opportunity to present your perspective, which expresses rejection of the occupation in a sophisticated manner. Your family doesn't want your photos to be exhibited?"

"They do. But what they want most of all is safety."

"In what way is the exhibition a threat to their safety?"

"Safety is the combination of money and anonymity. It gives people a protected, stable life. They have enough money not only to provide for the family but also for good health and pleasure; and no one takes an unwanted interest in them. They don't stand in anyone's way. That's the safest place. If the exhibition draws too much attention, annoys Jews, Arabs, possibly both, my family's safety will be compromised."

"Don't they find it important that your voice is heard? After all, it concerns them. They are torn between solidarity with the Palestinians and a desire to live in a modern state, the difficulties of an Arab minority among a Jewish majority, discrimination, extreme Islam."

"Important? Yes, but other things are more important. Providing for the family and a safe life is more important."

"But how will your voice be heard? I have an idea! Let's approach one of your leaders, a spiritual leader, someone accepted by everyone, and ask him to support the exhibition."

Hamid smiled bitterly. The young man suddenly aged; he looked like an older man who had born the consequences of human folly. He sat erect, crossed his arms, and said, "A leader accepted by everyone? There is no such thing. There are tribes and opposing tribes. There are leaders who quarrel with each other, and each one believes in something else. If one leader supports the exhibition, others would immediately object to it. That's the way it is in our community. You know, just like among Jews—everyone looks out for himself."

Silence fell. The space between them was almost visible. Eventually, Laurie said, "You know, only rarely does the Tel Aviv Museum offer a solo exhibition to an unknown artist your age. It is a unique opportunity. I'm not sure I could arrange this again."

"I know."

As Laurie entered the elementary school's yard holding her daughters hand, she looked around, astonished. It was surrounded by bare soil, two peeling benches flanked each side, there were withering flowers along the path from the gate to the main door, and yellow dust covered the entire area. The staff was trying to create a festive atmosphere before the school year began, with colorful balloons and a big sign announcing "Welcome First Graders." But Laurie thought the school looked rundown. There were weeds along the fence with some thorns, pieces of papers on the ground, a shirt someone had forgotten was heaped on the bench, and a bottle sat next to the gate. Abigail seemed anxious, but she smiled when a freckled girl offered her candies, and followed her mother into the building.

The teacher, about forty, plump with curly hair, smiled and invited them into the classroom. After asking Abigail a couple of questions, she suggested that she draw a picture she would like to put on the wall. Had it been possible, Abigail would have run away in horror. Her dark eyes expressed curiosity and fear. Noticing, the teacher took a seat beside her and began to speak very slowly, enunciating every word with an exaggerated emphasis, as though she were a six-year-old child: "Abigail, eve-ry-one is nervous when they come to a new place. It is natural. All children feel this way. I want to tell you about our school. Children come here to learn, find new friends, and play. But do you know what is the most important thing in this class? To treat others respect-fully. We care about our friends; we listen to them, and we offer help when it's needed. And if we're nice to people, they're nice to us! You don't know your classmates yet, and they don't know you, but when all of us are here together we will be kind to each other, and make sure we all have a lovely time."

Abigail relaxed as she listened to the teacher. She began to draw small flowers on her piece of paper: long straight stalks from which elongated leaves emerged; at their ends were small red circles that added up to a red flower. The teacher turned to Laurie and said coldly, "This is the most impor-tant thing: that they grow up to be decent human beings," as if this was the right thing to say to worried mothers. But Laurie heard a shrill, unpleasant tone, words said only so that they would be heard and serve as evidence that a worthy cause had been set; words to be written in an invisible book that would be read in the future, readers turning its pages, nodding and saying, "Ah, yes, people used to talk like that in the past. Some tried to keep the exist-ing order, to encourage people to look after each other and restrain the sour, selfish spirit. But unfortunately they failed."

When Laurie and Abigail got home, loud voices were coming from the television and a black title spread across the screen: "Disengagement."[1] Women soldiers were carrying a screaming settler, soldiers were moving equipment, buses surrounded by a crowd were trying to drive slowly; crying girls were screaming at the camera and cursing an officer. Ariel Sharon appeared for a couple of minutes, and then it was the settler leaders making threats.

Ofir was standing in front of the television, absorbed by the news, his body stiff and frozen. Rather than relaxing on the sofa, he stood motionless, as if he were a soldier in the Gaza Strip. Arms tense, legs rigid, he looked as if he was getting summoned to evacuate the settlers. He noticed that Laurie was worried and said: "Finally, we're getting out of Gaza. I can't believe it's happening. I hope the soldiers won't have to be there another single day—it's a nightmare. Who knows, maybe it will also take place in Judea and Samaria, and then everything will be good" Laurie smiled at him and they watched the news together.

Despite Ofir's agitation about Gaza, he had generally felt calmer recently. His life had turned into a predictable path. Every morning, he went to work as if nothing had ever happened, ran Handex without exchanging a single word with Ben, had lunch with two programmers and an engineer in the same restaurant, returned home early in the evening, and spent time with his wife and daughter. The firm was doing well, with Ofir selling the arm to hospitals in North America, Europe, South America, and even China. The company hired more programmers, engineers, doctors, a lawyer, and another secretary. As there wasn't enough room on the premises, Ofir leased more space on the fortieth floor of Azrieli Tower. The team working on the new robotic arm was allocated three extra offices, while the team maintaining the present robot secured two. The transition was smooth and easy.

A new spirit prevailed at home, too. Simplicity and pragmaticism ruled. No more jokes that made Laurie burst into laughter, no more reading about a new topic until dawn; Ofir began to act in a predictable manner. He would return home, kiss his wife and daughter, put his briefcase in his study, have dinner, play with Abigail, watch television, and go to sleep. Morning, noon, evening, night; regular beats; a pendulum moving at a constant tempo. Food,

---

1   In 2005, Israel dismantled the settlements in the Gaza Strip and withdrew from the territory.

drink, driving, work, driving, girl, woman—every day the same as the one before. A moderate life with no turmoil, stretching from the center of Tel Aviv to Azrieli Tower and sometimes to Jerusalem. But when Gaza showed up on the television screen, the rhythm was broken; in a moment, Ofir would shout at the settlers who refused to leave Gaza. His strained muscles revealed his tension, his eyebrows knitted together. The restless spirit was back, disrupting the calm routine. But soon he would relax again, mutter that he didn't want to watch it anymore, and turn the television off.

Every three or four nights, he caressed Laurie, drawing her close to him. If she consented, he would touch her and ask, "Maybe we'll try this? Or this?" The practical spirit made him an inquisitive lover, but created a gulf between them; they were partners in a sensual pleasure that lacked fervor. A man and a woman in a wide bed, touching each other's bodies as if they were complicated machines that had to be managed skillfully, mechanisms with a hidden logic. When they finally fell asleep, each one curled up on the opposite side of the bed, the moon floating in the sky would close its own eyes, exhausted by the sight of human folly. Sometimes a siren would call in the distance, like a sounding shofar.

July 2006

This time I'll take two weeks off and travel to Israel. Natalie will stay here; no need to put her in danger. I will visit Laurie. Maybe I'll even manage to persuade my stubborn brother to come to Tel Aviv. Daniel is already seven months old. Laurie has to look after two children in a time of war, though, thank God, at the moment the Hezbollah isn't targeting Tel Aviv. But who knows how this conflict will develop?[1]

If it had been possible to examine Eric's decision to travel to Israel during the 2006 Lebanon War, the conclusion might have been drawn that it was partly determined by vague and ambiguous motives. Lately, a discontent, a sort of restlessness, had entered his life. Something wasn't moving in the right direction, but he wasn't sure what and why. Though his business was doing very well, and his life with Natalie was quiet and comfortable, he sometimes wanted to go on a journey he couldn't quite picture. Every time this obscure longing surfaced, he looked around, trying to find the flaw he knew existed but couldn't find. *Maybe I should start a new company?* An old dream about a bookstore in the center of London became vivid for a moment, but was immediately ruled out. Everyone knows that chain stores are taking over small bookstores; the shop is doomed before it opens. *Maybe I should learn Chinese?* Ah, I'll never need it and I'm never going to sign a contract that's not in English. Years ago, he'd aspired to be an actor. *Maybe I could join an amateur group performing in community centers?* Come on, it would be strange and even ridiculous for a man my age to go on stage, even if the audience was made up of family and friends.

Eric sometimes even considered having an affair. He always felt fortunate for having found Natalie, a woman who seemed to have been created especially for him. The harmony between them was evident, their life together was serene. They were crafted from the same mold, shaped from a similar substance. But lately, to his great shame at such an age, he had begun to look at photos of naked women on his iPad, seeking out women's parts

---

1   In 2006, a military conflict broke out between Israel and Hezbollah.

that appeared isolated from the woman who possessed them. *Natalie doesn't do this*, he thought, appalled by his own desires, which were slowly becoming more sordid. And though he eventually dismissed this mood, telling himself that it was a sign of old age, it generated a hint of hostility towards Natalie. A hidden brook of resentment began to flow, breaking up time and again.

When he attempted to explain to his friends how his Jewish self-perception had shifted, he was met with bewilderment and irony. He elaborated enthusiastically that, in his view, Zionism changed the entire Jewish people, even communities that opposed the ideal of the New Jew. Everyone listened silently. Then one friend said that it was an interesting idea and he had never thought about it; his sarcastic wife asked if he wanted to be an Israeli warrior-hero. Someone else added that they were paying for the stupid things Israel does and for the occupation of the Palestinian people. "No one knows when it will end—though, thank God, at least they've withdrawn from Gaza." And that friend's wife said, with a grim face, that perhaps it would have been better if Israel had never been established. On the way back home, angry and frustrated, he explained to Natalie that they'd utterly misconstrued his meaning. Implying that he supported the occupation was ridiculous. He deplored Israeli aggression. They all knew this very well. He simply believed that the entire Jewish people had changed, and was unaware of it. "And by the way," he added quietly, "since I realized that my life has changed."

"Changed? How? Do you feel closer to Israel?"

"On the contrary. I feel more British now. Acknowledging that I am not as feeble as my grandparents somehow detaches me from Israel. Oh, well, clearly, we care about Israel, always have, and even more so now that Laurie lives there. But this idea of us being stronger Jews, different from out ancestor, separates me from it."

Natalie was bewildered; they continued in silence to the Tube. After a few minutes, she suddenly said: "You know, you've got a point. Every time I come back from Israel, I feel a bit different. Not in the simple sense of adopting the Israeli militant spirit. But as if an ailment that I have here in the UK has been alleviated a little."

A strange gaiety overtook him on the plane to Tel Aviv. People were talking about the situation in the country, wondering if the flight would be altered because of the war, and joking about Nasrallah's threats to fire rockets at Tel Aviv. Eric took part in the lively conversation, expressed some firm views, and chuckled out loud at the funny stories a young man told everyone. An elderly woman sitting next to him kept muttering, "Let's hope everything will be okay"; and on the other side sat a young man chewing his nails. A religious man was praying. Young girls giggled quietly. Eric surrendered to the friendly atmosphere, their common fate creating warmth and affinity, as if for a couple of hours they were all part of a struggle against evil and were loyal to one another.

But after a while, the joy dissipated, and he became gloomy. He recalled that he had offended Natalie by saying that this time he would travel alone and that there was no need for her to join him. He'd upset Laurie by suggesting she and her Ofir wouldn't be able to take care of two children should anything happen, and clumsily offended his son by telling him he should visit his mother more often. This urgent trip to Israel suddenly seemed unnecessary. Surely Laurie and Ofir could look after their children and had a plan if the war reached Tel Aviv. And how could he help, anyway? He couldn't carry a baby at his age, let alone Abigail. Why, in fact, had he left in such a hurry and flown off to Israel?

A flicker of thought was made flesh and vanished before Eric could see it clearly. *The discomfort entering my life has made me escape to Israel, not concern for my daughter and her family.* Something was unraveling, but he wasn't sure what. Something was fracturing, but he didn't know how to fix it. What had been firm and stable was slightly shaking, and he was helpless to stop it. He was watching the onset of a disintegration he couldn't prevent. His life with Natalie, his successful business and affluent lifestyle, the Jewish community in Hampstead, his generous donations, the friends he met at the pub—an inner weaving, making a beautiful embroidery, was coming undone. A thread was loose and he was scared to death. Initially, he thought weaving it back into place would suffice. But in a moment of terrifying comprehension he knew that the pattern itself was outdated—and though he liked the old fabric, he felt an urge tear at it with his fingers and twist every thread.

He was a dedicated father, an attentive grandfather spoiling his grandchildren, a loving husband, dearly liked by his son-in-law. During his visit to Tel Aviv he devoted himself to Laurie, Abigail, Daniel, and Ofir, called Natalie often, and discussed the military conflict with Joseph and Sarit. But he couldn't please his own brother.

A year ago, Harry had sold the house in Ness Ziona, succumbing to threats from contractors who coveted his piece of land. First, they asked politely, offering a fortune, then they began to bother and pressure him, and finally they kept badgering him. They threw garbage at the front door. Letters were taken from the mailbox. A couple of times he found his car with a flat tire, and once, a bush in the garden had been destroyed. The contractors had connections in the municipality of Ness Ziona, which suddenly demanded a considerable sum for "utilizing urban land for agriculture purposes." Only the intervention of a local paper forced them to relent. Harry could have taken all this, but as he saw tall buildings rising up around his garden, dust covering his plants, and towers hiding the sunlight, he decided to sell the house and his orchards.

He planned to build a ranch in the Negev. Then he thought he would move with Nurit to the Jezreel Valley, near the kibbutz where she was born. After two months, they bought an apartment in Haifa overlooking the sea, and Harry sat on the balcony for days, gazing at the bay. Their only son moved to the United States with no intention of returning to Israel, and for a brief moment they thought that maybe they would follow him. They were now wealthy people, and they moved from one place to another for a couple of months.

Finally, they decided to settle in the Upper Galilee. Harry bought the home and beehives of a poor, desperate farmer on the verge of bankruptcy, and was determined to become a successful beekeeper. He could see the farmer was lying, claiming that the hives were new even though rust was everywhere, but cultivating bees and producing honey captured his imagination. He fixed the beehives, bought complementary equipment, and began to study the lives of these small creatures, which he thought were miraculous; a well-organized community in which every individual bee finds its place. Standing in the field in the early morning, looking at misty mountains and wide green meadows, the smoky, azure sky enveloping the hills and filtering into the valleys, Harry felt that the pain of leaving Ness Ziona was slightly alleviated. He turned his face upward and closed his eyes, allowing the sunlight to caress his body, feeling a thin, light web draw him into nature's bosom, embracing him tenderly. There would be no more "we have such a beautiful country." Erect in the field, surrounded by his humming bees, in his mind Harry had become a minuscule particle in a universe stretching to infinity.

And now that war had broken out, it never occurred to him to leave his bees. As rockets fell not far from their home, he persuaded Nurit to visit a friend at Petah Tikva, but he stayed on. When his brother called and begged him to come to Tel Aviv, saying that Harry's two Thai workers could take care of the hives while he was away, bitter anger came over him, and he suddenly yelled into the phone, "If you come here from London for two weeks, don't give me any advice!"—and hung up.

February 2007

A wide road, broad and comfortable, winds among buildings and streets, towers and hills. Paved with smooth stones, it is flanked by bushes and tall trees. The surface is carefully marked; walking on it one feels safe and relaxed, revealing the tranquility of affluent people. Simpers and smooth talk, swaggering and false modesty, feminine giggles and strong masculine scents—this is the path of luxury and success. But a closer look reveals that lately the way has narrowed, slightly converged into itself. Though it seems nothing has changed, new lines have been painted that cut off part of the route. No one discusses shaping reality, collective fate, creative management, or developing talent anymore. Nowadays, people talk about profit versus overheads, short-term investments, interest rates versus the price of land, the rise and fall of share prices, technology replacing workers— words that entail comfortable disengagement.

Ben's days became routine and efficient. He worked from morning to evening and spent the rest of his time with his family. Two years before, David had been born. Ben hadn't been sure if he should name him after his father— Sephardi Jews call grandchildren after living grandparents. But Sophia begged him to. She'd pressed her palms together, as if she were praying, wiped away a tear, and said that because her husband hadn't lived to see his grandson, he deserves to give his name to the child. She'd added quietly that maybe he could also carry the name of her father, who had died in a concentration camp. David Menachem Haddad was a chubby, healthy baby who developed into a mischievous, good-natured toddler. Blond curls surrounded his dark-skinned face; unlike his father and grandfather, he was sturdy. And when he was two years old, Eden was born, a delicate baby girl who slept for hours.

In the evening, when Ben returned home from work, Talia would fill him in about her day, telling him things that seemed very trivial: the package of diapers was too small, David loved chicken and potatoes, baby bottles at the pharmacy nearby were very expensive, Ben's mother had knitted Eden a pink sweater. She listed these unrelated impressions quietly, often smiling, as if there was no point in having a conversation that wasn't focused on life's basics. Though exhausted by the end of the day, she always expressed inter-est in Ben's work, asking all sorts of questions: Should Handex move to the outskirts of Tel Aviv to save money? Isn't the parking in the Azrieli garage too expensive? Would hospitals all over the globe purchase the new robot? Also in the Far East? Ben gave long, detailed answers, weighing his words, as if his explanations would fashion a stable world, free of envy, theft, and a dead friendship.

On the Friday night after Eden had been born, Ben was surprised to find that Talia had lit Shabbat candles. She didn't come from a religious family, and she looked at the dancing lights with embarrassment. Sophia was amazed, and said that the room was bright enough. Talia smiled at her sweetly and said nothing. Ben gazed at the candles wordlessly; he asked her why she had lit them. "It creates a nice family atmosphere," she answered, looking at him affectionately, holding Eden in her arms.

Suddenly, he was furious. The table was laden. Rogue peas were all over it, as were crumbs from the bread his mother had sliced. On the plates, there was chicken, potatoes, and greasy brown gravy, and annoyingly, between them, were the white candles. The small flames tilted sideways, turning their heads down, looking away from the food, which Ben found repulsive. "They shouldn't be here on the table," he said sullenly, and Talia quickly picked them up and placed them on the cabinet next to the window.

His father used to ask his mother to honor him by lighting Shabbat candles, and she always vehemently refused, saying that if he thought it was so important, he should do it himself. Sophia detested his religiousness, which had intensified through the years. Eventually, her husband had given up. When his daughter was a teenager, he suggested that she take on Friday night candle duty lights; and she responded with a snort followed by a loud laugh. He growled, let out an unintelligible mutter, and then collapsed, irritated, into his armchair. And now, Talia, unconcerned about this mother's eyes that always look at the world with the best intensions and now revealed her despair, lit the candles casually, thinking it make the dining room cozy, unaware of the fraught past.

Ben chided David for spilling his food, told Talia that the chicken and potatoes were too salty, and even grimaced as his mother spoke. The image of his father materialized in his mind, rebuking him for not studying the Torah or going to synagogue. A solemn, thin man who always wore faded gray trousers and a white shirt made of coarse fabric, Ben felt as though his father's image was embedded in him. Within him existed a dreary old man, who had died prematurely.

But as he went on thinking about his father, almost smelling the mothballs on his clothes, Ben calmed down. *Why not?* he thought. *Why not? What's wrong with Talia lighting the Shabbat candles?* His parents' arguments had been so depressing he had hidden for hours in his room. When they made up again, he would speculate as to when the next quarrel would occur. All the arguments about religion . . . If his father hadn't been so grim when he spoke about Judaism, perhaps his children wouldn't have rejected his religion. It was his emotional intensity that discouraged Ben, his unwavering belief in God and unwillingness to even discuss other perspectives. Ben's father only admitted to the power and sway of the Almighty, which he felt was the deepest truth. But when Ben thought about religion objectively, it didn't seem at all bad; and the candles *were* pleasing, the ambience was one of homey tranquility.

When dinner was over, Ben stretched with satisfaction and said the food had been excellent and that the candles were a good idea. Sophia looked at her son with bewilderment; she got up and said it was time for her to go home. Ben hugged her and said, "Come on, Mom, it's only candles—and it's nice."

This pragmatic state of mind also took root at Handex. No one chatted in the corridors or laughed over amusing gossip at lunch. People worked hard at their desks, eyes fixed on computer screens. All day, work went on without idle talk. Staff meetings were twenty-five minutes shorter since no one made jokes or commented on issues unrelated to the arm. Ofir ran the first part of the meeting, which was half an hour long. He then left the room and Ben came in for the second part. They exchanged the shortest of emails when communication was essential; a line or two at most.

The practical spirit proved highly beneficial. Sixty robotic arms were sold to hospitals worldwide. The financial report for the final quarter of 2006 showed ballooning profits and that more was to come. To cut costs, component manufacturing was outsourced to a Chinese company, and two programmers and an engineer were laid off.

All the work at Handex was broken down into parts, and then parts of parts. The week was divided into task units, each one devoted to a concrete outcome. Offices were sectioned off, so people could focus better. The arm itself was worked on by four different teams, each on focusing on one element. Meetings first addressed marketing concerns; the second half dealt with software challenges and product design. Each member of the order processing team was given a continent: North America, Europe, or East Asia. The recently appointed evening secretary was tasked with overseeing outgoing mail, while the morning secretary managed incoming correspondence. Development, production, and marketing was more efficient when the different departments collaborated seamlessly. The efforts of Handex's workers were clearly quantified, advancing steadily at a pace that could almost be felt in the corridors. Anything frivolous was vanquished. Every employee fulfilled their assigned role, which made the production process highly efficient.

Abraham always emphasized his allegiance to Ben. He told anyone who'd listen that Ben understood the entire production process from top to bottom. He'd add that Ben's ability to bring together skills from various fields was what had made the creation of the robotic arm possible. And he didn't conceal that he didn't like Ofir, who, at meetings, would always call on other people before Abraham.

When Abraham knocked on Ben's office door, he heard a strange hum coming from inside, neither inviting nor ignoring the knock. He opened the door, surprised to find Ben looking at him, arms crossed, as if he were expecting him keenly. The wrinkle across Ben's forehead deepened, almost as though it had been cut with a sharp knife. His normally tight lips were slightly parted. Abraham noticed that Ben's gray curls were thinning and that a small belly protruded through his shirt. *That's odd*, he thought, *I never imagined it possible. Ben was so thin.* Embarrassed, he stood at the door, fiddling with the kippah on his head, wondering what was going on.

"I came to show you how I think this inner screw should be . . ." Abraham began. But Ben interrupted him and said quietly, ignoring his words, "What's wrong? Are you okay?" Abraham's round face, which often contracted into a smile out of habit, fell. His body became tense; the hand that sometimes touched his belly unconsciously was now deep in his pocket, the other one playing once more with his kippah.

"No, no, everything is fine. My eldest son is about to get married." His voice was croaky. It was like a stranger was speaking from within him. He tried to adopt a pleasant countenance, but he twitched like someone suffering from toothache.

"Your son is getting married?! How old is he?"

"Twenty-one. For us, this is normal."

"You don't sound happy."

"With him getting married young? I'm fine with this."

"Ah, so you don't like the bride . . ."

"Not exactly."

"What do you mean?"

"I'm not happy with their relationship. My wife and I dated for a few of years before we got married. We met when we were fifteen and got married at the age of twenty. They met only a few weeks ago. They dated a couple of times, 'to see if they're right for each other,' as they said, and then decided to get married. They hardly know each other."

"That's how it is with religious couples, isn't it?"

"Among Orthodox Jews—but not us! It didn't use to be this way, but it's becoming more common. They are more observant than we are; there is something extreme about them."

Ben's grinned, and then stopped himself.

"You're talking about extremists? You're all extreme. All those settlements are evidence of your fanatical spirit. It's kind of funny. One day, the fanatics find out that their children are even more fanatical than they are. And they're appalled. What a joke."

"My son is an officer in the paratroops. There is nothing fanatical about him. He is keeping Israel safe. What has his religion got to do with anything?" said Abraham, annoyed.

"Come on. You can't deny it. You take the land from the Palestinians, making their life miserable. If you had your way, you would expel them or turn them into slaves. Don't you think that's extreme?"

"I can't believe you're saying this. Take their land? The Land of Israel is ours. God gave it to Abraham. And they are all terrorists; they hate us to death. If they had their way, they would kill us all, certainly kick out us out. It's them who are being cruel, not us."

"Why don't you ask Ofir? He served in Judea, Samaria, and Gaza." As soon as he uttered the words, the room felt oppressive and cold, as if biting frost had spread everywhere. Ben and Abraham looked around, as though someone else had spoken. An obscure presence was with them in the office, a sort of elongated shadow of Ofir. It was walking on the burgundy carpet or crouching behind the bookcase. Perhaps it was outside the window.

Ben leaned back in his chair.

In an instant, the abyss, which he thought was closed, had yawned open again. Ben could almost feel Ofir's questioning gaze with a touch of unpleasant humor and the pragmatic spirit that drove him to despair. On sleepless nights, waking up covered in sweat, he went out to the balcony. Staring at the sky, he begged for an answer, right at that moment, before was too late: *Why? Why did I steal? Why did I commit such a sin?*

"Never mind, forget politics," Abraham said, trying to push the embarrassing moment aside. A cloud passed across Ben's face. His eyes were moist. He was horrified that he'd mentioned Ofir so simply and naturally, as if nothing had happened. Abraham kept the conversation going and pretended he'd noticed nothing. "My son is about to marry a woman he hardly knows. I don't understand why they can't wait. What's the rush? They act as if they have a mission they need to accomplish as soon as possible. But marriage is not a mission. The intimacy between a man and a woman develops slowly, not within a month or two. I asked him what would have happened if he'd thought they weren't right for each other. Do you know what he said? 'I'll look for another woman.'"

Ben, now somewhat recovered and trying to pretend that an abyss hadn't emerged in his office—in a moment he would have fallen into it—said lightly, "You always told me that, unlike secular people, you live together and not by yourself."

"My son and his future wife will live together, but in the wrong way. They are devoted to an idea, not a person. But marriage is a relationship between a single man and a single woman."

"The settlers are also devoted to an idea which keeps you together. If you weren't so committed to your vision of Greater Israel, each one of you would live by himself. One day, you will stop believing in this silly idea and find that you are nothing but a suburban community where people don't care about their neighbors."

"That will never happen." Abraham was frowning; he was stressed and resentful. "We will forever believe in Greater Israel—God Almighty gave it to Abraham. Nothing will change our minds. And we are not another suburb—we are a very close community. I have good friends in the settlement."

"All this solidarity will vanish when the idea disappears, maybe even earlier. When you have to choose between your belief and . . . let's say, professional success, you'll find that the choice is not that simple. If you had the option of being poor in the settlement or moving into the 1967 borders and being wealthy, I'm not sure what your choice would be."

Ben was now amused; his eyes revealed a light that seemed to have died out long ago. He rocked back in his chair, and smiling he looked like a child planning a trick. It would be funny; even Abraham would burst into laughter. But Abraham was angry and hurt. He flushed as he nearly shouted,

"What kind of question is this? I don't understand. You can ask this about anyone. You believe in democracy, don't you? Would you be willing to live in poverty in a democratic society or be wealthy in a nondemocratic society? You believe in equality before the law. Would you be willing to pay the cost to live in a society that supports this view, or do your values have a price? You can ask this about anything."

Ben peered at Abraham. His eyes were those of a motionless predator watching his prey before revealing his sharp teeth. His nostrils widened and rattled, as if they smelled blood; the right side of his mouth curved down, the left side curved up. A whisper came out of his mouth, floating through the air like a separate being: "Of course you can ask this about anything! That's exactly my point. The problem is that once you raise this question, it can't be taken back. All of a sudden, great ideas are quantified in units: tens, hundreds, thousands, and you begin to wonder how much your values are worth. Add a bit? Reduce the price? Democracy costs more than equality? Or the other way around? Eventually, you will also make this calculation—even you! And then you'll see that your values are not so absolute. This calculation makes every belief, as passionate as it might be, flexible; all truths become relative, and sometimes even dubious."

When Abraham left, he was hunched over and his plaid shirt was damp with sweat. He was still touching his kippah obsessively, taking it off, putting it back on. Ben watched the door close, as though he was expecting someone who was late. He then shut his eyes, his body went utterly limp, and the wrinkle across his forehead softened and became nearly invisible. He sat still for a couple of minutes.

Then he opened his eyes, straightened up in his chair, and called Talia. "How about we try out the new Italian restaurant on Shenkin Street? I heard it's great. Can you make a reservation? Around seven o'clock? Perfect!"

March 2007

In rare moments in early spring, the Mediterranean Sea nestles into itself and refuses to reflect the sky. Heavy dark clouds and a navy sea, light blue sky over dim yellowish waves, bright sunlight beating down on gray water, the mirror stretching onto the horizon won't let the immense dome above it look down and see its reflection. Only in the distance, where sky and water meet, do the colors gradually mingle and turn into thick fog, a mist absorbing the spectrum, like a gate into an occult world.

Laurie sat on a deck chair on the beach at noon, her body relaxed, gazing at the waves. Wearing a gray sweater and black trousers that flattered her round body, the breeze tussled her black hair. Her eyes followed a ship on the horizon. Though it seemed immobile, once in a while, you could tell it was moving forward. Next to her sat a man about her age with wavy gray hair, his expression slightly embarrassed: a faint smile betrayed a wish to apologize, explain why he had chosen to do this thing and not the other, to illustrate his good will. He was slim, of medium height, and wore blue jeans and a light sweater. His clean white sneakers indicated that he might be a tourist, a foreigner who happened to find himself in Tel Aviv. He turned his head to Laurie, as if expecting her to respond. After a couple of minutes, he said in English, "This is so different from the sea in England, isn't it?"

"It's strange—when I came here sixteen years ago, the landscape seemed so alien, but I thought I connected with the people. Now it's the other way around. I love the sea, the city, but I feel more of a foreigner."

"That sounds familiar."

"What I used to see as superficial impoliteness is really something very fundamental. I got carried away and then was disappointed."

"My wife says I look like an outsider, but I don't care. This constant need to blend in with the locals is tiresome."

"True. It's extraordinary that a country of immigrants from so many places emphasizes the need to be like everyone else, adopt the same habits. I sometimes think it is a result of fear, the conviction that if everyone behaved like they wanted, society would disintegrate."

A relationship formed out of friendship, not passion. An affair born in an hour of loneliness, not contentment. A hidden alliance between two British people living in Tel Aviv. They'd got to know each other six months earlier, and since then, they'd met once a week at noon, in cafés, restaurants, and in a beach hotel. The old receptionist used to look at them suspiciously, but now she smiled and made conversation about the weather, as if it's not unusual for two adults to spend a couple of hours together in a hotel every Wednesday.

When Laurie first agreed to meet Michael, she whispered to herself, defiant and resentful, that there was nothing wrong in it; her life had changed so much that it wouldn't make any difference. Ofir's practical spirit kept penetrating their lives, hindering bursts of laughter or passing sadness. No longer did he wake her up in the middle of the night to watch a funny movie or kiss her fervently in the morning. Now every day unfolded according to a prearranged order. At breakfast, she knew what would happen in the afternoon or evening. Twice a week he held Laurie closely at night, touching her like a man who had known many women. Though he never concealed his past relationships, he used to make these women sound like they were from a distant past he could hardly recall. The present always brushed aside Ofir's old girlfriends; they became nothing but a setting for his life with Laurie. But now she felt as though she had been added to this long list of unknown women. Now Ofir stressed that she was the mother of his children. At a social gathering recently, he'd introduced her with, "This is Laurie, Abigail and Daniel's mom."

At a party in Abigail's class, Laurie sat in the corner, watching her daughter dance with other girls to loud, rhythmic music. She felt bewildered. The mothers all looked at their daughters with delight; she was the only one who was distracted. Laurie smiled at the other mothers and they greeted her politely, but they never made friends. They spoke with so few words, as if everything had been prearranged before they met, and now only a few syllables were needed. "Ballet at four o'clock?" "Today at our place?" At first, she tried to join the conversation, but after a couple of sentences, she smiled, embarrassed, and just listened without understanding. Abigail, however, was a very independent girl, making friends without her mother's assistance.

Michael introduced himself as the father of one of the boys, and sat beside her. Both British, they shared a sense of humor; they had a natural affinity that was obvious from the start. Although they were two strangers meeting for the first time in a room full of people, the air sweltering and the music loud, they felt as if they were in a distant desert or dense forest in which on one had ever set foot, finding each other with relief. Their ironic comments about the overdressed teacher, the mothers who endlessly photo-graphed their daughters—they both carried a foreign land within them and, miraculously, they had some of the same memories. He asked if he could call her and she gladly said yes.

An impartial observer might have thought that the adventurous side of Laurie prompted the relationship with Michael. Despite her refined appear-ance, an urge to come across a new experience and look for an unusual angle led her to unwanted places; embraced by arms she disliked, meeting girlfriends who turned out to be vulgar, traveling to unsettling places. But an invisible weight, hidden yet heavy, small but fully compressed, always restored the center of gravity to its proper place, protecting her from aimless wandering, making her life solid. She was inclined to adventures, yet disliked them; fascinated by charming places, but examined them closely. She was a woman of both yearning and critical thought.

At first, she and Michael were only friends. A slight sadness wrapped her then, a touch of melancholy in a woman who knew her life had for-ever changed. Ofir would never again be the man she had married. She and Michael found themselves absorbed by pleasant memories, sitting in a café in the center of Tel Aviv. It turned out that he had grown up near Hampstead; and together they recalled well-known streets and buildings made of dark bricks. The conversation was amusing, but very quickly it became serious. Their longing for London was obvious and they were left uncomfortable at their candor.

Yearning can be addictive; a bittersweet medicine, cheering and disgust-ing. On the shores of the Mediterranean Sea, dreamed of by so many British poets, London, with its old buildings, dark alleys, and elegant streets came to life. The weird cries of the Tube, neighborhoods deep in silence. Once in a while, someone comes out of a house, speaking loudly, but immediately looks around uneasily, as if they have been caught in the act, breaking the utter stillness.

A soft touch became holding hands; a friendly hug transformed into a kiss. Not passion, but a desire to become one, an urge to unite with someone who longed for a familiar home. Michael suggested they find a hotel where they could meet, and Laurie nodded. A slight, nearly invisible, smile appeared and then changed its mind and disappeared.

The hotel room in an old building on Hayarkon Street had a tiny bal-cony facing the sea, so small there wasn't enough room to put a table next to the two white chairs. Laurie and Michael laughed at the design of the room, intended for tourists who couldn't afford the fancy hotels on the beach. The bedspread was faded. The carpet had a couple of stains someone had tried to remove. Above the bed, there was a photo of a couple wearing old-fashioned bathing suits, and on the chest of draws stood a cheap statue of Venus. The bed sheets smelled clean, but the nightstands were slightly dusty. Yet the more wretched the room was, the more appropriate it was to spend time there—a sort of proof that craving a more elegant world wasn't an infatuation. Only the scent of the sea wafting through the room was contradictory evidence—a discovery that raises doubt, a detail at odds with the prevailing notion.

When the sea stormed the beach furiously, they sat on the balcony, watching the waves silently.

Michael's body was light and soft; his hand touching Laurie's body was somewhat hesitant. He always looked as if he were trying to guess what she wanted. His power was his uncertainty, his unpretentious curiosity. His wise eyes followed Laurie's countenance, seeking proof of pleasure. Even when his body spread on hers, he was alert, attentive, as if any moment he would receive an answer to a question that had been bothering him for years. And she let him study her meticulously. A woman who found that the path she had taken was so broken that she had to find another. She was facing a new valley, which, although narrow and slippery, appeared to have no hidden pitfalls.

An awkward silence fell when they finally lay on their backs, looking at the low ceiling from which hung a chandelier made of small crystal balls. The yearning for London in this graceless room, with nothing but a double bed and a chest of drawers, suddenly ended. Vanished. Gone. The wind pushed open the balcony door, and a strong sea odor filled the space, swallowing London's cold fog. The draft shook the cheap statue of Venus, almost toppling it to the floor. And the two naked people in bed, a man and a woman, covered themselves with a ragged blanket, wishing to fend off the spray emerging from the Mediterranean Sea. But the humming of the waves, clearly heard on the fourth floor, never stops, and the water, which always washes the shore and then changes its mind and pulls back, was entirely indifferent to the small tear that ran down the bright, feminine cheek and the masculine arm desperately covering a stubbly face.

December 2007

Utter bewilderment. A lack of words. Shock mixed with perplexity. A silence that can't be broken but suddenly transforms into open agitation. How was it possible? After years of hard work, innovative and exciting ideas processed with great effort into sleek software and brilliant creative engineering—and one day, just like that, almost by mere coincidence, it turned out that another company had developed a similar product, perhaps even a superior one. In a casual email sent to the orders department, an innocent line appeared: "We've decided to order the robotic arm from Handex after seriously considering the counteroffer of a competing company that has a similar robot but with additional features. While your price is slightly higher, we prefer to purchase the robot from Handex due to your company's extensive experience and a strong reputation."

The orders department forwarded the email to all other departments; immediately everyone searched for the competing company. Complacency, assurance of success—how come no one had thought someone would challenge them? After a couple of minutes, they found it was a well-known Swiss company specializing in medical equipment. The website revealed that it had produced a robotic arm very recently, similar to that of Handex.

Both Ben and Ofir were present at the emergency staff meeting. Ofir sat at the head of the long table, and Ben, arriving right after him, sat at the opposite end. The staff was so unnerved that they failed to notice that the pair were together at the same table. Though Ofir tried to open the meeting in an authoritative voice, a programmer immediately interrupted him and yelled that it was impossible: "Developing such an instrument takes years. Why did they keep it a secret?" A senior engineer knocked on the table with his fist and cried, "They'll make us go out of business; all that time will have been for nothing." A doctor cleared his throat and said in a quiet bass voice, making an effort to adopt a practical tone: "You realize it's over, don't you? If they sell a similar robot at a lower price, we're in serious trouble. It's important to acknowledge the facts, not fool ourselves"; and a woman engineer said in a loud voice, "We shouldn't give up, maybe we can reduce the price and compete with the Swiss company." Another programmer murmured, "We needed to check that they didn't hack our computers. It's simply impossible to develop such a product so quickly."

The words blended into each other: theft, patent, expert reconstructing procedures, malware, industrial espionage, the end of us, an unattractive price—all exposing the fear of Handex's workers. Horror was apparent everywhere, rising from each argument or quiet murmur of "How could this happen?" In a moment, their world could shatter; they would fall into an abyss and their lives would collapse: their professional pride, generous salaries, the satisfaction of being successful people. Eyes glistened; there were worried looks and choked voices; hands knocked on the table. Ofir and Ben were unable to manage the discussion, continuously interrupted by yelling. Eventually, they both went back to their offices.

After a few minutes, Ofir received an email from Ben: "What should we do? We need to work out how to deal with this."

"Right."

"There's a chance someone managed to break into our computers, though they're secure," Ben wrote.

"Could be. Will you look into it?"

"Sure. I'll need professional help, experts in information security."

"Sure. Anyway, I think the solution is reducing the price," Ofir suggested.

"Agreed. Maybe we should outsource further stages of the production."

"Let's give it some thought. It will require letting some people go."

"No choice. Otherwise, we'll be out of business," Ben stated.

"Agreed."

When Ofir left his office and walked down the corridor towards the elevator, he could still hear anxious voices coming out of the meeting room. As he passed by Ben's office he stopped, hesitating whether to knock on the door. Though he didn't entirely turn towards the office, he was tense. He stood still, his fingers running through his graying hair—and then he walked quickly down the corridor. A light shiver began to crawl from the right corner of his mouth to the left side, accompanied by a twitch that gradually faded away. He stepped inside the elevator, peering anxiously at his reflection in the mirrored walls, waiting for the doors to close.

Six months earlier, at the beginning of spring, Ofir had landed at Zurich airport late at night. Though he often made business trips, this time he was unusually nervous. The man at passport control was too severe and stiff, the taxi driver didn't say a word all the way, and the elegant hotel wasn't cozy and inviting.

He hesitated whether he should call Laurie and decided it was too late. The phone might wake Daniel. His sleep was so light that any noise made him cry.

After showering, he collapsed, as always, on the wide bed. He was about to turn on the television when he suddenly recoiled in horror. The doors of the closet next to the bed were covered with a huge mirror; and there was his full reflection, sharp and clear. It was as though he were lying in bed next to himself. He saw a slightly gangly, albeit athletic, man. His upper back was a bit curved, perhaps a result of accelerated physical development in adolescence. His arms were too long, his chest hair thin and curly; his neck very long. Face narrow, nose sharp, brown hair with plenty of gray. His dark eyes, set above high cheekbones, stared at him, bewildered, curious, daring, almost mocking. Finally they looked away. Ofir turned onto his back and stared at the ceiling until he was overcome by deep and dreamless sleep.

The next morning, he went from the hotel to the closest branch of the bank. As he entered, a draft hit him, and for a moment he thought he smelled an odd odor, like mildew. Ofir walked lightly, almost hovering, as if he were dedicated to an extremely important mission and would resist any attempt to stand in his way. Determined and tall, wearing a business suit, he faced a bank teller wearing makeup that made her look doll-like: "A couple of days ago I opened an account here. I would like to know the balance, please." The woman, observing him coldly, raised her eyes and said in her strong German accent, "Sir, there is no need to come to the branch for this. You can check your balance online or with your credit card."

"Yes, yes, I know, but I happen to be here and would like to know the balance."

"Of course. No problem. I will tell you . . . A million and . . ."

Compressed air that appeared smoky, stains of darkness that flickered and disappeared, a masculine voice saying *never mind, never mind*; The space surrounding the teller seemed too dense; her face loomed out of a dark thickness, her eyes surrounded by black and blue lines, her mouth bright red. She looked at him with unmasked contempt and asked, "Sir, is everything okay? Is there a problem?"

"No, not at all. Thank you."

The way to the café on the bank of the Limmat River passed in a flash, despite the twenty-minute walk. Ofir seemed to arrive at the café at the same time he had left the bank. His stride was long and fast; his eyes were concentrated on the map to see which way he should turn. His feet touched the pavement, his arms swung back and forth, cool sunlight from snowy hilltops softly caressed his head, and a gentle smile remained on his face all the way; miraculously, his mouth neither contracted nor expanded.

On arrival, he felt his heart racing. He had seen a photo of Mr. Habsburg, but he wasn't sure he would recognize him. A man about fifty years old; broad face with high cheekbones; small nose and wide mouth; downy blond hair. Christian Habsburg was sitting at a table close to the river, dressed in a business suit, looking aimlessly around. *He looks so German*, Ofir thought, suppressing the word "Aryan." Mr. Habsburg got up and shook Ofir's hand, who handed over a hard drive, which was quickly deposited in the German's briefcase.

Ofir expected Mr. Habsburg to thank him and leave. But to his surprise he remained seated, his leather briefcase carelessly at his feet. "Can I invite you for coffee?" he asked simply, as if his briefcase hadn't just swallowed the guts of the robotic arm, which now seemed to Ofir like a living organism. In a moment it would be born in the briefcase, its parts would be assembled, the unique screws would connect the metals, and the arm would begin to move and make its extraordinary sound.

I wish he'd go away, thought Ofir, looking at the man with near hostility; but he replied politely, "Of course."

While they sipped their steaming coffee, Ofir's eyes darted around blindly. Mr. Habsburg drank his coffee slowly, as if he had been asked for his opinion on the quality of the drink. After a couple of minutes, he asked, "Is this your first time?"

"First time?!" exclaimed Ofir.

"Seven years ago, I secretly sold software I had developed with two partners. Software for graph analysis. It can be used in many fields. Two American investors bought it. When the company went bankrupt, I had plenty of money. Well, you see, I didn't have a choice. I was madly in love with a beautiful woman fifteen years younger than me. I left my wife for her, and my children wouldn't speak to me, but I was so crazy about her I didn't care. And she loved money: jewelry, clothes, good hotels, exotic locations. If she'd asked for a castle, I would have robbed a bank to pay for it. I simply had no choice."

"But you could have sold your share of the company, couldn't you?! I'm sure it was worth a lot. There wasn't any need to rob a bank or even sell the software." Ofir found Mr. Habsburg's laughter repellent. His grinning mouth revealed small, sharp teeth that didn't correspond with his firm body. His nostrils widened, his small eyes almost disappeared, and his voice was shrill, broken yet rising.

"You know, after I cheated my partners and left my wife, I wanted to spoil my love—but she left me for a richer man. Funny, isn't it? I was devastated. I didn't know what to do. I was left with a lot of money, but no family or work. After I got over the crisis, I realized it was better this way. Everything is simpler. I don't owe anyone anything, no guilt feelings or endless thoughts on who is obliged to who. Now I have relationships with two women. I'm not complaining." Mr. Habsburg winked at Ofir, who put on a false smile and swallowed the words "German," "boor," "pig," "Nazi."

Ofir stayed in the café for two more hours after Mr. Habsburg left, gazing at the water flowing slowly and the houses on the opposite bank. He felt like he was in a cloud. He saw straight lines and geometrical shapes. A small boat sailing in the river seemed unstable. In a moment it would roll over and all the people smiling and waving would splash into the water. Bicycles passing swiftly left a stream of air in their wakes, transparent yet tangible; and though he saw people around him, he felt as if he was alone, a desolate man on the banks of an unknown river, its water flowing into a bottomless sea.

But as the cloudiness slightly cleared, he could hear the voices around him. The people were just silhouettes, but syllables and words penetrated an inner mist and he began to listen. He realized, surprised, that everyone was speaking German. The café was busy and bursting with conversation and laughter.

After about fifteen minutes, he whispered to himself, astonished, that he found the German language oppressive. He often traveled to North America, France, and China, but rarely to Germany. Now, in Zurich, he came to understand that he disliked German, found it repellant. He looked around, making sure that none of the patrons could hear his thoughts. They seemed indifferent to the fact that their language had been used by killers whose mere mention left his father ranting and raving. "May they rot in hell!" he'd say—and repeat that his parents and brothers were exterminated in the Holocaust.

In an instant, Ofir was back in the house in Beit Hakerem: the furniture, once elegant, was old, the formerly colorful Persian carpets his mother tried to maintain were faded. A pleasant breeze was coming from the kitchen window, passing through the corridor and going out through the living room window; white and purple Brunfelsia flowers sent their intoxicating scent into the spring air; and his father sat in the living room watching the television. Into the image of his parents' house filtered a memory of the argument they'd had a year before. They'd seen a news report on an Israeli family living in Berlin. Ofir's father had argued that he simply couldn't understand how Israelis could live in Germany, to which his mother had replied that the people who'd been Nazis were now very old and their grandchildren were not the criminals. Joseph immediately claimed that the Holocaust was a unique historical event. Nothing even slightly similar had ever taken place before—it was an unparalleled evil, incomparable to any other historical atrocity. "As far as I'm concerned, it's enough that a person speaks German for me to dislike them, even if they or any of their relatives weren't involved in the Holocaust." When he talked about the Holocaust, his voice always lost its authoritarian tone and transformed into a sort of wail, turning and tangling and gradually howling like a dissonant flute.

Ofir was pleased with this recollection of his father loathing German. If in Switzerland with him, his father would've told him how he detested these people speaking the Nazi language and that he didn't care a bit if they'd had nothing to do with the elimination of European Jewry. He would've mocked them for their increasing tendency to forget history. "Suddenly, no one knows what their grandparents did during the war. Or even worse, they believe that their grandparents objected to Hitler but couldn't do anything about him!"

This imaginary discussion developed as Ofir added more details: his father would be pleased upon learning that Ofir also felt uncomfortable in a German-speaking environment. The old man would chuckle and add that one had to admit they made great cakes; but then get serious again and assert that Israelis living in Germany were morally destitute. Finally, he would spell out the flaws of the Israeli educational system, which insisted on referring to the Holocaust in terms of victory instead of sticking to the historical facts. Ofir felt relaxed. Agreeing with his father was reassuring, creating a homey atmosphere. This made the café seem even more foreign. He nearly forgot the joy of being in accord with his family.

But to Ofir's dismay, this imaginary dialogue suddenly took an unexpected turn. His father asked him what he was doing in Zurich. Unsuspecting, he wondered what had brought his son to this Swiss city. Taken by surprise, Ofir braced himself for what the old man was going to say about him selling the robotic arm software to Mr. Habsburg—a German rival.

The murmur of the river, the tumult of people around him, a woman next to him speaking into her phone, saying *ja-ja* and laughing; a ship's horn in the distance, cool wind on his head. Ofir realized that his father wouldn't be surprised at all. For years, his parents had believed that he should have gotten a job rather than run a business. And ever since he had become a businessman, even if successful, he'd led a life of deception and dishonesty. It was inevitable. Someone driven solely by self-interest would ultimately resort to theft and deceit. There was no way to be honest and do business. Ofir's parents even discounted Ben's terrible betrayal, seeing it as a natural consequence of their decision to start a company together. Since the two childhood friends had deviated from the right path, rejected proper jobs, and made their relationship partly commercial, the crisis and betrayal were to be expected. If he told them what he was doing in Switzerland, his mother's expression would probably reveal reservation and pain.

And his father? He would have groaned: "But why the hell did you have to sell it to a German? Why a German, of all people?"

May 1, 2008

As Natalie and Eric left the building, they looked as if they were leaning against each other. A tall, slightly bony woman and a chubby man; she held his arm, but by his posture it was impossible to tell whether he was clinging to her or supporting her. Their feet moved in harmony, as if they were marching to a beat. Both were wrapped in beige coats. Human silhouettes, masculine and feminine, walking down the street on a cold, bright spring day.

They had just cast their ballots. For the first time in their lives, they hadn't voted for the UK Labour Party; they were walking quietly, overwhelmed. Though they'd discussed the election for the London mayor extensively, considering both options and their implications, they were stunned. It had never occurred to them that an envelope placed in a box would create such agitation. One cannot apologize, mutter that it might have been a mistake, or ask to take the vote back. No, it was over and done with.

Panic made them walk faster. They had both taken a day off. The plan was: vote in Hampstead for the mayor of London; visit the National Gallery; have a late lunch in a French restaurant a few minutes away from the museum. But now it seemed that the plan had gone awry. They walked without knowing where they were heading. Eric coughed, clearing his throat, and Natalie swallowed spit. After a few minutes, Natalie suggested that maybe it wasn't a great day for the museum. Eric didn't answer—he just turned around and walked off in the opposite direction, back to their house on the hilltop.

They hesitated on how they should vote. They had always voted Labour, and it had never even crossed their minds to vote Tory. But lately, a certain need for a change had come into being. Their shared dissatisfaction became a source of subtle jokes. Natalie had profound reservations about Ken Livingstone's antisemitic views. "He is not a true antisemite," Eric would say to Natalie's distress, pushing up his glasses. "He's just anti-Israel with a touch of antisemitism." She was increasingly sensitive to anything even resembling antisemitism. Not that she hadn't encountered it before. She had heard comments at high school and college, but she'd learned to ignore them over the years. If an impolite customer mentioned "a Jewish lawyer," she went on with the conversation without blinking, absorbing the disrespectful words.

But Eric's observation that Zionism had changed the entire Jewish people implanted an unexpected seed of happiness within her—a seed that later generated resentment. Initially, she rejoiced thinking of herself as a new person. A new vitality existed within her, a feeling she ascribed to powerful people. But with it came a buried anger at the neighbor who asked her, time and again, when are *your* holidays. Words that were often completely innocent became an explicit reference to her being Jewish, and any criticism of Israel seemed like an attack on Jews.

Listening to Ken Livingstone, she contemplated voting for the Tories. She kept telling herself that she shared some criticisms of Israel; occupying other people for so many years was unjust; and if there was a threat to Israel's security, the country should seek a solution other than controlling a civilian population. Expanding Jewish settlements robbed the Palestinians of their land. However, any insinuation that there was a Jewish character type made her blood boil. She recalled her mother seeing photos of concentration camp survivors: she'd held her head as if she wanted to peel off her skin, collapsed into an armchair, and lit a cigarette that almost slipped from her shaking hands. "We should never ever keep quiet, Natalie," she kept saying to herself. "Never give up. Never be silenced." So Natalie had decided not to vote for Labour.

Eric listened patiently to Natalie's arguments, adopting a sympathetic expression, though bitter poison was already coursing through him, boring new pathways, outsmarting any attempt to block it. Something was changing, and he didn't know quite what it was; a certain truth, which used to be simple and obvious, was disintegrating. He kept asking himself what had gone wrong, but all his efforts to formulate a clear answer were futile. At night, he lay fully awake, trying to make sense of the change taking place in his life. Every moment a new observation emerged, replacing the previous one: people don't appreciate integrity anymore, the world is indifferent to the gap between truth and deception; people aren't rational—they only believe what they can see; whatever isn't on television doesn't exist; spilled blood is worthless if no one catches it on camera; dying children are tragic only when their distorted bodies are on the nightly news; the immense weight placed on visibility erodes confidence in simple truths; a man can get away with lies if he's brazen enough about it; sometimes it seems that assertiveness is the new god everyone worships; you can speak complete nonsense as long as you do it forcefully; devious politicians understand that nobody cares what they say as long as they seem confident; leaders don't even pretend they are working for the benefit of the public . . . Eventually, Eric closed his eyes and listened to Natalie's breathing. She seemed so much older when asleep. A slight movement of her mouth made her look like a toothless old woman.

Eric's firm was considered one of the best investment banks in London, and he was renowned for his financial acumen. He was teased when he invested in a small computer company, but it ended up yielding significant profits. An Indian insurance company, teetering on the brink of bankruptcy, made a remarkable turnaround and became a lucrative income source for the bank. He personally possessed shares in a minor bank that ultimately transformed into a prominent corporation. Friends sought his financial council. Investors followed his economic ventures religiously. He was a man who never failed to identify the potential of small businesses, and he never made reckless decisions.

But a few months earlier, there had been an unforeseen twist of events.

On a wintry morning, a man representing an African country approached Eric. In excellent English, he explained that his nation, ruled by an autocrat, intended to make a substantial investment in Britain, and the ruler had asked Eric's bank to manage it. Though Eric and his two partners were wealthy, this investment was entirely different, one that only countries and selected individuals could make. The partners called an urgent meeting, wanting to scrutinize the proposition, amazed at the magnitude of the offer. They began to gather information about the African ruler, who turned out to be rather dubious: he wasn't too mindful of human rights, deprived people of their property, and had no objection to children toiling from dawn to dusk.

Only the three partners were present at the meeting the next day; they'd sent the secretary home. Mr. Willis locked the meeting room door, and they all reclined into comfortable armchairs, looking at each other in embarrassment. The words that came up in the conversation—he is a dictator, indifferent to the suffering of his people, he takes advantage of children, transfers the country's fortune abroad, leaving his people hungry—floated around the room, hitting a door or a window and then fading away. It was all said so it would be heard; serve as evidence. A future report would include these words that were nothing but a thin veil covering what had been decided and could not be overturned: the firm would handle the African ruler's investment, ignoring the nature of his rule. Each partner gave in to greed, facing the enormous fortune, knowing that it was beyond his power to give up this unique opportunity. An immense, ancient wheel was turning; its axles, made of lava, never creaked or curved. *Rota Fortuna* had stopped this time for them, reaching out with a hand full of coins and precious stones, and if they didn't hurry and grab what had been offered to them, the wheel would turn again, and all that fortune would fall into the hands of others. Who would dare refuse Fortuna? Only a fool would turn down her presents, and who knew? In a moment, the wheel would turn again, and they might find themselves steeped in agony.

After the contract had been signed, Eric was in a contemplative mood for a couple of days, holding long debates with himself. At first, he mumbled that his weakness was fully exposed. Throughout his life, despite his secure financial situation, Eric advocated a fairer allocation of resources between the poor and the wealthy, made many donations to charities, and lately even joined an organization committed to supporting the education of underprivileged children in London. He'd argued repeatedly that politicians should never overlook moral considerations; eventually they were more important than meets the eye. He fully supported the Labour Party—the only party that cared for the weaker segments of society. But now, in an instant, he'd sold his values for money. And there was absolutely nothing lacking in his life. Eric was a wealthy man, living a comfortable life. Many envied him for the capital he'd managed to obtain. The repudiation of his moral standards made him bitter and desperate.

After a couple of days, a small, nearly invisible, crack was created in this self-blame. Not a rift, only a slight reservation, a combination of words that weren't a justification, God forbid, but only expressed a certain understanding: even had his investment bank declined this lucrative business opportunity, the reprehensible autocrat would have faced no repercussion. He would have immediately turned to another investment bank, which would gladly have represented him in Britain. A private business, successful as it might be, can't inflict significant harm upon the dictator. This could only be done by governments, international alliances—entities beyond his control. In truth, Eric himself could have done nothing to weaken the African ruler.

One might have expected Eric to dismiss such an obvious and trite argument, revealing nothing but human weakness and hopelessness. But it grew and expanded, developed and rooted. He could easily imagine a rival company swiftly sealing a deal with the autocrat before he changed his mind, publicizing it to attract fresh customers. He and his partners would disclose that they were initially approached yet declined to represent the African ruler. Some clients would rally behind them; they might even earn a modest headline in the inner pages of some newspaper, but the bulk of London's financial community would react with a blend of amazement and disdain: How could an investment bank turn down such an opportunity? The very essence of such a bank revolves around achieving financial prosperity; big money unlocks endless possibilities, enables the realization of ambitious projects. Refusing to expand one's capital was like tossing it all out the window. No doubt, a wealthy man was a blessed man, revered and adored. A person whose talents found complete and utter affirmation.

Strangely, though all of Eric's career had been dedicated to making money, only at the age of seventy did he clearly articulate its place in his life. As he was considering retirement, it turned out that having a fortune had far-reaching consequences. He tried to determine whether it had always been like that or that change had taken place in the last couple of years, but past deals were intricate and complex and difficult to recall, and his attempt always ended with a deep, liberating sigh. *Be that as it may, we all know a man is nothing but dust in the wind, and sometimes one has to accept one's fate*—he kept repeating these words, pondering how he would invest this newfound fortune.

His gradual distancing from his social activism generated skepticism mixed with some humor. Eric suddenly scorned those fighting for the weak, struggling for the underprivileged. The rights of the working class? Its leaders would give up their struggle if offered enough money, and indeed so would the blue-collar workers. Equality for women? Wealthy men like beautiful women. The failing public education system? If the teachers were offered positions in private schools, they would quickly trade their principles for higher pay. A constant protest against anyone who wasn't acting for his interest came into being as if it was a ridiculous and even slightly childish pretense. How could any intelligent person ignore the most fundamental human instinct to get the most for himself?

As the election for the mayor of London was close, Eric felt uncomfortable and even irritated. Every time he thought about the election, a variety of complaints against the Labour Party piled up: not only was Ken Livingston an antisemite, but the principles of the party were too inclined to the socialist Left, detached from reality. An unrestrained support for any decision the unions made, an unquestioned solidarity with any socialist party worldwide, a tendency to adopt archaic socialist ideas—Eric kept listing the ideological shortcomings as if they served as evidence of something recognized by all but left unspoken. A new spirit prevailed these days; efficient, determined, lacking hesitation, every man for himself.

Standing in line to vote, he still considered voting for Brian Paddick, the independent candidate. He detested Boris Johnson. But suddenly, he felt he had been put to the test. A rapid pulse, an unfamiliar heartbeat—Eric felt he was standing at some crossroads, though he waved his hand in contempt and muttered to himself that it was only the mayor of London they were talking about. The line got shorter, and Natalie held his arm somewhat excitedly; he kept telling himself that at his age, there were no tests, but a quiver indicated that he was facing a decision. And though he kept asking himself in bewilderment what exactly the test was and what the desired outcome was, after he deposited the envelope into the box, he couldn't tell if he had passed the test or failed it.

January 2009

The investigation had a single conclusion, leaving no room for doubt. For two months, Ben had examined Handex's computers and consulted a friend who had served with him in army intelligence. He looked into every possibility and found no trace that Handex had been hacked. Therefore, Ben could only come up with two possible explanations: one, that the computer was hacked by professionals who could disguise any evidence, and act without leaving a trace. This would be a professional job requiring significant funds. The Swiss company was very successful, marketing numerous products in Europe and the United States. It had been established at the beginning of the twentieth century. Years of accumulating assets and two world wars that generated profits, they most likely had a fortune.

The other possibility, a more distressing one, was that the software had been stolen from Handex in a different manner. Possibly one of the workers had managed to copy it and sell it to the Swiss firm secretly. Ben lay awake for hours at night, wondering who could have stolen the software. The loyalty of every worker to Handex was examined, focusing on family conditions that might require extra cash, unreasonable hours at the office, an unexpected relationship between employees. A couple of weeks ago, he accidentally overheard that a senior programmer was having an affair with an engineer. Someone mentioned it at lunch, making everyone chuckle, as Ben tried to conceal that he knew nothing about it. Later, he reproached himself. They're having lunch alone, sitting side by side at staff meetings; he'd once entered the engineer's office and was surprised to find the programmer there. He made a lame excuse and left.

A young orthopedic doctor with some knowledge in engineering was often seen doing strange things: opening and closing the photocopy machine, assisting the secretary in filing documents, fumbling at the locker that held old parts of the robotic arm—what was he looking for? One worker and another, they all turned into suspects. Every employee could have an urgent need for money. Nava was a single mother saving for her daughter's future. Since the crisis between him and Ofir had taken place, she hadn't bothered to conceal her reservations about the firm, arguing that the creativity had been lost. All her demands—we should provide social rights to self-employed cleaners, we should employ Israeli Arabs and make sure we don't discriminate against them, why doesn't Handex have a disabled worker?—may well be a smart disguise for a simple motive. Even Abraham could betray the company. He had six children; clearly, he needed money. He'd find it easy to justify himself. He felt he was devoting his life to a higher cause. The settlement of Israel fulfilled an ancient divine vision. He may have stolen the software to support the settlement in Judea and Samaria.

But the more he thought about it, the more an idea began to take shape, despite his desire to suppress it. Why not Ofir? Maybe he sold the software to the Swiss company. The suspicion, which at first was only a crumb of thought, began to expand and thicken until it became a well-defined idea. Yes, it was Ofir, no doubt. Naively, he didn't suspect him in the first place. Examining Handex's workers made him ignore the most obvious option, one which was nearly self-evident. How hadn't he thought of it?! Ofir's thirst for revenge was unquestionable. He must have felt like a fool for failing to see that his best friend had betrayed him. It must have been a terrible humiliation, a sort of abscess that even when it seemed that it had been fully cured, kept festering within, emitting bubbling stench that would eventually break and crack open.

Lying awake in bed before the rays heralding the sunrise filtrated into the sky, watching Talia—fast asleep, she wasn't smiling; her feminine face looked plain and ordinary, her mouth slightly open, her graceless peasant's hand with its short fingers resting on the blanket—he flew with Ofir to Switzerland to sell the software. The elegant hotel he must have stayed in, the head of the company who probably met him at a disclosed place in Zurich. Was the money given in cash? Did he carry it in a briefcase? Did he demand they sign a document that would never acknowledge where the software came from?

As a soft, pink light slowly mixed into the black, starless sky, envy materialized again, a monster with two heads drooling thick, dark spit. Surely Ofir had received an enormous fortune, but he had had to return what he had stolen. Ben was positive Ofir was giggling as he collected piles of cash, whereas he had been tormented for years. And though the robotic arm resulted from years of mutual effort, Ofir would be a wealthy man, but he would only be an affluent one. The anger that envy generated was so familiar as if six years hadn't gone by since a long friendship had been exposed for what it was—a locked jewelry box carefully guarded, stories passed by word of mouth about the stones hidden in it, diamonds plucked from the bowels of the earth, immense and unpolished, yet one day one drawer opens accidentally and it turns out to be empty. And as the other drawers are pulled open, they reveal nothing but mildew and dry dust.

The sudden wrath that overtook him drove him out of bed and carried him to the kitchen. He looked into the fridge and then slammed the metal door with a kick. The last cry of a night bird before dawn came from the yard; rain pelted the windows. Ben looked around, wanting to throw a plate or a cup to the floor, but remained motionless. Finally, he went to the children's room. He stood by David's bed, watching the golden curls surrounding his face. Sleep deprived it of its mischievous nature, and now Ben thought his son looked sad, reminding him of his father's bitterness. The muscular, childish body was sprawled across the bed diagonally as if he wanted to ensure no one shared his soft mattress. He then turned to look at Eden. She was sleeping on her stomach, breathing deeply, a very slim toddler with straight brown hair dispersed on the pillow. She seems so fragile, he thought, and then reproached himself. Talia must have looked like that at her age, and she'd developed into a very healthy woman.

Watching his children deep in sleep curbed his anger. He turned to the living room and lay down on the cozy sofa. With body fully relaxed, he tried again to guess how Ofir had sold the software: Did he tell Laurie about it? Did she travel with him? Did they go to a ski resort in the Alps? Did he buy her a super-expensive piece of jewelry? As he added more details to this imaginary journey, it gradually became an obvious development of past events. Clearly, a man who is betrayed by his best friend seeks revenge; there is no other explanation. And what better way is there to get payback? It's an elementary human response; when a child is hit, he wants to strike back, even when the quarrel has ended. Ofir processed his disappointments into a plan. When he returned to Handex after discovering the theft, he looked bony; a body of a young man with a dreary old man within it. But apparently, he'd managed to conceal the pain and create the illusion that he'd overcome the insult.

Strangely, the thought of Ofir acting out of revenge created a sour disappointment. Though Ben kept telling himself it was ridiculous—he more than anyone could understand how frustration and bitter envy can drive a man to wrongdoing—despair overwhelmed him. He crossed his hands behind his head, his body tensed, and his left leg shook uncontrollably. The light dispersed across the sky revealed dark, dense clouds. In a moment, a storm would break, and light capillaries would slit the sky. How come Ofir betrayed his parents' moral principles? They used to disdain people who went astray and mock corrupt public figures. More than once he had heard Ofir's father argue that a liberal society rests upon two pillars: moral values and a genuine concern for fellow men. People must care for each other, not only for themselves. They believed this was the true meaning of an advanced society. And now, their son had ignored the moral imperative prohibiting theft, and he didn't care that his acts resulted in laying off a third of the company's staff.

But delving into moral judgments was uncomfortable; Ben knew it might lead to calculations he preferred to avoid. Thus, he decided to stop at once this inner conversation about Ofir. A moment before a cry emanated from the nursery, he concluded that Ofir used to embody a promise that ceased to exist. And though he couldn't quite tell what the promise was and how it was to be fulfilled, he had to admit that his envy of Ofir was cut to the size of this promise, and its length and width became part of his own body.

In the evening, as he drove his new SUV on Ayalon highway, he was smiling. The morning's heavy clouds had disappeared, and, as often happens, they left an empty sky and thin air. After a storm passes, the sky reveals what's missing: intense winds mixed with huge water drops and the sound of thunder. Ben left Michelle lying naked in bed, on a bedsheet made of pure silk, covered with a fine down duvet. After her divorce, she invited Ben again into her house. She kept the spacious apartment in the center of Tel Aviv; her ex-husband had purchased an apartment in Jaffa. Two successful lawyers, they had enough money for both of them to live comfortably after they split. When Ben asked her mockingly if she still "sees life as it really is," her face tightened, and for a moment he thought she would cry. But, to his utmost surprise, she elaborated in great detail how she wouldn't let anyone take what she'd earned with hard work. "Poor people always think they deserve more and must be compensated for their hardship. But it's not true. We shouldn't give them what isn't theirs. If you donate some money, they immediately ask for more. You give them a finger, and they want the hand."

"Who are 'they'?" Ben asked.

The strange mouth curved again, part up, part down, with a mixture of displeasure and contempt.

"Poor people who don't have money because they don't try hard enough, but they envy those who do have it," Michelle replied.

"I thought there were those who get everything easily and those who have to struggle for everything."

"I've worked hard and made good money, and I have no intention of sharing it with anyone. Surely not with people who think they deserve more only because others are more affluent. Someone will always argue that what you have is theirs. But we should never accept this. If they want money, they should work harder."

From Michelle's place, he went to meet a friend, a businessman who invited him to a Likud Party meeting before the coming election. Despite Ben's protests—*I'm not really interested in politics, I object to the settlements in the West Bank*—he promised to go to the event in Ness Ziona. Commotion filled the place as they got to the main town hall. Though only a minority of the Ness Ziona residents supported the Likud, an apparent attempt had been made to make the place look crowded. Uplifting Mediterranean music came from loudspeakers at the entrance to the building, Likud flags were flying everywhere, and young women offered stickers. Ben was taken aback by the loud music and nearly stepped back, but the friend laid a heavy arm on his shoulder, pushed him inside, saying, "Come in and take a look, just once. If you don't like it, you can always leave."

When he'd been in the hall, against his better judgment, he'd felt a childish joy. He laughed out loud at any silly joke, overpowered by a spirit of unrestrained unity; whoever was there was a partner and a friend. He couldn't help but observe that there were almost no Ashkenazim in the hall, and he quickly answered an unasked question, *So what? What's wrong with that?* The Israeli flags around the podium were nice and bright. He felt that the massive sign with the slogan "Strong in security—Strong in economy" expressed a simple, undeniable truth. The loud cries of "Hu, ha, who is there? The next prime minister of Israel" as Benjamin Netanyahu entered the hall almost made him deaf, and he too began to shout. An older woman sitting in front of him, her hair as yellow as lemon and her face wrinkled, turned back and smiled at him, showing crooked teeth. Next to her sat an obese man yelling "Well done" at the podium as each speaker finished. At the end of the meeting, overcome by exaltation, he walked to the parking lot with his friend, who put his heavy arm around his shoulders again and said, "So you're happy you came, aren't you?"

But as he began to drive, the exaltation vanished. It was raining heavily. Irritated, Ben turned on the turn signal instead of the windshield wipers, and as he tried to fix it, he accidentally turned on the high-beam lights. Finally, the SUV glided between the puddles and headed for Tel Aviv.

An impartial observer might have thought that Ben was shamefully exposed. Such a successful and talented man yelling like a boor, uncovering a side of himself he usually concealed. Maybe he would even have looked into Ben's life, wondering where else he exhibited such unbridled enthusiasm, a penchant to be part of the crowd, a need to remove emotional inhibitions and be caught up in this atmosphere of unity. He might have thought that the struggle within Ben's spirit, torn between a Sephardi father who wished his children to study the Torah and an Ashkenazi mother who encouraged them to get professional educations, contributed to this emotional nakedness. He might even think of Ben as a man who'd returned to his spiritual origin, which he had previously suppressed.

But not so Ben.

He examined these arguments briefly and didn't rule them out. But in his profound wisdom, he knew that tonight he had finally managed to find the abyss in his life, which despite his many efforts, he had failed to detect so far. He was like a man attempting to reach another continent; and to do so, he had to walk on cracked, arid earth. He stretched a leg forward and carefully touched the new land with his toes, but then he found that it had changed beyond recognition and was no longer the place he had been eager to reach. Though the streets and buildings were prettier and shinier than ever, well-lit and glittering, a sour spirit prevailed, dry and cold; every man for himself, improving his own life and watching others distrustfully. Immediately, he leaped back, trying to hold fast to his world. But the apprehension that he had ventured to leave the old world was already deeply rooted, and the only thing he could do was look down and see the ground opening beneath him. Ben gave a short harrumph to illustrate a strange, almost absurd, thought: *I miss Ofir's parents*, he said to himself. *Not Ofir, but his family, his father's ridiculous speeches about a progressive society, his mother always hesitating and commenting about her husband's arguments while preparing dinner, and their constant exploration of questions of truth and justice. I wish I could meet them now.* And though Ben adopted a strange smile, tears filled his eyes, eclipsing their strange glamor when they saw what couldn't be refuted.

As the car approached Tel Aviv, the heavy rain stopped, but the wet towers still seemed blurred, and the tiny lights mixed into each other. Dark clouds passed in the humid sky, insisting in vain on drifting eastward to remote deserts. Ben relaxed in the driver's seat and drove slowly, immersed in thought. The glowing buildings and the glossy road gradually dissolved the impression of the Likud meeting. His eyes were half closed, and he didn't pay attention to the road, driving almost automatically. *Why should I care?* he heard his own voice say, whispering to himself in a slightly humorous tone. *It makes no difference who wins the election; life won't change. Why not vote for the Likud? What's wrong with their slogans?* Every party has a couple of sentences people repeat. True, the populist atmosphere was a bit excessive, vacillating quickly between hatred of Arabs and Leftists and an intensified unity of people who were called "Israel lovers." But the atmosphere was warm and homey. And come to think of it, there's nothing wrong with a party encouraging members of the lower class to take part in politics. But in truth—here the inner voice grew louder and adopted a more determined tone—*the only thing that matters is what would be good for me; which party would prove beneficial for Handex.* Any other aspect should be ignored. Strange things proved beneficial; like the Swiss company stealing Handex's software.

The theft of the software led to an improvement of the production process, resulting in higher profits. Another component of the arm was outsourced for manufacturing in China. To cut down costs, several programmers were laid off, and a portion of the software development was outsourced to an Indian firm. The apprehension about potential layoffs motivated everyone to put in more effort. A senior engineer suddenly came up with idea of employing lighter metal for a specific section of the robotic arm, which enhanced movement precision. Ultimately, by the final quarter of the year, the company's activity increased by two percent.

Thinking about the success of Handex encouraged Ben. Despite some obstacles, Handex was a highly esteemed firm with a wide range of economic endeavors, a company where successful programmers and engineers were eager to work. The profits increased, the forecast was very optimistic, hospitals around the globe placed orders for the new model of the robotic arm and occasionally faced a year-long wait for its delivery. The Swiss company's service lagged behind that of Handex, and now the cost of the robotic arm from the two companies had become nearly identical.

Ben's satisfaction with Handex's success always embarrassed him. He found it hard to admit how much he enjoyed his professional success. When he reflected on it, he sometimes forced himself to think of his children to tame his pleasure, his strong son and delicate daughter; David's courage, Eden's sweet face. But all those cunning tricks aimed against himself were only helpful for a couple of moments. Then the images of his family vanished, and he pondered about further developing the robotic arm, using new materials, and the many hospitals interested in purchasing it.

Odd, he said to himself as he was driving along Ayalon highway, his SUV splashing water on both sides, merging into a bottleneck of cars, and slowing down as heavy rain began falling again; *the pleasure of success isn't all about money.* People tend to think the reward is a luxury lifestyle, but it isn't entirely true. He now realized beyond any doubt that his satisfaction was almost unrelated to his affluent lifestyle. If I didn't have a family, I could live very modestly, like my father, he whispered to himself. Had I won the lottery, I would live extravagantly without a sense of achievement. No, money was only a pleasant consequence. A clear confirmation that he'd managed to fulfill his ambitions. A social stamp. The unequivocal success of Handex was a sort of blessing, an irrefutable affirmation of his talent—maybe even a divine signal. Perhaps this was how a man received a sign from God, letting him know he was walking on the right path? A divine message that despite everything, he was living his life properly? Maybe it was a reward for good deeds?

As he parked his car at home, he suddenly heard a man's voice behind him. He looked around and saw no one, and then he chuckled. It was his father's voice that he had been hearing, weak and slightly rough, emerging from within him, from an inner pocket that never heals, telling him sullenly, reproachfully, almost angrily: *God helps whoever helps himself, how many times do I have to say this?! How many times?!*

February 5, 2009

A man of about forty-five or fifty stands in the alley where he grew up, looking around in irritation and bewilderment. His gaze roves over familiar details: the tree, the stairs, the parking lot. He looks around, anticipating an inner echo, but nothing emerges. Stillness. Utter alienation. Estrangement. He silences any internal conversation, listening expectantly to a forgotten tune, longing for his childhood, but the only thing that surfaces is vague resentment. In his desperation, he decides to focus on the details: the stone at the end of the stairs is still loose despite letters sent to the municipality for forty years requesting it to be fixed; a fragrant shrub next to the fence withers entirely in the winter and recovers miraculously in spring; the green leaves of the tree at the top of the stairs rustle pleasantly in the wind; on a particular stone in the alley, a heart is engraved; even the two stairs leading to his parents' house are so familiar, made of white stone with dark spots. But it's useless. Though he knows this alley perfectly well, he is in a foreign land, in a city he's never visited. The more familiar things he sees, the deeper is his feeling that he's never been here before, and today is the first time he has ever set foot in this place. His childhood memories of leaping up the steps that once seemed high, or balancing on the fence that appeared to be such a huge hurdle, only generate a vacuum, a sort of boredom mixed with slight ire. Where, he wonders, is the web that connects me to this alley? To my childhood? He looks up at the rustling tree; maybe a memory that would awaken joy or agony is hiding there. But the tree top waves gently, making a rustle sweet to any human ear.

Joseph Stern had passed away following months of recurring appointments with senior cardiologists, consultations on a malfunctioning heart valve, and numerous medical tests. He was found dead in bed one morning. The Filipina woman looking after Sarit, who had been diagnosed with Alzheimer's at a relatively young age, went into his room and found him lying on his back, pale and cold. She immediately called Ofir's sister, who told her two brothers that their father was gone.

When Ofir told Laurie in a choked voice that his father had passed away, the growing wall between them cracked slightly. She stretched her round arms out and hugged him firmly. At an early morning hour, engaged in the daily routine, the very pragmatic state of mind had shattered as tears filled his eyes. They hadn't hugged like that since Ofir's mental collapse. His recovery had been marked by practical conversations, well-phrased questions, and an endeavor to avoid impediments. Yet the effort to skirt pain generates indifference; an over-practical spirit often transforms into disappointment. But, as Ofir put his cell phone down on the table and said, "my father is dead," the vigilance that had become a part of him halted, and he let her embrace him, his body limp and a single tear running down his slender cheek.

He sometimes looked at Laurie and wondered what had gone wrong. How did this relationship become so comfortable, lacking the emotional intensity from which it was born? He used to watch her thinking this was true love, two souls knotted together. Her devotion after his crisis created not only gratitude but a belief in the healing power of love. Her kiss, touching his sandy lips in the dark room, was burning and sweet, and her tears that dropped on his face soothed his acute pain for a single moment.

But all that was over now.

Come to think of it, he reflected, *love began to dissipate even before that.* He couldn't tell exactly when, but he was sure that a couple of months earlier he had felt a sort of distance, not from Laurie but from the emotional element that produces such intense emotions. An inner pattern began to crack, inadvertently letting the fervor out and keeping the practical intentions in. His world became narrower, and he liked it. It's easier to deal with mundane questions, running Handex, assisting his parents, taking care of Abigail, and enjoying sex, than with the soul's inexplicable turmoil.

A couple of months after he began to recuperate, this pragmatic side of him, which counterbalanced his restless spirit, took shape. Managing Handex without exchanging a word with Ben, taking part in household chores, and looking after his mother with her Alzheimer's, became more natural every passing day, gradually removing past anguish and resulting in a certain satisfaction. He and Laurie ran the family in a sensible, comfortable manner, almost without any arguments; each person had his own role. The practical spirit generated some tranquility, as if the family was an efficient factory, making the most of each person. A man, a woman, two children—each had his place. Twice a week, he and Laurie had sex, giving pleasure to each other skillfully, as if it were a mission to make each other emit a deep moan. They then fell asleep on opposite sides of the bed, the vacuum between them relaxing comfortably, stretching its arms and legs, every time taking a slightly bigger part of the wide bed.

But when he turned to her that morning and said in a broken voice, "My father is dead," a different light flickered in his dark eyes. For a single moment, the Ofir whom Laurie had known in the past surfaced; a man as sharp as a razor yet inclined to be sentimental, brave yet alarmed by a baby stumbling and falling. Laurie's arms held him close, and he clasped her like a child. But then he stood erect, detaching himself from her motherly body, saying, "I need to take care of the funeral," again driving a wedge between them.

The funeral was postponed by a day so Laurie's mother could come from London. Ofir stayed in Jerusalem with his mother, who kept asking why Joseph wasn't making her a cup of tea and insisted that Ofir call him immediately. At night, he wandered restlessly around the house, sitting by his father's desk and looking into the drawers. In the upper drawer, he found his collection of pens. His father loved stationery and had pens, pencils, and erasers. For his seventy-fifth birthday, Ofir had bought him a lovely Mont Blanc pen with his name engraved on it. It was now inside the box at the center of the drawer. The second drawer had letters his father had gotten for his retirement, printed on paper with The Hebrew University logo: a note of thanks from the president of the university and the provost, an album with photos of him with renowned visitors. In the third drawer, Ofir found the last years' paychecks divided into years and months, organized in transparent binders, every year arranged from January to December. The lower drawer was locked. Thinking that maybe it should be left locked, he tried to open it. After several failed attempts, he decided to look for the key, but couldn't find it anywhere.

The fear of the locked drawer, holding secrets his father wished to conceal, made him shake it hard and try to break it. He couldn't tell whether he feared it would open or rather that it remain locked. As he was about to give it up, a strange click was heard and then a scrape, and the drawer slid open. Old, frayed photos lay inside the drawer. Ofir held them gently as if they were living people. An elegant woman with two children smiling at the camera. The same woman on her wedding day, with a very grave expression. The two children at a slightly older age. The photos' borders were ragged as if they had been handled endlessly, and small tear-like spots covered them. The last photo was of a young man resembling Ofir, with dark eyes, a narrow face, and straight hair. Ofir turned the picture over. On its back, his father had written: *My cousin, Herschel, who the Nazis, may they rot in hell, killed in 1943.*

As he collapsed onto the sofa in the living room it made a light wail, crying quietly. In the silence of the night he could hear the springs sigh, surrendering to Ofir's body. He put the photos in his wallet, but then changed his mind. His father's family members who had died in the Holocaust were now placed again in the lower drawer, and Ofir stretched out on the sofa, looking at the ceiling. The paintings on the wall, the faded carpets, the furniture that used to be elegant, the ticking clock next to the window all seemed so familiar and unreal. *I could close my eyes and describe each detail in this room,* he thought, *and still, it seems as if I'm in a strange place, a hotel I used to visit. Only a couple of days ago I sat here with my father, watching the election broadcast on television.*

The coming elections had sparked a vitality Joseph seemed to have lost. In his last years, he looked neglected, maybe due to his wife's illness. A man who was always dressed stylishly, a blazer and tie in winter and summer, now walked around at home wearing gray sweatpants and a shabby, mustard-colored shirt. A close friend from his time in the kibbutz passed away. He met another one living in Jerusalem very rarely. Apathy overtook him; he surrendered to old age. But political discussions always generated both excitement and temper.

"Look at Barak and Livni![1] It's impossible to win the election this way. Two people who have nothing at all with the values of the Left. Will they fight for the interests of the people?" Though Ofir knew precisely how the conversation would unfold, beginning with a general complaint and quickly developing into a speech about the Left losing its fundamentals, for some strange reason and unlike his usual self, he openly disagreed with his father, saying, "Dad, you also left the kibbutz. Despite your support of socialism, you chose to live in Jerusalem." Now, after his death, Ofir was tormented by the memory of his own words. But only a couple of days ago, sitting on the sofa he was now lying on and his father relaxing in his comfortable armchair, he had felt somewhat content. He'd had enough of the sentimental memories of the kibbutz, which in his old age became more vibrant, embracing new details. To his utter surprise, his father had turned his eyes to the television and said nothing. As Ofir watched him, bewildered, a small smile spread across his lips shaped like matches, and he replied, "It doesn't matter if you live in a kibbutz or in Jerusalem, on a farm, or in Tel Aviv. The question is if you want to help others. It's true on a personal level and even more so ideologically. Are people willing to work for others or only for themselves?

---

1   In the 2009 election, Tzipi Livni was the leader of the politically centrist Kadima Party and Ehud Barak was head of the left-leaning Labor Party.

Are politicians willing to act in a way that isn't purely advantageous for themselves? The heart of the matter is concern for other people, which affects everything: social rights, economic justice, investment in education, and even the struggle to end the occupation! It is all derived from this question. Barak and Livni are no worse than others, but they are a product of an ideology that consecrates self-interest, and therefore they won't lead the Left to win the election."

Ofir concealed a smile.

"Dad, you don't really think that people who don't believe in socialism don't want a better world?"

"I think that their ideology presupposes that if every individual were to act in their own interest, society would be better off. Each person could fully develop their talents, leading to a flourishing society."

"Isn't it obvious that people try harder when they act for their own benefit? When they compete with each other and eventually make more money? If you had stayed in the kibbutz, you couldn't have lived in such comfort," Ofir said.

"Yes, apparently that's true," Joseph said and fell silent.

Ofir watched the television. Ehud Barak was speaking, but he couldn't tell what he was talking about. Suddenly he heard his father's agitated voice, high-pitched, shaky yet determined, "But who needs all that if a man lives alone? Who needs achievements if you have no one to share them with?"

"Lives alone? Who lives alone? A man acts for himself and his family. Competition is only with strangers, not with the ones closest to you," Ofir replied.

Now, a couple of days after Joseph's death, these were his farewell words; he had deposited in Ofir's hands questions with which he would have to struggle for the rest of his life. Annoyingly, the entire conversation was fixed in his mind and couldn't be removed. Though he tried to disregard it, telling himself that his father's arguments were ridiculous—he even chuckled out loud thinking about them—the words "live alone" were fixed in Ofir's mind, rooting and creating doubt that quickly transformed into a heavy burden.

And as if his father were going out of his way to be proven right even after his death, Ofir was irritated by things he typically ignored: Eric called to apologize; he was sorry, but he couldn't attend the funeral; he had a business commitment he couldn't cancel; if he traveled to Israel he would lose a fortune; he was sure Ofir knew how sad he was that Joseph had passed away. His wife asked to postpone the funeral by at least a day; if she traveled to Israel she would stay longer, which required special arrangements. Very few friends of his father came to the shiva. Most were ill and could hardly leave home. Only ten workers from Handex attended the funeral, though Ofir arranged for transportation from the office to the cemetery. The Hebrew University sent a representative to the funeral who had never known his father, and in his eulogy, he spoke about loyal administrators. During the shiva, Laurie had asked a several times if he would be staying in Jerusalem; she couldn't take a week off, and they had to decide where Abigail and Daniel would stay. Abigail kept asking when they would return home; she was bored, and Daniel wandered restlessly among the mourners.

Ofir could ignore all this. The lame excuses, the embarrassing apologies, the house he could hardly stand, even the oppressive walk on Hakhaluts Street. He looked at two remote stone walls. As a child, he'd been so proud that he could jump from one to the other. Now he gazed at them, and all he could see was chiseled stone and cement. The childhood memory had disintegrated and turned into dust.

But the new idea created anger as if he were caught in the act.

An obscure thread existed separately from fleeting thoughts, a form of reflection that twists and rolls in an unseen space, spiraling beyond joy and sadness, hope and longing. Once it surfaced, it was unimaginable that it hadn't always been there. *The advanced digital community Handex had established to aid hospitals using the robotic arm could also serve alternative purposes.*

Unintentionally, Handex had generated a medical platform. Why should it be limited to the distribution of complementary products? With considerable effort, they fostered global communication among hospitals, facilitating medical clarifications and offering guidance on operating the robotic arm. Doctors were able to consult each other. Why not use it to sell and distribute medical equipment? The potential profit would be huge. Medical equipment is complex and requires superior skills; thus, the interaction among professionals unrelated to Handex is imperative.

Months later, when this idea was applied successfully and had begun to generate a substantial profit, Ofir admitted that his father's death had caused a burst of creativity. But in the shiva, since he'd immediately understood the potential profit, a strange fury had spread quickly, as if his dead father had defeated him. Here, not only was no one attempting to alleviate his pain, treating the funeral and the shiva as nothing but burdens, but when he had such a brilliant idea, he had no one to share it with. Except Ben. Of course, he would have to share it with him. He wasn't anticipating any disagreement.

Ben was immersed in developing the software, uninterested in any other aspects of the firm. And if he objected, Ofir could always force his way.

A man has thousands of conversations in his life, endless words are spoken, reflections surface, opinions articulated, disputes echo, and still—annoyingly—one conversation is ingrained in his mind, fixed in some inner closet, and can't be removed. "Live alone," these words sank into Ofir's spirit and wouldn't be wiped out. To make matters worse, they were associated with his professional achievements. Already in the shiva sitting next to his mother, who now wasn't hesitating anymore but rather smiled at everyone and asked why they were paying her a visit, the link his father set between achievements and solitude was fully established. Ofir could see himself as an elderly man, adorned and lonely, wealthy and desolate. And though he shouted at himself silently that he was a family man, married and a father of two, he couldn't drive out the older man who had settled within him, with brilliant ideas yet living in solitude. When Laurie served him coffee and cake, he'd raised his eyes and said quietly, "You can go home with the children. There's no need for you to stay here." He'd found affirmation of his convictions in her response: "All right. We're leaving." As Abigail pulled her mother out of the apartment impatiently, saying, "Mom, let's go. It's boring here!" he sighed, and told himself that though he found it hard to accept, his father might have been right.

December 2010

It was the hottest December ever. Yellow desert winds pushed away rain clouds slowly advancing from the distant north; the air was full of sand particles, and dust lay thick on the ground. Thorn bushes that couldn't quench their thirst raised filthy black nails, and trees, their leaves plucked by the wind, shivered like bare skeletons. The soil crumbled, allowing huge ant colonies that mistakenly thought summer had never ended to dig out grains. And, as a minuscule spark ignited, burning fires swept across bare hills and pine tree forests, sending a gigantic tongue of fire into the sky, swallowing the entirety of Mount Carmel.[1]

Laurie and Ofir's divorce was unbelievably simple and quick. It's hard to imagine how two people who had been married for fourteen years, had two children, and had accumulated so much wealth, could separate so easily. Two hard-working lawyers handled the legal documents, though there were no disputes. They quibbled over a minor article to justify their excessive fee until Ofir determined it made no difference. Laurie remained in their apartment; Ofir bought a new apartment a few blocks away.

Laurie thought separating from Ofir had evolved naturally; a man and a woman who no longer lived as a couple but rather had become tenants sharing an apartment. Both were thoughtful and disliked quarrels, making their comfortable life easy. Laurie met with Michael several times a week; Ofir never asked where she was or how she spent her day. The daily routine was kept almost without glitches, making Abigail and Daniel tranquil.

Ofir's new vitality in the last year had broken a hidden balance, placing a heavy weight on one side of the scale and turning over the other. He was immersed in work again, as he was when Handex started. Laurie hadn't seen him smiling like that for years, telling jokes that made everyone laugh. A touch of light was shining now in his dark eyes; his body was upright, and he dressed elegantly, hurrying off to the office in the morning, kissing his children, closing the door, and whistling in the hallway.

---

1 In 2010, a deadly fire broke out in the Carmel Mountains, claiming many lives.

The man living next to Laurie, absorbed in his new project, was now full of the joy he had seemed to have lost. The new challenge, using the digital community to distribute medical products, created fresh energy, which made him happy. Once again he was joking with friends, going to work early in the morning and returning home late at night. But this energy, like a man waking up after years of slumber, wasn't directed at Laurie but only at his work. Executing the new idea, its many applications, potential partners, skillful management—Ofir was absorbed by an exciting world that did not include his wife.

Since she had become the contemporary art curator five months ago, Ofir's inner solitude had deepened. He'd never expressed reservations about her career, though the source of their wealth was the profits of Handex. On the contrary, years ago, he had asked his father to take advantage of his connections to find a job matching her skills. But when she told him she had been appointed curator, he looked at her with some hostility and said casually, "Very nice." An almost philosophical curiosity made her ask him if he was happy for her, a sort of provocation between people who hardly ever quarreled. He stood up stiffly and replied politely, "I'm sure you will be a great curator," put some papers in his briefcase, and turned towards the door.

"Suddenly you became a competitor," Michael said, and she smiled, wondering how a curator could compete with a successful businessman like Ofir. "Now you are professionally successful, just like him. Not in his field, but still very successful. He finds it hard to digest."

She and Michael were relaxing on the balcony of the small apartment they'd rented together in the northern part of Tel Aviv, gazing at the eucalyptus trees shading the entire street. They weren't sure if they wanted to live on such a dark street, where sunrays never penetrated the broad branches. But the green dome covering the passage produced deep tranquility. They met every day at the small apartment, and it gradually became their home. An old quilt that Laurie had kept was now spread across the bed; she served lunch and dinner with porcelain dinnerware she'd brought from London and never used. A poster of an exhibition in the National Gallery Ofir disliked was now hanging on the wall, and Michael's many books accumulated on the shelves. And as Michael was an amateur gardener, after a couple of months, pots full of blossoming plants filled the balcony. The disturbing memory of the hotel next to the beach faded away. The smell of the sea was replaced by the fresh odor of green leaves with a touch of smoky air—the scent of the eucalyptus' trunk's bark falling to the ground.

On a hot winter day, they sat on the balcony and watched the trees bowing their heads down and stretching their arms to the ground, overwhelmed and exhausted by the unexpected heat. Dust filled the sky in the early afternoon; the air was heavy. Sparrows drank water from a tiny puddle around a hose in the yard. Under the green dome shrouding the street, a yellow desert that somehow arrived on the shores of Tel Aviv materialized, waiting silently and impatiently for the wind to carry it back to the open space, where everything lay bare and nothing conceals the sun and the moon.

Laurie relaxed on the straw chair and put her feet on a stool. The small wrinkles around her eyes shrank in the heat, and sweat accumulated on her pale, nearly transparent skin. Her black hair was pulled up in a ponytail; her body was full but graceful. She wore a dark dress that emphasized her feminine figure. Michael looked at her, always fully focused, as if she carried a hidden secret. Since they had rented this apartment and spent much time together, an unfamiliar happiness had engulfed him. He no longer seemed like a man who found himself in a foreign land, his appearance displaying his desire to remain a stranger. Now he often smiled, sometimes laughed, and was not taken aback by inquisitive, rude words. As the old lady living on the first floor asked him if they were a married couple, he smiled kindly at her and replied in a humorous tone, "No, but we're good friends."

Watching eastern winds blending with Mediterranean haze, sand and dust vortex under clouds wandering over from Europe, Laurie turned to him and said, "You won't believe what I did today. I fired my assistant."

"What?! I know you can't stand her, but you fired her?"

"Well, not exactly fired—transferred. She has tenure and won't be left without a job. But I told her I didn't want her as my assistant anymore. She's a horrible woman; lazy, always gossiping, and takes advantage of having tenure to skip work. I really can't stand her. I asked her to list very few artworks in a storeroom a week ago. Today she said she hadn't had time to do it!"

"But what will the director of the museum say? And who will take her place?"

"I will insist that I can't work with her. And as for replacing her, I was thinking of Hamid. I want him to be my assistant."

Laurie and Hamid became friends, ignoring captious looks and open criticism. Hamid's parents wondered why the curator had visited him at home twice. Ofir inquired about their relationship, saying he had no objection and asking if it had to do with him being Arab. People at the museum were surprised that Laurie had invited the young Israeli Arab into her office. She often argued that the connection between artists and the curator should be limited. But a similar way of thinking of two people, even if they belong to different worlds, creates affinity: the books they both liked, a partiality towards particular artworks, a reservation of discussing only the technical aspects of art. Hamid was interested in the principles of artistic expression, the potential power of photography, combining the artistic and documentary perspectives, and its main disadvantage: the role of random circumstances. He deliberated whether he should take color photos that create an illusion of reality or black and white photos that make the spectators aware that they are looking at a world processed especially for them. Consulting Laurie led to long conversations, emails, and book exchanges.

When he told her he had been engaged a year ago, unintentionally she uttered a cry of surprise. He had never mentioned a girlfriend or a spouse and only portrayed his job at the family furniture factory with humor. When she asked who his bride was, it turned out Hamid hardly knew her. His parents had found a match, a girl from a respected family; her parents owned a restaurant, her brother was a doctor, and she studied social work at the university. Laurie's eyes were full of surprise. It never occurred to her that a man like him would marry a woman his parents chose. Hamid laughed as he saw her amazement and said, "I know what you're thinking, but I am happy. You could think of marriage in different ways. I want a stable life. I work hard, and I want to keep photographing. I need a woman who will support this desire, and there is no reason why my parents shouldn't help."

"You don't want to choose your wife?"

"They know exactly what I'm looking for; there's no reason they can't help."

"But what about your feelings? Different women may be suitable, but only one would make you fall in love with her."

After the words were spoken, silence fell. The gulf between them had been exposed. If Hamid had said, "That's the way we live" or explained that he's giving in to his family's expectations, Laurie would have nodded with sympathy and sorrow. But his simple, unequivocal wish to lead an uncomplicated life without emotional turmoil left her speechless. Not only did the distance between her and Ofir suddenly materialize in a very vital way, but annoyingly, it now seemed like a justification for Hamid's choice. Her relationship with Ofir, born out of true love, had lately dissipated and dissolved, leaving her disappointed and somewhat desolate.

Her contempt for a marriage that resulted from matching seemed like an empty sentiment, and her reservation about life without passionate love appeared questionable.

A month later, Hamid was pale and cheerful on his wedding day. Jumana, his bride, was a beautiful young woman who smiled bashfully at everyone. Laurie thought there was some affinity between them; they whispered to each other and giggled when no one was watching. Ofir had sat beside her, amused and indifferent to the general excitement. After a couple of minutes, he was absorbed in his phone, ignoring the wedding ceremony. The abundance of food, loud Arab music and colorful lights made Laurie dizzy, as if she found she was participating in a juggler's performance. And though the boisterous sounds were wearing as she and Ofir left the wedding, the silence between them was sharp and distressing.

When she approached the museum director, asking if she could take Hamid as her assistant for a part-time job, a flicker of scorn surfaced in his eyes. He leaned back in his chair and crossed his hands with amused anticipation, as if she was about to tell a joke. But instead of apologizing, Laurie began to speak assertively, and after a couple of sentences, she switched to English: No Arabs are working in the museum. Such a liberal institute must hire Israeli Arabs. How would it look if an Arab candidate were rejected? It might be misunderstood. Hamid is a very gifted artist with a profound understanding of art; he could contribute much to the museum, and it might create problems if he wasn't hired. Most donors would dislike it if he was rejected, maybe because he was Arab. The director immediately sat erect, the mockery absorbed in his face, and now he wore a worried expression. "No, no, of course not," he said. "We wouldn't want anything of that sort to happen. It would be unimaginable. When exactly do you want him to start?"

Now that she was divorced, Laurie met Michael daily in the apartment they rented together, a few minutes away from the museum. They usually had lunch together. They spent the night together when Abigail and Daniel stayed at Ofir's place. Michael had now been divorced for a year.

Their apartment became a meeting place for a group of Brits living in Israel. Laurie's three girlfriends, two couples from London living in Israel for almost thirty years, an elderly man from Manchester who had immigrated to Israel after his retirement, two lesbian women who had fallen under the spell of the liberal spirit of Tel Aviv, a forty-year-old journalist reporting from the Middle East for the last ten years, and a young woman who traveled around the world and ended up on the beach of Tel Aviv, and now didn't want to leave the group that felt like family. They had dinners together nearly every week, discussing British politics, exchanging books, joking about rude Israelis—a group of people that, a couple of years ago, were not acquainted with each other, had become a small community with an affectionate atmosphere.

Friendship abroad, even if a person has been living there for years, is like the affinity between siblings; the intimacy is bare, small details of everyday life discussed without pretense, distress unconcealed and fear uncovered. The mother tongue is spoken with much awareness since it bears the friendship. Longing for the homeland becomes a shared feeling—either nostalgia or a yearning for a place that exists in the imagination. The words "in the UK this couldn't have happened" came up repeatedly, in laughter or with sadness, and were always mixed with childhood memories, descriptions of houses and streets, and often photos of children, grandchildren, parents, brothers. The group of friends adopted each other's memories as if they were their own, supporting each other.

Laurie often thought this friendship couldn't have been born in the UK. After years of living in Israel, she suddenly felt that longing for London had faded away, leaving room for a new, pleasant comfort. Sarcastic words, insulting remarks about her British accent, she wasn't facing them alone anymore. In this small British community, she'd found a homey spirit she had never encountered before.

As they sat on the beach in the evening, stretching out on blankets spread on the sand with food and drink, the haze emerging from the Mediterranean Sea turned into a warm, intoxicating scent. A vibrant silver carpet expanding onto the horizon under a warm red sun, sprinkling burgundy powder as it set, swallowed London's gray air and old buildings. The waves that always invade the shore and then change their mind made a quiet, delicate hum, a graceful sound seeping into the heart, implanting happiness and hope.

August 2011

Glass-like blue eyes, with a tiny spark at their heart, with thick eyelashes and straight eyebrows stretching above them. A deep wrinkle dividing the forehead horizontally revealed a constant concern with the future. Thin white curls granted the face a spiritual expression. Ben was standing on the balcony watching the crowd on the street below, people hurrying to the demonstration for social justice.[1]

Looking at the stream of people, and against his better judgment, an unfamiliar excitement overtook him. An ancient tune surfaced, a primordial instinct of the human herd that makes people stick together and march forward gradually intensified, silencing any argument or explanation. Men and women could be seen from the balcony, young and old, striding towards the demonstration. And though it was clear they hadn't come together and didn't know each other, their common wish fully materialized in the street. In a moment, Ben would have joined them. Happiness filled him. Seeing people joining forces for a shared aim awakened a childish joy. He was about to run down the stairs, hurry to the demonstration carrying a "We demand social justice!" sign.

But as Talia stood beside him and asked what he thought about the demonstration, the joy vanished and was replaced by silence. She said, "I agree with them. Everything is so expensive here," then added, "I hope they won't block our parking lot," and finally concluded with a smile, "Some parents from David's class are going there together," as if it was a class trip, oblivious to her husband's unsettled spirit. While he was leaning on the rail and looking down, somewhat gloomy, she began to chat about David's class, indifferent to the people marching down the street.

A bit later, when the masses in the streets of Tel Aviv appeared on television, the spark in his bright eyes died out, and all that was left was a glazed look. Ben explained to Talia that the demonstrations were pointless, and she nodded politely. It was true that the prices of some products were too high, but there

---

1   In 2011, a series of demonstrations involving hundreds of thousands of people protested against the high cost of living in Israel.

were contrary examples. And generally speaking, what was it that the demonstrators wanted? Some wanted a socialist government, and clearly there was
nothing more ridiculous than that. The capitalistic spirit was spreading worldwide; the rich and developed countries were more capitalist than ever. Sweden
was always brought up as a contrary example, but the Swedes had gradually
come to understand that they paid a heavy price for their social rights. As
for the allegations that a few families had taken over Israel's assets, they were
unfounded, to say the least. That was how modern economies worked: a few
entrepreneurs generated prosperity for many, and they made a lot of money in
return. Would it be better to live in a poorer world with no wealthy entrepreneurs? Each and every one of the demonstrators would give up his protest if he
were given a choice to live comfortably next to rich people. And if segments of
the free economy were not working properly, they should be fixed. No need to
change the system.

The stream of arguments got stronger. Unlike his usual self, Ben talked
at length to Talia, who continued to nod. When he finally stopped, he seemed
exhausted. He lay on the sofa watching television silently and fell asleep after
a couple of minutes despite the loud cries for social justice that echoed in
the room.

The following day he woke up with a headache. As he strolled along the
corridor to the kitchen, he could tell something irksome had happened yesterday, but he couldn't remember what it was. All he could recall was that he
was immersed in a new software. He made himself a cup of coffee, sat with
the steaming cup facing the street, and then the memory surfaced, enveloping him at once. The masses that had filled the streets, hundreds of thousands
marching together, the voices coming from the megaphones, and his profound desire to join them, which had utterly gotten hold of him for a second.

His bright eyes closed at once, as if he had been whipped, and pain
twisted his face, his mouth tightening and his back hunched. Once again that
damn wish to be part of a group was unearthed; a desire to act for the benefit of others, an urge he secretly called "a fruitless need." For a moment, he
thought that he hadn't been born in the right era; a generation or two too late,
maybe even three. This absurd thought made him chuckle. The image of his
father materialized in his mind, and his words about a man taking care only
of himself and his family were whispered, along with an answer that he would
have acted differently. But all these reflections were relinquished to Ben's
rational and systematic thinking, which determined decisively and unequivocally that there was absolutely no sense to his own words.

He heard people talking about last night's demonstration in the elevator going up in the Azrieli Tower. A woman declared, "It's amazing how many people came," and a man's voice replied defiantly, "People are bored. They have nothing better to do." The man and the woman left the elevator, and it ascended. Ben was hoping to hear some more, but nothing was said. A middle-aged man exited on the twenty-third floor, three young women got out on the thirty-second floor, an elegant woman left on the thirty-eighth floor, and he was left alone to exit on the fortieth floor.

A few minutes after he entered his office, a knock on the door was heard and immediately it opened. Abraham asked, "May I?" without waiting for an answer, entered the office, and sat in the leather chair facing Ben's desk. His hair was now completely gray, his chubby body strained at his plaid shirt, and his unintentional movement of fiddling with his kippah was repeated again and again. His face, normally beaming, looked troubled now. "We've secured the new version of the software. I think someone is breaking into our computer. It'll be a shame if years of hard work go down the drain."

"Why do you think someone is breaking into our computer?"

"I can feel it. I can't prove it, but I know it's true."

"Abraham, come on, 'feel it'?! First of all, we raised the level of security, and it's harder to hack us now. Also, the previous software was stolen in a different way, not by breaking into our computer."

"What?! Do you know who stole it? And how?"

"I know that someone gave it directly to the Swiss company. And no one broke into our computer."

Abraham's face flushed even more. His eyebrows shot up, and his hands tensed, grabbing the chair's armrest. "You know that someone in the company stole the software? How? Who? Why don't you report to the police?"

"You are so childish. Turn to the police? I want what's best for Handex. If the police come here and investigate people, our reputation will be damaged beyond repair. Also, Handex hasn't been harmed by the theft. On the contrary."

Abraham's body quivered. It seemed he couldn't take Ben's cold look, watching him indifferently, maybe with some disdain. "It's not a question of damage. There are things beyond that; truth and lies, honest people and thieves. The thieves must be caught and punished. If you had listened to your father, you would know I'm right," said Abraham.

The amusement in Ben's eyes completely vanished when his father was mentioned. He crossed his arms on his chest provocatively and said, "Well, you really are an example of moral standards. You take the Arabs' land, conceal the money you extract from the state, discriminate against Sephardi children in Ashkenazi schools—an exemplary society." As he saw Abraham's anger, he began to move his legs back and forth like a child annoying his nanny. But the voice that came from Abraham's mouth, pitched and broken, resembling a blowing shofar, caught him by surprise. "We're not moral? Is that what you're saying? We live by the rules of the Torah. Nothing is more moral. I don't understand how you can say such things. For us, a thief is a thief, and an honest man is an honest man. The Torah orders us to act justly and care for others. We look after each other, not like you."

At first Ben looked tense as the words were thrust into the room, with force and effort. Every syllable was intentional; the breath between the words sounded like gasping. But after a couple of moments, his body relaxed again and the eyes adopted a detached look. "You think that because you live by the laws of the Torah you care more about others? You're wrong! It's the other way around! Religious societies don't focus on man but on God. The main thing is the link between God and man, and caring for others comes second. Arguably, a belief in God implies solitude. Secular society is all about people, and therefore is more attentive to their needs. You may give to charity, but secular culture created a social welfare system, providing the basic necessities for everyone—and also some minor values like equality before the law, the basic right to freedom and education, and more . . ."

"I'm not saying you don't have values, only that we live by the laws of the Torah, which are moral laws," Abraham insisted.

"This sheer madness of the Greater Israel! Years ago, religious people were normal people. Religious families in Beit Hakerem were like everyone else, only with different habits. Now you are secluded in your settlements and don't care about anything else. A one-principle society. But this won't hold. There is no such thing. Societies that were built on a single principle have either vanished or changed. You're influenced by extreme religious ideas. Come on, admit it, your children are more religious than you are, aren't they?"

"I think I've heard you are attending Likud meetings. Is that true?"

"Sometimes. What has that got to do with it?"

"It's related."

"I enjoy the atmosphere there. The noise, the speeches, people hugging—it's nice."

"Will you vote for the Likud?"

"Probably."

"Why?"

"I don't know. Anyway, it doesn't matter. A single vote is meaningless."

"Because Ofir deserted you? Because he's not your friend? I've noticed that you've been working together recently."

When Abraham returned to his office, he stood by the window, looking over Ayalon highway. The busy road went by the tower, but the sealed windows stopped the noise. *No, not the extreme religious belief, that's not the problem*, he whispered to himself as if Ben were in the room with him, and he was trying to prevent the satisfaction that would appear in his bright eyes. *A lack of passion, a spirit too practical, a sort of aggressiveness that isn't channeled at building the country but nourishes itself.* The excessive religious devotion is only the symptom, an indication of a limited spirit prevailing among orthodox Jews, which the settlers used to ridicule. But now his sons argue that the price of real estate in the settlements is rising and living there turned out to be a good investment. They wonder how they could extract more money from the government. They see marriage as a sort of contract. And his youngest son, whom he always thought was exceptionally talented, left the yeshiva and wanders around Samaria with some friends, throwing stones at Arabs and uprooting their olive trees. *The problem is not the radical religious habits, but that the once thrilling and engrossing path has become overly calculated, breaking down the great vision into minor details and fostering aimless aggression,* he thought.

Ben remained seated as Abraham left the room, closing the door so forcefully that it hit his leg. He leaned back, gazing at the ceiling. A tiny spider was hanging by an invisible web, swinging slightly in the air. *What on earth went wrong,* he kept asking himself. *What went wrong? How did the inherent human inclination to assist others become scornful and despicable? How did anything that isn't motivated by self-interest become ridiculous?* Something one should never ever admit? Of course, the right words had been found; a good deed gives a man a "positive utility." How had *love thy neighbor as thyself* turned into these meaningless words? How?

Out of the dry air coming from the air conditioner surfaced a bitter sensation of disintegration; the past dissipates and is replaced by a pragmatic spirit, leaving him breathless; it is as though he were carrying a heavy load he found worthless but struggled to heave. Despite covering his inner abyss with wealth, on sleepless nights he wondered how the crater he was facing had been created. Every time he turned to God, sometimes complaining, sometimes weeping, he saw Ofir, his childhood friend, who had turned into a stranger he couldn't understand.

A few months previously, a conversation had started between them. In a moment of distraction, standing beside the coffee machine together, suddenly, words not related to Handex came up. Ofir muttered something about his father, how he was sure he would have liked this coffee machine gushing, steaming, and pouring dark, bitter fluid with a fine, strong taste. Ben, nearly dropping his cup in surprise, replied that he remembered that in the afternoon, the scent of coffee had filled Ofir's home and his father watched the percolator attentively, waiting for the exact moment the coffee would be ready. Ofir then said that coffee at four o'clock in the afternoon was a sort a ceremony at his parents' house, a small ritual that marked the end of the working day. The conversation continued, meandering through the streets of Beit Hakerem, making its way to Tel Aviv, pausing in Canada, France, and finally returning to Handex with a smiling and relaxed atmosphere, very simple and with a touch of humor.

An unbiased observer would have thought that this was closure. A circle of life was completed. Two childhood friends founded a high-tech company, a past experience made them quarrel, and now they forgave each other and found common ground again. Their firm's success was, after all, a result of the intimacy between them; Handex endured despite the harsh split. After years of disappointments and heartache, they managed to overcome the painful past and restart their friendship. This very short conversation, which only lasted a couple of minutes, was heralding an old-new companionship that might adopt a new character.

But not so Ben.

Returning to his office, he contemplated these nearly self-evident observations, all the while fending off a horrible fear that started in his feet, crept slowly through his body to his stomach, chest, and head, and then emanated from his eyes. Ofir has changed. He was not the same person. He was a stranger. A different man. A person who didn't resemble his childhood friend. A man he couldn't figure out. Though his face had hardly changed, and the wrinkles around his eyes and graying hair only made him more attractive, someone completely unknown to him existed behind his eyes. His familiar gestures—stretching his back as he spoke, one hand leaning against the desk supporting his long body—only emphasized the complete alienation.

Overwhelming anxiety made Ben pale and his heart raced. He sat down, trying to restore an inner balance that had broken while talking to Ofir. It was the very simple exchange of words, the few agreeable sentences that provoked horror that gradually thickened, threatening to fill him completely, and then was transformed into gloom.

In the months after this conversation, they began talking with each other almost every day. At first, the workers of Handex observed them with interest. Though they were all used to the company functioning well despite the discord between the two owners, a silent sigh of relief seemed to emerge from the corridor as the change in the relationship appeared permanent. Each one still ran half of the weekly staff meeting, but the tension that had characterized the encounters between them vanished, and discussing work issues became routine.

But Ben, who felt the stares following them, seeking confirmation that the old conflict had ended and a renewed friendship was stirring, looked at his employees with resentment. It was an error. A grave mistake. An empty pretense, that's all; it would be better if the conflict between them had persisted, a remnant of true friendship that existed in a past world. This new Ofir had shed any residues of intimacy, the bits of betrayal, the vestiges of solidarity, and now he was smiling again, joking and making everyone laugh. Who knows? He may have even cut the thread connecting him to his children. Maybe he gave them expensive presents, and waited for them to return to the home that had once been his. He stood erect; he wasn't too thin and his clothes fit him well. He was absorbed by work from morning to night, developing the distribution network he created and supporting the expansion of the robotic arm's third-generation software. A handsome, successful man. Women were attracted to him; again he walked lightly, his gray hair falling gracefully on his forehead, but his gaze was blank, with neither laughter nor sadness. His eyes watched the world with impartial curiosity, examining everything in a pragmatic manner, searching for how to make things work better for him, add utility or profit. The conversations he initiated were very practical. He disliked theoretical discussions; a dialogue with him was always like a negotiation. Even in political debates, which in the past had made him angry, he now expressed his opinion moderately in passionless language: "We must withdraw from Judea and Samaria unilaterally. It's pointless to wait for a moderate Palestinian leadership. We should leave and formulate a security arrangement." Not another word.

On sleepless nights, Ben looked at the sky, following tiny twinkles in the distance as if they held a hidden message, a signal intended only for him; if he could only decipher it, a cure would be found for his growing fear. The image of his childhood friend who had turned into such a stranger was terrifying. His friendly smiles, funny jokes, personal charm, blank eyes, an insatiable hunger to expand production, develop more products, improve the software, raise the price of the robotic arm, make the company more profitable, lay off unnecessary workers . . .

For the first time in his life, Ben wondered if the wheel could be turned back. The practical spirit that provided support in moments of weakness— spurring him into rushing forward, inventing, achieving, and removing whoever stood in his way—suddenly seemed shallow and unimaginative. His father's words about a man caring only for himself and his family, which he always believed to be innocent and profound, were now aggravating. Money, a comfortable life, and Handex's success all diminished as he recalled Ofir's blank eyes. He calmly suggested firing some workers who had been with them for years—Abraham and Nava included—to save on costs.

Resentment gradually transformed into animosity. Though Ben's face revealed anger, he couldn't tell who he was mad at. He sat on the balcony and looked down at the dark, empty street; cats lay on the pavement, indifferent to prey hiding in the bushes. Suddenly, a strange idea came into being. He would apologize to Ofir. Ask for forgiveness. Try to appease him. Explain how years of envy impaired his judgment and made him betray his best friend, the other part of himself. Forgiveness was the answer, the solution. Even in Yom Kippur, there was no atonement for transgression between people unless they forgave each other. To remove the blank look of his childhood friend, a pardon was needed. Maybe he would suggest a good deed as compensation, a joint effort for those in need, in Israel or in remote places around the globe. Perhaps they could build a hospital? A school? After all, they had created Handex together.

But Ofir's blank eyes in the darkness, two murky holes in the sky, looked back at him with utter indifference and maybe even a touch of scorn. Hospital? School? In a moment, he would burst out laughing at these ideas and suggest they start a new company that would do even better than Handex; a brilliant original idea that they could execute together. Ben stared down at the street, which seemed motionless at this early morning hour. Clouds didn't move in the sky, leaves didn't rustle, night birds didn't soar, and insects didn't crawl in the dark. Complete silence. Stillness. Even the air, which seemed to be full of mist and dust, was stagnant. And from the utter silence loomed the echo of a grim solitude that enveloped him until he could hardly breathe; a heartbreaking moan, like a weeping trumpet emerging from a dirty, deserted street corner.

April 2012

It's heartening to find that the innate human desire to assist others endures, though at times it seems to have disappeared. The primary urge to help fellow men without expecting anything in return, driven purely by goodwill, manifests in surprising circumstances.

When Ofir decided to use the digital community Handex created to market medical products, he knew it would be an excellent business opportunity. But it never anticipated that the "General Medical Advice" section of the software would develop into a new digital community. Physicians from around the world shared medical information and advice, nurses found a platform for communication, and caregivers from Africa and other developing countries sought assistance and occasionally received help. This segment of the software became an integral component of Handex's distribution network. A subtle smile filled Ofir's eyes as he read the numerous medical suggestions put forth by healthcare professionals. *Yes, yes, the part of the human spirit that struggled for people's rights and encouraged self-sacrifice for the sake of justice still existed.* And though Ofir was proud about creating an entirely new platform, he still formulated a question: Why are people willing to help others without receiving anything in return?

Beside Ofir, who lay in bed reading his iPad, Hadar was asleep on her stomach, revealing her curved back. Her short hair was messy, like a child after a wild game; only a sparkling earring in a gentle earlobe indicated that it was the head of a beautiful woman with exquisite facial features. Since his divorce, he hardly went on dates. Very rarely did he spend the night with someone, and then he left early in the morning without saying goodbye. From morning to night, he was absorbed in his work, living in a world made of numbers, graphs, software, new markets, profit and loss; a daily routine devoted to work that generated a deep satisfaction. More than once, he thought nothing was lacking in his life. When he was young, he used to think his world would be incomplete without a woman to share it. But it turned out that wasn't true. At the age of fifty, good-looking and successful, he knew his life differed from that of his parents. Every time he recalled how they had coffee at four o'clock in the afternoon and shared a piece of cake, walked along shaded streets in

Beit Hakerem, he felt a burning drop sliding inside him, absorbed in his body. Embarrassed, he whispered to himself that he didn't want to live like them. His life with Laurie had simply ended, a man and a woman who became one entity and then broke apart into two shapes that didn't fit each other anymore. To his surprise, he was relieved when he learned she had a partner. No, he wanted to live differently, free from a binding relationship. It was enough that his children spent every other weekend with him. Though he had designed a nice room for each of them, in the evening they asked to return home.

Hadar had sat next to him at a bar late one night. A beautiful woman, about forty, with short hair, penetrating eyes, and a shapely body. A casual conversation begun; Ofir was already thinking that he didn't want to spend the night with her, and just out of habit, asked her what she did."

"I'm a physician," she said.

Hadar didn't like Magritte; she thought his works conveyed a sense of emptiness. She disliked haphazard decoration. At her house, every picture decorating the wall harmonized with the colors of the furniture. She stirred away from synthetic fabrics; only cotton was fit to wrap the human body. Eating meat made her nauseous and was unhealthy. She had been an ardent vegetarian for years. She argued that people who didn't engage in physical activity looked limp even with their clothes on. She found women who devote their lives to motherhood ridiculous. She wasn't sure whether they were unaware of what they were missing or they simply adapted to common patterns. She certainly didn't want any children. Interruptions to her work made her angry and often ended in a heated argument. People with a dependent disposition simply put her off. She would never consider a relationship with a man who needed her, and she didn't like to commit to one man. She found the bourgeois attitude towards sex revolting. Sex was an art, the ultimate form of self-expression, the most profound pleasure a person could have.

After a few dates with Ofir, with encounters that left them breathless is bed, gasping with eyes closed, she told him directly that she was also seeing other men. In a tone neither provocative nor apologetic, she said she didn't believe is long-term relationships. She didn't want to offend him, so she was informing him that he wasn't the only man in her life, and he never would be. Ofir was completely taken by surprise by her very pragmatic tone. The echo of his own words thickened and swelled, infiltrating into her sentences. It was he who normally declared that he wasn't interested in a long-term romantic relationship. Since he had undergone an emotional crisis that led to his divorce, he wanted to live alone. But hearing her, an inner pillar had cracked, one that he often leaned upon—women are softer; they need a lasting relationship with one man. Their motherly side is reflected in their romantic relationship. But now, a truth he thought prevailed even in a world with successful independent women had been challenged, and he was left lying in bed, wondering whether the world had changed or if Hadar was an exception.

Even after spending time together for months, sometimes seeing each other a couple of times a week, they never became friends. Ofir thought there was something barren about her. She lacked the warmth he needed, a tenderness he expected a woman to have. But, then, he contradicted himself. He was the one who wasn't interested in a long-lasting relationship; he was always careful not to delude women. It was better this way; Hadar didn't need him and she wasn't emotionally attached to him. In rare moments of sobriety, in which a window into the future opens for a split second and then closes and disappears, he saw a lonely old man surrounded by people but with a sealed heart. The memory of Hadar's naked body removed these gloomy thoughts. Still, the more he enjoyed having sex with her, intense and intoxicating, the emptier he felt when it was over.

Two different people began to exist within Ofir, uniting and separating. During the week, he was a successful, charming man, talented and energetic. People gathered around him; women looked at him seductively, his funny stories amused everyone. But, late at night and on weekends he spent without his children, the spirit of a solitary monk took over, living in a world of shadows. In the last couple of months, he'd begun to hike alone. He purchased an SUV for driving on unpaved roads, and on the weekends, he went places he had known as a young paratrooper. The wilderness of the Negev, the Judean Desert, Ayalon Valley, the hills of the Galilee, Mount Gilboa, Mount Tabor, streams on the Golan Heights—Ofir walked slowly but with determination, looking around and letting the landscape sink in until it no longer seemed miraculous.

One step after another, carrying a backpack with food and water, he walked by himself in the burning sun or in the rain. Mountains and valleys spread before him; sometimes he climbed a steep hill, sometimes he slid down a slope. He tried to remember how he felt as a young soldier walking with his comrades, carrying heavy military equipment, but the memories disintegrated into shapes and colors—the hue of his uniform, the square backpack of the person walking in front of him, red paratrooper boots—and evaporated. All he could remember was a couple of words. The spectacular landscape blurred the memory of the military service and left him staring at it as if he had never seen it before.

At times, he sat down for an hour or two looking around, allowing the sun to caress his body and the wind to dishevel his hair. Light, bright clouds produced tenderness and calm; he would tilt his head back, looking at them moving across the sky. Dark, heavy clouds created a feeling of lurking danger; his body became tense and he watched them galloping forward. The desert sand awakened an adoration of material formation—here he was, facing a wild land, a primordial landscape that no man had ever set foot on, one person facing the yellow-brown sand. And though each grain making the desert was almost invisible, millions of grains laid one upon the other formed infinity right here in front of him, tangible yet incomprehensible. The green landscape in the lower Galilee was so inviting, with winding paths between round hills. Walking them was like strolling in a mysterious garden; in a couple of steps a small vantage point would be found, an open cave or a bird nesting on green branches. Looking at the Sea of Galilee evoked only one vibe: a deep-set wish to swim in the pure water that revived the memory of the womb. The bare hills of the upper Galilee, with their hidden meadows, were often covered with gray fog. Early in the morning or late in the evening, enveloped in clouds, it seemed as if the earth and sky had fused and once again become a single entity.

Normally, as Ofir went on hiking, he felt calm and relaxed. A reflection that takes place in nature expands without being painful, taking shape without extending its limits. Thinking of his life while looking out on a valley or a mountain, any error or sin was forgivable. Only once, sitting on a rock and looking at Makhtesh Ramon,[1] was an inner lining torn and his spirit left uncovered; a formless consciousness, a bare soul facing the primeval landscape, unable to fend off sun rays that penetrated it and ignited a new, unfamiliar light, a sharpness he had never experienced before.

Boards covering an abyss aligned next to each other, flexible and long, moving together. The depth beneath them seethes slightly but doesn't pour out, dust melting in water, parts of rocks floating on vapor, a constant movement containing itself. In the fraction of a moment in which the boards move away from each other, an ancient glare penetrates them, shedding a glimmering light in the depth of the

---

1   A crater canyon in the Negev Desert.

soul. Man—universe, man—mountains, valleys, streams, merging with nature,
drowning itself in the chasm, constantly duplicating itself and filling the abyss,
creating a full and complete consciousness of being a particle of the infinite. This
apprehension, which exists within itself and depends on nothing, produces a sense
of freedom infused with fear. The rays gradually withdraw from the chasm, and
the covering boards remain in place, but the glare that enveloped them leaves radi-
ant traces that would never fade away.

Ofir often tried to reconstruct that moment, the strange illumination he
experienced in the canyon. He sat silently in the desert, closed his eyes and
opened them, explored thoughts and then struggled to remove them, turned
his face to the sun, and then turned his back—but in vain. The inner light
never returned, though the memory of it was deeply engrained in him as if
it had taken place only a moment ago. Though he scoffed at himself, thinking that, like many before him, he had lost his clarity in the blazing desert,
the essence of feeling a minuscule element of nature was rooted in him and
never lost.

On weekdays, he worked until late at night, often with Ben. Since the
first conversation between them, a new dialogue had started, moderate and
restrained. Once again they planned to expand the company, but now they
used a pragmatic and dispassionate language. The lack of affinity improved
their cooperation. Ben asked for Ofir's advice regarding possible direc-
tions for developing the software and how each would affect Handex; Ofir
shared with Ben his hesitations regarding the distribution network: Should
the number of products be limited? Again, they perfectly complemented
each other; Ofir's daring thought, venturing to break the boundaries, and
Ben thinking logically and systematically, removing obstacles and deepen-
ing foundations. Only as they discussed the free medical advice in the digital community, given very generously and asking for nothing in return, did
embarrassment spread across their faces, as if they were caught in the act;
like two high school students who'd failed a test though the questions were
ridiculously easy.

At the end of the workday, Ofir often sat on the beach, watching the
black waves. An inner string loosened, making a soft sound. Cool breeze
gently caressed his forehead and cheeks; he listened to the water whispering, his legs stretched forward and his body relaxed. But one night, he turned
alert. As he sat by the water, he saw a woman walking on the beach holding
the hand of a girl of about ten. She seemed very familiar, but he couldn't tell

who she was. But she recognized him. As she saw him, a broad smile spread across her face and she approached him. Only as she stood beside him did he realize it was Carine. Astonishment made him stand up, almost leap up, trying to conceal his embarrassment.

She looked older—still beautiful, but very different. Her hair was in disarray, her face had no makeup, and she was dressed very simply, wearing only a necklace made of carved wooden beads. It was hard to believe this woman used to wear exquisite clothes and expensive jewelry. Ofir looked at her and said nothing. A strange woman emerged from Carine's eyes. Her face, once impassive, was now warm and innocent. Seeing Ofir's amazement, she laughed and said, "Yes, I know. I look different now."

He stared at her with eyes wide open, trying to follow the unfamiliar woman that had spread within Carine's body, removing the elegant lady and throwing away her expensive jewels. This new woman told him that after divorcing Ben she had remarried, had a daughter—she caressed the girl, who hugged her with love—and then divorced again. She found it hard to explain, but one day she had had enough of the luxury life. She suddenly had no interest in expensive garments. It was strange; she didn't quite understand the nature of her transformation, but it seemed to her that she was free like she had never been before. Lately, she also had begun to paint. She was not very talented, but it made her happy. When she recalled her past life, she was dismayed. Life drove her to that path, but gladly, she'd managed to break free. She would never want her daughter to live like that.

A full moon peeked from behind the soft clouds, stretching its velvet beams onto the dark water, dropping light driblets into the sea, which expanded and faded away. As they said goodbye affectionately, Ofir watched the mother and daughter strolling at night along the waterline, embracing on the wet sand, and tears filled his eyes. *I wish I could walk like that with Abigail and Daniel,* he thought, surrendering to a painful longing, a yearning for yesterday, last week, last month, last year, past years before the invisible gear that he was trapped in began to move slowly, at a constant, moderate pace. He used to think it could be stopped; now, he was sure all hope was lost. To comfort himself, he made himself think of the successful company he had created with Ben, and the fortune he had made. Finally, he sighed deeply and decided to go home.

May 2013

A bride and a groom under a canopy on a balcony overlooking the sea. Laurie, the bride, is getting married for the second time. Her body is full and round, she is wearing an ivory straight-cut dress, elegantly simple. A forty-five-year-old woman, her face retaining its pleasant freshness and skin still glowing, yet years of despair now emerge from her eyes, visible despite her delight. Her former husband, who had had a breakdown; her loneliness and suffering; the simple, unemotional divorce—they are all pushed aside now, replaced by a full and deep happiness that fills the heart. A bliss that ignites light. As she looks at Michael, the groom, her eyes gleam.

Her daughter Abigail stands beside her and smiles at the guests. She has her father's sharp facial features and her mother's fair skin. Her eyes are dark and penetrating, her eyebrows look as if they were painted by an artist; a straight nose and a full mouth, and a narrow, slim body. She wears a light blue dress. Her face reveals excitement and some awkwardness. The guests congratulate her; she flushes and becomes tense. But she can tell everyone likes her; her body loosens, and she holds her mother's arm. A young woman, slightly stiff and bitter, but now she is fully relaxed, watching the rabbi conduct the ceremony. Her father's breakdown had created grief within her that later transformed into stubbornness. Her parents drawing apart and divorce produced uninhibited outbursts, for which she was almost expelled from school. But the British group had banished her loneliness and provided comfort. They had adopted her and became a sort of extended family. Abigail speaks fluent English with a British accent. Her friends think her English is perfect, but Laurie corrects her errors. Now they all look at her and smile, and she returns an affectionate glance.

Next to Abigail stands Natalie, her grandmother, who has come from London to attend the wedding. She is still tall and bony despite her old age. Though standing still is not easy for her due to severe varicose veins, she refuses to sit down. She wishes to stand beside her daughter as she marries again, a marriage she believes will be more successful than the first one. The first husband wasn't right for her; people who have similar backgrounds have a better life. Though she's looking at Abigail and Daniel, her two grandchildren, with pride, a forbidden thought passes: for a moment, she imagines the life Laurie might have had in London. She quickly pushes it away and reproaches herself for thinking about it. It's a sin. Tempting fate. Her granddaughter is so beautiful and gifted; her grandson is charming and mischievous. As the rabbi conducts the ceremony, she gazes at the sea. The vibrant colors look like a flame burning above water. The sea adopts a darker color; the waves are high and vigorous. Natalie observes the foreign landscape with profound affection. There were times when she couldn't look at the sunset in Tel Aviv without thinking how different it was from London. Now she allows the strong colors to sink in uninterrupted; orange, purple, and light blue become an appropriate background for her daughter's glowing face. Natalie would have moved to Israel and settled in Tel Aviv had her husband agreed. Two of her good friends passed away. She retired as her husband began to make a fantastic amount of money. Her severe varicose veins and heart disease prevented her from being a part of the Belsize choir, and her London grandchildren had left home. She often feels something has ended in her life and she needs a change, regardless of her age. But then she waves her hand in dismissal and immerses herself in reading books.

Eric is standing beside her, looking around with curiosity and some irritation. Though he is happy for his daughter and can see her joy, he finds the stay in Israel burdensome. He fully objects to Israel's policy in the occupied territories and believes the blunt vanity of its leaders is bound to end in catastrophe. If he could, he would move Laurie and her children to London. But he has accepted the fact that a substantial part of his life will remain in Israel and that every time he flies to Tel Aviv and back to Hampstead, his inner struggle will be revived. First, an inclination to identify with Zionism, moving him and bringing tears to his eyes. Then a certainty that he isn't a part of the movement and never would be. A sense of belonging to British culture surfaces. Britain is and always will be his true home. He'll never leave Hampstead. And words regarding Britain not being part of the EU leave him both anxious and proud. He is a strong Jew and a loyal Brit.

But a certain remorse that always blended into his inner dialogue on the role of Israel in the Jewish world made Eric purchase a lovely apartment at the center of Tel Aviv for Laurie and Michael. Though Laurie argued it wasn't necessary as the divorce from Ofir left her a wealthy woman, Eric was determined to buy the apartment and nothing could change his mind. And despite his advanced age, he insisted on joining her as she searched for the right place, ensuring there was plenty of room for Abigail and Daniel. Eventually, his daughter decided not to offend him, and he purchased the flat.

Now, standing under the canopy beside Laurie, he's glad he bought the apartment, as if he finally found a justification for the fortune he made representing the African dictator, though he made up his mind he'd stop thinking about him. He reflects that the wedding could have taken place in London rather than Israel. He bought the tickets for his son, his family, his friends, and the rabbi conducting the wedding. Laurie's British friends stand around the canopy, embracing the married couple with warm smiles. He once asked Laurie—a slip of the tongue—why she didn't move back to the UK if all her friends were British. To his surprise, she replied that their deep friendships couldn't have been formed in London. In Tel Aviv, they became a group tied together by both intimacy and alienation.

His brother Harry is facing the canopy, a tired smile on his face. Nurit is in the US. She often spends time in New Jersey with their only son, his wife, and two children, while he is devoted to his beehives, waking every morning to hear their beloved humming. His face, as always, is tanned and wrinkled. His body, muscular despite his age, resembles an ancient giant. He has huge and rough peasant's hands, flat feet with broken nails, but eyes with a soft glow. The sunrise he sees every morning removes the bitterness and sadness from his gaze, and his countenance remains somewhat childlike.

Michael is dressed in a tailored suit with a red pocket handkerchief. He looks around calmly. He is very sorry his son refused to attend the wedding; he wanted him to share his joy. But marrying Laurie is like medicine for a disease that broke years ago: an unhappy marriage, a sense of alienation from Israel—and suddenly, a cure came from a surprising source. Years spent trying to adopt foreign habits and make friends with people he has nothing in common with—and all of a sudden came an unexpected turn of events. A love affair with a British woman and friendship with a group of Brits generated a deep sense of being part of Israel that he never thought possible. Gone was the yearning for London, reflections on how life could have been different. He found full justification for his life in Tel Aviv; it truly had become his home. In a moment of intimacy, he'd asked Laurie if they could have a child, and she replied she was too old. He hugged her firmly and they remained motionless for long minutes, listening to each other's breathing.

Laurie is holding Michael's hand. She wishes to capture the moment but then changes her mind; extending the present into the future is impossible. Anticipating future memories distracts from the present joy, which she is resolute to savor to the fullest. Beautiful Abigail is holding her arm as if she is about to fall. Daniel sports a mischievous look, and her parents' expressions reveal excitement. Michael's face is flushed—he probably had some drinks to moderate the thrill—friends look at her affectionately, colleagues from the museum stand far from the canopy and look at everyone with curiosity, the workers of the refugee assistance organization in which Laurie has been active gather at the far end of the balcony with three Eritrean women, one carrying a baby. A glow spreads on the balcony, a glistening trail engulfs the guests, transparent radiance facing a sea—the waves that always invade the shore and then change their mind are already dark and secretive. "If I forget thee, O Jerusalem, let my right hand forget her cunning. Let my tongue cleave to the roof of my mouth, if I remember thee not; if I set not Jerusalem above my chiefest joy," Michael says in a trembling voice, in Hebrew with a strong British accent, and Laurie knows that a question she doesn't quite understand but has been there for years has finally found an answer and would never rise again.

August 2014

———————

Do you mind? I'll pay you. I promise. I'll give you fifty shekels every time you get him off me.

I don't need money. My dad gives me as much as I want.

But you'll have more. If you get him away from me twice a day, once in summer camp and once in the afternoon, you'll have another hundred shekels every day.

I told you, my dad keeps asking me if I need money. Why don't you ask Idan? He doesn't have much money.

But Idan isn't my friend. You're my best friend.

I'm your best friend, but I don't need money, and he does.

But he'll take the money and won't help me.

So, if he does this once, don't give him any more.

But then they'll beat me up.

Okay, if Idan will cheat you, I'll help you.

The childish voices coming from David's room filtered through the closed door. Ben stood behind it, listening to the conversation between David and his best friend. Since first grade, they'd met up every day. Because he didn't want to miss a single word, he put his ear against the door and held his breath. His forehead was sweaty, and he felt a sort of heaviness spreading within him as if a thick fluid permeated his organs, and soon he wouldn't be able to move. *It's my fault, it's all my fault,* he muttered to himself and knocked on the door. The childish voices fell silent.

Later, as the friend left, Ben sat beside his son on his bed. It's strange that he is so muscular, he thought. My father and I were so slender, while he looks strong and robust. It's no wonder his fragile friend asked him for protection at school. At just ten years old, he already has a masculine appearance. Trying to ignore the heaviness expanding within him, creating discomfort in his legs and chest, Ben turned to his son and said in a fatherly tone, "David, friends should support each other. Someday, when you need help from your friend, he'll be there for you. Some things cannot be bought, regardless of how much money you have."

One word after the other, explanation on top of explanation, an argument he articulated in very simple words so that his ten-year-old son would understand; but the words broke and disintegrated as they were pronounced, transforming into a bunch of syllables that became vowels and consonants. His mouth uttered sentences that evaporated before he could hear them. David, who stared at the wall indifferently, wasn't listening to him. In between the sounds he was producing, he could hear his son saying, "But just a few months ago, you promised to pay me if I did my homework. So, what's the difference? I'm supposed to do it for free." Then his own voice grew louder, trying to be authoritarian, but annoyingly it came out squeaky. He explained that this was an altogether different issue. School was like work, but friends were like family. "You wouldn't even consider asking your own sister to pay you for defending her, would you? David, can you hear me?! I can't hear your reply. I'm talking to you!"

A couple of minutes later, Ben sat on the balcony. The inner heaviness made him forego the air-conditioned apartment for the hot summer air, which he felt was as heavy as he was; filled with minuscule water drops, neither falling nor ascending. Sweat ran down his back and legs, his thinning hair was moist and slightly oily, and his son's words echoed in his head. As his relationship with Ofir materialized in his mind—Jerusalem-Tel Aviv-crisis-recuperation—he closed his eyes and murmured that despite everything, when they were children, boundless friendship had made Ofir protect him.

Like a man scared of a passing shadow, he began a lively and somewhat aggressive conversation with his dead father. First, he complained about his son not respecting him like he respected his own father, and he was met by a bitter scorn. They would have behaved differently had he been religious and raised his children in the spirit of the Torah. This maddening response only created further anger. Clearly, some well-behaved children respect their parents without being religious. His father's frustration and hatred appeared again, shamefully simple. Irritated, he chuckled to himself to illustrate how ridiculous the argument with his dead father was, who remained silent and said nothing.

The setting sun left a rosy, misty glow in the sky, lying above the buildings. Streetlights spread beams and cast shadows; dusty trees shed dry leaves. *A man looks after himself and his family. Everything else is nothing but hypocrisy, an attempt to exploit you.* Ben could hear his father reproaching him, explaining time and again he shouldn't fall for it: *Don't believe smooth talk, don't trust those who act for the sake of society, socialism, ideals one should be willing to die for. I look after myself and my family. You'll do the same when you're an adult.* The words hit him now, burning and bitter. His father's disappointment was so obvious, a life that did not evolve as he expected, living in a world indifferent to his religious sentiment, blind to the biblical characters who were so vivid in his mind. He'd held on with all his might to looking after himself, his wife, and his children as if this would ensure an ever-lasting order, the deepest instinct of life: parents look after their children, who look after their children

Imagining his father's words only further thickened the density that filled Ben. He thought he would never be able to move again. Closing his eyes and shuddering, leaning his head against the headrest, Ben was struck by lightning; his spirit was split open, revealing an inner membrane.

Why him and his family?

Why not only him?

Every living creature possesses a basic animal instinct to survive, so why look after anyone other than oneself? It has already been argued that human beings are selfish animals with physical and psychological survival mechanisms. So why assume they will look after their families? Here, his son David didn't rule out the notion of charging his sister, his own flesh and blood, for protection. Come to think of it, his relationship with Talia, though stable and pleasant, was, in fact, a contract: he provides for his family, and in return Talia runs the home and looks after the children, enveloping him with a homely atmosphere. Annoyingly, he suddenly imagined all sorts of disasters: he would lose his fortune, Talia would catch a terrible disease, he would become disabled, and she would have to nurse him. He was now absolutely sure that in all these cases, a cold and practical calculation would be made; each one would do whatever was best only for them.

The heaviness that continued to spread within him nearly paralyzed him. In a moment, he would burst out crying. He swallowed a moan and looked up, searching as always for a divine message in the heavenly bodies. But the dense air and murky darkness concealed any answer that might have been hidden in the sky, and a thin moon sank beyond the horizon. "I wish I could tell myself without a doubt that a man looks after himself and his family," Ben muttered in tears. *Mom and I are like Abraham and Sarah,* his father used to say. *We stay together no matter what.* He recalled the words, but their weight made him feel as though he might never rise again.

Then a blaring siren echoed through the city, an oscillating sound rising and falling, signaling that Hamas had launched rockets from Gaza towards Tel Aviv. Now there was only a minute and a half to find shelter.[1] Out of the unbearable heaviness, Ben leaped up and ran from the balcony into the apartment, searching for David and Eden to take them to the stairway and descend a few floors. David shouted to his father that he was already hurrying to the stairway, but Ben couldn't find Eden. He rushed from room to room, quickly looking everywhere, pushing open doors, accidentally kicking a paper bin and stepping on the television remote control, and bursting into the bathroom. *Eden, where is Eden?* Time ticked away, one second and another. They must find shelter! Where is she?

A deep, hidden vein was about to explode, blood spray bursting forward—it seemed that the vein walls wouldn't be able to contain the growing steam; a primordial instinct to protect one's offspring from a predator emerged and moved his body, which was ready to strike an enemy that might be hiding in a corner. *Where is Eden? Where?*

He found her sitting in a corner, caressing her big doll as if she couldn't hear the loud wailing. He carried her, a slim eight-year-old girl, and ran to the stairway. The doll fell as they were running and, although she wanted to pick her up, Ben moved with a strange agility, leaping like an animal. He reached the stairway swiftly, and began to descend. Ben could hear David's voice echoing: "Dad, I'm going down!" *"But not to the first floor, David. Not to the first floor!"* he shouted.

Death prevailed on the first floor. Ben was ashamed of his words but couldn't stop himself. A soldier living in the building had been killed two weeks before. At midnight, the stairway was filled with screaming the likes of which he had never encountered; it was impossible to tell if they were human or were the cries of an animal being torn to pieces alive. Army men came in and out of the building. Family members and a neighbor had whispered that he died in Han Yunis;[2] a huge explosive had gone off next to the soldier. He was severely wounded and died in the hospital. Obituaries were plastered on the entrance door; people whispered in the stairway. The neighbors decided to attend the funeral together.

---

1   In 2014, a military conflict broke out between Israel and Hamas, during which rockets were fired from Gaza towards Tel Aviv.
2   Khan Yunis is city in the southern Gaza Strip.

First, shame was born; sullen, introverted, sad. A humble spirit suggesting that even if he wanted it, it was impossible. Ben couldn't attend the funeral. He was very sorry. He had a commitment that couldn't be postponed. The thought of the body of the young soldier in the casket made him shiver; the sight of the mourning parents was disheartening: the mother's eyes were wide open, as though she could never close them; the father's eyes appeared like two elongated slits that would close and vanish. The crying at the funeral would be unbearable, a young life ending too soon; the wailing that would accompany the casket being lowered into the ground would be heartbreaking; the sound of his comrades firing their rifles three times in his memory would provoke a desire to lie down under the wheels of a passing car. He was sorry—Ben apologized to the neighbors, distantly related family members, Talia, and even his children—he couldn't make it.

But profound shame could never endure for long. To remove it, or at least to reduce it, resentment was awakened; the simple truth was that Ben hardly knew the family. The father once asked for his help opening the garage gate. The mother ignored him. He hardly knew the soldier. Once in a while, he passed by him in the stairway; like most teenagers, he was absorbed in his world. So why did he have to attend the funeral? If he had known them, naturally, he would go, but they have lived in the same building for years and never become friendly neighbors. And expecting all neighbors to attend the funeral was almost ridiculous. *What does he have in common with this family? With the young man who got killed?* His resentment grew, but was kept within the bounds of a tragic case involving the untimely death of a young man, taking a concrete but restrained shape.

But there was something fickle about resentment. One argument developed into another, one complaint created another complaint, and suddenly Ben found himself wondering what would happen if it were the other way around: *Would the neighbors come to David's funeral?*

His question left him in shock. He was short of breath, his heart was racing, and his left foot trembled uncontrollably. The fear was so intense that he could vividly imagine his son's body in a casket. In a minute he would have cried. As he lifted his head, he made an oath: *Never. Ever. He won't let this happen. A man looks after himself and his children;* everything else is nonsense, just like his father said—utter nonsense.

August 2, 2015

It was sweltering in Tel Aviv in early August. In the evening, bars and restaurants on Rothschild Street were bustling with people. Laughter blended with quiet conversations; jokes intertwined with soft music creating a hubbub accompanied by the aroma of food. People sauntered in the park in the middle of the avenue with heat-exhausted dogs, mothers pushed strollers, bikes weaved through the crowd, and the air hung still, heavy, and hazy.

Ofir sat in a bar, sipping cold beer and watching the television screen. The events of the last couple of days had created a sort of indolence, an inner silence he couldn't understand. Every couple of minutes he tried to mutter something to himself, even a single syllable, attempting to generalize the situation in Israel, but his endeavors were immediately replaced by exhaustion. Fatigue made him order more beer and look around apathetically. This may be a result of my canceling my weekend hike, he thought, but the memory of driving to Jerusalem made him shiver.

On Thursday afternoon, he was surprised to see Laurie calling him. A mixture of English words with crying emerged from the phone, saying "Abigail" repeatedly. Sometimes, a single moment could comprise endless disasters that pile up one upon the other: car accident, terror attack, disease, rape—they all merge into a single imaginary event, full of blood and crushed organs. He yelled into the phone in horror, begging Laurie to calm down and explain what had happened. Finally, he understood: Abigail had gone with friends to the Gay Pride Parade in Jerusalem. Laurie heard something had happened there, but she couldn't understand what it was.[1] Abigail wasn't answering her phone, and the news reported someone stabbed a couple of people. She's afraid something happened to Abigail. Could he find her, leave everything and drive to Jerusalem now, immediately, without delay?

The SUV crawled out of the Azrieli's garage tunnels, rudely blowing its horn at a car driving slowly and almost breaking through the exit gate. A light hit Ofir's face, a blinding midsummer sun. He put on his sunglasses and took

---

1   In 2014, six people were stabbed at the Gay Pride Parade in Jerusalem by an ultra-Orthodox Jewish assailant.

a sharp turn, pulling dangerously onto Ayalon highway, and speeding south-ward towards Jerusalem. Towers on the side of the road, giant billboards, cars changing lanes—Ofir was so absorbed in his driving, thinking that if he got to Jerusalem quickly, he would find his daughter safe.

The radio broadcast news of an Orthodox Jew assaulting people with a knife. It remained uncertain whether he had acted independently. While there were reported injuries, the exact number remained unclear. It appeared that no fatalities occurred. Ofir's heartbeat gradually calmed, and his breath-ing became regular. The road to Jerusalem stretched before him, shining in the burning sun and covered with dust. Yellow fields spread far on both sides, farmland already harvested and awaiting summer's end to embrace new seeds. The phone ringing was followed by Laurie's crying, asking time and again why Abigail wasn't answering her phone. No, she didn't know the friends she went with; she only told her they were going to the Gay Pride Parade in Jerusalem. Yes, now she's sorry she didn't ask for more details.

Jerusalem.

He had to get to Jerusalem to help Abigail.

The SUV careened forward, overtaking cars, blowing the horn at whoever slowed it down. Wheels turning, steering wheel moving right and left, white lines flashing left, right, left, the road curving and straightening, becoming narrow and wide. As Ofir passed Latroun, suddenly a snapshot of Abigail's birth appeared in his mind, and the car seemed to drive itself. *Here is the moment she came out of Laurie's body, a light-skinned baby with black fuzz covering a delicate skull, looking at him, astonished, with dark blue eyes, fluttering and scared.* As he kissed the porcelain-like cheek, he felt pure light engulf him and his newborn daughter. He then recalled Abigail in kindergarten, a quiet, shy girl inclined to stand by the wall and speak very softly in British English, like her mother. At her birthday party, she looked around in dismay, sitting at the center of the room as the children waited for her to blow out the candles.

As Ofir passed by Sha'ar haGai, he was suddenly jolted; looking around with surprise, he realized that he had already covered half the distance. In elementary school, she changed. She wasn't shy anymore and had turned into an assertive girl, organizing social activities and rebelling against teach-ers. He recalled the strange moment of tracking an unfamiliar personal-ity trait in a child, a quality so different from her mother or father. At once, Abigail became an independent human being, not only a mixture of her par-ents. In fifth grade, she organized a class strike to protest against too much homework. The many conversations with the teacher and the principal, in which he promised to persuade her to change her mind, never concealed his immense pride.

The road curved among the Judean mountains, their slopes yellowish; pine trees were sticking out their gray-green needles, and the sun cast a blinding light. In the last few years, Abigail became active in leftist circles. He had never had a political argument with someone holding more leftist views than himself. Political talks with friends were more of an affirmation of what everyone thought: the Likud party winning the election was a disaster; Israel is doing nothing to end the occupation; even if there is no Palestinian partner, we have to withdraw from the West Bank and stop expanding the settlements; Israeli society is changing its character, becoming more conservative and religious—all this was said with some desperation. But Abigail's questions were uncomfortable: When you served in the army, weren't you part of the occupation you objected to so much? How did you behave when you served in Gaza? Did you humiliate Arabs? Did you say something when you saw inappropriate behavior? How will the situation ever change if we don't fight to end the occupation? Ofir could imagine her wearing ripped jeans and a colorful tank top, hair disheveled and eyes heavily made-up. Tears filled his eyes, and he accelerated even more. If he managed to get to Jerusalem quickly, her tormenting question might find appropriate answers, and her strange stubbornness would be replaced by a light, almost invisible smile.

A road crawling up among the hills, dry shrubs and cracked soil, dust everywhere and trees bending down their tops, blackbirds flying above; for a moment, Ofir thought he could hear a strange cry; maybe human, maybe a bird. Sweat ran down his forehead, his hands holding the steering wheel were wet, his back curved . . .

The phone rang.

Laurie.

Thank God, thank God, Abigail is fine. We can take a deep breath now. As the attack began she ran in panic, dropped her phone, and couldn't find it later. But now she is on her way back to Tel Aviv with her friends. There was no need for him to get to Jerusalem. Maybe he would like to come for dinner? Abigail sounded very frightened, even though she said everything was fine. Something about her voice revealed that she was unsettled.

When Laurie opened the door and invited him in, he was struck by the life he had left. She smiled at him kindly and introduced Michael, who seemed shy and fragile. *Strange that she had chosen him,* he thought. He had always assumed that the pain of their divorce led to this relationship, but he couldn't help but observe their affection. He looked around, examining the room. Some of the furniture used to be in his home, but they'd shed their previous abode and now fitted perfectly to their new home, which was homey and charming. Plenty of green pots placed next to the window, a wide sofa that made you want to slump down, soft carpets, a lovely white dining table—Ofir looked around, astonished. More than once, he had thought that her second marriage was brought about out of agony and loneliness, a refuge from his breakdown and emotional transformation, maybe also a result of her feeling like a foreigner in Israel. There were even moments of painful remorse. But looking around, he suddenly realized he was wrong. Laurie's face didn't show a trace of bitterness. Her eyes resembled gentle autumn clouds covering the sun, affectionate and tender.

Abigail, who had shut herself up in her room, invited Ofir in with a broken, sobbing voice after he knocked on the door and whispered, "Abigail, it's me, Dad." His daughter was lying in bed, covered by a summer blanket, only her young face visible. Her long, narrow body was curled up on the bed, her knees folded, her arms holding tightly around her legs. Tears began running down her face, mixing with makeup and dirt, as she saw her father. The festive spirit that had transformed suddenly into a horror, the tangible feeling that people were willing to kill her because of her opinion, a hostility she had never encountered in Tel Aviv—she surrendered to his loving embrace, listening to her father whisper in her ear, "Thank God it's over; luckily you didn't get hurt; we should be thankful that you are safe."

Curled up in his arms, now relaxed and calm, closing her eyes and speaking while almost asleep, she mumbled softly, "Daddy, can I tell you something?"

"Sure, sweetie."

"I did something that I'm a bit sorry for."

"Did what, sweetie?"

"I took the money."

"What money?"

"From your drawer."

"You took the two thousand shekels I left in the drawer?"

"Yes."

"But why didn't you tell me?! I told you that if you need cash, you can take whatever you find at home. But you should have told me. I fired the cleaning lady. I was sure she stole it."

"I know. I'm so sorry. I was there one day and needed money. I found the bills in the drawer. I took them and forgot all about it. After you blamed the cleaning lady and fired her, I couldn't admit it."

"Why?"

"Because you would have been angry with me."

"Abigail, I mistakenly accused a woman who had worked for me for years, and she lost her job."

"I'm really sorry, but you would have been terribly angry with me if I told you. Don't look at me like that. You always said that, first and foremost, I need to take care of myself. Dad, you've repeated it ever since I was a child. Since that morning when I was five years old; I can remember it clearly, as if it was yesterday. The shades were closed, the room dark, and you had a strong smell of the sea. When I hugged you and asked what was wrong with you, you opened your eyes, grabbed my hand, and said, 'Abigail, sweetie, you should learn to look after yourself. And don't trust anyone else.' I didn't understand what you were saying. I left the room looking for Mom; I was going to ask her to explain what you said, but I found her crying in the kitchen. But gradually, I got it. You've been repeating it for years: 'First, make sure you're fine, then think of others.' I knew you would be angry at me for not admitting I took the money and for wrongfully firing the cleaning lady, so I said nothing. That's all. I'm sorry, Dad, but what could I do?"

The dim lights in the bar were switched on as the sun set. Small lanterns hung on the wooden walls. The air was heavy, all the tables were taken, and noise filled the place, blending with soft music. Ofir had another beer, looking around and discerning nothing but human silhouettes surrounding him. Abigail's words remained engraved in an inner space, emerging time and again, innocent and provocative, nearly funny but frightening. And the sincere tone in which they were said, full of sorrow yet revealing such a ridiculously simple truth—he was the one who had implanted this plain, uninhibited selfishness in her. In a moment of profound love, he came to understand that it was also directed at him, transcending any moral consideration or fear of punishment.

Slightly drunk, he became even more sullen, attempting to understand what had gone wrong. All he had done was give his daughter some advice, and share with her a simple self-evident lesson he had learned the hard way. But in some mysterious and unclear way, this simple advice lost the innocence in which it had been given; it grew and expanded, crawling into every inner room, pushing aside the natural human inclination to seek justice, removing friendship, ridiculing self-sacrifice, and even threatening to tear the thousand transparent capillaries binding together parents and children.

The television screen featured video clips from the Gay Pride Parade after the stabbing had taken place. People running in panic, cries echoing through the air, ambulances rushing down the street, and then the beautiful face of the murdered young woman: sparkling eyes, a fresh smile, soft red hair, the face of benevolent youth.[2] A pleasant voice was heard: "Shira Banki, a sixteen-year-old from Beit Hakerem, Jerusalem, had gone with friends to the parade." Ofir watched the screen but could hear nothing but the music, which grew louder. A certain flicker of thought—I might buy a house in London or New York. I've had enough of life here—materialized into images of fancy homes in foreign cities. Gazing at the screen, he felt that absolute emptiness, silent and deadly, gradually encroaching on him. A fading world was leaving him orphaned and neglected, as though he were abandoned alone in a dry desert.

"Excuse me, are you okay?" the waitress touched his arm lightly, looking at him anxiously. Seeing a man with such an air of success, with blank eyes and head leaning against the wall, was frightening. "Yes, yes, I'm fine," he replied out of habit, straightening up and asking for the bill. She was a pretty young woman with blue eyes and light hair pulled back, dressed in black with colorful sneakers. She observed him, and then she turned her gaze to the television. "Yes, I know how you feel," she said. "It's awful. I want to cry when I see this. What a shame, isn't it? God, what a shame."

2   Shira Banki was stabbed in the Gay Pride Parade and died three days later.

May 1, 2016

A phenomenal deal. An outstanding success. A unique achievement. A pinnacle of Israeli industry. A dream come true. Who would have thought it possible? A company born in a small, run-down office in Jerusalem was acquired by an American firm specializing in robotics for one billion and one hundred million dollars. The news broadcasts opened with a report on the acquisition of Handex. TV crews gathered on the fortieth floor of the round Azrieli Tower, taking photos of the workers entering the offices with restrained smiles. The management had prohibited any interviews, but their faces revealed their joy. Ministers and public figures congratulated Handex, praising the enterprise, talent, courage, resourcefulness, teamwork, combination of skills, determination, original thought, cautious yet imaginative management, and more words pronounced with grave expressions. The prime minister called Ben Haddad, a businessman affiliated with the Likud, congratulating him on this remarkable accomplishment. In a photo in the paper, the two partners sat side by side, relaxed and smiling.

From the Azrieli Towers, you can get a good view of Tel Aviv. Under a dome of clouds on a cool spring day, a carpet of buildings stretches to the horizon, square cubes split by roads, white, gray, and green dots. On cloudy days, rather than in the summer, a sigh of relief emerges from the city. It isn't the air of a sensual beach town that brings comfort, but sunset against the clouds, a water pitcher left on a table in a café, rusty bicycles tied to a pole with a "Do Not Touch" sign, fat street cats relaxing on a fence, a barefoot toddler running around a playground, an old man on the beach, stretching his arms up, bending forward and then standing. The shore extends pointed fingers into the Mediterranean Sea through which the waves flow, sliding over the wet sand grains and always retreating to the depths of the sea.

Ofir and Ben were standing on the roof of the round Azrieli Tower looking westward silently. They both gazed at the sea. Finally, Ofir said, "What an achievement, huh?" And Ben replied immediately, "Who would have thought we could sell Handex for so much money?!"

Only a graceful breeze whistle could be heard in the pleasant silence.

Ofir's eyes were narrowed as he asked, "Is it true that the prime minister called to congratulate you?"

"Yes."

"Well done. Are you a member of the Likud?"

"Member? No. Sometimes I attend their meetings."

"You used to oppose the settlements in the West Bank. Did you change your mind?"

"No. Not at all. But I like the atmosphere in the Likud meetings, that's all. I think of my father when I'm there. If I don't go to the synagogue, at least I spend time with people who cherish tradition. For over an hour I feel that there are 'we' and 'them,' and that I belong to a group that sees me as part of it. Ten minutes after I leave, the feeling dies out."

Together, they emitted a short, loud chuckle.

"Today is May Day," said Ofir. "I think of my father on this day. It's unbelievable; he genuinely believed it was a day to celebrate. Years ago, when my mother claimed she had nothing in common with the workers in China, he asked her what people have in common. I hate to admit it, but I'm still searching for the answer."

Again, a mutual hum of laughter was heard, a bit longer and more relaxed.

"People don't understand the magnitude of the social change taking place," Ben replied. "Out of several foundations of the Western world, there is one that eliminates all the others: self-interest. It wipes away common values, gradually swallowing everything else. Anything is allowed if a person is acting for his own good. Anything is forgivable if it is an act aimed at improving one's situation. It's scary."

"Frightening," Ofir said quietly, almost whispering. "When people act only for themselves, society disintegrates. Any human value stands in contrast with the simple bestial instinct to be better off: justice, government, defending the weak—everything. Human societies are based on restraining bestial selfishness."

A moan emerged from two throats.

"And this selfishness makes people lonely," Ofir added. "If you act only out of self-interest, you quickly find that you've lost all empathy. And you avoid relying on others. Every person exists in his world." Ben quickly added, "And if you act for the benefit of others, you expect a reward. It flattens emotional relations, making them nearly superfluous."

Silence fell, heavy and transfixing.

After a few moments, Ben cleared his throat and said, "Do you remember my parents' house in Beit Hakerem? I was there a couple of days ago. I was standing on Hakhaluts Street, and suddenly, I was overwhelmed by longing. I looked around; the street was so green and quiet, I almost started crying." It was impossible to tell if the bright eyes that turned to Ofir were covered with a film of tears or a reflection of a single sun ray, thin and pinkish, that emerged from behind the clouds. The ice at their bottom had melted for a moment, replaced by an inner light. Ofir looked at him with dark, nearly black eyes. "Yes, yes, I know the feeling. You have to watch out. It's so easy to burn with longing, but so difficult to wake up and find that that world no longer exists. In Beit Hakerem, Tel Aviv, London, New York, whatever a person does that isn't directed at their own benefit is considered stupid or hypocritical."

Stillness enveloped them, an awkward silence that lasted a couple of moments.

"On the other hand, without the urge to fulfill our talents, we wouldn't have created Handex and wouldn't have sold it for a fortune," Ofir said excitedly with a choked voice; and before he even managed to complete the sentence, Ben replied passionately, "So true!"

"So, what do you think? Was it worth it all?"

The four eyes turning westward revealed both fervor and alarm. Beyond the buildings of Tel Aviv, the sea could be seen, and above it stretched a soft, gray sky. Only on the far horizon did thick, dark clouds accumulate, suggesting that the seeds of a coming storm could be forming.

"I don't know. What do you think?"